CRUSHING CURIOSITY

By

Denise Greenwood

ISBN 978-1-9997416-4-8
Copyright ©2017 Denise Greenwood

This work is a work of fiction. Names and characters are the product of the
author's imagination and any resemblance to actual persons, living or dead,
is entirely coincidental.

Published by
Llyfrau Cambria Books, Wales, United Kingdom.
Cambria Books is a division of
Cambria Publishing.
Discover our other books at: www.cambriabooks.co.uk

Cover design by Carolyn Michel

DEDICATION

To Bal Lotay who provided encouragement and feedback during the first few chapters.

Also to Steven, wherever you are... I only remember you as a strange little boy.

CHAPTERS

1. Pucker-Up

As children leaned across desks to whisper or gazed out dirty classroom windows, one small boy sat with military stiffness in a front row chair. Without blinking he stared directly ahead. The skin of his rigidly held knees touched the underneath of a cold wooden desk.

'Barry? Barry? Are you present?' A teacher's shrill voice held constrained annoyance. Miss Rogers refused to move her eyes, pinpricks through thick lenses, from a longer name on a quivering register. As she gazed at it, her upper lip twitched. *I won't say it. It's like something from a soap opera cast list.*

Miss Rogers gripped the clipboard tightly then brought it up to her face to hide her expression. Her knuckles were white, as white as the dorsal hump on her nose. She could feel the boy's stare on the back of her clipboard. She caught sight of his blond head and her upper lip curled but she continued to wait for an answer.

The boy remained silent. With his spine erect and head held at a slight angle, his expression was as rigid as his knees. Ice-blue eyes blinked slowly but remained fixed on the back of the clipboard until whispering and fidgeting around the boy stopped. There was a charge of expectation in the air. Knuckles around the register appeared whiter.

Eventually, the teacher's eyes smarted and she had to blink several times. After a deep sigh the clipboard slowly lowered. Pinprick eyes turned downwards to look at an expressionless boy.

'Barry, you MUST answer *Present Miss.*'

The boy moved by merely upturning his chin and as he did so raised a piercing glare to meet reflective spectacles.

'I'm Barrington George the Third,' he replied in unemotional monotone. 'My name is NOT Barry.'

Instantly children erupted. Laughter spluttered, snot bubbled then flaying arms thrashed across desktops to send paper gliding before chanting began. Bar-ry... Bar-ry... Bar-ry...' It was quiet at first.

No, no, not again. Miss Rogers inwardly groaned but as Barrington stood then climbed onto his desk, the chanting increased in urgency and volume. Small feet stomped on wooden floorboards until their pounding thundered.

'Stop it, stop it instantly!' Miss Roger's high-pitched objection drowned in the din but Barrington was not to be deterred. Watching his teacher with the calculating coldness of a shark looking at its next meal, the calm boy unzipped his shorts to lower them and his briefs until they creased around his ankles. As he did so he bent his knees to take centre position and without flinching, pushed a peachy behind into the air.

What the hell is he doing now?

The bum was met with a shocked response. Busy mouths were instantly silenced when Miss Rogers shrieked: 'Stop!' Her voice momentarily buzzed in her ears.

As Barrington leaned forward, his warm breath blew against cold knees and he blinked. Glancing sideways he was then suddenly transfixed by a new girl immediately to his left. *Elspeth,* he remembered her name.

Caught in a shaft of sunlight spilling in from a window, her red hair was magnificent, like bright copper against flame. The boy gasped. Just a hint of uncertain smile lay frozen across the girl's features but her eyes shone with the bashfulness that Barrington should have experienced. In that instant, looking into the boy's eyes, she adopted his unused emotion. She felt what should have been his deep-rooted embarrassment. His blank expression changed, she saw the corners of his mouth turn up then, her adopted emotion somersaulted. She was struck with breathy and loving admiration.

Drinking in the girl's aura of copper burning bright, Barrington felt warmth. It was strange, enticing and almost dangerous but the boy hadn't yet finished expressing his rejection of teacher and class. Barrington opened his mouth to address his stunned audience. The only other sound in the room was the ticking of a clock and although the young voice was arrogant, the boy's attention remained solely on the enrapt girl within her halo of flame.

'Go on... Touch it. You know you all want to.'

Elspeth's mouth dropped open. Sunlight shifted and suddenly the shadow of Barrington's bum lay across her freckled face. The girl's copper locks shook with indignity but, Barrington hadn't finished.

'Kiss it. Why don't you ALL... just kiss it anywhere you like,' and he returned a cool gaze to Miss Rogers.

There was an explosion, an instant uproar. The teacher yelped, unable to comprehend. *There's something wrong with him.*

'Pull up those shorts immediately! What on earth do you think you're doing?' Without looking at the panic-stricken teacher, Barrington retorted.

'If none of you can remember my name then I'm giving you something you can,' and he sniffed with indifference.

Fifteen minutes later, Barrington waited patiently in the dimness of an unused classroom. Tops of rigidly held knees touched the underneath of a cold desk as he stared directly at a blank blackboard. Then, like a blast of cold air, the boy sensed that eyes were upon him. He slowly turned his head towards a window in the classroom door. Miss Rogers stood on the other side, her face now haggard but she stared with repressed hatred through thick lenses, through thick glass. *Why is there always one problem child in my class?* This boy unnerved her.

Barrington moved only his head, tilting it to one side while arching a chiselled blond eyebrow. Miss Rogers watched his lips slowly mouth: 'Kiss it.' Then, he pursed his lips to blow her a kiss. The teacher's nose turned as white as her clenching knuckles. The window steamed up but Barrington had already returned his blank expression to a blank blackboard.

3

A further fifteen minutes later, Barrington's mother sat in a neat office as the Headmistress animatedly explained why her little boy would be excluded for two weeks. The Head brandished her biro like an instrument of torture about to be tested. Mrs Barrington watched it form small circles in the air before it made short stabbing movements in her direction. She released a sigh and during the Head's heartfelt diatribe cast a furtive glance at an empty chair next to her. *I wish my husband could for once make an effort.*

During the past four years, Barrington had attended two local primary schools and at each Mrs George had received requests to either speak about or pick-up her son. She had always arrived alone, even at parent's evenings. In this school, the Head's patience had worn paper thin but Mrs George excused her husband's absence with a sentence that now glided effortlessly from her lips: 'He's so busy at work.' This time the Head ignored it completely.

'I have no recourse but to exclude Barry, he's a disruptive influence, his behaviour continually defiant and rude. This latest incident has escalated our need to address this problem once and for all and quite frankly Mrs George, Barry pushed boundaries too far!' The pen then swirled in the air and the Head's face turned a light shade of peachy pink, not unlike Barrington's bum as she realised she would now be able to spurt her favourite explanation of school ethos. 'We pride ourselves on our pastoral care, which is predominantly formative rather than reactive'. She looked smug for a moment. 'However, I have no alternative but to arrange for an Education Welfare Officer to visit you. The Officer will discuss with you *and your husband*, all possible solutions.'

The Head laid down her well-chewed biro and both she and Mrs George watched it roll to the edge of the desk then, fall onto the floor. Both women sighed with frustration.

On the way home, Barrington sat in a rear car seat with his usual stiff air, taking care that his seat belt didn't ruffle a pristinely laundered shirt. His mother avoided looking in the rear view mirror. She was aware of her son's strange presence but unlike Mrs Rogers didn't want verbal confirmation. 'Don't you dare say a word!' she ordered as she stared directly ahead at the road. Barrington looked blankly at his mother's red lipstick in the mirror. Again, came the warmth and with it an instant recollection of Elspeth's copper hair. He decided that it was his favourite colour. His warmth spread.

During the journey, Barry's mum inwardly thanked God that she'd produced an only child then released a sigh when she thought of a caesarean scar that ruined her otherwise perfect figure. She also avoided looking at her hands at the steering wheel; because of Barrington she had to cancel a nail appointment. Without an acrylic tip on her index finger she felt partially undressed. *I don't understand it. He has everything a child could want.* Then, she thought of her husband and how he had given her everything she could want.

The car travelled through the centre of Mistlethrop, bumping over cobbles then turned west into Crossley Road. Mrs George released another sigh because she was nearing home, preferring to drive along a road with canopies of branches than drive through the old minster town, once famous for wool mills. Barrington was lost in his thoughts.

At the end of Crossley Road, Paxton Park appeared, and then the car turned right into the leafier Dandelion View. The town centre was now left behind, prompting yet another sigh to escape from Mrs George's highly lip-glossed mouth. She still felt tense and kept her eyes firmly fixed on the road ahead as they entered the affluent suburb of Hogarth.

Detached, double-fronted period residences adorned the side of the road opposite the park. The largest of these residences, Radburn House, belongs to the George's. It is named after the family business, Mistlethrop now known for Radburn Confectionery, predominantly chocolate and toffee. After Great-Grandma had married, the Radburn surname had been lost to the family. One last turn to the right then the car drove along a side driveway, past a sweeping front lawn. It was

5

as finely manicured as nine of Mrs George's fingernails except for one huge solid oak tree closer to the road than the residence.

Barrington released himself from vehicle confines, planted feet firmly on block-paving then trotted behind his mother and into an impressive house. Mrs George wouldn't speak to Barrington until later that evening. *I won't waste another word. It will be up to Barrington's father to lay down the law.* She dreaded her husband's wrath but couldn't see any other way to get through to their son.

The boy hesitated on the staircase as though to speak but instead stared silently at steps. It was a moment when a normal young boy would have felt the severity of his situation hoping that it hadn't influenced his mother's capacity to forgive. Mrs George inspected her nails, immediately casting her son from her mind. Barrington climbed the stairs to his room.

The dutiful mother hastily clicked high-heels across parquet to enter a little-used parlour. She used a false nail to tap keys on a Motorolla Star Tac. 'The mountain will have to come to Muhammad today.' She waited for her manicurist to answer.

Meanwhile, Barrington lay on a high four-poster bed trying to ignore its Paddington Bear drapes. He practised a new signature; the idea had come during the journey home. 'If they're going to shorten my name then, I'll say how it's spelt!' The tip of his pink tongue licked the corner of his mouth as he focussed. His favourite book, a Ladybird edition of *The Human Body* was open at its first blank page and within minutes several versions of *Barri* were written across it in red ink. Next to the book, a small white plastic skeleton minus an elastic loop lay in a fold in the quilt.

Mr George arrived home promptly at seven-fifteen for the evening meal. A creature of strict habit he discarded a fine worsted jacket and silk tie to open his shirt collar by two buttons. Then, he removed gold and lapus lazuli cufflinks to place them next to a gold-trimmed dinner plate.

Nothing was said about Barrington's incident until after a main meal of chicken in pesto had been eaten and then a cheese selection placed on the table. Mr George sat at the head with his wife to his right and his son to his left. The other fifteen chairs remained empty. By this time Mrs George's equilibrium had been restored and her French polished acrylic nails pristine. Mr George was staring at the screen of a newly acquired pocket-PC. It lay next to his cufflinks. As he finished a second glass of Anjou and contemplated what to drink with the cheese: Chateau du Bourg or Ruby Port, he pushed back his chair, shifted position to cross one leg then looked keenly at his wife.

'So, what did you get up to today?'

Mrs George was used to the routine. A family dinner ate in silence until the question at the end.

'I was called to the school yet again. Barrington misbehaved and as usual, the school didn't know how to handle it.' Mrs George examined her new acrylic tip and shook her head with disappointment.

'I don't understand?' Mr George raised a finely chiselled blond eyebrow. 'Surely we must get to the bottom of this.'

'It's funny you should say that,' Mrs George remarked. Barrington smirked. His father ground his molars but helped himself to a slice of Brie while thinking: *It would have been nice to have been able to finish a meal in peace.* He listened intently as his wife related the full details.

Barrington used a cheese knife to slice Gouda then a thin wedge of cheddar. A few white grapes and one Melba toast were added and he nibbled quietly. He didn't have to look up to see red lips moving; lips rarely without lipstick and seldom used to kiss him.

When her new-born's eyes had changed from baby-blue to unsettling ice, cutting through her with the same intensity, Barrington's mother had been glad that she hadn't decided to breastfeed. Her strong sense of society prominence, her perfect facade meant that she hadn't sought a professional to explain why her maternal affection also iced over. She now had something in common with Miss Rogers, an inability to rid her mind of worrying thoughts.

Mr George tried to remain calm while he spread Brie onto a peppercorn cracker then he turned to look at his son with the same cold eyes as his offspring.

'Your grades are still excellent?'

Barrington raised his piercing eyes and replied: 'Yes father.'

'And you're still happy to go to a local school?'

The boy's expression remained constant. He was about to reply when his mother intervened: 'He should go to a boarding school. He'd receive a superior education and could mix with children of his own standing.' Mrs George didn't necessarily have her son's best interests at heart but her husband had a different view.

'We've been through this before. I don't want Barrington to go through what I did at his age. We have plenty of time to decide where he should be educated long-term.' He then turned back to his son. 'Well, what say you?'

Barrington was also used to his mother's opinion. It didn't deter him. 'I'm happy to go to the school,' he lied.

Mr George licked his lips and instead of clenching a fist, which he would normally do, he helped himself to the last piece of chicken and cracked its bone while thinking: *I should have stayed at work.*

A sharp snap made Barrington suddenly take interest in his father's hands. Mrs George noticed a fleeting change to her son's face. *He's just like his father. Perhaps misbehaviour is his release?* She didn't think of her own inability.

'So, tell me your version of what happened?' Mr George's lips were moist with pesto. He waved the broken chicken bone in the air while Barrington watched it closely. His mother had deboned his and he looked ruefully at his discarded plate before answering.

'They call me Barry. I told them hundreds of times that it's not my name but they do it anyway. If they couldn't remember it then I thought I'd show them something they could. I made sure they all saw it; that's why I climbed onto my desk.'

8

'And then what?'

'I told them to kiss it.'

Mr George lay down his chicken bone, wiped his fingers on a napkin before slapping the table which made his wife jump. Barrington, unperturbed, looked admiringly at the bone.

This was a surprising turn. Mr George had also grown tired of repeatedly hearing about his son's exploits but this latest incident had hit a nerve. 'Your name is important,' he said seriously. 'The first point of respect is one's name. How can you respect yourself if you do nothing when people disrespect it?' Barrington nodded innocently.

Mr George was reminded of an old Radburn employee who had gravely misjudged him while learning the business. He'd made his opinion known to co-workers. *The further up a tree a monkey goes, the more you see of his arse.* Judging by the man's expression when he'd turned, Mr George had known instantly that he was the monkey referred to. The remark sealed the man's fate. He then found it difficult to achieve good performance reviews resulting in his eventual release. Mr George now suddenly experienced a sense of pride. *Christ! If he's this assertive at his age then imagine what he'll be like when I teach him the business.*

Mrs George was surprised by her husband's reaction and restraint. He carried anger constantly around with him but lately, his anger had become a new source of annoyance then a self-perpetuating cycle. Mr George was relieved, chuckled then slapped the table again.

'Listen son, you did right. You showed it to them at the earliest possible opportunity. You see, you do have a name, a superior life. They're important. There are leaders and followers, people who do things and those who just talk about them or worse still, do nothing but complain. They can't take your name away from you. Most of your classmates will work at Radburn one day, work for you, so you did right to show them your arse. Sooner or later they'll have to kiss it.' Mr George threw his head back and laughed.

Barrington's mother closed her eyes and winced. *I would have preferred anger. He'll return to work tomorrow without worry whereas I'll be stuck at home with the problem.* 'What about the visit from the Welfare Education Officer?' she asked. 'Are you going to deal with that?'

Mr George stopped laughing, snorted in derision before pulling his chair back to the table. 'Of course, I'll speak to the headmistress first thing tomorrow.' He flaunted his napkin with a dismissive wave. 'She'll soon see sense after I've spoken to her. If she wants all the extras for her summer fete then she'll have to see things my way. Now, let's have a glass of red and push this nonsense from our minds.' Mr George reached across and patted the top of his son's head. The ends of Barrington's mouth turned up although his lips remained tightly closed.

While his parents withdrew to the sitting room with a bottle, Barrington went to his tree-house secluded in the heights of a huge oak tree. The only feet to cross manicured lawns were the gardener's and Barrington's. He carried his Ladybird book and plastic skeleton plus one other item neatly secreted in a napkin, a discarded chicken bone.

Using only one hand to steady him, the boy balanced the small burden carefully against his chest as he climbed a tree-house ladder. He'd made plans earlier to squash five snails waiting for him in jam-jars but he had a new project in mind. It would need intricate planning. He climbed higher. A look of bliss swept across his face as he felt the sharpness of a bone through the napkin.

'Yes, red is definitely my favourite colour.'

2. The Birthday Presents

It was two years before Mrs George's wish was finally granted, her son efficiently packed off to a boarding school. Two incidents forced the issue; the former a disturbing precursor to a tragic latter.

Three weeks before Barri's tenth birthday, Mrs George had swapped high heels for silken pumps then climbed the tree-house ladder out of curiosity and mistrust. Small wooden crucifixes beneath the hydrangeas had grown by one too many. Three rabbits, one guinea pig and a cat lay buried, another cat missing and one puppy escaped to the park. Barri caught his mother rifling through his collection.

'What are these?' she demanded with horror.

'Bones,' Barri replied innocently.

'Where did they come from?' Mrs George looked out of place kneeling on a coir mat; rough bristles ate into her thin Capri pants.

'It's my school project. They're from the bins,' her son lied convincingly but Mrs George was used to his matter-of-fact tone. She anxiously looked about her. The tree-house interior was as neat and clean as any room in Radburn House. A low table held a box with compartments and each contained bones. A stool was next to the table, too small for Barri's mum to negotiate comfortably. A shelf held jam-jars, stacks of plastic take-away tubs and a box of tools.

It even smells good not the leafy, mouldy smell I remember. 'It's so clean in here,' she remarked and sniffed loudly, narrowing her nostrils then holding her breath to emphasize that she knew the air had been clinically perfumed.

Barri had finished his project, he preferred less mess. His pale eyes blinked but then his mother saw a brief look of rapture when he lowered his eyes to her neck. 'I can't ask the cleaner to come up here,' but Barri was quick to add: 'I do it myself. After a while it gets smelly.'

'I see,' Mrs George reluctantly assented. She opened her mouth to say something then her mind went blank, unable to see past what was in front of her. She stared ruefully around and slowly nodded. 'Well, do whatever it is you do up here. Later, you have a job to do.' Barrington looked questioningly at his mother. She shuffled past then paused to look into his face. He couldn't avoid red lips. 'You have invites to write.'

'What to?'

'Your birthday party, I've had fifteen printed so you'll need to write one for each of the children in your class.' Mrs George continued a stooped shuffle to the doorway. She couldn't see her son's crimson cheeks.

That same day Barri erected a barrier around the tree trunk by shoving unused junior golf clubs into the grass then tying a length of string around them. A cardboard sign was hung over the string: *Keep Out.* The tree-house ladder was safely secreted behind the row of wooden crucifixes beneath hydrangeas. Although Mr George remarked to his wife that the sign looked ugly and Barri's clubs were meant for golf, he thought Barri's barrier another boyish whim.

'The boy's growing up...' he reasoned, 'trying to find his own space and that's a good indication that he's growing some balls.'

'And I suppose you won't mind him flashing them to his class mates,' Mrs George muttered.

'What?'

'I'd prefer he learned how to mix with other children than communicate with signs.'

'Nonsense, there's nothing wrong with it. Why, I remember distinctly...' Then, Mr George waffled on about his childhood before ending with: 'I turned out fine, so will he.'

His son's whim lasted until the day of the party. Although Barri's behaviour had improved since his bum-bearing, his arrogance persisted. Children thought him too clever to bother with. Teachers tolerated him but didn't go out of their way to bring him into the fold. It was his parents' responsibility to sort him out, a dismissive policy unusual for that time but now accepted as the norm. Mrs George innocently assumed that a birthday party would be the solution. Barri would learn to mingle. His classmates were more eager to see where Barri lived, what toys he had and what they could eat than take notice of the birthday boy. Barri was annoyed with his parents and classmates.

The party would last from two to four. Thirty minutes for play, fifteen for food, another fifteen to watch a magician then an hour to play games or take turns in a bouncy castle in the rear garden. Presents were unopened and piled high on the parlour table except for one, stored in a young girl's pocket.

The first ninety minutes passed without incident. Barri reluctantly participated in a game of pass-the-parcel, pin the tail on the donkey then swung a bat at a piñata. As children scrambled to snatch sweets from the patio, Barri made a hasty escape among swarming bodies to avoid being frog-marched to the bouncy castle. He kept a close eye on a present from his father who'd been surprised at the request. Barri had wanted a wristwatch with a stopwatch function.

The tree-house would be his hideout. Barri could spend the remaining thirty minutes undisturbed. Cars would then arrive and their drivers begin a painful process of peeling away disgruntled kids. The bouncy castle only held eight at a time and children now queued impatiently for a turn.

Mrs George underestimated the amount of energy required to keep children both occupied and contained. For Barrington's sake she had assumed the martyrdom of a domesticated mother. Unused to torrents of squabbling and spillages, she regretted not hiring help then found another reason to resent her husband. Mr George couldn't resist a live experiment for his confectionery. He busily shoved small questionnaire cards into giant goody bags.

Meanwhile, Barri almost felt happy, relief and happiness

being related. He carefully manoeuvred the tree-house ladder from under bushes and gently propped it against the tree trunk, but, as he climbed Barri became increasingly uneasy. Some thinner branches were broken. A thicker limb half-way had a small piece of blue material hanging from its splintered bark. Barri paused, stretched out his hand to pluck it away but as he did so felt a creeping sensation around his ears. He stopped just before his fingertips touched the shred then he knew that his favourite colour was rising to his face. Someone had climbed the tree and had partially broken the branch.

Warmth may have been his closest emotion to love but heat was anger and Barri hadn't yet felt its burn. Pulling back his hand then looking upwards with a snarl he adopted stealth mode while trying not to grip the ladder too tightly to cause creaking. When he reached the top Barri pulled his head slowly upwards so that he could peak over the threshold.

Shadows of branches with masses of leaves made it dim inside his den. Barri wanted to reach for a large power-torch he kept strategically at the side of the doorway. He could shine it upon an intruder but, once again he stopped his hand short of touching it. The intruder wasn't as expected. The boy held his breath then pulled himself silently across the threshold.

Elspeth Rush sat on a small stool with her back towards the entrance; she was bent over Barri's box of bones. Her long copper hair spilled across the table. A shaft of light fell across it from a square window hole in the opposite side of the tree-house.

'It's good for you so you should eat as much as you can.'

Barri was confused but when Elspeth sat up he saw that she had put bones in three plastic tubs as place-settings. A stuffed toy sat behind one and at another, Barri's white rubber skeleton. Elspeth talked to them in soothed tones. 'Would you like some more?' and she immediately reached for another bone.

Barri couldn't contain searing rage. His home and time had been stolen by children he perceived as inferiors and they'd tested his self-control but now, his last bastion was taken. He

14

shook, blinded by emotions left to fester too long. He hurled himself forward then came to an abrupt stop one inch away from Elspeth who had jumped up, spun around and was standing with her mouth open. He didn't hear her say: 'I... I was just setting a place for you. I've got a present for...'

In a mist of pure hatred the livid boy saw a burning copper flash from the intruder then, she was lying flat and he on top. His right forearm leaned across a white freckled neck, pinning the trespasser down. Sunlight steamed across Elspeth's throat.

The young girl was dumbstruck, not knowing whether to be frightened or delighted. She felt the brush of a sleeve against her throat; saw Barri's lips tremble then expected them to kiss her. She hadn't felt the force of her fall. It had been too sudden, too unexpected. She lay across the coir mat with her arms spread-eagled, her head thrown back and hanging off the edge of the mat.

In an instant Barri's rage changed but its aftermath remained as a red throbbing mass surrounding him with its thickness. He hadn't felt anything like it before. Adrenalin surged through his veins as he gazed down into Elspeth's shining eyes. His eyes lowered to her throat where only the lightest of freckles were gathered in small clusters across soft, alabaster skin. Beneath delicate epidermis he saw where voice-box cartilage pushed out. He felt warm breath on his face, sweet with butter-cream and icing. He knew that just below his sleeve a windpipe was fragile and vulnerable.

He leaned harder, rolling his arm, taking his eyes back to Elspeth's and she opened her mouth to say something but his arm hardened. His fist clenched as he leaned with greater force, feeling a vibrating sound of vocal-cord rasps as first her voice-box then windpipe were crushed. The expected chicken-bone cracks sounded like music.

Barri felt a flutter beneath his sleeve and his expression changed from absolute bliss to one of awe and wonder. He gazed into Elspeth's final moments, enthralled as her eyes widened then changed from abject terror to confusion. A

15

shudder ran through the body beneath him. A warm icing-coated breeze brushed against his face. The girl's eyes glazed but remained open, unfocussed. The thrill of it ran through every fibre of Barri's being. He lay still for a while thinking that maybe it would have been better if he'd rolled up his sleeve.

It took forty-five seconds for Elspeth to die even though Barri didn't look at his new watch to verify. It would have taken longer, as long as it took for her to hold her breath but shock and pain accelerated the process.

Barri was brought back from the twisted sensual to the harshness of his situation. Reluctantly, the boy pulled his body away from the intruder. Then, he noticed something had fallen onto the mat. A small soft package, more sticky tape than wrapping paper lay on the coir matting near Elspeth's fingertips. Barri hastily picked up the package, shoved it into his pocket then looked about him. His brain synapses raced into overdrive.

Three cars drove along the driveway past the sweeping front lawn. Their occupants didn't notice a small crumpled body at the foot of the tree. Only on a car's departure did a cry of alarm ring out. Elspeth's battered and broken body was discovered. She lay spread-eagled where she had landed after being thrown out of the tree-house, facing the sky, her eyes open. A large broken branch lay across her throat, a scattering of smaller branches and leaves over and around her. The branch had crushed her windpipe but the fall had broken her back. The tree-house ladder was in its hiding place and the golf club barrier remained intact around both tree and body.

There was only evidence of a tragic and fatal accident. Tell-tale shreds of material upon a partially broken branch then one large broken branch confirmed it. She had fallen from the tree-house and a branch had given way to fall mercilessly across a fragile throat. The furry toy was found in the tree-house, still sitting at an empty place-setting. Plastic tubs were empty.

While all the commotion went on outside, Barri sat on his four-poster bed with his nose in a book. He wore a thin friendship bracelet made from two leather strips braided together, one copper red and one a pale yellow almost the same colour as his hair. It was the only birthday present other than his watch that he took interest in.

As he read, he paused now and then to run a fingertip along a ridge of tightly wound leather. He thought about cricoids and tracheal cartilage, how it leads into the trachea and the intricate relationship of bone, muscles and gland. Rapture passed over his face as though he was immersed in a wonderful dream.

3. Out of the Frying Pan

Fourteen years later, the sky was so dark that a train's harsh interior lights discharged a stark aura. The blackness outside disguised pelting rain yet it was still afternoon. A young woman was soaked to the skin. She quickly deposited her case in a luggage cage then took the nearest vacant seat to keep an eye on it.

There was a bright flash of lightning. Caprice strained to see through rivulets chasing each other from the top to the bottom of a window. There was a second flash and for a second she saw a skeletal face staring back at her. She jumped and squealed with terror before shrinking down into her seat. Holding her breath, she froze, now aware that she had been as equally visible under the train's interior lights. *He's found me.*

Seconds passed at an excruciatingly slow pace. Caprice was torn whether to leave her case behind and spring to the next exit or remain frozen. An old man slowly ambled past her seat, his thin white hair so wet that it couldn't hide a dripping white scalp.

'Oh, thank God!'

'Sorry dear?' The old man looked back at Caprice who nearly wept with relief.

'Filthy weather,' she offered. The man nodded before continuing his way down the train.

Slowly the train pulled away from the platform. Within minutes a guard announced that due to flooding ahead the train would terminate at Mistlethrop. Transport to destinations farther down the line wouldn't be available. The only alternative would be a bus ride back. Caprice shrank into her seat then closed her eyes to allow a solitary tear to trickle down her cheek. She felt crushed but quelled further tears. She would

18

have to alight at Mistlethrop then figure out her next move.

The first ten minutes of the journey were uneventful. Caprice had the luxury of having almost an entire carriage to herself. The old man had chosen a seat at the opposite end. The train travelled through a hillside tunnel instantly plunging it into black pitch while interior lights glowed orange. The outside roar of train on track entered the carriage to rattle teeth fillings. Caprice was exhausted, closed her eyes but resisted the temptation to doze. The train emerged into a grey world and the interior roar retreated to its rightful place.

Two heavily hooded men boarded the train at the next station and made a beeline for a table in front of Caprice. They swore, sprawled opposite each other, taking up two seats apiece to spread dripping water across the table. Caprice shifted in her seat, disturbed and suddenly uncomfortable. She looked ruefully at empty seats around her. Then, one of the men turned his head to peer through a gap between seats. She smelt something foul and stale, then alcohol. The man stared out of a wet hood and into Caprice's face before turning back to his companion and grinning. 'We've got interesting company,' he remarked to his friend and winked. The friend stood and feigned an exaggerated stretch, pushing clenched fists into the air. He looked over at Caprice then sat down again.

'I like red meat.' He pointed to his head.

Caprice's long hair was still wet and shined with scarlet intensity under lights. She rummaged around in her pockets for a train guide and nervously tried to peel wet pages apart. Meanwhile, the man who had peered through the gap turned then knelt on his seat. He placed his elbows firmly on the top while he looked down at Caprice. He watched her fumble.

Keep your cool, Caprice thought, trying her best to ignore confrontation. *You've dealt with worse than him,* a thought that did little to ease anxiety. *Maybe I can get through the next fifteen minutes.*

'What's your name beautiful?' the man asked, his face still enshrouded. Caprice lowered her train guide to look directly at her questioner.

'That's none of your business,' she replied coolly and she held his gaze but the man didn't budge. She saw a glint of mockery in his eye.

'Ah but you see it is, coz you and me gonna get acquainted and once we're friends then I can introduce you to my mate 'ere.' The man remained kneeling but his friend moved to two seats to the far right of Caprice where he plonked his behind then stretched his legs into the centre aisle. The only escape would be by clambering across. The redhead's anxiety increased as the train travelled into a second hillside tunnel. A grinding of train against track amplified and they were plunged into orange eerie light.

'Ah, come now,' the man persisted, raising his voice to be heard above rattling. The odour of pungent alcohol and damp dog filled the air around him. 'You have to tell me your name otherwise I'll have to look in your case.' He looked at the only luggage in the cage.

'Do you want me to look?' the friend asked eagerly and quickly stirred.

'No, you stay put for now. I'm sure I'll get a name soon.' The man maintained his stance but Caprice wasn't going to allow a stranger to bully her. She was just about to say something when she saw the old man approach their table. The train emerged from the tunnel but the darkness outside was equally oppressive. Rattling immediately stopped but a dull roar continued.

'Thanks for looking after my case. Are you okay sitting here as I prefer to sit nearer the loo.' The skeletal face with thin white hair didn't look perplexed. Caprice opened her mouth to answer the old guy.

'I'm just having a polite conversation with my new girlfriend here,' the hood interrupted and smirked. 'I'm not bothering you, am I?' he then asked Caprice, who was torn by the question. She was afraid for the old guy.

'When we get to Mistlethrop...' the old man replied for

Caprice, 'you can explain to my son and his mates how you know his girlfriend.'

The hood reluctantly sloped back to sitting position. Caprice stood and stepped sideways to jump over slouching legs. She retrieved her case before quickly passing it to the old man who turned and returned to his seat. Caprice jumped back to sprint after him but caught a last comment from the hood. 'Guess we'll have to work harder for our red meat.'

Without looking behind her Caprice caught up with the old man, whispered something into his ear then they walked through to the next carriage. The next ten minutes passed peacefully after assuring her new travelling companion that she was unharmed and unconcerned. The only light she could see through streaked windows was the twinkling of distant vehicles as they travelled across hillsides.

As the train pulled into Mistlethrop, rain became steady splattering. The old man carried Caprice's case to the bottom of platform steps where she turned it on its side to yank a pull-along handle. Steps to the upper level were steep. The ticket office was closed, its monitors blank. The old man offered to share a taxi and Caprice looked with longing at the taxi rank but refused then walked towards a road junction. Her damp hair received a fresh soaking as rain turned to large icy splodges.

Beyond the junction a rising street shined with water still gushing along kerbstones. A dirty glow from stormy sky reflected up from slippery cobbles but the pavement wasn't much easier to walk on while trying to navigate a rolling case. All the young woman's belongings were in her case, not much for her nineteen years.

Shops had closed early due to a forecast of extreme weather. A few display windows were lit to reveal abandoned, darker interiors. Case wheels whirred over wet stones then made a grinding, laboured pace over raised uneven surfaces. They drowned out the soft tread of two hooded figures to the rear. A muffled cough came from behind. Caprice turned. Two hooded men were twenty paces or so behind her, both with hands in their pockets, hoods pulled closely and shoulders determinedly hunched against icy rain.

There was a turn to the right where spotlight fell on a green metal sign over a stone archway, *Market*. Turning off the main street Caprice began a steeper ascent through shadows towards the sign. Paving, kerb and street merged as she picked up her pace so that her case banged over newer crescent-shaped cobbles. She looked over her shoulder. The men had also turned. With rising panic Caprice surged forward ignoring a warning squeak from case wheels.

Just as she neared her destination Caprice squinted to see two tall iron gates past the sign. Pitch-black under the archway masked its dark guardians but she hurried towards them then pulled at iron Fleurs de lis between Yorkshire roses but to no avail. There was a smaller sign pinned to the gates, *Market Closed. Mistlethrop Corporation, No dogs allowed in this market by order*. She quickly turned and backtracked but her new tormentors were confident and took their time. She could hear one of them chuckling while the other sang: 'Here kitty-kitty, come to daddy. I love a ginger pussy.'

Looking wildly to her left then right, Caprice saw a narrow alley threading from a side street along the back of shops. Instinctively, she darted towards it, launching her case into the air and wrenching her arm to swing forwards. Momentum would force her wobbly legs to move quickly.

Increasing their speed and now laughing openly, the pursuers parted. One sprang away, ran back down the main street to look for a left turn while the other headed into the alley. 'Our red meat will be trapped,' a voice shouted.

The swinging suitcase dropped heavily onto old cobbles, too heavy and wet to manoeuvre easily. As Caprice ran, it squealed and churned behind her. Just as she neared the rear of a pub she saw a black shape block the alley ahead. Out of breath and with her heart pounding in her ears she turned then to see a menacing shape behind her.

'Squeak, squeak!' The shape mimicked the squeal of wheels

and as he did so a wheel burst into pieces. A sudden shift of weight forced Caprice to slip on wet cobbles. She fell headlong onto stone. As she lost consciousness, Caprice fell into what seemed like a long black tunnel then continued to fall.

Barrington George the Third, or *Barri George* as printed on his business cards, had spent a few hours on a barstool. He'd calmly watched the progression of stormy weather from inside The Varsity pub. It was unusual for him to be out during the day. Weather had been so unpredictable that he had felt drawn to be part of it then taken strange delight in being forced to take shelter. He'd thought about the eight years since his compulsion had last erupted and like an alcoholic turned teetotal he knew exactly when, to the day, to the hour.

Humidity inside the pub had become uncomfortable. The landlord had reluctantly opened a door into the bar then a rear exit to allow equally reluctant breeze to flow through. Ceiling fans whirred overhead but did little except to disperse humidity. Barri slowly caressed an iPhone with as much reverence as his father had once treated a newly invented pocket-PC. He was bored. Weather had deteriorated with a bright flash. After thunder, lightning and heavy downpours, Barri had no choice but to sit and savour a bottle of Stella Artois much to the landlord's disgust. He considered his esteemed customer a tightwad. The door leading into the bar area slammed shut.

When a dirty glow filtered through windows, Barri took his last swig then headed for a toilet at the rear. At the end of a long narrow corridor he quickly poked his head out the exit to see if the rain had stopped. It hadn't. When he emerged from the toilet, Caprice was already running down the alley. Barri's curiosity was roused by squeals and laughter. He poked his head out again to see what was happening just as Caprice hit cobblestones then a dark figure quickly lowered onto hers. Without thinking Barri jumped out like a cork released from a bottle.

The hooded figure straddled a woman's body which was face down. He rifled through her pockets. It was this figure Barri brought both fists heavily down upon, clenched into a Thor-like hammer. The hammer hit the man in the square of his back immediately winding him. He fell across the witless form beneath but then threw his body sideways to roll against a wall. As he tried to stand up, his left foot slipped sideways on crisp bags around a blocked grid.

Barri reacted swiftly but as he pulled his fist back, something whizzed past his nose. Another figure had lobbed a discarded beer bottle but it had slipped through wet fingers. It momentarily caught Barri off guard. It was this moment of confusion the first man needed to make good his escape. He charged down the alley, stomping echoing feet to send sprays of water into the air. The second man quickly led the way. As he ran he picked up Caprice's case but it burst at the top and some of its contents fell out.

Barri watched two dark figures escape around the end of the alley. He felt heat throbbing along his arms while icy rain cooled his skin. Wet splodges on his shirt were soon added to like a dot-to-dot picture being formed. He then looked down at the victim. The woman was out cold. Her forehead had hit one of the cobbles. Barri bent down to gently roll her onto her back. His mind raced as quickly as the blood in his body. This was an unexpected opportunity.

After hours of being caught in vivid imagination and twisted perspective, Barri quickly surveyed the alley. His heart beat so hard he thought it would burst from his chest. Pausing for a second longer would make him question a rash decision. He re-entered the pub to turn off a corridor light then pulled the door behind him until he heard the clunk of an interior latch.

Without further delay Barri straddled his victim just as the hooded attacker had done. Slowly and carefully, he stretched his legs out behind him to place his wet torso against the girl's. He had to stifle a groan. A trickle of cold rain ran down the back of his neck then under his shirt to sensually enhance pure physical delight. Barri was so intoxicated with the unexpected that he shuddered then writhed with pleasure.

Barri's shirt sleeve was saturated and through it he felt the warmth of a throat. He also felt breath upon his face and he wanted to spend a moment to drink her in, feel life beneath him, feel the fragility. Just as he tensed forearm flexors, ready to roll an arm gently back and forth along the girl's throat, a thin stream of light spilled across the girl's face then disappeared. It happened again, a rapid pulse of light that stopped then flashed.

The pub door was still closed. Barri realised that the light had come from the end of the alley. A security light had momentarily burst into life, automatically set to switch on when the alley was dark enough but its sensors confused by the weather. Barri blinked and swore. The light was only a temporary intrusion. He returned focus to his unexpected opportunity but was caught by a sight that sent all yearnings for unnatural ecstasy, for a satisfying snap of bone into quandary. He gasped.

A spill of light captured the young woman's features like a flashbulb from a camera. An egg-shaped bump shined purple on her upper forehead but it was the wet, sleek, copper tones of her hair that drew his breath. It spread around her paleness like a halo. For a second his eyes played tricks and he thought he saw Elspeth beneath him. His breath caught in his throat as though it was he who had been hit by a hammer of fists. The intensity of a memory transposed to this young woman's face winded him.

The girl murmured. Barri knew he had to act quickly but the lure of seeing delicately-freckled eyelids open, to peer into eyes then witness last moments was tantalising. He couldn't resist, he faltered.

Caprice moaned. Something heavy was crushing her, something unfamiliar and powerful. As her senses gradually returned, she raised finely plucked eyebrows but her eyes remained closed. Barri watched fascinated, his face just a breath away, as neat arches of finely entwined copper raised then eyelids stretched, glistening with raindrops. Rain stopped abruptly. A blocked grid gurgled nearby, it echoed along the alley.

Sluggishly, eyelids opened fully and Barri was ready, waiting for a familiar sight of unfocussed pupil spring into awareness. He wasn't prepared for a vibrant flash of deep violet as the eyes opened wider and an intense expression of pain as the girl whispered a word. It sounded like: 'Mephisto.' Her breathy word was only just audible. It sent a shudder throughout the sinewy body on top of her. Then, the girl was suddenly focussed. Violet eyes showed mistrust as they ate into Barri. The young woman didn't move but neither did the man lying on top. At that moment Barri did something contrary to his black primal nature, he spoke: 'You're alive.' He felt embarrassed and it was foreign to him.

Still, the two bodies didn't move. The echo of gurgling drains dulled to a polite swallow. Barri realised his predicament. Caprice didn't know whether she was dreaming and felt numb.

'I thought you were dead,' Barri explained before sliding away from the young woman then quickly standing erect. He stretch out his right hand, palm up, as an offer to help her to her feet. *How am I going to explain what I was doing on top?*

The young woman looked at Barri's outstretched fingers. They phased in and out of clarity. Then, she bent her knees and slowly furled her stomach to rise into a sitting position. She winced, paused then pushed her knees to one side and eased into a kneeling position before standing up, ignoring his offer.

Barri took a few steps down the alley. He was on strange territory, shocked at his inability to act. Unfamiliar emotions overrode his disappointment. Now, he didn't know what to do or say. He patted the sides of his legs in confusion like an overgrown kid.

Just like a curious but suspicious cat would eye a predatory dog, the young woman slowly began to circle Barri. Her nostrils narrowed, almost sniffing him out. Barri was surprised but mesmerised. She looked at his soaked apparel ignoring her own wet and bedraggled state, arched her slender neck and throat instantly reminding Barri of one of his childhood pets. He shivered with a strong thrill of an old memory reinterpreted. His shirt clung to him and his jeans felt heavy with rain water.

Caprice was disorientated. She looked at the man but wouldn't look at his face. She saw an athletic physique, plainly visible through a soaked shirt. She could still feel his weight upon her. 'Where did they go?' she asked; the tone of her voice relayed mistrust. She raised her fingers to her forehead but didn't touch it then swayed as though to fall into a swoon. Barri jumped forward with his arms outstretched but didn't touch her. The young woman quickly pulled herself back then steadied herself by leaning one hand against a brick wall.

'They fled.' Barri was relieved that he could state some of the truth. 'I managed to get a swipe at one of them before he harmed you any further but then they ran off.'

'So what were you doing on top of me?' The young woman then experienced her first jolt of pain. Her hot head throbbed. Her skin felt stretched taut across her forehead like a saint being tortured on a rack. She winced when she touched a large tender bump. Barri reigned in his emotion and straightened his spine, feeling mental agility returning with a fresh surge of adrenalin.

'One of them floored me by bringing his fists down in the middle of my back and I fell across you.' Again, Barri was relieved to use some truth although it wasn't he who had been winded. He felt another surge of adrenalin, the satisfaction of covering his actions so plausibly.

There was something so weird and unexpected about what was happening that Barri was like a wasp caught in honey. This was the most conversation he'd had with a woman for some time, in fact with anyone. The novelty of it radiated nervous energy. He knew the girl had a presence. Immediately his unsettled mind attempted to adjust him to this strange series of events. *This could be an advantage. She could be something to look forward to, to savour*, like his bottle of Stella Artois. Just as he was warming to this idea another childhood memory unexpectedly surfaced, the first chicken bone he'd heard his father crush. He shuddered then thought: *I could have a*

27

pleasure to surpass anything I ever felt before.

'My things!' the young woman exclaimed. 'Where's my case?' Caprice's voice betrayed panic.

Barri looked behind him; a few contents from the broken case had landed next to the grid. Barri reached down to first pick up a small handheld hairdryer but it was broken. A black box lay on its side nearby. The box was cracked in two, its soggy red velvet innards ripped by splinters of black enamelled wood. He stooped again to retrieve a tiny figure lying among the wreckage. It was a ballerina with one leg folded, the other balanced on tip toe.

'One of your attackers ran off with your case.' He sounded almost apologetic. Barri handed the ballerina to the young woman but she swayed again and had to re-steady herself against the wall. A fresh dilemma challenged Barri's self-control. *What am I going to do with her next? Calling an ambulance is out of the question, if she reports what happened then I'll be asked for a statement.* It was coolly discarded.

'Look, you can't stay here, go inside the pub.' *It's the only solution, let others take over and I'll go home.* As soon as he'd made the suggestion Barri felt disappointed and sulky. *It's a pity I spent the afternoon in the pub. If she describes me to the landlord then he'll definitely know it was me.*

'No, no, I don't want that!' The young woman's hissed insistence surprised her saviour and for the second time Barri was lost for words. Before he had chance to ask her why, the girl realised that her words may have sounded strange and added: 'I couldn't face it. All I want is to find somewhere I can clean myself up until I can get the next train out of here.' She sounded pathetic but spoke the truth. Barri stifled his relief. The thrill of having a pleasure to look forward to returned. Again, Barri was shocked by his reaction.

'Then you'd best come with me. You can clean yourself up at my house.'

Caprice felt sick to her stomach. *Can this day get any crappier?*

4. Prelude

Fourteen years ago, in the sanctuary of his tree-house, Barri had sat at a small table and hugged himself.

He wore Elspeth's bracelet and stared down at a coir mat while trying to recapture a thrill. His father walked across the lawn to look at a symbol of his own childhood then came to a halt at the foot of the tree. The man brooded then looked back at the house waiting for anger to subside. Another argument with his wife had made him wish he was a boy again.

'Bloody-hell,' he swore when his wife appeared with a face like granite at Radburn's front door. He watched with seething as her high heels sank mercilessly into the pristine lawn. She was feeling bullish.

'I expect the next stage of our argument will be conducted more civilly in the open.' Her neighbours and friends had been surprised that the stigma of a child's death hadn't forced the George's to move.

'Why on earth would you want to move to a new build?' Mr George spat. 'Radburn goes back four generations. Do you want a house without character, a featureless box filled with cheap Swiss furniture and people drowning in debt next door?'

'But...the tree-house!' his wife pleaded.

'Rubbish! It was just one of those things.' Mr George crossed his arms to prevent them from flaying around. 'The girl had been here for what, an hour or so? Our family's been here for years. I'm not allowing that girl, who shouldn't have been up there in the first place, to destroy Barrington's den.'

'Why not, he won't be here to use it after next week?'

Mr George shot his wife a look that could have instantly formed skin on rice pudding then stormed back to the house. Mrs George watched her husband's determined stride then placed the palm of her left hand, with its polished acrylic tips, against rough crumbling bark. She stared up at the tree.

'You're another monstrosity in my life, one I have to put up with but another about to be removed. You should have been chopped down and burned,' she hissed between gritted teeth then looked at grass around her feet. 'I suppose the lawn would have eventually grown over but the roots would still be here. Removing something from sight doesn't get rid of the problem. You will be my penance. What else can I do?' She'd continually asked herself this question and preferred it to the more serious question of: *What should I do for Barri?* Barri had heard every word and worried about where he would be the following week.

Two days later, in a fit of pique Mrs George deposited her son at the reception of Radburn Confectionery, declaring: 'Your father can try looking after you!'

Ignoring the Receptionist's order to stay put until she'd phoned through, Barrington took the lift up, marched through winding corridors, passed numerous offices with brass nameplates until he reached his father's. There would be no need to knock. Barri expected his father to be overjoyed that his son had surprised him. *He'll sit me on the big chair then tell me how all this will be mine one day.*

When Barri turned the handle he was too young to understand what he saw. His father's grimace instantly brought to mind a wooden clown from a little-used jack-in-the-box. Beneath him a strange woman lay across his desk, her long neck and pink throat bent backwards like the arched spine of a pig. The woman's eyes were tightly closed and she wore the same bright lipstick as Barri's mum. A sharp crack sounded as something beneath the writhing couple shattered. Barri jumped back as though a bullet had shot through him. He swiftly sidestepped and turned to place his back against an outside wall.

Perhaps I should have coughed or something? He hadn't seen two humans touch like that before. *Were they touching?* Then, he heard his father grunt followed by an open laugh, full-throttle and strange to his son's ears. His eyes instantly filled with tears. The pig-like woman had claimed his father and stolen a moment of glory. The boy plodded slowly back to the lift.

'I've seen my dad. Can you telephone my mum? Tell her I'm ready to go home now.' The boy looked contrite and the Receptionist tried not to smile.

'Wouldn't you want to speak to her yourself?'

'No.'

He was quiet on the way home and although his mum didn't think anything of her son's silence she kept looking at her rear-view mirror. Barri's face was as pink as a freshly born pig. His mother basked in a small dose of victory. *He's learned a lesson at last.* Barri had been crushed to his core.

When his father came home Barri looked at him for a long time. Mr George sat in his customary chair at the head of the table, cufflinks neatly at the side of a gold-rimmed plate.

'I'm glad Barri came to his senses today,' Mrs George remarked.

'Did he misbehave again?' Mr George had no idea what his wife referred to.

'He did but perhaps in future he should have more time-outs at your office.'

Mr George's fork dropped onto his plate chipping its rim. He looked at his son for the first time since he'd arrived home. Barri's still-water eyes saw a quick change of countenance. Instead of the usual static expression, wrath surfaced through a red face and it stung Barri to his quick, his mouth dropped open. The father looked from the boy to the mother then back again.

'He will NOT visit my office again! That is a place for work and, if you...' Mr George leaned forward to jab a finger into his son's shoulder, '...want to frit away your chances to do something with your life... If YOU can't mix with people and work with them then, DON'T come to my place of work and expect sympathy!' Mr George picked up his fork, stole a sly sideways glance at his wife then continued his meal ignoring the chip in his plate. His son's eyes glistened. He played with food on his plate.

'Eat the dinner your mother has cooked,' his father insisted.

Afterwards, as Barri changed into pyjamas, he saw his father outside his bedroom. He wondered how long he'd been there and what he was doing at this far end of the hallway.

'I meant what I said downstairs,' his father hissed through a darkened doorway. 'What did you do at my office?'

As Barri rushed to button his pyjamas, he lied. 'I sat with the lady at the front desk.'

Mr George stormed into the room then loomed over his son, forcing him to look up at his imposing figure. Barri looked straight into his father's fury and trembled. Fright mixed with a strange excitement as he heard sharp snaps. His father menacingly cracked his knuckles. 'Your mother shouldn't have taken you there. It's no place for a child. You won't be able to do that again, you hear?'

'I thought chocolate factories were for children,' Barri tried to reason wondering what his father meant by *won't be able*.

In an effort to calm himself, Mr George stretched to touch his son's hair but Barri, unsure of the intention, pulled back. His behind plonked down hard on the bed. Like a whip lashed, the hand sprang back to form a tight fist but Mr George tottered, ready to launch an attack as soon as he saw a signal. The boy cowered lower, petrified that his father had been replaced by some kind of alien or devilish monster. He'd seen it on *Invasion of the Body Snatchers*. Mr George leaned back with fists still clenched then abruptly spun round and left. Barri shivered with terror but more importantly, he shivered with the sudden absolute conviction of a small boy that his father hated the sight of him.

The first night at boarding school came as a shock. Earlier that day, Barri's mother had attempted to placate her son's worried expression. Although she hadn't seen him so upset before it hadn't plucked at any heart strings. 'Don't worry, you'll love it. You'll mix with boys just like you.' His father had said:

'Things will be different from when I was a boy. If nothing else you'll learn how to deal with people.'

Barri had to share a room with three other boys. He wasn't allowed to wear Elspeth's present but it was in his hands after dorm lights went out. It dulled abject misery as he recalled snap and crunch.

Following the Festive season, Barri took a fancy to Brazil nuts and for his eleventh birthday asked for a nutcracker much to the amusement of his parents and dorm mates. When refrigerated, nuts provided a more satisfying crack, a familiar sound to keep darker yearnings at bay. A mini-cooler was also requested then placed on a window ledge behind his bed. Barri earned a nickname, *Brazil* but it was pronounced like *Basil*. It assisted Barri's integration into a new environment but whenever he heard someone calling it from the end of a corridor his facial muscles tightened. He remembered children chanting.

It soon became apparent that Barri had an avid interest in science. He absorbed lessons with the ease of a kitchen towel soaking up spillage and although he excelled at every subject, science remained his favourite. With all his cerebral activity it could be assumed that he would become a nerd with aspirations but physical activities were high on the school's list of normal and healthy pursuits.

Barri quickly realised the benefits of a strong physical presence. He threw himself into sports with the gusto of a man released from prison into the yard. It came as a surprise to other boys, particularly a tall lanky lad with sinewy limbs and a self-assured smugness that he would be the alpha. Like all threats, the lanky lad dealt with it as only a bully knew how to. First, he'd put the fear of God into a new victim.

'Why bother?' he snarled at Barri in the changing rooms. Barri's expressionless face arched an eyebrow and it was taken as a question. 'Don't bother looking at me like that; you know you're a faggot.' No reaction, the lad interpreted it as fear. 'Faggots like you can be easily crushed to a pulp, so why bother trying to be something you're not?' Still, there was no reaction.

"Faggot" was a word bandied as only light insult or friendly banter but Barri knew by the lad's threatening posture and decreasing distance between them that it was an excuse for a more meaningful dialogue. Barri wouldn't need words.

The lad now stood inches away and looked down on a blond crown intending to thump it hard with both fists. Barri raised his head. His cold eyes pierced a moment of uncertainty and it was enough. Without hesitation, Barri quickly turned and walked away intending to fool the lad. A smile broke through the bully's snarl. Barri walked only so far. He swiftly turned and, dipping his blond crown, charged like a ferocious but silent bull. Within seconds, the lad was knocked off his feet. 'Yow!' Before he knew it, Barri was on top peering down, unyielding, unemotional but with a glint in one eye. Sinewy arms thrashed upwards but Barri brought one clenched fist down so hard that an instant crack confirmed bone had shattered. The victor jumped up to one side then strode confidently away to leave his victim splattered with blood.

The beaten bully writhed, choked then tried to find his legs but reeled from the rapidity of the attack. He wouldn't bother Barri again nor admit to anyone that he'd been defeated. Everyone knew it was so easy to slip in a damp changing room. Little-did-he-know that he was lucky to escape with only crushed nasal bone and cartilage. Afterwards, his lankiness developed into a distinct hunch; a heavy secret pulled him down.

Armed with an excellent knowledge of impact upon bone, Barri excelled in Rugby and gained a reputation as a tough but brutal player. As protective gear wasn't a requirement as it is in the States for football, Barri could get away with continuing his release on the field. He was vigilant to only injure when an opportunity presented itself and it was by no means personal. He neither liked nor disliked any of his school mates, he tolerated them.

'That lad doesn't open his mouth much.' A teacher spoke to a colleague as they watched a match. 'Not even on the field.'

Yells and guttural grunts exploded around the teachers but Barri remained focussed. His silence added to his aura of strength and confidence. After several seconds, the teacher's colleague responded. 'I wish they were all like that, getting them to shut-up during lessons is a full-time job. As long as he's doing what's expected of him and he continues to play like THAT...' Just then, Barri wrestled the ball from an opponent and carried it away like it was glued to him. Opponents were caving-in easier. 'There's something odd about him though.'

'D'ya think? I've always found him polite and thorough. The other lads seem to look up to him.'

'Are you sure that's not fear?' and the teacher smirked.

'Yeah, fear of him out-running, out-playing and out-performing them all!'

During school holidays Barri's parents agreed for once, that their son should avoid Mistlethrop until he'd acquired social skills. Mrs George had been constantly uneasy even in close friends' company. She grew morose. At the slightest provocation she suffered fits of exasperation followed by sinking despair, usually after a silent meal at the dinner table aided by two large glasses of wine.

A second residence was purchased in Whitby; the Yorkshire East coast preferable. It held fond memories for Mr George and he could quickly drive back to work if needed. On occasion, the family would also vacation abroad but never longer than a week.

Mr George continued his fascination with a pocket-PC. His wife grew to hate her husband's anal routines particularly the sight of his cufflinks next to a plate. She counted the seconds until the pocket-PC joined them. Her husband became increasingly concerned by his perfect wife's decline. It affected his ability to focus so he did what he always did; he threw money at a problem until it disappeared.

Mrs George was sent to stay with her sister in Italy and it gave her husband a chance to make a change. An annexe was added to the far side of Radburn then the drawing room wall knocked through for a door. Light flooded in through floor-to-ceiling windows overlooking the lawn, the interior fitted with geometric parquet and oak panelling. Plum leather sofas and glass side tables were positioned to take in the view, some angled on a higher split-level towards a cinema screen.

When Mrs George returned home she was immediately ushered into the new annexe by a proud and excited husband. 'I've been busy while you were away,' he boasted. A project manager had done it all whereas Mr George had signed cheques. His wife, pumped with enough anti-depressants to plaster a smile permanently upon her face, had been given enough distance and time to develop a new perspective.

Perhaps my suspicions were over-zealous? She turned slowly to take it all in. *It's romantic in a way, a gesture.* She was overcome with the simplicity but elegance of her husband's choices. 'You did all this for me?'

'Of course, you needed a change at home too.'

'Will things change?' Mrs George looked anxiously at her husband.

'They already have.' Mr George rocked on his heels with his hands in his pockets and beamed. *I've done everything within my power. It's now up to her to move past a difficult period in our lives.*

Mrs George's eyes were drawn to the tree at the end of the lawn then, when she looked at interior walls was instantly reminded of the tree-house. 'Oak wouldn't have been my personal choice.' Mr George's facial muscles tightened and twitched.

'It's in keeping with the house.'

Barri began to record experiments. He created a chronicle of observations and results, he being the apparatus. During a half-term holiday in Whitby he purchased a leather-bound notebook and was particular when choosing it. Leather binding reminded him of Elspeth's gift. The A6 book became precious cargo. It was small enough to be carried in a blazer inside-pocket and only temporarily released to a padlocked locker. An electronic version would be a risk. Barri preferred the tactile feel of pen and pencil against his fingers. It added another dimension to remembering how he had arrived at results.

At first the chronicle was written with perception after facts. It held a record of Barri's earlier experiments upon pets and stray animals from Paxton Park. Elspeth was referred to as *"Subject Fifteen."* Later, it detailed rugby experiments and he would linger over his words while savouring the sound of nuts cracking.

When Barri reached his fourteenth birthday, he'd formed a template for future endeavours. *"Victim"* wasn't in his notes. Nothing had been as satisfactory as his first human *Subject* but he seized an opportunity three weeks after his birthday.

The school janitor added his niece to the cleaning staff. Ironically, she was forced to undertake menial work at the school to fund a distance-learning course. The girl worked afternoons when Barri had lessons. The logistics of finding a suitable locale for the movement of his subject relied on too many unknown factors. The yearning to relive his experience with Elspeth clutched at Barri's innards whenever he caught sight of the girl between classes. Eventually, he had to yield.

After pilfering roofies from a boy who boasted about their sedative effect on women, Barri placed a chocolate-chip muffin in a red organza bag then added a bow. The gift was placed on the handle of a floor buffer and when Barri's lesson ended he rushed to the Orangery at the back of the school. Once through the exit, the teen clambered through tall shrubbery until he was on a dried mud track at the other side. Shrubbery and the hidden track ran the full course of the school then along a gravelled courtyard at the front. Vehicles used a tarmac road on the opposite side.

Barri thought he'd been thorough in his research. He knew how long it would take for the effects of his gift to kick in. The girl would be on her way home and according to plan, she was semi-conscious at the end of the track. He was prepared and blew into thin surgical gloves then slivered his hands into them before dragging the girl into shrubbery. Throwing his blazer to one side, he sat astride a semi-lifeless body. Using a bare arm was out of the question, Barri's forearms had a thin layer of cling-wrap. Unfortunately, he was ignorant of one fact; the girl was asthmatic.

His subject had suffered a reaction, in distress after only a mouthful of muffin. Suddenly, a sweet smell of chocolate rasping onto Barri's face lost its appeal. The throat he'd fantasised about while in a dormitory bed stroking a friendship bracelet, became a bucking bronco of choking spasms. The subject's eyes were unfocussed but in obvious pain. They and she disgusted him. Barri retrieved the red organza bag and its bow, donned his blazer then returned to his dorm. He made a note in his chronicle: *"Say no to drugs."*

The janitor found his niece on his way home. She was beneath a large creeping passion-flower that grew through the shrubbery. When he found her she was festooned with purple flowers, her inhaler still in her pocket. A coroner later advised: 'To some asthmatics passion-flowers can be lethal. They must be avoided.'

Two years passed. At last Barri found his rapture again and with it some of the passion the flowers covering his subject had failed to pass on. Exercise and the endorphins Barri's brain produced after it, helped to relieve abnormal desire. His daily ritual now included an early morning run and his Head Master had a theory. 'I've said it once and I'll say it again, a high level of physical activity is the reason why that boy is so laid back during exam times. Why can't all my pupils be like him?'

His run would take Barri past playing fields and tennis courts to woodlands beyond and it was there the ideal pupil saw his next subject. She was at that age when a teenager wants to make the most of a budding physique and so she liked to run too. She made an exaggerated deal of it whenever she emerged from her semi to run through her estate to the edge of the woods. Barri discreetly watched, got to know her route and running times. His efforts were noticed and the girl was flattered. *He's one of those posh schoolboys. He must have money, not like the plebs at my school.* She kept her thoughts to herself not wanting to raise the interest of a rival, but, that wasn't the only draw. The boy was handsome as well as muscular. Barri's hair had darkened to dirty-blond. His face had matured from sullen arrogance to a cool awareness of self and abilities, apparent in pale-blue eyes.

At first the two runner's paths crossed unexpectedly in the woods. Then, as Barri moved into the observation stage, he kept his distance. The girl was used to closer attention from the opposite sex. She used her mum's hair-lightener to give mousy locks a lift.

One morning Barri put on his lightweight field gloves. They disguised another. Taut surgical gloves against fingers were highly pleasurable. Again, timing was everything, the exact location for his fall and how long he would have to lie across it before the girl ran around the corner. Barri was careful to ensure his watch dial wasn't obliterated by the long sleeves of his rugby shirt. This time it was personal, he'd studied the art of flirting. The girl knelt to help him, blew gently on his grazed knee.

'Keep still,' she said between slow puffs of air. 'It'll take the sting out.' Soft brown eyes flicked over him before she returned to her task with a blush in her cheeks.

What a stupid thing to say, Barri thought as he looked at the girl closely. His cheek muscle twitched when he saw that her hair was two-toned and dull under sunlight. *It should be red.* His eyes lowered to her face and lips, then her neck. Her skin looked soft, supple and covered in the faintest down. He had an urge to lean forward, lift her chin and brush his face against it but he hesitated.

As the girl raised her head, there was an almost-kiss, a moment when two people are drawn by invisible force. Barri instinctively wanted to rest his lips upon a slightly open mouth, feel breath meet his before sliding the kiss lower until lips rested against neck, her throat. The sheer headiness of the encounter was electric. The girl was eagerly receptive; she read the signals

39

of attraction. Barri was, for the first time, aware of his power to attract.

'Let me help you.' The girl had a syrupy voice. Barri nodded but didn't say anything and it was interpreted as bashfulness. They stood up together. Barri limped pitifully, his subject with the misconception that she held all the power. He leaned on her shoulder as she guided him and she did all the talking. 'They won't mind me bringing you into your school will they?' Her eyes glistened with the prospect of more handsome, muscular types seeing her in the role of heroine and nurse. *This one is too shy.*

Barri nodded. They didn't go far. He stumbled again but grabbed onto the girl to make it seem that he was trying to prevent a fall. Instead, he engineered it into a joint tumble into long side-grass. The girl giggled. Their two bodies lay as one. Barri lay across his subject, pinning down a willing body. He remembered his prep-notes: *"There is one constant - a willing subject or one taken so unaware that the suddenness and rapidity of following actions come as a total surprise."* He could relish the seconds it takes for his new subject to repeat Elspeth's last moments. The girl's face was pink with pleasure.

Perhaps he's not so shy after all.

Barri pursed his lips to blow a slow stream of breath against the silken throat. If his lips had been closer then he would have tasted perspiration. Instead, he inhaled a sweet essence of scented soap, a clean fresh smell. As he blew he leaned up then pulled up a sleeve. To his surprise the girl's body responded by lifting her pelvis slightly. He became aroused, but not from the closeness of the body beneath. It was the excitement of feeling his arm take position, gently at first, then gazing into trusting eyes. A halo of hair surrounded a susceptive and yielding face.

The dull crack, the drainage of life, the shudder and retreat into death was more than any physical union could provide. It went beyond a joining of bodies. Barri was the institutor, the bringer of death and the girl's final gurgles, music. He relished it for as long as he could then dragged the body farther into the woods, piling wood and leaves over and around her. He gave his subject a gift and placed it around her wrist, a friendship bracelet. Then, Barri returned to a shower, clean clothes and his study-period. The penknife he'd used to score skin on his knee had been cleaned and put away.

Experiments stopped. Barri was sensible enough to know that to repeat them would be a mistake. His last experience would sustain him. The more he thought about it in the darkness of his dorm at night, the more he was convinced. *It will take a special subject to prolong agony and joy.*

Time passed, boarding school was replaced by university then... within a week of his parent's car accident, one of Barri's first decisions was to change office layout. He wanted open-plan and the only private office would be his. Two of his father's office walls were replaced with glass so that during the night Barri could look out at banks of unoccupied desks minus dividing barriers. He preferred to work at night.

During the day desk occupants looked directly into Barri's office but their new boss didn't think it mattered if he wasn't there. Table-top computers were replaced with laptops and a clear-desk policy introduced.

Sometimes at night, Barri walked between banks of desks to look at the personal touches a few die-hard employees still clung to. He picked up a family photo to then replace it face down or flipped open a desk diary annoyed that it hadn't been shared electronically. Secrecy was his privilege. The only paperwork he valued was a leather-bound notebook secreted in his bedroom at Radburn House. It was in a place even the cleaner couldn't stumble upon.

Nearing his twenty-fourth birthday, Barri was despondent. *I have the world at my feet but, it isn't the world I'm interested in.*

5. Curiosity and the Cat

From the moment Barri first caught sight of Caprice's vibrant halo of red then looked into disturbed violet eyes, his world expanded. He was caught in time, in the seconds when fragility lay beneath him and he knew he could crush it. He also recognized that she would be The One.

In this surreal new world, air was charged with high-frequency energy. Barri was sensually and acutely sensitive, like a plasma globe with a hand placed upon it to the young woman's presence. He began to hear and see through the duality of both hunter and prey.

What could have been awkward silence during their car journey wasn't acknowledged by driver or passenger. It was late afternoon, drawing into early evening. Rain ceased for brief respite. Wispy blue sky appeared and was then swallowed by oppressive slate-coloured cloud as humidity returned with a vengeance. Caprice stared out of a car window.

'You have a name?' Barri's thought became audible and to have spoken it shocked him. *Did I just say that? Do I need to know her name?* His next thought offered: *Elspeth.* He had to quickly glance at his passenger to check if she'd heard. He was then unsure whether he had actually said or just thought it. *Did I leave it too long?*

Caprice heard herself tell the stranger her name. It was a normal thing to do, to introduce oneself but she didn't pay attention to a reply, not that her saviour offered a name in exchange. 'I need to go to Bradbury as soon as possible.' She didn't get a response. *Why did I tell him that?* She didn't elucidate, said nothing about using that city as a stopgap before deciding what to do next. Each journey in her life hadn't yet taken her far enough away from her damage. *Is that what it is, damage?* Her damage was unbearable and she drove it like a stampede of wild horses from her mind, otherwise she'd be dragged and crushed underfoot. It was like looking at the space where a deformed and shrivelled limb had once been. Better off without it, she bitterly mourned what it could have been.

They passed Paxton Park. Black pools of stagnant water smothered grass and only became visible when silent lightning flashed from a billowing black mass overhead. The car turned right into Dandelion View. Caprice kept her eyes firmly fixed on a leaf-strewn road. Another turn to the right and the car drove along a side driveway, past a sweeping front lawn smothered in leaves and broken branches. A huge old oak tree's limbs had been victims. Barri noticed and suddenly felt his old warmth followed by panic. He became a child again, remembering what the tree had once meant to him. He had to stop himself from running out the car to check it was okay.

The bleakness of the man's home roused Caprice's interest, she thought of Rebecca's first glimpse of Manderley. Without that fictional mansion's stately grandeur and twisted thread driveway, it held the same shadow of secrecy and silence. *It must be apartments.*

Barri had a guest and as such only the front entrance would do. He struggled with keys in the semi-darkness. Caprice looked up from a step. *I can't see any wall buzzers.*

The right key was found, a light switch flicked but followed by a brief delay before a hallway became bathed by chandelier. Barri strolled in and deposited a plastic bag containing what was left of Caprice's belongings onto a gentleman's tub chair. Creased and cracked leather didn't detract from a luring temptation of comfort. It stood near a walnut grandfather clock against walnut half-panelling. Barri dropped his keys onto a table. The entrance was so formal and old-fashioned that Caprice immediately groaned. 'You live with your parents?' She looked about, dreading meaningless introduction and small-talk.

'No.'

Radburn House was Barri's home and no longer just somewhere he visited. A lorry-driver, asleep at his wheel, had ploughed into his parents' car. In two years, their son hadn't changed anything except his room and his father's cinema screen, replaced by a sixty-inch plasma TV. The rest of the house was touched only by a cleaner who visited once a week and only in the evening. Barri had insisted.

As he looked at the young woman in his hallway Barri became confused. New sensations mixed with old. Suddenly he wanted to run to his room, rummage about in drawers until he found Elspeth's gift. *Have I set myself too big a challenge?* He hadn't encountered one since school. *Perhaps this is exactly what I need?*

'I'll leave your bag here. The main bathroom is at the top of the stairs, first door to right. Do you need anything?' Barri looked at Caprice's wet and smeared jacket and patches on her jeans, wishing he hadn't given all his mother's clothes to a charity.

'I could do with a shower, if that's okay?' Caprice assessed smears to her clothing. Patches were superficial not ingrained but she couldn't see that the purple bump on her head had formed into a black shiny mess. 'I can dry off my things while I take it.'

'Do what you have to.' Barri hadn't seen romantic movies where a soaked heroine is obliged to wear the hero's oversized shirt after showering.

The young woman climbed a staircase opposite the tub-chair, fighting overwhelming weariness. All she could think of was a cold wet facecloth on her forehead to sooth swelling and throbbing pain. Barri watched her ascend then walked into a long dining room through to a spacious kitchen. While the kettle was boiling, he looked up *National Rail Enquiries* on his iPhone then, *Latest Travel News*.

'She said she was...' Barri shivered. '...Caprice said she was on her way to Bradbury. It will be a problem for her.' Saying the young woman's name out loud sent a shiver down Barri's

44

neck. He thought of the rain in the alley and a similar sensation. *Is it a problem for me?* Judging by her clothes and lack of belongings, Caprice wouldn't have much money for an overnight hotel which suited him fine. 'Think, think!' he said to his phone. 'It was so easy in the past.' Now, when Barri envisaged a stranger spending a night under his roof, his stomach churned.

When Caprice had showered, shampooed, brushed dirt from dry clothes and was re-attired, she made her way back down the stairs. A clock ticking echoed around her and she wasn't sure where to go. Not knowing Barri's name, she asked hesitantly: 'Are you there?' with a polite but raised voice.

Poking her head around a door, she peered into dense blackness so she backtracked and tried another door. It opened onto a dining room and as she hadn't received an answer, she asked again but a little louder.

'Through here,' a male voice replied from a doorway at the end of the room. Caprice walked through the room, admiring a long dining table. She counted eighteen chairs, eight along each side and one at either end. She wanted to feel what it would be like to sit at the head of a grand table in an elegant room but resisted the temptation. Candelabra wall-lights twinkled her way to a kitchen and when she entered, she was equally impressed.

Brushed-steel appliances and a white centre-island lifted the heaviness of dark wood cabinets. Limestone floor and a wall of cream stone reflected light from a white ceiling with centre light-panel. After the elegance of an old-fashioned hall, the dining room and kitchen held a mixture of traditional and modern design. Her host poured coffee from a carafe.

'Bad news I'm afraid,' and the host turned his head to gesture at an iPhone upon the island. He didn't want his smirk to be noticed. Caprice picked up the phone, not sure what to do. Barri brought two bone-china coffee mugs over and quickly relieved Caprice of her puzzle. *She doesn't know what to do with it.* He was surprised.

45

'Here.' He handed it back to her. Caprice slowly drew her breath as she read its screen while Barri's eyes went to her hair, now scarlet under bright kitchen lights. He gasped, so taken with its colour that he had to stop himself from reaching out to touch it. Again, he felt flesh-tingling awareness of the young woman's presence. The hairs of his forearm stood to attention as he waited for her to say something.

'I'll find somewhere to stay for tonight,' she sighed. The young woman had enough money in her purse to pay for a hotel room but she had deliberately disposed of bank and credit cards before starting her journey. 'Do you know a hotel near the station?'

Barri caught a tantalising whiff of soap just used, a fresh clean smell he had enjoyed with his last subject. He didn't want to release it by exhaling nor release this fresh new victim back into the world. 'Stay here, there are plenty of rooms.'

Caprice then looked into her host's cool-water eyes. It was the first time she'd looked at him properly. *Perhaps I'm now in the right place at the right time.*

'Will anyone else mind?' Her eyes narrowed.

'No, I'm the only one here.'

'I'll stay but I'd appreciate a lift to the station first thing tomorrow?' Staring back into his coolness, Caprice thought that this inconvenience may not be so bad. Then, Barri made another rash, snap decision.

'I must go to work now. Choose one of the bedrooms on this side of the house. I won't be back until late.'

'Aren't you going to eat before you go?'

'No, but help yourself to anything you find, but I must go... now!' He sounded impatient which took Caprice by surprise. She stood to one side as he quickly brushed by.

The normally confident young man was unsure of himself and what was expected of him as a saviour or host. He had to have room to think, to plan, to gain control over a furore of unfamiliar emotions. Like the weather, he was neither day nor night.

46

On the journey to his office, Barri couldn't stop thinking about his first night at boarding school. His room to breathe and think freely had been snatched away by demanding strangers. Barri shrugged it off. 'I must be coming down with something.' Later, when he entered his office, he was greeted with an unexpected but cheery comment from his assistant.

'You've made an exception today!' Barri looked angrily at the man, who immediately regretted speaking then looked at his watch. It was only five-thirty. The boss preferred to work alone in the small hours when Radburn's offices were abandoned and silent.

Office staff didn't miss what was never there. Overnight factory hands were accustomed to seeing Barri's car enter then leave the car park. He was considered an eccentric who preferred to only communicate by email, phone or via his proficient assistant. He was nothing like his father.

'Why not work from home? Why does he bother to go into the office at all?'

His assistant had one explanation: 'He prefers the discipline of an office.'

'Are you sure he's not one of them True Blood types?'

On rare occasions Barri made an appearance earlier than usual but only if a business appointment demanded it. He sent nightly instructions to his assistant who found them in his email inbox the following day. Signed papers were piled neatly on his desk. The assistant was empowered to act on Barri's behalf but only if he first cleared it with him. The boss still found people difficult to be with but was at ease with how he dealt with them. His personal presence often caused unease. Demure quietness and a look of intensity meant he was deliberating the meaning of every word spoken.

Since leaving The Varsity Barri hadn't paid any attention to his appearance. His assistant refrained from asking except for: 'There's a spare shirt in the cupboard behind your desk.' Barri experienced angry embarrassment, another first. He barged past his assistant.

'I got caught in the storm.'

Meanwhile, Caprice was alone in Radburn House and unsure how to occupy her time. Her first inclination was to find a room to temporary call her own. She didn't know whether she would be able to sleep that night but she felt secure. *My tormentor won't be able to find me here.*

Taking her coffee with her, Caprice re-entered the dining room then pulled out a table-end chair, careful not to lay her hot cup on grained wood. She spread her free hand across it, stretching fingers to feel smooth coolness while looking directly ahead. She imagined guests and a table laden with a feast. This was a first for her, to imagine wealth and a superior position. She sat in the chair Mr George had once occupied then, like Barri's, her perspective tilted. She saw through the eyes of both hostess and guest.

Barri washed in his private bathroom then changed his shirt. With some order restored he paced his office not realising that he was pacing. His assistant looked nervously through a glass wall. Barri hadn't switched on his office light. Something was wrong. The assistant didn't like an unexpected visit then brooding. The rest of the outer office didn't like it either.

Barri paced and when he passed his desk a fourth time, he realised what he was doing. He looked up to see his assistant twitching an overfilled folder and the rest of his staff flicking eyes between laptop screens and his office. He'd been buried too deep in thought, trying to collect spilt apples. As soon as he stopped pacing, his assistant flew from his seat and tapped on the office glass door before automatically allowing himself in. Barri clenched his molars. 'What is it?' The assistant licked his lips before replying.

'We... You... received a business proposal from Mandrake Bakeries. It came today. They want a response by the end of the week.'

'Do they now?' Barri purred the words with contempt and placed his hands in his jean front pockets. 'It will be up to me when I give them a response. Leave it with me.' This was Barri's

48

favourite expression, good for most occasions. The assistant hovered with the folder before placing it on the desk. 'I'll let you know if I need to speak to you,' Barri confirmed as the man retraced his steps.

Barri walked to his glass wall to stare out and waited for all eyes to return to their work. Then, he sat at his desk but ignored the folder. Instead, he opened his laptop, waited for Windows then stared at a blue screen. He felt exhausted, as though he'd survived a trauma. Tiredness enveloped him while looking through a desktop screen into the back of his mind.

What am I going to do about Caprice? Ironically, a song from an old school musical popped into his head and he found himself mentally humming: *How Do You Solve a Problem, Like Maria?* Barri shook his shoulders. *Where the hell did that come from?* His thoughts then continued to amble until he drifted uncontrollably into the soothing memories of his first kill. It was warm around his ears, a dense steam surrounding his face. Then, he opened his eyes and realised with alarm that he'd dozed. With a start, he looked across at the office but only his assistant's eyes were on him. Barri sat up and glared.

The wall clock showed six-thirty. Barri was amazed. Staff had already gone home. Barri tapped his watch face and his assistant took it as a hint. He quickly cleared items into drawers then went. 'And a good-night to you too,' he said under his breath as he headed for the lift.

Radburn's boss remained seated behind glass with only the blue glow of a laptop screen to light his face. Desks outside were now lit by dimmed fluorescence. 'Now, I can think!' He looked at the banks of desks outside his office and remembered his classroom at primary school. *My desk was at the front and Elspeth's next to mine.* He also remembered how he had resented other children with their smiling, inquisitive faces.

Barri was sat at his father's old desk. Just as Caprice spread her hands across his dining room table at home, he spread his across grained oak. He stretched fingers to feel its coolness. The memory of seeing what had happened upon the desk was

49

an old and painful one but now, it changed. Suddenly, Barri had clarity. It had been but one pebble thrown into a still and stagnant pond.

Some people have a disposition for the macabre. Some prefer fantasy to an unfulfilling existence. Some find that a single moment injects itself into their lives repeatedly until all they live for is that moment. Is that me?

'Why am I sitting here?' Barri now asked himself audibly. 'When I could be enjoying myself?'

First, before his enjoyment could begin, Barri would call briefly at The Varsity to see if his presence encouraged questions about earlier events. If someone had seen him, Caprice or the two men then he needed to know about it. He would stay at The Varsity for no longer than necessary but it would be both an agony and a thrilling delay to the inevitable.

Radburn House was dark and imposing. From the dining room, Caprice moved back into the hall then mounted the stairs. She could ramble around an impressive house without intrusion or feel guilty about her intrusion into privacy. She smiled as she swept her hand along a walnut banister.

At the top of the stairs, light from a low chandelier was of little benefit. She was plunged into blanket darkness but when she reached for the light switch she was momentarily thrilled. *Imagine what it would be like to live in this house, to know where to lay my hands on any light switch, in any room.* Caprice hadn't known a home, having only occupied a succession of four walls. It was an evening for new emotions. She walked along the upper hallway and opened doors.

Light spilled across thick shag carpets and wide beds in high-ceiling rooms. Grand dark furniture, crystal lamps and silvered mirrors were in every room, each with curtains pulled tightly across windows. She looked at four rooms before finding one she liked. Although the mattress was bare, a pewter bedstead with simple metal curls appealed to her. The young woman flicked a light switch. Two lamps spread golden warmth into a musty room.

Walls were plain mushroom and furniture, light teak. A round table with two curved chairs stood in front of a window. Plush curtains had some of their heaviness curtailed by their hue, the cream of Lancashire cheese. Three cushions, the colour of apples left to lie too long on the ground, lay across a chest at the foot of the bed. It held sheets the same colour as walls plus a duck-down quilt, the same colour as cushions. She prepared her bed for the night, spraying a fine mist of rose-scented fragrance from a bottle she'd found between bedding.

With her sense of security now bolstered, Caprice continued her journey of discovery, keen to satisfy her interest in her host's residence. Past the bathroom, along the hallway into the opposite side of the house there were a further four rooms, each with tall heavy furniture and tightly-drawn brocade. Finally, she came to a room at the end of the long hallway but before opening its door she turned to see her bedroom door in the distance. She shivered. 'Somebody just walked over my grave.' She decided not to touch the door then made her way back along the hallway until she reached the stairs. Another flight led upwards.

On the third floor, all rooms were part of house eaves. Lower sloping ceilings contained canopied windows but again, each room had tall furniture and thick curtains. Caprice didn't spend long looking at them, suspecting that her host's room was the one she'd ignored. She returned to it with haste. Before the untried door she hesitated then slowly turned its knob to be greeted by the gloominess she'd seen in all rooms. She was instantly disappointed and ready to close the door but an inner voice told her: *Is it wrong to be so curious about a stranger?* She thought about it, weighing up whether it was rude and unnecessary. *If I don't satisfy my curiosity then it will play on me.* She reached to the side then was surprised to feel a row of switches.

The room was instantly bathed in light. Caprice blinked. A cartwheel with four upright candle-lights hung from the ceiling, cascading light upwards. Lamps besides the bed, in corners and on an expansive dresser radiated arcs. A vast four-poster looked inviting with its ruby eiderdown and pillows, the only bright colour. Everything else was plain beige, walls papered in rich fabric, a garland design on mottled butter-cream.

Just as Caprice was about to further feed a starved imagination, a loud crack jolted her and she froze. It had come from downstairs. She hurriedly switched off the lights, silently pulled the door to and tip-toed along the hallway until she reached the stairs. Inhaling deeply, Caprice stretched over the banister then held her breath to listen. There was silence except for the echo of a grandfather clock.

Sticking her right foot out, Caprice placed it on the top stair then repeated her inhalation and silent listening. Still, there wasn't any sound except a laboured creak followed by hollow ticking. She remained silently hovering, using sheer force of will to quell her fear. *Has he traced me to Mistlethrop and found me?* It seemed impossible but her stomach felt queasy.

Slow hollow ticking took reign of the young woman's imagination. She fought harder to hold on to reason. She looked anxiously down at the clock and empty tub-chair imagining a grotesque figure would appear stealthily and silently then look upwards. She tried to calculate how long it could take her to run down and out the front door. Then, the clock chimed. Loud metallic notes made her almost slip with fright.

Following a flush of pins and needles, the pressure of holding still bended toes was too much. Caprice repeated her stair-by-stair descent, thinking the noise must have been a door or window not closed properly then slamming shut. With each step, her confidence grew and she was ready to frolic the last few steps when she heard another loud crack. It sounded like a window breaking and it came from the kitchen.

With the dread of one who had spent so many tender years on the brink of hell, Caprice wanted to run.

I can't. What's the point? He'll only find me again.

6. Hunger

A middle-aged cleaner also made an unexpected decision and arrived at Radburn House earlier than usual. Gales, thunder and lightning had been a warning but a forecast of plummeting temperature was the decider. Her employer had found it difficult to find a domestic to work the hours he'd required. She knew that if he complained then she could use it as leverage.

Lights were on when she placed a key in the rear door. Barri would still be at home. She prepared herself mentally for the intensity of his steely eyes even though she hadn't spoken to him in person for a year. Like his Radburn employees, the cleaner found there was seldom need for direct communication. Her salary was credited to her bank and a payslip posted to her home. She came under the banner of "*Confectionery staff*" and felt special, the only person to see how the boss lived.

Routinely, instructions were left in an envelope on the table next to the tub-chair. Barri hated handwritten notes but texting was too personal. He'd be at work when she arrived and still be there long after she'd returned home, but, once his cold blue eyes had been looked into then they couldn't easily be forgotten, the cleaner saw them whenever she read his notes.

A second bout of severe weather was already making its way across the Pennines, creeping across moors then building momentum. Low winds were the first sign as they whipped across the saturated lawn to test the strength of a few leaves remaining on shrubs and trees. The door slammed shut behind the cleaner. Her teeth chatted as she nervously looked around the kitchen.

'Hello there!' she called out but it was a feeble attempt. The thought of those steely blue eyes made her feel colder. A coffee carafe and used mug confirmed her suspicions so she quickly removed her feet from squelching shoes to place them in slippers from her bag. Delaying a face-to-face for as long as possible, she busied herself by cleaning the mug and carafe so that she could feel more at ease when Barri appeared. *Should I try again to let him know I'm here?*

In a nervous state, the woman progressed to the dining room to first spray a fine mist of polish onto the table before sweeping a soft cloth across wood. She paid close attention to rooms she knew Barri frequented and ignored the rest, as did he. It was a big house, three hours per week inadequate to maintain a thorough state of cleanliness. Her employer had made it clear that she could work only one evening each week despite her willingness to earn extra. With each sweep of the cloth, the cleaner's anxiety increased.

He'll be in the drawing-room or his bedroom, the bedroom was the only room he insisted she didn't touch. She'd investigated during her first week despite being told not to go in. It was just a bedroom, a grand bedroom she could fit both her lounge and kitchen into. But, if she'd continued to pull out a dresser drawer and seen past rows of neatly bunched socks then she would have seen a locked lid.

A large terracotta pot outside the kitchen door split in two when a wheelie bin blew over. It was enough to make both women in the house jump. 'Oh God what was that?' The older woman quickly shuffled to investigate.

Opening the kitchen door was an arduous task. Fierce wind blew hard against her efforts then eagerly grasped the door once opened wide enough. Due to heavy wood and its propensity to shrink and grow according to season the door stuck half-way. She struggled just before it sprang back to hit the cleaner squarely in the face. 'Jesus!' It took seconds to see what had caused the commotion outside then the cleaner put her shoulder to the door to heave it shut. When she turned, a young woman was standing behind her. Both women looked at each other with equally shocked expressions.

'Ah!' the cleaner exclaimed. 'Who are you?' She anxiously

looked to the dining room doorway expecting Barri to appear but was also surprised at seeing a woman in Barri's house. It disproved her theory that Barri preferred his own gender.

Caprice hid her relief but worried that she'd now have to explain her presence to her host's mother. She didn't even know her hero's name. The air changed and Caprice felt like an intruder.

'I was invited to stay for the night,' she offered sheepishly but added: 'He's at work and said he'll be late'.

'Oh, don't mind me. I'll be gone by eight-thirty. You can let Barri know I came early because of the weather.' Caprice couldn't hide her relief. Hired help wasn't a threat plus, she now knew her host's name. The cleaner was relieved not to speak to Barri. His guest however, would source her proclivity to gossip for the next few weeks.

Caprice's curiosity quashed, her hunger was suddenly replaced by a more physical one. Not having eaten anything that day, her stomach growled loudly. Embarrassed, Caprice patted her middle and smiled nervously.

'Hasn't he fed you then?' the cleaner asked and burst into a wide smile. Caprice licked her lips and shook her head. 'You know Barri!' the cleaner delved and she looked closely at Caprice's face for a tell-tale reaction but the younger woman gave nothing away. 'You won't find anything in the fridge to feed the soul, but I must get on.' The cleaner returned to the dining room to take up her basket of canisters, sprays and cloths. It was tempting to stay and drop a few friendly questions but she wanted to give a good impression just in case the young woman became more than an overnight guest.

If he's brought her home then she must be special. There would be plenty of time later for carefully worded questions if she was The One.

Caprice thought: *Close call, I've had enough of talking with strangers for one day.*

Opening every kitchen cupboard door and drawer, Caprice eventually found crockery and cutlery. A cupboard held cereals.

Some of the boxes had been opened but tightly covered in cling-wrap. Another held tins and jars. Contrary to what the cleaner had said, the fridge was stocked with roast chicken, honey-roast ham (both on the bone), crusty cobs, olives and five different types of cheese. Everything tightly covered in cling-wrap. A chiller housed white wine and mineral waters. She pulled out a piece of chicken, cut slices from the ham and the only two cheeses she recognised. She reluctantly opted for mineral water but looked at the wine.

The cleaner moved on from the dining room. Caprice took her plate and glass through once she found where placemats were stored, not wanting to dirty a beautiful table. She could now sit in peace and grandeur at the head of the table.

So, he does live alone in this huge house and, can afford a cleaner. However, the cleaner's last words had hit a sore spot. *No, I won't find food for my soul in his fridge.*

Caprice had only recently discovered that she did own a soul and wasn't an empty puppet at the mercy of a puppeteer. If it wasn't for the fact that she'd escaped his shadow then she may have considered Barri a viable target. Placing her knife and fork down, Caprice chewed slowly and savoured not only her meal but her surroundings then sighed that such a golden opportunity should be discarded. She'd been taught to play with emotions, use physical magnetism she knew she possessed to lure potential players to her tormentor's twisted games. Disturbingly, she'd enjoyed a fleeting moment of power in an equally twisted sort of way. It was the only kind of power she knew she could wield if predisposed to but worthless if she couldn't now use it to rid her of misery.

Another woman had considered her viable target from the chair Caprice now occupied. It had offered the same fantasy when first looking down the long table. However, the chair had belonged to the then head of Radburn. Although Mrs George had seen her plans come to fruition, her wish had come at a harsh price. Caprice may have recognised something in Barri's mother but been reluctant to acknowledge it. There were now far greater things to worry about than the size of one's abode, a label on a dress or how many noughts were on a bank statement. Caprice craved riches of a different kind.

The young woman shifted her weight from one buttock to the other then felt something eat into her leg. Pulling the offending object out of her jeans pocket, she examined it before propping it against the side of her plate. A tiny ballerina with one leg folded, its other stretched into pointed tip-toe toppled over.

I have a lot in common with you. The tiny figure used to rise and dance whenever its music box opened then *Carousel*'s famous theme tinkled. Caprice would watch it bob and rotate in front of mirrors until music slowed and the gentle tap-tap-tap of the dancer's mechanism laboured. When the lid closed the small dancer sank into the interior.

Barri was delayed. A tree had fallen across the main road and his car diverted to side-streets crammed with tooting cars edging forwards at a snail's pace. It would have been quicker to abandon his car and walk. Most people preferred to spend an hour or so moaning about the weather in a pub then have a clear journey home later.

Meanwhile, the weather steadily grew angrier. Roaring gales shoved Barri through pub doors and towards throngs surrounding the bar. Barri swore under his breath. It took ages to attract a barmaid's attention then he ordered his usual bottle of Stella taking it to the end of the bar where it was least congested. He stood back like an abandoned trolley in a crowded supermarket and fumed. *If it wasn't for that cursed woman then I wouldn't be here. I wouldn't have had to change my routine and, I'd still have some common sense.*

'Didn't I see you in 'ere earlier?' a man on a high stool shouted over chatter then gestured at Barri who looked around him before realising that the man was talking to him. 'I've been 'ere all afternoon.' The man beamed. 'Only on my fourth though,' and he held up an almost empty glass. The man's rosy cheeks and happy expression were proof enough that he'd passed time comfortably. Barri hadn't paid much attention to

57

anyone in the pub earlier that day but now that he looked at the man realised that there had been someone sitting in the same spot. *He could be useful. The landlord is busy but this man will know about anything unusual.*

'Can I stretch you to a fifth?' Barri offered and joined the man. Barri was head and shoulders taller even though the man sat on a high stool.

'Very civil!' and the man held his glass out until the barmaid saw it.

Barri peeled another note from his wallet and handed it to the girl. 'Keep the change.' The girl flushed and the man raised an eyebrow. The rosy-cheeked man didn't know whether to be impressed or laugh at the young man's generosity. Barri remained deadpan. 'You're right, I was in here earlier.'

'Thought so, I've seen you a few times.' The man looked Barri up and down. 'You're not a big drinker.'

'It's too gassy.' Barri attempted a smile, turning up one side of his mouth to match an arched eyebrow.

'You should drink the proper stuff,' the man stated with confidence. 'Lager's alreet now and then but a pint o'bitter won't give you ill side-effects, especially the brew they serve 'ere. It's creamy, goes down like milk to a baby.' The man held up his glass, pursed his lips and blew a kiss at it. Barri was genuinely amused, another emotion he hadn't experienced in any capacity. He was reminded of his isolation in the darkness of an unused classroom then Miss Rogers staring at him through thick glass.

Another strange emotion made its slow ascent from Barri's toes to the tips of his ears. He leaned an elbow casually on the bar. Holding his bottle of Stella, he watched the man tilt his head from one side to the other in admiration for a full glass before pursing his lips again to plant them firmly on its rim. Oddly, Barri became caught in a web of sensual awareness as though Caprice had entered and stood next to him. He looked through the man and saw her clearly. He also thought of the heady days he'd spent immediately following Elspeth's death.

The enormity of what he'd done had lain for many years like a thick coat of goose-fat applied to a channel swimmer; all else washed over him. The layer prevented his secret and memory from washing away. He was protected and slippery. At first it had felt like a weight but then, as light as a final breath. Only he knew what he'd done and there would always be a longing to relive it. Looking through the man on the stool at his lovely vision, he knew that he would have to relive it soon.

'So, how is she then?' The man's attention changed from his pint to Barri who felt his words like a bolt of lightning.

'Who,' Barri asked, his strange emotion vanished.

'Young lass who took tumble out back, was she alreet?' Barri stopped leaning on the bar.

'A bit shaken, I managed to get her to a taxi at the station.' He searched the man's face. The man was too comfortably ensconced and full of his mother's milk to be disconcerted by Barri's intensity.

'Good, glad to 'ear it. Just saw you fetching 'er things; looked like she'd flake out again any minute. Ere, let me buy next one.'

'No, I'm not stopping,' Barri intervened but the man didn't listen.

'It's a rare thing, to find someone willin to 'elp without wantin summit. Take my wife for example, she passed out in front of Town Hall steps, but did anyone stop? No, just stepped right over as though she was a lush.' While he was talking, the man gestured at the barmaid. Another pint and Stella were placed on the bar. Barri had no recourse except to politely accept then try to make good his escape. He felt anger rising.

Early evening ebbed and with it the throngs who occupied the pub. Only diehard regulars remained, the man on the barstool included. Outside, weather squalled and fought with everything in its way. Rain lashed sideways and pelted car roofs before turning to thick hail shot from the sky like miniature meteorites.

Barri looked at his watch, his father's gift replaced by a more expensive model. Its bevelled face sparkled under lights. It was

59

almost eight-forty and despite simpering anger, Barri saw the wisdom of staying away from Radburn until he was sure what he wanted to do when he got there.

Caprice had finished her meal and remained seated in the dining room until the cleaner declared she was done for the evening. She made a toothy grimace before bidding a hammy farewell. 'Nice to meet you, tell Barri I gave the bathroom a good going over.' In the older woman's experience, young men with free reign over a huge house and fortune, who didn't bring home every piece of skirt, would have to think a girl special to invite her to his home for the night. The cleaner was confident that she'd made a good first impression. It wouldn't be long before there'd be an addition to the Radburn family tree.

At last Caprice felt safe enough to continue wandering through rooms. She returned to the hall and opened a door only just noticeable because of its knob. It was within walnut panelling but when opened led to a narrower extension of the hall.

A door opened to an L-shaped study with book-lined walls. It smelt of yeast. Caprice sneezed and quickly closed its door. A games room snooker table was covered in brown dust. A dartboard didn't have any holes, housed in a wooden frame with clean chalk-board panels. A curved bar had a layer of dust thick enough to write one's name in and its well-stocked rear shelves held bottles last opened when Mr George was alive. It was the third room Caprice was drawn to, the music room. This room had been a whim of Barri's mother.

Caprice entered and looked enviously at a display of instruments before stretching her fingers towards a violin. It rested across the top of a grand piano. Her fingertips brushed its strings then she wiped a tear from her right eye. She thought of a time when music had been her only solace, before her tormentor had made it an accompaniment to his perversion. Like the ballerina, she'd been expected to perform. Then, she remembered she'd left the ballerina on the dining table. *You've stopped dancing, I hope never to again.* As she stood in

Radburn's music room she realised: *I've never felt this safe.*

After walking back through the hall, Caprice discovered that the opposite end of the house was clean and dust-free. She smelt pungent furniture polish then sneezed again.

A door led directly into a parlour, far bigger than any rooms she'd already seen. Walnut panelling continued but only on three of the walls but her eyes were drawn to a monumental stone fireplace, it dominated the room. Two armorial griffins sat upon rising pillars supporting a long and bare mantel. Above, a limestone plaque depicting a row of Yorkshire roses covered the remaining expanse. Carved into aged stone, these roses were easier on the eye than the black iron roses at the entrance of Mistlethrop market.

Caprice stepped across parquet to feel the soft give of an Afghan rug. She looked down at bunches of lilac grapes woven through green leaves then up at two stately wingback armchairs placed side-by-side. She sat down, pressing her spine into a tall back, pushing her rear into a horse-hair seat. Raised on cabriole legs, their silver-grey velvet was slightly worn but luxuriant to the touch. Caprice looked at the empty chair beside her. *I'm a queen without a king.* She sneezed again and it echoed.

The deeply impressed young woman looked around the back of her chair and saw another hidden door in a panel. Her hungry curiosity had another course to look forward to. The door led to a less formal drawing room and when she pressed its light-switch, decor wasn't as cold or ostentatious. This was a room to take drinks into at the end of a dinner party but there was another room beyond, through glass doors. She could hear tapping like fingernails on glass. A low light penetrated through a gloomy interior to show the ends of leather sofas.

When Caprice stepped into the annexe, she couldn't find a switch but gawped at its magnificent windows. She looked into a wall of swirling hail rapidly turning to snow. Looking out, the world had shrunk and it seemed that all that remained was inside the house. Stumbling around sofas, she banged her knee on a glass side-table then groped a reflection to find it was a cold steel base. When she found the lamp switch, she blinked with surprise. This was a room for relaxation. Long leather sofas were arranged so that sitters could look at a sixty-inch plasma.

It was cold. The fireplace, a hole in the wall beneath the TV, held a stack of fake logs with a gas burner. Caprice was trigger-happy, another switch to master and she enjoyed seeing the fire spurt then flame. Behind her, a bum-shaped crease in a settee looked inviting. Reaching for a remote she aimed it at the TV.

A wall of white outside windows, rhythmic tapping against glass, flickering fire and solitary lamp-light, made a comforting ambience. When the screen burst into life Caprice was in yet another magazine photo. Her starved imagination got the better of her. *What would it be like to live here?*

As she sank her body into leather then laid back her head, she looked at the screen. Its volume low and whispering, she could dream fully, to be a woman without a past, without pain, without habitual dread. An involuntary giggle gurgled in her throat. As soon as she heard it, she shook herself free, the reality she'd come from too strong. The TV came into focus. A film had just ended on Movies Twenty-Four, another would begin in ten minutes, an old Jane Eyre film from Nineteen-Seventy. Caprice relaxed again and focussed on trailers.

The streets of Mistlethrop were white and silent. Nobody in their right frame of mind would be out after nine. Barri had made good his escape from The Varsity ten minutes before.

Stinging flakes of ice hit his face then made Barri gasp. He swallowed as the gassiness from his two bottles of lager tried to escape then clutched at his chest and grimaced. He had to use the back of his sleeve to wipe crusty snow from his car door. Turning blowers up full, he sat and waited while his impatience ballooned. Just as Caprice leaned her head back against his sofa, Barri hit his head backwards against a headrest and continued doing so. An open display of frustration wasn't in his nature. It spilled uncontrollably, his frustration compounded.

The drive home did little to relieve stress. It was difficult to see through a snow blanket. Flakes flew towards his car window like a swarm of white bees then accompanied by a hard volley of hail as though someone had thrown gravel.

Radburn's lawn stretched towards the front door like a white bib pulled to a mouth. As Barri neared he noticed a light radiating through busy air at the far end. A flicker of expectation was replaced by resentment, an emotion Barri knew well. His home was no longer his castle, it had been invaded. He was reluctant to leave his car. He saw a broken pot, an overturned bin then felt crushed, crushed by circumstances he couldn't control, not dissimilar to the time he'd seen a pig-woman with his father. When he placed a foot outside his car he winced, he heard a crack but it was ice beneath his shoe.

Finding Caprice, her strange pull and his reaction, resurfacing memories and with them unexplored emotions, fell as heavily as freak weather on Barri's equilibrium. They rolled back and forth, crushing him further. He sat in his car and stared out a window filling with snow. Then, Barri pulled himself together.

It was cold inside Radburn, central heating not needed when he was at the office most nights. Barri thought of his guest. *Whether she's cold or warm when I lay my arm across her throat doesn't matter. I'll look forward to the warmth of her last breath.*

7. Seeing Red

A plate and cutlery were next to the sink. As soon as Barri saw a bottle of Mr. Muscle he remembered what night it was. *The cleaner must be here.* The master of an unloved home threw back his head and stifled a low growl. He wanted to turn on his heels and leave. *Where would I go?*

His house was infested. Anger and frustration seeped through his pores then, there was that damn stupid song in his head again: *How Do You Solve a Problem, Like Maria?* It was a ludicrous annoying tune he couldn't shake from his head. He felt pathetic, out of control. *I've allowed two females to rule my actions and one of them has infested my brain as well as my house.* He looked down and grabbed his balls in case he'd been castrated on his way in. 'No, they're still there,' he said and grimaced.

The tinkling of melodramatic music didn't reach Barri's ears until he'd passed through the parlour. Light from the TV and a flickering log fire didn't infiltrate the dullness of parquet and panelling.

'What on earth are you watching?' he demanded as he strode into the annexe, his annoyance still surging but he thought he'd done well to restrain it in his voice. Barri stared at the plasma, avoiding eye contact. His guest seemed engrossed but started.

'It's a film. It's not been on long.' Caprice's body stretched upwards as though pulled by unseen strings as she first raised limbs then posture from a relaxed slouch.

'Yes, I can see it's a film!' Barri's impatience resurfaced.

Caprice looked at him open-mouthed and had to stop herself from uttering: *He's so rude.*

He could feel the weight of her eyes upon him and although his remained fixed on the screen Barri imagined deep violet before feeling a micro-second of guilt. Then, he became ashamedly pleased and couldn't account for either emotion. Barri sat down abruptly at the end of a sofa to await the next electric jolt of his emotional rollercoaster.

Caprice returned to her slouch and put her host's sullenness down to a journey home through foul weather. *If he wants to talk, he can make the effort.* Reverend Brocklehurst made his appearance on TV. His nasty character outmatched Barri's bad temper.

Barri wasn't able to relax and turned his head slightly so that he could look at the TV but instead, honed his hearing towards the glass doors. *The cleaner will go home in a couple of hours.* He couldn't think of anything else to do but sit on his childish anger and watch a film with his guest.

'It's Jane Eyre, by-the-way,' Caprice volunteered then returned her head to a leather niche.

Barri hadn't watched a film in years. Other people's stories or imagination didn't interest him. It was painful to sit still and feign interest but without realising it Barri began to listen to dialogue but without the emotion Caprice experienced.

On the screen, Jane Eyre and her friend Helen were enduring punishment on *pedestals of infamy.* Jane, dressed in a dowdy pinafore, stood balanced in an empty classroom while consumptive Helen did the same in an open courtyard. Then, thunder cracked and heavens opened. Caprice stole a glance at the harsh winter night outside Radburn's windows and shivered. Jane stole an anxious glance at her friend through a window. She was coughing violently in the downpour. Jane watched in horror as her friend's clothes were soaked.

Caprice reacted to the scene, made a small noise and Barri immediately looked at his guest. A voice involuntarily rising along restricted throat was caught before escape. He'd heard it before, almost a squeak but not mouse-like. His guest politely coughed to disguise it. Barri had to stifle excitement but then, he saw a sparkle on her cheek. TV glimmer illuminated a tear as it trickled and Barri couldn't understand why it was there.

He quickly looked back at the screen, nervous excitement turned to discomfort. He gritted his molars to send a pulse through one side of his cheek. 'What's upsetting you?' he asked the screen. Caprice answered without thought but with naivety.

'For most of my life I've felt like that girl on the stool.' It was an odd statement. Barri was thrown completely.

What does she mean? He thought of rain earlier when they'd both been drenched then, his puzzlement grew. 'You were a gypsy, living in the open?'

'No, no, nothing like that, I mean...' and Caprice released a sigh of exasperation. Her statement was akin to pulling a plaster from a half-healed cut then it smarting. It would have been wiser to have not said anything. 'I meant... most of my life I waited for something to happen. There was a lot to endure while I waited.' She was surprised by her candour; her words had poured freely. *Why did I open up?* Quickly, she tried to cover her tracks. 'Have you never felt that way?'

Barri struggled to reply, furrowed his brow then arched it. 'No, I can't say I have,' he lied and cleared his throat. 'If you could compare me to anything in the film, then I'd say I'm the stool.' Barri looked fully at Caprice who arched her eyebrows in surprise. She had to think about her host's puzzling statement in case he was somehow being clever and she, thick.

'How can you compare yourself to a stool?'

'Easily,' Barri stated nonchalantly. 'I keep all legs on the ground and maintain a solid base. Unlike that girl up there, I don't allow outside elements to affect me. Sooner or later, life will come to me, as did she to the stool.' Barri looked at Caprice eyes seeing only a flash of vibrancy lit by shimmering TV but her hair was glorious and as red as a burning kettle on an open fire. Its warmth immediately melted pent-up tension. He wanted to sit and bask in its glow.

Still, Caprice was uncertain what her host meant but he'd given the impression that he was unflappable, reliant. He was capable of providing the type of security she'd only dreamt about and equally secure in his own knowledge of self. It was

66

one of the most attractive impressions he could have bestowed without realising it.

As Barri gazed at the red-head he began to see what she meant about the girl on the stool, his solid base toppled. Heady, swirling emotions rained down upon him.

Caprice was as equally captivated by her host's expression and found it difficult to fathom. With dirty-blond hair brushed across his forehead and feathering his right cheek, the bridge of his nose furrowed but left eyebrow sharply arched, she appreciated his good looks.

When she'd first come round after her fall, her eyes hadn't fully focussed. Later, she'd talked to a car window, too absorbed in her troubles to examine Barri's face. She now noticed deliberately unshaved stubble across his upper lip. It continued neatly down both sides of his mouth to form a U-shape underneath then around the cleft of his chin. Without it he would look a lot younger so she could see why he favoured that style. It was a stern, serious but attractive face. His pale eyes reminded her of a blue margarita. Then, as Barri relaxed his eyes portrayed a glint of mischief, the furrow between brows lifted. He posed a question:

'If you feel so vulnerable to life's weather, then don't you think it's time to step off the stool and head for shelter?'

'I've never had the opportunity,' Caprice answered and she looked beyond Barri towards the windows. His eyes followed hers. The blizzard had entered its fiercest phase. Snow the size of a child's hand hurled against glass then slowly slid downwards to form a Tetris of white tiles. Caprice's heart sank and Barri felt the change.

'You have the opportunity this evening.' A chink opened in Barri's armour, just long enough for him to also say: 'Let me be your stool for now. You're safe here.'

'I appreciate your hospitality.' Caprice looked amused but appreciative. 'You know you're weird right?'

Barri returned his eyes to the TV but Caprice knew he was taking in everything in his periphery. The young woman sensed

67

he was interested in her but there was something her sixth sense wasn't yet telling her. Barri didn't flirt or play games and she was so used to both but, she instinctively recognised a wall when she saw it. He chose words carefully, took time when speaking and although he exuded confidence she guessed his wall could be due to distrust or a secret.

The film lost its potency. Caprice fidgeted and Barri shifted weight from one buttock to the next until he could keep still no longer. 'I'm getting a drink, do you want one?' He stood up.

'I'll have whatever you have,' Caprice replied.

'You may not like it,' Barri warned.

'I like most things. I doubt you can give me anything I've not tried before.' Caprice thought of a Snag-Tooth Nell she'd been asked to make when working in a Bistro. The memory of the trouble she'd taken to get it right then the customer's unreasonable behaviour made her flinch. She cowered when she thought of what had become of him.

Barri's deep-rooted resentment of having to share made his mouth twitch but when diluting spiced rum with coke he imagined Caprice's lips touching the glass. His innards reacted as though he'd swallowed a large mouthful of pure alcohol. *It's bloody ironic. Anything I do for her chokes me.*

He returned ten minutes later with two tall glasses. As soon as she saw them Caprice thought of her tormentor's favourite tipple. Tentatively, Caprice took one of the glasses and sniffed to receive a heavy aroma of spice. 'What is it?' An ice cube cracked, forcing a slice of lime to spin around.

'It's Black Kraken with coke.' Barri settled into his former seat. 'It's spiced rum with more oomph.' Caprice sipped and liked it. 'You've had this drink before?' Barri asked, doubting she had.

'Well, not this one, exactly, I've had Bacardi.'

It became easier to sit through the film. Caprice didn't want to converse unnecessarily. *There's no point in trying to get to know him.* Her host had put her at her ease and in doing so he felt equally relaxed.

There's no point in talking to her. Apart from a few casual comments about the film they spoke little but at ten-fifteen Barri remembered the cleaner. He looked anxiously at his watch. *Where is she?* He went to investigate but when he'd quickly used the bathroom and looked around the house, he realised she wasn't on the premises. He hurried back. 'Did the cleaner come tonight? he asked, bringing with him two fresh glasses.

'Eh, yeah, she was here earlier. Sorry, I forgot to tell you. She said she had come early because of the weather.'

'So she saw you then?'

'Yes, we didn't speak long. I told her I was here for the night and she got on with her work.'

Barri's first inclination was to slam down the drinks but he didn't and groaned inwardly. *Everything seemed so simple when I was at the pub.*

The man on the barstool had also seen Caprice but it could be glossed over. Barri had privacy and time to dispose of a body. Or, he could if he wanted to, keep hold of his subject. He had thought about it but an opportunity had never presented itself until now. *What would I do with her?* After waiting for The One it would be a shame to just let her go but: *What will I do with her?* He thought of Bates Hotel and shuddered. *That could be too much to handle.*

He could also have told the cleaner not to come due to the weather, but his usual logic had been as clouded as a snow-filled night. *Why didn't I remember the cleaner?* Everything involving Caprice seemed to begin or end with a question. Matters had become complicated and his craving would continue. Barri's throat made the same tight squeak as when Caprice empathised with Helen upon her stool. He turned to watch the snow Tetris form rows then columns. *This has got to be the oddest day of my life and I have no idea if or how it will end.* He looked back at Caprice then again at the window. He was no longer interested in the film or what happened to Jane and Mr Rochester. *Is she enjoying it? It's so hard to tell, more tears?*

Eventually, it occurred to Barri how pleasant it was to just sit and do nothing, to have ignored his office. This was a fleeting sensation. Inwardly striving so hard towards an impossible end had been hard work.

He remembered that he hadn't eaten anything. *It's too late to eat. It's too late to do anything tonight but there will always be tomorrow.* Barri smiled; another rare event. He gazed out at the snow and wished he could see his tree-house.

8. Change of Plan

Barri awoke with a start, he'd overslept. Pale luminescence crept under heavy curtains to send tapering fingers across the floor and up the side of his bed. He'd forgotten to flick his alarm-clock switch and he glared at it.

Being primarily a night-creature, Barri was attuned to working overnight, arriving home between two and three then sleeping until eleven. His routine rarely faltered, breakfast replaced by brunch, tea-time his main meal. Sweeping sheets to one side, he stamped both feet on the floor, fingers of light reached his toes. He rubbed his face hard, feeling lighter bristle where he didn't want it.

Outside, snow had fallen on sodden ground then frozen. Icicles hung as crystal stalactites from ledges. Barri had to rub windows to see out. Jack Frost had trashed every clear surface and the sky was as white as the spread of frozen snow. It was difficult to differentiate where the road ended and the park began.

Two skeletons stood stark against the harsh white of their surroundings, the leafless limbs of the tree reaching upwards to keep tight hold of its tree-house and, a play-frame over the road. It was a modern addition to an old park but made of reclaimed wood in keeping with the mood Mistlethrop officials wanted to portray. Way beyond the frame, blended with snow and horizon was The Peoples Bandstand. If a giant ogre happened to amble by and wanted to play skittles then he could have stood at the foot of Barri's window and bowled, to take down first the tree, the frame then the bandstand.

Barri rubbed his face again and reached for his phone. Trains weren't running. News headlines warned of further severe weather, dangerous conditions and the havoc freak floods, ice

71

and snow had reaped across The North and Midlands. Barri looked out at his snow-peaked tree-house. *Life was a lot simpler when I was a boy* then, his stomach howled.

It was past noon. Barri hastily showered and shaved to ensure his groomed stubble remained intact. All the while, he thought of the problem, the Maria-type problem and that song at the back of his scheming mind. He formed a rudimentary plan. The exhilaration of imagining its execution pushed to his surface like champagne bubbles in a fluted glass.

When Barri stood in his bedroom doorway to look at the door opposite, he wondered about his guest. The night before, she'd silently waved goodnight from her end of the hall. A smell of cooked ham arrested his attention then he knew she must have been awake for some time.

'You don't need to tell me, I've seen the news on TV and used the kitchen phone to find out about trains.'

Barri gaped at his guest. He'd forgotten how arresting her appearance could be. Bright kitchen fluorescence set her hair alight. Champagne bubbles of feverish anticipation soared through his body. All he could do was stand and stare but he didn't feel foolish. He felt powerful, the master in his house again.

Caprice was unnerved by Barri's stance and stare. His ice-blue eyes hadn't been as noticeable the night before. The master of the house didn't blink but his eyes shined intensely.

'You'll have to stay.' The monotone of his voice wasn't in keeping with the look on his face. He continued to stare at Caprice who felt warmth rising to her face so she turned to the oven.

'Thank you. I've made some breakfast. Do you want to eat here?' Caprice gestured to the centre-island.

'No, this is a kitchen,' Barri stated as though it was a ridiculous suggestion. 'I'll take mine in the dining room where food should be eaten.' He turned and left the kitchen. His abrupt decisiveness seemed like a criticism.

Who the hell does he think he is? Caprice shovelled slices of

72

grilled ham onto hot plates of scrambled eggs. *I go to the trouble of making breakfast and am treated like a maid.* With a sniff, she carried a tray to the dining room where Barri was seated at the table head with his arms outstretched. Reluctantly, Caprice served the contents of her tray using a tea-towel, which Barri disapprovingly pursed his lips at before tucking into his first meal of the day. *I must be drawn to men with personality problems,* Caprice told herself then winced.

Breakfast was eaten in silence. Caprice assumed position to the right so that she was nearest to the radiator. She'd enjoyed flicking a tiny plastic switch with her fingernail when she'd found the heating controls.

The silence was deafening. Barri's eyes flicked between his plate and the far end of the table. Although he ate quietly, masticating slowly so that food slipped down easily, his rollercoaster was in motion for a fresh ride. Since his parents' death Barri had sat at the head but hadn't realised how lonely it was until the seat to his right was occupied. He thought of his mother sitting there and it was unsettling.

Remembering his mother brought a new appreciation of his childhood, his reliance. Whenever he was in trouble, she'd brought him home. That day in the tree-house he'd known that he could always rely on her. He saw her whenever he took his eyes from his plate. *Why do I keep remembering years ago?* Barri spluttered and choked. Coughing violently into a napkin, he quickly stood almost knocking his chair over then downed his orange juice.

'That last piece of ham was over-done,' he snarled then left the dining room. A loss of control threatened Barri so forcibly that he had to storm into the parlour before it overcame him completely. With hands on knees, he stared at the Afghan rug through watery eyes then clenched his teeth until he regained equilibrium. A few minutes later, he returned to the dining room a lot calmer but stared, expressionless at Caprice.

'Thank God you recovered,' she stated. 'I don't know the Heimlich manoeuvre.' It was her attempt to lighten the situation, her patience with Barri's swinging demeanour wearing thin. Her host had only just managed to pull himself together, his sense of mastery almost destroyed by delayed grief. He sat down and pushed his plate to one side. The taste of uncontrollable emotions didn't help digestion.

'I have to go to work,' he told his guest quietly.

'You work odd hours then?' Caprice asked, wondering what he did for a living.

'I work the hours required, and business is my priority.' Barri was only half truthful.

'And what is your business?'

'Radburn Confectionery.'

'What do you do there?'

'I own it.' Caprice's lower jaw dropped. It was a name on contents of shop shelves up and down the country and beyond.

He must be worth millions' her mind shouted. She closed her mouth before a squeak of excitement escaped. *What a totally wasted opportunity.* Just as Caprice couldn't allow herself to think of both wasted and new opportunities, Barri couldn't allow himself to uncork his returning champagne energy.

Small steps, he told himself. It was a lesson in business management. *Every successful manager breaks down a large goal into small steps to make it achievable.*

'Anyway,' Barri continued. 'I'll be at work until late.' Then, Barri thought about practicalities. 'I'll bring fresh groceries but there should be enough food in the cupboards.' He didn't mention trains or alternative transport, his mind was on other things. 'You will have to...'

'I have just one small problem,' Caprice interjected.

'What's that?'

'I don't have any clothes to change into.' Again, Barri regretted donating his mother's wardrobe to charity.

'Leave it with me,' his favourite expression, good for all occasions.

Caprice was left alone in the warmth of the house with dirty

74

dishes. Barri put on his Mont Blanc boots and sheepskin-lined jacket to apply chains to car tyres before taking a walk around the grounds. He waited for his car engine to warm up. He couldn't remember a snowfall so treacherous and heavy. It had drifted up the front of Radburn to form a thigh-high slope. A small child would have been tickled pink to use it to make snowmen but when Barri touched it, the tips of his gloves instantly stuck.

When he'd walked around Radburn's perimeter he returned to the front then took steady paces across the lawn as though marking out paces to buried treasure. The tree-house was in need of a carpenter's touch and preservative. Barri was both bitter and nostalgic. He should have been allowed to use it long after his tenth birthday. He took a step back to look beyond the tree.

Usually the view at the end of the garden was obscured by a row of tightly knit hydrangeas. They were bare of leaves but buds had appeared before heavy snow formed on stubby, severed stumps. Barri looked across the road at the park play-frame. Even covered in snow it looked impressive. Its lower platform had a small playhouse at one end with a door and two holes for windows. It could be accessed via a wooden ladder to the front. From the platform, a chain and rope-ladder led to a higher platform stretching to the side on thick stilts. There was a slide, climbing wall, fireman's pole, monkey-bars and two swings underneath.

Lost in a fog of memories, Elspeth and the fantasy of what it would have been like to kill her in the frame playhouse, Barri lost track of time. He stood rigidly still while his breath formed clouds that floated up over his head.

There were two pairs of eyes upon him, one a violet pair that watched him from the annexe. 'What's he staring at?' The second belonged to a woman in her early thirties. She worked in a care-home next to Radburn.

A stretch as wide as the side driveway, separated two houses, both impressive in structure but Radburn retained distinct superiority. The house nearby had recently been converted to an old people's home, its lawn replaced by a parking lot. One of the carers found more interest in the exterior than its interior. Dressed in navy polyester, the carer stood rigidly still as she stared out of an upstairs window. Unbearable heat within the home prevented frost.

Within a few months the carer had escaped her two shrill-voiced children, given them to the care of an after-school club while she'd gained a basic qualification. She now considered herself a benefit to the community and a qualified nurse. The woman harboured smug pride. She had a selfless, caring job. If she went home with the contents of some Old Dear's party buffet or ordered an expensive main course when on a shopping and dining trip, then she deserved it. No good deed should go unrewarded. Her working life had become one huge good deed. The Christmas shopping she'd recently volunteered for included purchases itemised on an expense sheet as: *"jumpers for grandchildren"* and *"underwear replacements."* She knew nobody would bother to check.

Judith Gormey watched Barri intently, preferring it to the task of cutting an old woman's toenails. Instead, she half-listened to the Old Dear prattling about whether to have sugar-almond nail-varnish or luscious-red.

'He's strange, what's he staring at?' Judith thought out loud. The Old Dear continued wittering. The subject of Judith's inquisitive nature was oblivious to the attention he received from both houses. If he'd known, then perhaps he would have been wiser to have shelved his plans. *"If"* was a word Mr George senior had once venomously banned from conversations and it had riled Barri considerably.

'There are no ifs in life,' his father would say and Barri would think:

Well there's an "if" in the middle of life, so what does he mean? Barri currently pushed aside his fantasy of: *What if I'd crushed Elspeth over there?* He returned to his car, now surrounded by a sea of exhaust and purring like a contented cat.

The drive to work was slow and laborious. Roads had been gritted but not enough, cars without tyre-chains were sliding.

'Get someone from the canteen to make me a coffee!' Barri ordered as he strode past his assistant's desk. The aftertaste of ham still lingered. 'I see some people didn't make it in?'

The assistant smiled weakly. This was a second unexpected visit. 'No, the phone's been busy, many are working from home.'

'I see.' Barri looked down banks of desks, recognising a couple of faces from photos he'd seen. The forced journey into work had cleared his head and he felt more cheerful. One employee was bent at a drinks machine at the end of the office. Barri watched as he raised a plastic cup to his lips then pulled a face.

'Tell the canteen to also make coffee for everyone in the office. Tell Marketing to bring samples of new products.' The assistant looked surprised. People within earshot of Barri's orders smiled but kept their heads down.

Cheerfulness was the descent of a rollercoaster where Barri's pupils had expanded while sailing the heights of a new plan. He swooped through it on his way down to an even keel more accustomed to but, he wasn't prepared for the shudder as it ground to a halt. Three hours later, Barri still sat at the bottom then, he remembered he had groceries and clothes to buy. A new mission re-ignited his passions.

Caprice had an uneventful day. After depositing plates in the dishwasher she didn't know what to do. She'd watched her host through an inch of clear window. He'd trudged methodically across the lawn then stared into space. *All this, loads of money and not a care in the world. I bet he's never known what it's like to be on the outside looking in.*

The guest braved the snow to see how feasible it would be to continue her journey. Suddenly curious about a view of the house in daylight she ignored tingling in her feet. Her thin shoes weren't up to the job but Caprice used Barri's footsteps to get through the snow.

A large patio at the back was an ice-rink. Tracing giant peanut-shaped holes, the end of the house was overshadowed by thick holly. At the front, she then looked up to see *Radburn House* engraved in slate over the front entrance.

The hop, to the tree was difficult. Where Barri's Mont Blanc boots had plundered, Caprice felt ice shards. Finally, she looked up at the tree-house then beyond it. As she mimicked Barri's reverie, a pair of eyes appeared at a window in the care home. Judith watched with even greater interest. Wool was slowly wound around two outstretched hands.

'Anything interesting out there?' an Old Dear asked.

'No just snow.' Judith continued to watch Caprice and thought: *I wonder who she is, don't say he's actually got a girlfriend.*

The younger woman noticed a row of small crucifixes protected from a battering of snow by a mass of stumped hydrangea. She took sinking steps until she reached them then bent to read faded names. Judith strained her neck to see what the young woman was doing.

"Are you sure there's nothing interesting out there?' A frail voice repeated its question.

'Yes.'

'Well don't get your nose too close to that window, I don't want smudges on it.'

Judith glared then continued to crane her neck.

Once she was shivering uncontrollably, Caprice returned to the house. When she was bored of TV, walking around the rooms, opening drawers, cupboards and examining shelves she was drawn to the music room.

Barri became feverishly purposeful as he walked past the train station to the town centre. When he arrived at the entrance of a chain-store known for affordable designer clothing he thought of his mother and how she would have walked by. Taking the advice of a ghost in his head, Barri continued until he reached East Gate Walkway then he saw a small boutique with a tasteful display of mannequins.

'Show me casual clothing suitable for a young woman,' Barri ordered the owner of the boutique. The woman was helpful but the girl assisting her more so. 'The young woman is the same size as you.' Barri aimed his intense stare on the girl assistant. This was another task for Barri to execute but to the women, it was a chance to shine.

He came out of the boutique with three large bags containing a variety of clothing and two small ones containing underwear. The girl had saved him the embarrassment of visiting a lingerie shop. He'd explained: 'The young woman had an accident and is laid up for a while.' Barri wasn't concerned by strangers knowing this; his plan was as yet, in its earliest stage.

Shopping for groceries took considerably less effort. He deposited his purchases in the boot of his car before making a second entrance into the office. Again, his assistant was surprised, assuming his boss had gone home. Most people had or were getting ready to. 'Mandrake's secretary called and asked if you had looked at their proposal.'

'What proposal?'

'The one I gave you last night.' Barri searched his memory while searching his assistant's face but couldn't recall. He felt his good mood flat-lining. The assistant went straight to the proposal where it had lain untouched.

'It's time you went home,' Barri ordered, returning to his usual abruptness.

When the office was a dark silent room of furniture only, Barri read the proposal then threw it on his desk. He looked at the folder, thumped it hard then turned to his laptop while cracking his knuckles. It sent a shiver up his arms.

His email was short. He selected *Send* then opened the top drawer of his desk, rummaging at the back until he found what he was looking for. Elspeth's bracelet was at home but he did have something tactile enough to provide a small pleasure, a rabbit foot key-ring. It had been his father's. Twisting soft coney between finger and thumb then rubbing along stubble beneath his chin, Barri re-read his sent email. He allowed his fantasies to take charge for a while.

It was after nine when Barri placed his key in the kitchen door. He hadn't seen light from the annexe windows, the kitchen was in darkness. He put groceries away then went to look for Caprice. She'd been cooking, that much he could tell by a spicy smell.

As he walked through the dining room, he saw that the table had been set for two and it strangely pleased him. As he progressed to the hall he stopped. He listened then recognised the muffled but eerily magical strains of a violin. It was played with such expert soulfulness that he was forced to sit down in the tub-chair afraid that his presence would somehow dispel the magic. He had to breathe shallowly to hear properly. 'It's got to be her.'

Weeks had passed since Caprice last played a violin, the memory of it so painful and humiliating that it had been tattooed on her soul. Only in Radburn, with snow surrounding it like a comforting cloak of seclusion was she able to seek out her old and only solace. She was lost in Tchaikovsky's, *Meditation*.

Music floated on air then touched a part of Barri he didn't know existed. Until then, it had been a noise in a school lesson, in dorms, at musicals he'd been obliged to sit through then a background annoyance at The Varsity. To now hear the manifestation of a tortured soul through the weeping of a violin was a strange but humbling experience. It penetrated Barri's house and his being. He sat with elbows on knees, his head bent in reverence and his eyes closed.

Will my experience of her be enriched by this or lessened by the crushing of one so capable of expression? With a heavier heart Barri went to the music room then entered to find a red-haired goddess posed in an ageless, artistic stance. Her eyes were closed tight against the music. He waited.

Eventually, Caprice came to the end of the piece and with dreamy violet eyes, raised her head from the instrument. She saw Barri with bewilderment, her arms dropped.

'You have a habit of suddenly appearing,' she observed, sucking in her surprise. Her seclusion was broken.

'I could say the same for you,' Barri replied. 'I certainly wasn't expecting to see you when I emerged from the pub yesterday. Come, we need to talk.' Accustomed to his orders being followed without question, Barri returned to the hall, selected a bottle of red from a hidden panel beneath the stairs then sat at the head of the dining room table. He carefully uncorked the bottle while waiting for Caprice.

I'm under his roof, using his things and if he hadn't been in the right place at the right time then, where would I be? She was conflicted. *Is he that arrogant to sit and wait for his meal to be served to him or does he deserve to?*

'You haven't eaten then?' she posed.

'I don't get chance to at work,' Barri responded. 'Have you?'

'Not yet.'

'You'll find new clothing in the kitchen. We must talk.'

'Don't you want to eat first?' Caprice asked, acutely aware after the breakfast fiasco that Barri followed strict rules about dining and talking.

'No,' he surprised her. 'We can talk over dinner,' and he surprised himself.

Caprice went to the kitchen but resisted looking into bags strewn across the centre-island. She was pleased her host had gone to such trouble. From what she could see from a label spilling out, he'd chosen clothing far superior to any in her stolen suitcase. She smiled. *The thieves did me a favour.*

A culinary concoction was ladled into wide bowls. They were sprinkled with finely chopped basil, a touch that didn't go unnoticed. Barri had chosen an Italian Barolo to compliment a meal he guessed would be served from its scintillating aroma. As he lifted his fork, he said: 'I've been neglectful. You must tell me all about yourself.' His plan moved into its first stage.

'There's nothing to tell,' Caprice responded nervously.

'What, nothing? Where are you from?'

'I was last at Macefield but I travelled about.'

81

Barri's face twitched, Macefield wasn't too far away. 'Who did you travel with?'

'Family mainly...' Caprices nervousness increased.

'Do you have a lot of family? As you see, I do not.'

'No, hardly any... now.' Caprice said this last word with such finality that Barri guessed she'd recently suffered bereavement.

'My parents were killed a couple of years ago. They were my only family.' This fact could solicit sympathy and Barri was now open to it. Caprice stopped eating and tried not to stare.

'You seem to be coping well.'

'Work conquers all.' Barrie glanced at Caprice to see if she was sympathetic. He noted that she looked indifferent so he tried a different tack. 'And, it is work that brings me to my next question.'

'Oh?'

'Was your journey taking you to somewhere specific, a new job? You obviously play the violin with skill.'

'No,' Caprice filled her mouth with pasta as an excuse not to speak.

Keeping his cold blue eyes upon her, Barri watched his guest chew her food then watched her creamy throat when she swallowed. 'So, you have nothing in mind, no goal, no plans and no purpose.' He said this while searching her eyes. She felt a magnetism that she knew she owned but hadn't seen in anyone else. It felt almost holy. Caprice heard his words but their meaning fell heavy upon her. She had fled, escaped. Suddenly, the vulnerability of having no set future gripped her. She couldn't eat and put down her fork.

'I have a proposal...' Barri paused deliberately. 'Your journey is obviously not urgent.' He paused again to add accent to his next point, he wanted to get it across in a reasonable and suggestive way. 'Jobs aren't easy to come by so close to Christmas and I have much at my disposal.' Again, Barri paused to carry weight to his reasonable suggestion. 'I'm not offering a permanent job, but I do need someone to manage the house until New Year. I'll decide then whether to remain or move.'

'You would sell this house?'

'There are six weeks until New Year. I'll make a decision then. Do you need time to think about it?' Barri avoided Caprice's eyes but curiosity about her reaction was too much to bear. He wouldn't wait six weeks to achieve his goal.

Caprice picked up her wine glass and tentatively sipped. Her logical side said: *Yes, go for it. This is a chance to earn something and have a secure roof. The only drawback is that it's so close to Macefield.* Her illogical side, plagued by insecurity and the terror that she may be found out, said: *You need to go as far away as possible.* The logical side won. *Distance made no difference in the past. You can only gain from this.*

'Yes, I'll accept your proposal as long as it is only until New Year.'

Barri's lips parted into a lop-sided smile. His champagne excitement returned. 'Good. Don't worry you will be dispensed with by then.'

Caprice gave Barri an odd look. *What a funny way to put it.*

9. Playing Safe

A mini Michelin Man fled across virgin snow, his billowing padded coat and waterproof trousers squeezed by elbow and knee-pads. He headed for the play-frame struggling to keep his piss-pot helmet on. Its buckle ate cruelly into his flesh. His pursuers were hot on his trail; a group of four foul-mouthed lads bent on burying their victim in snow once they'd relieved him of his helmet and pummelled his head. Ahmed fled for his life and wheezed in pain.

Aged five when his family moved to Mistlethrop it had taken another five to get used to discrimination reserved exclusively for him. Older boys on his estate couldn't accept anyone who challenged their idea of a close-knit community. 'You've got nowhere to run!' one of the boys shouted, quickly followed by a hoarse roar. Shouting was detrimental to breath-control while running.

The young boy ignored burning under his chin. He kept his eyes focussed on the play-frame not realising that it was already occupied. It hid children of a different ilk to the red-faced ruffians who regularly exercised attitudes older than their years but rarely stretched stunted IQs. Chasing a younger boy through ankle-deep snow eventually slowed the hot pursuers. They bounced off each other to maintain balance. Each secretly marvelled at how swiftly their prey glided across icy snow even with his over-zealous body protection.

As Ahmed neared the frame, heads appeared from the side of a playhouse, another appeared at its round window. The boy stopped as soon as he saw potential danger but the next few seconds quickly changed his mind.

'Ere mate, get to the ladder and we'll cover you!' a confident voice shouted from above, followed by more encouraging yells of: 'Yeah, we'll get 'em!'

Heads with stretching necks emerged from the side of the playhouse like a three-headed tortoise then dipped down so low that Ahmed couldn't see any torsos. Suddenly, a volley of snowballs sailed past him, narrowly missing his head. He knew from foul language behind him that their targets had been hit. His pursuers quickly scrambled up snow then pounded it into lumps before beginning fierce retaliation. One hit Ahmed in the back but missiles were mainly aimed at the play-frame's lower platform.

Ahmed roasted inside his layers, his face deep puce but little could be seen of it beneath protective headwear and a rigid coat collar. A welt of thick blood oozed beneath his chin but panting was more painful. The exhausted boy tentatively placed a snow-caked shoe upon the first rung of a wooden ladder. As soon as he put full weight on it there was a loud crack. The rung snapped. Ahmed fell back into snow but as he looked up he saw a missile hit a face at the playhouse window. He caught a glimpse of its features before another snowball spread like a custard pie. It belonged to a pretty girl with ginger hair. Ahmed swallowed hard and his panic, exhaustion and humiliation immediately vanished.

Without a second thought the boy arose, turned to look directly at his enemies while raising both arms to form a human crucifix. Then, he took a few steps forwards, stopped and yelled: 'Come on you cowards, give me all you got!' It caught his enemies' attention. Resuming their initial hatred for the boy, the lads grabbed fresh fistfuls of crusty snow and hurled. Ahmed's bravery had also spurred on his new allies.

Although the face at the window had retreated into a torrent of tears, three children remaining were infused with unifying strength. The largest, a thick-set boy who looked a lot older than Ahmed even though he was the same age, jumped towards the rope-ladder. 'You hold the fort,' he instructed a tall wiry girl crouching near him. 'And you...' he ordered a shorter boy, 'Come with me.'

85

When they reached the upper platform, the larger told the smaller to remain and resume firing then rushed to a slide at the end. During his descent he forced snow downwards to finally land in a pile at the bottom. With this new ready-to-hand ammunition and a body big enough to add power to his efforts, the boy gathered and formed volleys with precision. The enemy were now hit from three levels.

'You think you're 'ard?' the large boy taunted. 'You're as 'ard as my Nan's rice pudding!' He released a grudge against enemies of old. With each missile, painful memories resurfaced then, the large boy was driven by anger at seeing those memories re-enacted with a new victim. Six months earlier, he'd been the new arrival having committed the terrible sin of speaking with a posh accent. He'd gone to great pains to get rid of it since.

Still, Ahmed stood his ground. His head bowed so low that his oversize helmet protected his face, thick body-wear a bullet-proof vest. Clumps of ice pounded him with sickening thuds. Their intensity almost knocked him off his feet but he determinedly twisted his heels into snow.

Within minutes the enemy lost steam. They were open targets, being hit from above, middle and below. The face that had retreated from the window now returned upon the lower platform and it was twisted into an ugly scowl. The beetroot-faced girl had overcome humiliation and was now keen to help. Two girls stood valiantly side-by-side and pelted snowballs filled with rocks. This was not the time for a clean fight; that was for the boys with their superior strength. 'Get back to the bandstand,' they screeched like banshees. Shrill voices penetrated ears, adding another dimension to their assault.

One of the ruffians lowered his arms having recognised the larger lad, who stood sideways but looked directly at him. His arms swung with the precision of a baseball pitcher. The lad had grown fierce and confident as well as in mass. Quickly weighing up whether to charge and attack then, the chances of being hit in return, he shouted: 'Don't fink this is over. We'll

86

get you when you least expect it then we'll see who's 'ard!' With that, the rough boys turned in unison. Only one looked as though he could have stayed for another round but he too, reluctantly trudged back through the snow. The victors watched them retreat.

Ahmed lowered his arms to enjoy silence and soothing cold air. Hot breath swirled into wisps about his head. He thought he saw steam rise from his coat. The large boy spoke first. 'What's your name mate?' The weight of Ahmed's helmet had forced itself to the front of his head, almost obliterating his vision. He turned and said: 'Ahmed.' The girl with the ginger hair giggled.

'Armoured!' She laughed and clapped her gloved hands, sending puffs of powdery snow into the air.

'Sick name,' the large boy remarked. 'Guess the armour came in handy today.' and he gestured to his new friend to come and join them.

And, that is how *Armoured* got his nickname, from layers forced onto him by an over-protective mum. The sore beneath his chin became a wound from glorious battle. He smiled so broadly that beneath his helmet, the children could only see two rows of teeth as white as the snow.

'Well, Armoured welcome to our gang!' another voice rang out. Ahmed pushed up his helmet to see a boy standing on the upper platform. He had an uncanny resemblance to the girl with the ginger hair only his hair was dark brown. Armoured bowed. It seemed a superhero thing to do and the girl with ginger hair giggled.

'He's my twin!' she shouted from the lower platform but the girl next to her frowned.

'It's not fair; everyone has a cool name except me.'

'There's nothing wrong with Sophie,' the large lad commented and Sophie's frown disappeared.

The children gathered on the lower platform then sat to swing their legs over the side while *Rosebud*, for that is how the girl with the ginger hair introduced herself, used the sodden end

87

of her scarf to clean around Armoured's wound. He loved the attention. 'So how come you're called Rosebud?' he asked shyly, but the girl's twin answered.

'It was Mum and Dad...'

'No, let me tell 'im, I like to tell it!' Rosebud interrupted but her brother ignored her.

'I'll tell it, he insisted. 'Anyway, before she butted-in... Mum and dad like a really old film...'

'Citizen Kane,' Rosebud interjected and her brother glared at her.

'And...!' The boy paused and glared again but his sister kept quiet when she realised it could come to blows. 'They liked the name of the man who was in it, Orson.'

'And...!' Rosebud interrupted mimicking her brother's tone, instantly forgetting any concern for personal safety. 'They also liked Rosebud, also in the film but I'm not sure why. They didn't name me that, they named me Rose but they always call me Rosebud.'

'Oh!' Armoured exclaimed. 'I thought it was because of your hair.' The children had to think about their new friend's statement but Rosebud blushed. Her face and hair were ablaze. She dropped her scarf to grab a handful of her hair then twisted it around her fingers.

'That's the nicest thing anyone has ever said.' She smiled bashfully but her brother snorted.

'I was named Orson but I prefer *Awesome* and, people call me that anyway.' The boy arched an eyebrow as though his awesomeness was a matter of fact.

'That's only coz they haven't 'eard of Orson and think you're saying Awesome. You deliberately say it the wrong way if anyone asks.' His sister was pleased with herself. The glare reappeared but her brother couldn't argue. Armoured kept quiet, his name also due to mispronunciation.

'Our dog's called Citizen,' Rosebud offered. She looked enviously at Ahmed's golden skin. Each time she entered the playhouse it was a tower and she, a princess in a fairy-tale.

She'd waited patiently for an exotic prince to rescue her, loving the stories of Rapunzel and Arabian Nights equally. She twisted her hair again and Ahmed's eyes shone with appreciation.

The large lad was ominously quiet. He held onto his secret. Sophie gazed lovingly at the large lad and remembered the first time she'd seen him. He'd been running from the bullies during a hot summer day.

'So what's your name?' Armoured asked the large boy, now recognising he was in the same year as him at school but a different class. He'd already recognised the twins and Sophie as in a lower year. He wondered if any of them recognised him. It had been so hard making friends. Kids mocked his foreign accent. The large boy was suddenly reluctant to tell his story but Rosebud came to the rescue.

'He's Inky.'

Inky took off his gloves and held up his hands. They were covered in blotches of various colours but only he knew the error of his friends' assumption. Six months earlier on a hot day, the large lad had fled across the park with the alacrity of a jack-rabbit chased by dogs. His largeness then had been due to puppy-fat which had since solidified into muscle aided by a growth spurt of two inches. Inky now loved to climb, swing, slide and run.

Six months ago he'd exercised an unknown talent that could disperse enemies with deadly timing. It had proved useful whenever about to receive a beating. Inky was a flatulent boy. They weren't the quiet expulsions that don't linger. They were violent rasps of lethal intensity that could instantly make eyes water, nostril's narrow in disgust and the backs of throats gag. His favourite snack of cheese and peanut-butter helped enormously. Inky had previously been known as, '*Stinky.*' Stains on his hands, on that particular day, had been incidental. He also loved to draw with a set of felt-tips, having eaten his crayons.

Stinky had fled and three children playing in Paxton Park had watched him run, change direction, run, change direction again, double-back then disappear into the distance, swiftly followed by an angry pack. 'Stinky! Stinky!' Voices had been too far away to clearly hear what they cried.

Ten minutes later, the large lad had headed directly for the play-frame. He'd outwitted his pursuers which hadn't been difficult. When he'd arrived at the ladder, he'd clung onto it to catch breath. When Sophie had descended half-way, it was the stranger's ink-stained hands she'd noticed. They'd reached up to offer assistance. Sophie had been flustered but once on firm ground she'd found she was still holding a multi-coloured hand.

Returning to the present, Inky held up his hands and thought there was no need to explain. His secret was safe; his talent a weapon to be used in dire circumstances only.

The children weren't still long enough for bitter coldness to affect them. After introductions and a few minutes of leg-swinging, Inky introduced Armoured to the pleasures of the play-frame. All the children explored every inch as though a new experience. When they came to the playhouse, Rosebud took charge and blushed when Armoured entered. 'Wouldn't it be great...' she said eagerly, 'if there was a bridge between 'ere and that tree-house. Armoured followed a pointed finger.

'It's too far,' he observed. 'It would have to go right over the road then into someone's garden. It would be too dangerous. Whoever owns that garden would go mad.' They were valid points and said with such conviction that Rosebud was instantly swayed. He'd been the only one to take her suggestion seriously enough to bring logical arguments against it.

'I saw a lovely lady in that garden this morning.' Sophie popped her head around the corner.

'The lady with red hair,' Rosebud sighed with envy. 'I saw her too but I don't think she saw us. She looked sad.'

'How do you know?' Armoured asked.

'Oh, we women can just tell,' Rosebud stated and Sophie nodded. 'Only women recognise true sadness.' This time Rosebud nodded to acknowledge her friend's wisdom. Armoured nodded as though he understood. The girl with ginger hair fascinated him.

'Perhaps we could ask the sad lady if Rosebud could play in the tree-house?' Armoured suggested and all three nodded.

The new gang member soon learned the hierarchy. Inky was ringleader and Awesome, second-in-command. He was protective of his sister but frequently belittled her only to apologise afterwards while looking longingly at Sophie. Sophie was quiet but worshipped Inky. She tried to impress him but became easily exasperated when he played hard to get. Rosebud had found her exotic prince but she felt hard done to by her brother. She could be snippy and trite until he was forced into a bout of insults. All this was learned in one afternoon.

Armoured was bewildered but extremely happy when he later returned home to his overprotective mum. She was surprised when she tried to relieve him of his layers. He told her: 'I want to keep them on.'

His parents had to hide their amusement at the dinner table when he'd sat in full battle dress during their meal.

10. The Beast and His Castle

Before leaving at five p.m. Barri leaned across the kitchen isle to hand his guest a piece of paper. She hadn't seen him all day and had wondered where he'd been hiding.

'Read this. If you have any questions text me, the number is on there. DO NOT ring me! I'll be in the factory and unable to talk. I won't be home until the morning so I'll speak to you tomorrow.' Barri's authoritative tone and serious expression was enough for Caprice to accept the paper without question. Plus, it would be embarrassing to tell him that she didn't own a mobile. Her old pay-as-you-go had been a portal for her tormentor. Even putting her mouth near it had been enough to turn her stomach. Among other items it had been disposed of.

When Barri had gone, Caprice reluctantly sat at the head of the table to read. The printed paper was entitled, "*Housekeeper Duties.*" Barri had included his phone number at the bottom then in brackets wrote "*TEXT ONLY.*" Although his guest had looked flustered when faced with his iPhone, Barri had assumed Caprice used an older mobile without a touch-screen.

Barri had been torn about changes to his household affairs. He'd also been acutely agitated when compiling the list. His assistant was a recipient of impersonal instructions whereas he would have to speak to and look at Caprice regularly.

'I need to find things for her to do,' he'd told the screen on his iPad. 'Why can't I quickly knock something together then leave it on the hall table?' Nor was he used to the luxury of observing a subject so closely. Just knowing Caprice's was under his roof had made Barri's hand quiver with repressed excitement. An old comforter had hung from his wrist. Its soft leather twill had caught his eye as the screen filled. When pausing to reread, his left fingertips had automatically stroked it.

"1 - Make a list of food required for two people for a week. Calculate cost."

Barri used a local Tesco, open twenty-four-seven and at the ridiculous hours when he visited, he was usually the only customer.

"2 - Personal products, i.e. toiletries, etc., and cost. Add to list."

He didn't want Caprice to wander freely around Mistlethrop and so he added this point as an afterthought.

"3 - Prepare one meal per day, to be served in the dining room at 4."

'So, he wants a cook too,' Caprice muttered under her breath. She stopped reading and furrowed her brow, suddenly disappointed but couldn't logically explain why. Her eyes darted across the room then across the table until they rested on a chair at the opposite end. Then, she understood the root of her upset.

Barri wasn't the only one to relive childhood memories. Caprice looked at the chair and clearly saw the first school teacher to have made an impression. He was quiet-spoken but strict. Her time with him had lasted two terms. Forced to move around, her education had been snatched from a number of schools.

Mr. Kerraine stood at the end of a classroom table and watched Caprice. She could now feel his eyes as though he wasn't an apparition conjured. She also remembered she'd sat with hands under the sides of her knees, too engrossed with watching children's mouths animatedly chatting. She mimicked children she hardly knew by opening and closing her lips in silent unison. A blank sheet of paper lay untouched.

'Can't you think of anything?' Mr. Kerraine asked. 'Didn't the tune make you think of anything?' Caprice shrugged her shoulders then the teacher had a troubled expression. He went to his desk and returned with something in his hand. 'Perhaps if I play for you...'

He raised speckled maple to his cheek. As soon as horsehair

93

moved gently across synthetic strings, a lonely shy pupil was captivated by purity of sound. When it finished, her teacher gestured to her to pick up a pencil but instead, she looked down and shook her head. Before long, his open hand was before her. With eyes still cast downwards she saw fingertips through her lashes.

'Come on,' he coaxed. She sheepishly accepted and her small hand was encased in warmth and strength as it guided her to her feet. Caprice remembered its touch vividly. She'd been singled out and in doing so the teacher had raised her to a plane much higher than merely out of her chair. The rest of class ceased to exist.

Gently instructed how to hold the violin against her jaw, her fingers guided to their correct positions, she only had eyes for her teacher's hands. Then, as the first feeble strains vibrated through her cheek and across her shoulders, Caprice found something to love. Mr. Kerraine had been correct, her mind unlocked.

When she'd lain on wet cobbles behind The Varsity then opened her eyes to see Barri's open hand, she had felt a modicum of that same special extraction from the mundane.

"4 - Manage household accounts - see filing cabinet in the Study."

Caprice's eyes returned to the list and her memories dispersed like smoke from a bonfire.

'*It's not as if Caprice would have the purse strings, just access to the paperwork,*' had been Barri's decisive thought.

Accustomed to a position of forced servitude darker and more menial than domestic, Caprice had already accepted that gift-horses do not exist. Through her disappointment at putting herself into this position, a tiny voice inside her cried out: 'Prove me wrong!'

"5 - Supervise cleaner and provide additional cleaning where and when necessary."

'So I'm nought but a skivvy!' After reading number five, Caprice's potential gift-horse bolted.

"6 - Do laundry."
Barri routinely dropped his things off on Monday then collected them on Friday but, that would have to change briefly. The list was short, but there was an addendum: *"Salary paid in cash weekly on Thursdays. Any additional expenses will be discussed."*

Caprice continued to stare at the list long after she'd finished reading but she was relieved by the last point. 'How would I have explained that I don't have a mobile or bank account? She rubbed her face with both hands then stood with purpose. 'Well, if he wants a housekeeper, he's got one!'

Another long evening stretched ahead but swallowing her pride, Caprice dug deep to find determination. After she emerged from the Study with a pen, paper and clipboard she went directly to the music room, more specifically a shelf of CDs beneath an outdated stacked music-system.

'Hasn't he heard of iPod or Wi-Fi?' Caprice asked the air as she pulled a fingernail across a row of CDs then thought about her own pitiful state, without a phone and bank account. 'Surely this can't be what he listens to.' Thick undisturbed dust proved that Barri didn't listen to music. After much humming she chose a moderately acceptable compilation disc then had a fresh set of switches to play with. She examined the dust on her fingertip. 'What on earth does that cleaner do?'

Earth, Wind and Fire's *Boogie Wonderland* blasted out then Caprice squirmed as she turned the volume so loud that she had to immediately vacate the room. It thumped deep base throughout Radburn as she first moved to the top of the house to inspect each room with the eyes of responsibility.

Throwing open doors and striding in with intense efficiency, Caprice tugged at heavy curtains in time to bellowing music from the depths of the house. Clouds billowed from creases and soon the air was thick with dust. As she wrenched each curtain Caprice rebelled against her past then her demotion from guest to employee.

'It may be dark outside...' she explained with a wide smile to

95

the curtains, 'but this house is as dark as hell.' She peered through grimy windows into navy sky dotted with sparking pinpricks then smiled wryly at the snow-laden ground. Reflected light entered the room, enough for her to write on the clipboard paper: "7 - *Source window-cleaner and costs.*" Then, she flicked every light switch she could find, continuing rebellion against everything that had brought darkness.

Each room was examined thoroughly, allotted a number and a note made of their contents and respective position in the house. When she came to Barri's bedroom door she hesitated, spat at it, wiped spittle away with her sleeve then ignored it.

David Sylvian's mournful voice sang the opening of *Ghosts* just as she stepped onto the bottom stair. The efficient young woman sat in the tub-chair to complete her list. Haunting music soaked her in its intensity and her mood changed. She looked up at the grandfather clock, surprised that time had passed so quickly then noticed that panelling hid another door. It opened to a flight of steps and when Caprice flicked another light switch she saw that it led beneath the dining room. 'So this is where you were hiding.'

Caprice opened a hamper at the bottom and saw a crumpled vest and joggers. A whiff of body odour forced her to close it quickly but, as she stepped back from the pong she saw a display of three, randomly placed wall-clocks. Each had been set at a different time but didn't appear to be working. A large distressed vintage dominated the middle, its neighbours smaller but each distinct with shabby-chic design. Then, she saw an empty hook. Cracked plaster around it had received a fresh blob of filler and it was dark in comparison to the rest of the wall. Caprice pushed her finger into it, still pliable enough to take her imprint. After a quick look around a basement gymnasium, Caprice returned to the ground floor then went through her lists.

Judith Gormey was about to begin an overnight shift but before she entered the care-home she stopped to look at the neighbouring property. *That's the first time I've seen the place*

96

lit. Light spilt across snow but that wasn't the only novelty, loud music accompanied the light. *What's going on? Is he having a party?'* Doubling back, Judith trudged across the driveway, dodged two parked cars to then slink into a gap between one and a dividing hedge loaded with snow. She had to stand on tiptoe to peer over. She searched her knowledge of music. *Edwin Star.*

It was difficult to see much despite craning her neck. Peering up, Judith could only see interior ceilings and when looking across, only panelling. There was a distinct lack of human presence. *Unless,* she guessed, *they're all at the back.* She'd check from the home's rear conservatory but just as she turned, music stopped and, one-by-one, Radburn's lights went out. 'Weird.' Judith's curiosity continued to smoulder throughout the night and was then inflamed as she left work.

Barri had walked to the base of the oak tree to look up at his tree-house. Rain made the lawn a mass of mini-potholes. Old footsteps had filled and fresh tracks laid bare a thick sludge, grass so saturated it was difficult not to slip. It would be dark soon. From an upper step, Judith could just see him over the hedge. She took her time to pull on gloves, struggled to place her fingers into the correct holes because she tried to move only her eyes. Her neck had stiffened painfully after its exertion the night before.

A voice rang out: 'Hey mister!' Barri looked about him, unsure where it originated and if directed at him. Judith didn't hear it. The Old Dear's bingo caller was in full voice: 'Clickety-click!'

'Hey mister, we're over here!' Two children stood on the play-frames upper level and flayed their arms as though ready to take-off. Barri stepped to one side to look around the tree then the arms caught his attention. He had his hands in coat pockets trying to determine whether the children had shouted at him or at some unseen person further along Dandelion View.

'We need to talk to you!' a young female voice yelled but still, Barri remained static and unsure. 'It's about your tree-house!'

A van whizzed by and exploded slurry of frozen leaves mixed with crushed ice. The child's voice was momentarily muffled. Barri just caught the words: 'tree-house' then reluctantly pulled one hand from his pocket to wave. One of the children returned his wave so frantically that her hat sprang from her head. Ginger hair wound into a coil beneath sprang out. The hat landed on a wire fence dividing the park from the pavement but, it wasn't the hat that caught Barri's attention. Long locks of bright red stood out against the stark white of the girl's surroundings. Barri gawped then, without hesitation he turned and marched back towards the house. Frantic voices continued but he ignored them.

Judith, however, saw something quite different. Barri's sudden interest in the tree-house had been a puzzle particularly as she knew he didn't have any children. After seeing him wave at the children in the park, Judith's mind took a leap in a direction only the most suspicious of people could. Even then, only a person with an ingrained sense of jealousy would be so keen to extend it. The sour, podgy woman turned the side of her mouth up into an ugly smirk then nodded with evil intent. It sent her neck into fresh spasms.

'It's disgusting! Girlfriend my arse! She's an excuse so people won't suspect what you really are.' Judith couldn't relinquish the reigns of wild surmising as she climbed into her chocolate-wrapper infested Ka. 'He's never had a friend let alone a girlfriend to the house. At his age, that can't be natural.' She based warped reasoning on idle gossip that had inflamed a jealous and bitter nature then, her nosiness. She recalled the time she'd shouted 'hello' only to be glared at then ignored by Barri's cleaner. 'That stupid cow thinks she's too good to speak to me because she works for 'im and who's he? No one! Take away his house and business and what do you have, a bloody pervert!' Then, Judith nodded. 'That tree-house is a trap,' discarding the fact it had been there for years. 'He'll get kids to look at it but all the while he'll be looking at them.'

Judith's leap placed her on a dangerous precipice but she

bolstered it by further false reasoning. 'It's always the ones you least suspect. They're everywhere, in the news, on the telly. Having money won't shield him. Christ, when I think of decent people who work for an honest day's pay and he's there lording it up.' Judith's own honest living wasn't in question. 'Jesus! If he touched one of my kids, I'd kill 'im!'

As Judith's car emerged from the driveway onto Dandelion View, she slowed then lowered the driver's window. The children were trying to tip Rosebud's hat from the wire fence with a stick.

'Don't you go anywhere near that tree-house!' Judith shouted out the window. 'If he talks to you again, call the Police!' The window went up and the Ka raced away leaving the children bewildered.

'What's up with 'er?' Awesome asked his sister.

'Don't know.' Rosebud's mouth stayed open while she thought about it. 'Perhaps the old people who live over there would be cross if they see us play in the tree-house. They don't like noise and stuff.'

'Who did she say to call the Police about?'

'Perhaps someone's living in the tree-house and that's why that man and that sad lady were looking at it.'

'I haven't seen anyone.' Awesome shrugged but took a long look at the tree-house. Rosebud followed her brother's eyes and wondered too before a light bulb went on in her head.

'Remember when mum told us someone died there, a long time ago.'

'Oh yes!' Awesome now also illuminated. 'His ghost must haunt it.'

'I thought it was a girl who died?'

Awesome shrugged again. 'Perhaps we didn't hear that woman right.' Then, the boy thought again and concluded: 'I still don't see why we'd call the police about a ghost though.'

Children shouting had surprised Barri. He'd been in the thick of old memories which had become increasingly trance-like, so much so that they smothered his capacity to think of

99

anything else except Caprice. Rain hadn't threatened his plan, it only added to it, more heavy snow forecast for later. As he placed a muddy boot over the kitchen threshold it seemed as though he was stepping from the past into the future. Caprice almost dropped a pan when Barri flung open the kitchen door. 'Oh!' she exclaimed, 'I didn't realise you'd been out.' Barri chuckled inwardly.

'Just for a breath of fresh air, before I eat.'

'Then sit at the table, I've almost finished.'

While Barri pulled off his boots, Caprice pulled a salad bowl from the fridge and laid it next to two hot plates on the centre-island then waited for a comment of appreciation. She watched in amazement as Barri strode silently past not offering to take any of the plates with him. 'Unbelievable!' Barri just caught what she said as he disappeared through the doorway but didn't think it was directed at him.

Caprice gathered her dignity then hastily donned an old tatty apron she'd found in a drawer. It was canary yellow with white daisies across its bib and pockets. Although she'd been extremely flattered by Barri's choice of clothing, thinking that she was seeing herself through his eyes, the old apron would help her make a point. She then sashayed into the dining room with her head held high but her lips squeezed tight.

The table had been set for one. The master of the house sat perplexed at the head with his elbows either side of his placemat, his fingertips touching to form a triangle. 'Where's your place?' He glared at the apron, it clashed horribly with Caprice's hair.

'I'm eating in the kitchen,' Caprice said grimly. 'It wouldn't be right for a housekeeper to eat with you.' Barri was speechless.

What could have happened to change the balance so drastically? He was reminded of the time he had walked through a dark office to look at photos. Caprice felt a weird sense of triumph. By the look on Barri's face it was like taking a sweet from a spoilt baby then saying: 'It will be better for you in the end.'

'No, this won't do,' Barri insisted as plate was laid in front of him. 'Take off that ridiculous thing!' Barri shook a hooked finger at the apron. Caprice looked down in mock astonishment.

'This is protective clothing; Health and Safety and all that. I could try to SOURCE and cost a maid's uniform if you'd prefer?' The young woman towered over Barri whose anger bubbled dangerously. His former guest could hear his nostrils expelling air.

'This is absolute nonsense!' Barri suddenly felt as though his father was in the room. He had to stop himself from springing out of his chair. The conflict of emotion was too much; panic at thinking his long awaited pleasure would scarper if he said the wrong thing but simultaneously, furious at being trapped in a situation he'd invented to keep her there. 'You are NOT a maid and you're NOT a housekeeper. Take off that bloody apron and set another place at the table before OUR food goes cold!' Barri slammed his left palm on the table. Salt and pepper cellars jumped.

Caprice quietly returned to the kitchen where she removed the apron, placed items on a tray then returned. Barri watched with shining eyes and pink complexion while she ceremoniously laid a fresh place at the far end. The tray was then propped against a table leg. Barri didn't object to her new choice of seat. He'd surpassed his previous shocks by a sudden flare then demonstration of frustration. His heart continued to hammer as he picked up a fork to stab a broccoli floret. The meal was eaten in silence until Barri noticed that he didn't have a drink. 'Didn't you choose wine for the meal?'

'No, I wasn't sure if you would want any, seeing as you have to drive to work.'

'I can have a glass with the meal and so can you. One glass isn't going to affect my driving. A good meal should be accompanied by good wine. You can put a stopper in the rest, that way one bottle will last two meals.'

Barri raised his napkin to his face then went to fetch wine while Caprice thought: *With all his money, why worry about how long the wine is going to last?* It was fastidious but she was ignorant of his rigid routines.

Before Caprice's arrival, two glasses would accompany a main meal but now Barri had company it became another leap into sharing. Wine helped to diffuse a prickly atmosphere but Barri worried that he may have upset his subject. Caprice was complacent. *I made a point but was it worth the hassle?*

During the rest of the meal, Barri had time to contemplate how to handle a misconception. *She is a subject,* he told himself then realised it inferred he was a monarch, he balked. *She's the right one,* then he realised it was a description of a bride, he balked. *I did employ her,* he reasoned, then: *What is she?* Elspeth's face came to mind. Barri welcomed the same sensual excitement as when he lay across a willing girl's body in woods.

After Caprice had removed all evidence of their meal, Barri savoured the last of his wine before pausing to think whether he should top-up his glass. 'Have you any questions about the list I gave you?' Caprice was prepared.

'First...' She raised violet eyes to her employer who appreciated them from across a long table. He wanted them to be closer so that he could run his eyes from them to a pale throat and back. 'What am I?'

Barri raised an eyebrow and felt uncomfortable. *Did she read my thoughts?* 'What are you talking about?'

'If I'm not a housekeeper or maid, then what am I?'

'You want a title then?'

Barri's question puzzled Caprice who paused then coyly said: 'Yes, I think I do. I want something to put on my CV.'

'You think a few weeks work is worthy of a note?'

Caprice didn't intend to completely lose her previous taste of twisted triumph too soon. 'Any job, no matter how temporary is worth a mention. You own a company; I'm at the other end of a greasy pole. It could help me find a proper job when I get to where I'm going to. So yes, a title would help.'

Barri pursed his lips and thought about it. 'How about Residential Manager, will that suit?' He couldn't resist upturning one corner of his mouth.

'Yes, that will do nicely.' Caprice returned the lopsided smile then went to the sideboard to retrieve Barri's list plus her clipboard. Barri topped up his wine, now calmer but amused. He pulled back the chair he would have preferred Caprice to have and waited for her to sit in it.

They discussed her lists. Barri was further amused and slightly impressed that his former guest had spent time to prepare paperwork, even though he disapproved of it. She'd made lists of repairs and possible renovations required to Radburn before an estate agent or potential house buyer walked round it. There were lists of room contents. She'd researched removal companies, storage options and where to sell furniture.

'You've been busy.'

'Yes, it needed doing if you're going to sell-up but, I had one problem.'

'What?' Barri felt himself drawn into violet eyes, feeling no small measure of Caprice's ability to weaken a chosen subject if she'd wanted to.

'I only had the house phone so you may have a large bill.'

A smile drifted across her employer's face as he allowed the pull of Caprice's eyes, hair and oh so milky skin to tantalise a now totally open imagination. He had to stop himself from saying: 'Leave it with me.'

'You should have said something sooner.'

Then, Caprice continued to go through her lists. Barri watched her closely. To have said it was sexual would be too uncomplicated as Barri's appreciation of his subject went far deeper than physical awareness, chemistry or the thrill of having someone so attractive so near. Each time she paused to draw breath Barri felt his heart surge. He drank wine as he listened but also drank her in until she became part of him. It was almost like experiencing that last breath when blissfully crushing life so that it cracked beneath him.

'Who gave you that?' Caprice asked out of the blue. She ran a finger along the twisted twill on Barri's wrist as it rested across the table. Barri resisted the urge to withdraw his hand then had to will his wrist to remain. He shivered when he felt Caprice's fingernails touch his skin. Hairs on his arms began to rise beneath sleeves.

'It was an old friend.' Barri didn't lie.

'He, she, must have meant a lot judging by how worn it is.'

Still, his wrist remained and Barri felt warmth circulate around his neck from beneath his shirt as it travelled upwards like fingers softly caressing a scalp. 'She,' Barri confirmed but didn't say anything more which intrigued Caprice. It sounded so final. Her fingers withdrew and Barri felt their absence like the death of a loved one.

'I have a question, Caprice slipped-in then, still keeping her eyes on the bracelet asked: 'If there's a problem when you're at work and I can't text you, is it worth me getting a mobile for the sake of a few weeks?'

'Worth - you've used that word more than once. So much is measured in monetary value but true worth lies elsewhere.' Barri looked at his bracelet then at Caprice's hair imagining it twisted into thick plaits around his wrist. 'I digress; how come you don't have an essential that defines a person these days?' He was curious about the answer.

'My phone was in my case.' The lie ran effortlessly from her lips and Caprice wondered why she hadn't thought of it sooner.

'Don't you have any relatives who would phone or worry about you?' Barri waited with bated breath.

'No,' Caprice said with as much finality as when Barri had said '*she*.' He felt new warmth swell in his chest.

11. The Thaw

Two weeks passed uneventfully and Barri didn't know why he had allowed them to. He worked each evening, leaving Radburn House at five and re-entering before three a.m. His usual routine melted. His new routine included a drive around Mistlethrop, often sitting in traffic. Being trapped with other stationary cars made him feel part of something larger than the life he had at home or in the office.

When he arrived at Radburn Confectionery he would walk around the factory, at first to avoid a busy office. Office personnel assumed that their boss had returned to his usual habits. Once everyone had gone the factory became unexplainably preferable to sitting in a glass box in front of a row of dark desks. When peering out of a car window Barri took comfort in seeing people do likewise, all patiently waiting for a car in front to move but, in the office he saw empty chairs and more worryingly, Elspeth looking back at him.

After a couple of nights he progressed to conversation with factory supervisors, interrogating them about production problems before trying to solve them. His presence on the factory floor caused unrest then speculation and when word reached office personnel, Barri's assistant suddenly became tight-lipped and glum. He developed a theory.

Prior to Barri's change of routine his assistant had been an important person, the key to all business operations with a finger in every pie and an ear to the ground. His customary discretion was the only reason Barri trusted him. With a boss akin to Howard Hughes, rarely seen in the flesh, gossiped about and an enigma to all, the assistant had gradually supplanted himself into a misguided notion of being a force behind the throne. It was a role he was glad to make the absolute most of and he told himself that he deserved all perks that went with it but, secretly resented not having the word "Manager" in his title. It was he who had followed Barri's instructions so efficiently that he'd reaped regular praise from all departments. It had been his name at the bottom of emails and letters (with a c.c. to his boss). It was him people now turned to for a discreet answer to the question of everyone's lips. 'So, what's he up to then?' He remained coy and tight-lipped.

A new Barri had emerged, his assistant the last to find out about factory inspections. The assistant's pique was compounded by an influx of emails where his name was demoted to c.c. Communications flooded in from people who'd felt previously rudderless. They wanted to now gush at Barri's direct instructions and prove their worth but, his assistant didn't have a record to look back upon. He grew increasingly surly. He shrugged-off colleague's questions which only increased curiosity. Rather than admit his boss was taking a more active role, the assistant decided that his personal theory could be the only explanation. Barri was preparing to offload his business.

When at home, Barri slept until one then used the basement gym for an hour before showering. Afterwards he remained in his room until three-thirty before repeating his walk around Radburn and the tree-house. Routines, routines, his world revolved them. He clinged to each change imposed upon him until he felt confident that he could control it but, somehow his routines continued to evolve.

His path altered slightly when the lawn began to look worse for wear and so Barri took the driveway route then side-tracked. It was a new habit Judith Gormey clocked and each time she saw her enigmatic neighbour she looked at the play-frame.

Half-term was over and children disappointed that snow hadn't stayed longer so that school had to close. It ended at three-ten and by the time children were relieved of uniforms and had their cheeks bulging with biscuits; it was too dark to play out.

At first, the four p.m. meal only took twenty minutes followed by ten of conversation but, as each day passed, Barri would appear slightly earlier than expected. He would read online news either in the annexe or seated at the table then, he would remain seated for longer.

Throughout the meal, Barri's conversation was purely cordial, enquiring how his employee's day had been, if there was anything he should be informed about, but, by the third day it wore thin. He didn't have anything new to say. His only input was a formidable presence followed by a repeat of the same couple of questions. Caprice wondered if he was deliberately secretive or didn't feel comfortable enough in her presence to speak about anything personal. 'You don't say much do you?' she ventured one afternoon.

'There's strength in silence.' It was another of Barri's odd responses that left Caprice with little avenue to continue talking. As she thought about what he'd said, she realised there was a lot of truth in it. *How many years did I remain silent?* Whereas this island of a man, secure and strong, lord of his domain, chose to keep his. Caprice thought how the dining room was his space. She'd lost hours just sitting at the table, keenly aware that it was his space and staring into it while Barri was at work. The music room was hers. *It's so good to be able to sit and be alone without fear.*

Snow thawed. Caprice remained under Radburn's roof and her time passed by fulfilling her listed duties. She now had the benefit of a new mobile and iPad. Both items Barri had given her within a day of their first discussion, ever keen to remove as much paperwork from his life as possible. His next instruction had been for Caprice to transfer all clipboard information to the iPad so that it could be added to household files. She could email Barri.

Caprice's salary wasn't included in business payroll and as her employment was temporary Barri paid cash but treated it as an expense. It was recorded as: "*property management and services.*" As with any business expense, it was up to the payee to take care of tax declarations.

As snow thawed so did Barri but he didn't realise it. It was the time of year when winter arrived with a mighty blast then retired early to regroup for a fresh attack. Barri plotted, allowed his imagination to mix freely with childhood memories. His thoughts and expectation surrounded him like the Boy in the Bubble. He hadn't been this indulgent before.

Every step was towards the inevitable and it was all he could see ahead. Anything outside his new cocoon of plotting was of little importance. He learned not to resent the new presence in his house, his life, the disruption to his perfected routine. Yet, in a short period, that presence became a craving beyond a physical and psychological desire to kill. He wouldn't acknowledge to his devious self that it also disturbed him. He didn't have time to ponder the disturbance to his psyche, ask why it was there and what it meant. It was shooed away like a persistent fly around a lion's mane. Dogged reliance on new routines and persuading his inner darkness that each was a step towards his goal, helped ease unfulfilled craving.

'So, what are you doing for the weekend?' Caprice asked Barri over a plate of steaming spaghetti and meatballs. She reached for a slice of garlic bread, dipped it in red sauce then manoeuvred into her mouth without splashing.

'I have shopping to do.' The words spilled out before Barri could stop them. He was so at ease with Caprice and new routines that his guard had collapsed like the meatball speared onto his fork. Weekdays, weekends, days had blended into one long unending routine and yet, Barri responded to Caprice's question as though he acknowledged weekends were a time for leisurely pursuits.

Prior to the meal, Barri had taken his walk around the gardens, commencing with the back and working his way around to the base of the oak tree. It had become a pleasant routine. Judith had seen him from an upper-storey window and busily made her way to a room with a better view. She'd remained busy near a window making a note of the time. Her interest had already been raised to a new level. That morning, she'd hyper-ventilated when she espied two workmen at the base of the tree. She'd watched agog while they'd taken measurements, proof that her assumptions had been correct, the tree-house would be bait.

The tree had a new barrier around it, red and white safety cones equal-distance apart. Barri had walked up to one of them and placed a toe tentatively against it as he recalled his old makeshift barrier. A smile that followed had been tried and tested over a number of days but become more easily expressed.

Returning briefly to his bedroom before dinner, Barri had pulled out a drawer then re-read his chronicle with the happy nostalgia of a granny flicking through a wedding album. Then, he'd reached for a small bag scrunched at the back of the drawer and to his dismay found it empty. 'I'll have to buy some more.' He'd toyed thoughtfully with a treasure upon his wrist. 'I could have sworn I had a couple of bracelets left.'

When he'd paused in his bedroom doorway to look across as Caprice's door, he'd noticed a coffee mug on a side-table. Alarm bells had sounded. The mug was between two similarly-sized vases and it contained an inner sticky bottom that had offended his nostrils. Barri had mentally walked the seven paces it would take back to his bedroom, looked again at the mug interior then presented it to Caprice. Her response had been logical and allayed his suspicion. 'I must have left it when I was cleaning one of the rooms. Don't worry Barri I would never go into your room.' Now, between mouthfuls of food, Barri couldn't help but lay down his fork to touch his bracelet for reassurance.

'Is there anything in particular you have to shop for?' Caprice asked innocently, sensing an opportunity to get out of the house.

'No, just a few basics.' Barri thought of a fresh batch of friendship bracelets.

'Would one of them be a clock?' Caprice remembered the hook in the wall outside the basement gym. Barri stopped eating.

'What makes you ask?'

'I saw the display downstairs. It looked like you're ready to make an addition.'

'No, I removed one. It wasn't working,' Barri lied.

'Oh? Then what about the others, they don't work either?' Caprice looked earnestly at Barri who hadn't considered that she would notice the clocks.

'They should be working,' Barri lied again then said abruptly: 'They must have stopped since I last looked.' He returned his attention to his plate but Caprice was pensive then looked around the dining room. 'What are you looking for?' Barri asked when he saw her fidgeting in her chair.

'Now I come to think of it, I can't remember seeing a clock in any of the rooms except the hallway.' This included Caprice's bedroom. She used her watch propped up against a bedside lamp. 'Why are all those clocks downstairs?'

Barri shot Caprice a look that she couldn't interpret then said coyly: 'They're mementos of happier times.' The answer took both Caprice and Barri by surprise but Caprice immediately thought of his parents and loss.

'They belonged to your parents?'

'No!'

Caprice guessed by his curt response that it was a closed subject. The grandfather clock in the hall decided to chime the half-hour. It broke an otherwise awkward silence. She waited, then said over a decreasing pile of spaghetti: 'There's a few basics I'd prefer to buy in person, I'd like to come with you tomorrow.'

Barri's surrounding bubble of inward perspective suddenly raised him off his seat then plonked him down again with brute force. A brief levitation had brought a glimpse of a world where he could walk with Caprice along Market Street like any other shopper. The thought both repulsed and appealed and as quickly as it came, it went. Barri's snow hardened again. *I must handle this,* he ordered his lax resolve.

The clocks had become a trophy case of sorts, with Elspeth

he had a bracelet and tree-house but with the other two, his memories were frozen at pacific times so that he could revisit them. He could look fondly at each clock and become lost in its time while slowly pushing his bracelet over the prominent bones on his wrist.

'I'll leave at one p.m., so make sure you're ready.' Barri pushed away what was left of his meal with disgust, more at his inadvertent slip into normality.

'You didn't like the food?'

'It was fine; I've had enough for today.'

When at his office, Barri regretted being lured into domesticity. He now faced a difficult weekend. If he couldn't maintain physical distance then he could at least maintain mental distance from his subject. His iPhone pinged in unison with his laptop.

New email roused him from his dilemma. Fastidiously zealous about all email, Barri was a stickler for working methodically through his inbox so that it only contained a handful. Minor communications were immediately forwarded to his assistant or allotted to subject folders he could later look at. Talking to people on the factory floor had prompted him to respond personally to emails. He'd taken great pains over some of them, however, there had been a clamour and now people copied him in on every discussion. This latest email was something different: *"Mistlethrop Civic Trust Awards."* Addressed solely to Barri, he was immediately torn whether to forward or open it.

"Dear Mr Barrington George,

Mistlethrop Civic Trust Awards are given annually to individuals or organisations responsible for high-quality new building, the reuse and restoration of old buildings, landscaping or any other work which makes a significant improvement to our town or countryside.

It is therefore our great pleasure to inform you that you have been nominated for the restoration of Hebble Mill and the creation of a moorland garden at the rear of the property. The new apartments have rejuvenated an otherwise disused section of our town and will benefit the local community by providing affordable housing to our residents.

This year, another of our nominees has kindly offered to cater for the awards ceremony, which will be held at his newly renovated Whiskers Hotel, formerly Whiskers Mill.

An official invitation for yourself plus a guest will be sent to you via Royal Mail in due course. We look forward to seeing you."

Barri stared at the email.

"Our residents" and *"'affordable,"* having no concept of community or what was affordable; Hebble Mill was a viable project that he'd been asked to fund. The mill renovations were mainly for Radburn employees who wanted to purchase a home nearer work. As yet, all apartments except one furnished to a high degree to tempt buyers, stood empty for final touches after New Year.

The read email remained in his inbox. Barri didn't want to add yet another new folder to his archives and felt annoyed but obliged to do more than just forward it.

'I'll go.' Barri's life became even more complicated.

12. Curious Collectables

Going to shops with Caprice was another excursion to foreign lands. Barri hadn't experienced anything like it since his first holiday with his parents. Caprice was nervously expectant as she climbed into a passenger seat. The driver focussed on the road but relived the night when he'd first felt the young woman's presence whereas Caprice looked at numbers on bus stops. She wanted to remember the route. She craned her neck each time a bus appeared in the side-mirror then noted whether it followed them. 'Everything looks so different in daylight.'

When they entered a car park, Caprice was disappointed. 'I thought we were going shopping?'

'We are, but it's best to park here at my business then walk across.'

There he goes again. Caprice remembered his request to cork wine so that it would last. *He's now saving on parking.*

As Barri strode across the car park he shouted over his shoulder: 'I don't have time to waste walking about. I know what I want and where to get it.' His words trailed into breeze.

Long athletic legs strode across roads towards Market Street which was busy with shoppers so Barri took side-streets instead. Caprice had to trot but remained behind despite her busy feet. They walked across cobbles she'd fallen on. When they'd passed the rear of The Varsity and crossed a road, she saw an arched entrance to Beacon Cloth Hall.

'Why don't we meet at this arch when you're done?' Barri shouted over his shoulder.

'I'd like to look around this place first. It looks interesting.' Caprice went through the arch but Barri had already entered. *It's as though he doesn't want to be seen with me.* As she entered a middle spacious courtyard she saw a quadrangular

113

stone building built in the neo-classical style. That much she'd remembered from her chequered education. Each side had a rustic basement story then two upper, fronted with interior colonnades. Benches in the courtyard were occupied by a man busy with his phone and a woman waiting for friends. It was too brisk a day to sit out long and Barri eyed them nervously.

'I doubt there's anything in here you'd be interested in. Go and sit on a bench or something. I won't be long then I'm going straight home so, decide now!' There was that cold, curt tone again. Caprice was disappointed and so was Barri but he didn't know how to soften his tone. Turning abruptly to the right, he headed for steps at a corner. Caprice ran up behind him.

'Where are you going?'

It took a moment or two for Barri to answer then, it came to him. 'I have to buy a present for someone at work,' he lied. 'I'll meet you here in thirty minutes. Will that be long enough for you to get what you need?' Caprice nodded then watched Barri climb steps. His provision of clothing and underwear had been thorough but she didn't have socks to wear with jeans. The excursion had been an excuse to get out and about.

Caprice walked along the quadrangle edge, peering through narrow windows before going to the next level. Upper walks led to arched rooms which two-hundred years ago were used for marketing cloth from local mills. An interesting sign beckoned, *Heaven's Cakes*. She bought a vanilla cupcake and ate it while walking to another sign, *Baa-Baa Black Sheep*. She chose three pairs of knitted socks from a basket in its doorway then returned for another cupcake. Looking through the window of *Curious Collectables*, she finished eating it while staring at the back of Barri's head. A paper bag lay on top of a glass counter but Barri was peering into a wall cabinet.

'I never had you down as a sci-fi fan.' Caprice sidled up then looked too. Barri didn't have a clue and was annoyed that she'd found him. He'd been admiring an unusually shaped blade wondering what the words etched into it meant, *Klingon Batliff*. He pretended to smile as though he'd known what she meant then straightened his body.

'Have you finished shopping?' Barri stared at Caprice's lips, devoid of lipstick but pink and plump. Caprice thought she had a blob of vanilla icing at the side of her mouth and quickly licked it.

'Yes, I got what I wanted.' She was dying to ask Barri what he'd bought. If she didn't ask now then she'd never know; his conversational skills were non-existent. 'So?' she hinted. Barri had moved his cold eyes from her lips to her hair.

'Did you find something?' A woman's voice interrupted before Caprice could elucidate. The shop owner, a smiling woman with a twinkle in her eye, had emerged from a doorway behind the counter. She held a small carousel stand.

'You may want to look at these. They came in yesterday and would go nicely with the bracelets.' Barri swung around but tried to remain calm as he returned to the counter. The woman ran her fingers along the stands contents. 'See, this one would match the bracelets.' She draped plaited leather across her palm.

When Barri saw it, he held his breath. 'What is it?' he asked, unsure if it was a bracelet, it seemed too long.

'It's a choker,' the woman replied. 'Here, let me show you. Do you mind dear?' The woman looked at Caprice.

'No not at all.' *Strange thing to buy for someone at work; I wonder who she is?* With a sinking feeling, Caprice suspected that Barri didn't just go to work in the evenings. *He can't have a girlfriend, why doesn't she come to the house sometimes?* She felt slightly better but still perplexed. Despite bending down, strands of Caprice's hair flopped forward to interfere with the operation of a delicate clasp. The shop owner was short and had to reach up.

'When you tie a friendship bracelet around the wrist of a friend they're supposed to wish for something.' The woman paused in her task, hesitant to catch Caprice's hair in the clasp. 'A bracelet should be worn until it falls off by itself then the wish will come true. I like to think that these chokers reinforce the wish.'

Barri's hand went immediately to his wrist. He smirked again as he thought: *I got mine but could do with another.*

Giving up, the woman handed the choker to Barri. Caprice was even more perplexed. *A friendship bracelet sounds romantic but, is he buying it just for friendship?*

'Here, why don't you have a go, I'm sure your girlfriend would prefer you to do it.' Barri glanced at Caprice and for a moment looked odd. Caprice noticed. He accepted the strip of leather then waited while Caprice gathered her hair to lift it. Barri didn't correct the woman's assumption and Caprice's heart leapt. Barri stood behind his subject to weave leather between upright arms until two ends met at the back of her neck. A silver loop was pressed gently in the middle. It opened and was then hooked onto a loop at the other end. As Barri's fingernails caught the silver, he caught a whiff of sweet vanilla. He gasped.

'"Okay?' Caprice asked, pulling her chin close to her chest then raising it.

'Hmm,' Barri replied. 'Keep still.' Enamoured with the crimson down along her nape, delicate wispy hairs that tickled his fingers, Barri asked the shop owner: 'Is it supposed to be so tight?'

'Yes, that's why it's called a choker. They're supposed to lie snugly against the throat but not be uncomfortable.'

Barri was reluctant to remove his fingers from the twisted leather thong. It was soft and snug against Caprice's warm skin. Her arms remained in the air then, she turned to show Barri the choker's full effect.

'What do you think?' Her violet eyes were as close as the first time he'd seen them. Barri stared at the choker and envied how it held fast against his subject's throat. Vanilla filled his nostrils and he felt the muscles in his right forearm stiffen. A dreamy perspective descended then closed around them both, it seemed to draw his subject nearer.

Penetrating personal magnetism combined with the lure that an open wound presents to a beast starved of food, Barri

116

reacted. His forearm stiffened but to his dismay it wasn't the only part of his anatomy. The unexpected movement was enough to render him momentarily speechless. *Thank God I put on a three-quarter coat.*

'Leave it on,' he rasped hoarsely. He would have a new fantasy to drip-feed his craving until it was time to feast. 'I'll take the necklaces and bracelets,' he informed the shop owner, who had taken her correct place behind the counter. She smiled widely but Barri then said: 'Make sure you count them.'

'I thought you were buying for just one person?' Caprice asked in surprise, lowering her arms so that her hair cascaded across her shoulders.

'Yes I was going to,' Barri answered assertively then, looked odd again.

13. Inviting Trouble

Saturday afternoon, Caprice's restlessness lingered following her too brief re-acquaintance with fresh air. She'd suggested lunch out, asking if The Varsity provided meals but Barri had insisted they return to Radburn House. Then, when she asked if they should see a movie somewhere, he'd looked bewildered and replied: 'The cinema is miles away. Why on earth would you want to go when there's a sixty-inch TV here?'

'Don't you get bored, just hanging around?'

'No and I won't be hanging around!'

'You're working again tonight? You're the boss! You can work when you want to.' She wondered if she'd guessed correctly about his evenings then brooded.

'By being the boss, I have to work harder. If I didn't, the business would soon fold.'

'I'm sure one evening off wouldn't harm it. Everyone needs time to unwind. What would you do if you didn't have a business to go to?'

During the choker-fitting Caprice had thought about succumbing to her old ways. She could have milked one of her two talents. The violin had needed regular practise whereas her feminine wiles had come naturally, shaped and forced by her old tormentor from an early age. *Am I out of practise so soon?*

She'd seen Barri's expression, felt his fingers quiver at her neck which had taken an inordinately long time to complete a simple task. Then, her bodily turn towards him, a slow release of long hair, her stance with knowing gaze, enough for his eyes to betray want. It would have felt good to use her talent without knowing it was part of some sick game. She'd experienced an unexpected release. Small physical acts initiated a concept of power when she'd previously experienced only helplessness.

118

Without the reward of material or mental accomplishment, Caprice had been hungry for any morsel.

Later during a meal, Caprice sat in silence. Barri noticed how she ate methodically but occasionally fidgeted. Her new choker bobbed gently with each swallow. Barri attuned his food mastication to hers with a dreamy impression that her choker beat time. *This is madness,* Barri confirmed when he realised he'd lost grip again. Her earlier question had played on his mind and stirred restlessness.

When alone in his childhood home, Barri had already lost his reality. Memories of his first kill had beat relentless time and dominated his nights. Suddenly, he knew that he couldn't trust his constraint much longer. He wanted to feel free. *What would I do if I didn't have Radburn Confectionery or the house?* Despite possibilities and excitement from the unknown, Barri was a creature of binding habits. It didn't deter him from escaping to the office as soon as he could.

While Barri worked, Caprice found a potential friendship although its interpretation was questionable. She took a walk along Dandelion View to see what was at the other end. Her car journey had provided information in one direction only. She dressed in clothes worn on her arrival then set out from Radburn's front door with more confidence than when she'd first entered.

November is an undecided month. Autumn wouldn't acknowledge winter but the latter season's early arrival allowed it to return for a last lingering kiss. The early evening sky was star-speckled and the park, a flat expanse, black beneath moonlight. Caprice took a moderate pace and passed a sign, *Fernlea Rest Home.* She passed four mansions before the road bent sharply to the right. Opposite, was a walled entrance into the park but Caprice wanted to see homes, look through windows to see families sitting in front of TVs.

She followed the bend and after walking several minutes houses appeared on both sides of the road. They decreased to four-bedroom sameness, each with a white garage and a strip of

119

garden with the same shrubs repeated. Curtains and blinds were closed. Disappointed, she continued to a row of four shops, two closed but two open, one an off-license.

People passed with bags that chinked and then Caprice felt lonely. A tantalising smell of vinegar drew her to a doorway where she joined a queue. At the front two teenage girls tottered on platform shoes, their long hair back-brushed into billowing bouffant.

'Do you want salt and vinegar?'

'Yeah on both,' one of the girls fluttered eyelashes that were too long and thick to be natural then she snatched a chip from greaseproof paper. She popped it into her mouth. 'Oh Fug,' she tried to say through her blowing, 'too hot!' She waved glittered fingernails in front of her mouth. Caprice was envious and despite not being much older than the girl, she felt suddenly old. She had nowhere to go and no one to talk to on a Saturday night.

'Hello there,' a whining voice said to her chest. Caprice instantly thought of the noise geese make when flying in formation. It was a voice that could be loud if released. She hadn't noticed a small dumpy woman staring up at her.

'Hello.' Caprice looked down. She tried to avert her eyes from the woman's round bulbous orbs; they were too wide apart on a flat pan face to be considered human. Badly-dyed hair pulled back severely made her eyes prominent. The woman stared brazenly, examining Caprice's face with the same anticipation as the girls with their chips. 'You live at Radburn don't you?'

Caprice looked at her questioner. Wide eyes didn't blink. Caprice changed her mind. *She's not a goose. She's a reptile.* 'Yes, for now.'

'Ah, so you're just staying for a while?'

Caprice nodded then waited impatiently for the queue to advance. She'd judged the woman within seconds, an emphatic gift honed by living with a deviant who'd instantly judged and was rarely wrong.

The third person in the queue said: 'Yes' to salt and vinegar.

Teenage girls moved to the window where they tried to eat without squashing potato under their fingernails.

'I work at Fernlea,' Judith said as though it held gravity but quickly followed with: 'Are you a relative of Barri's?' The woman said his name as though she'd known Barri for years. She hadn't spoken to him. Once she knew a name she banded it about with familiarity.

'No,' Caprice replied simply. The woman looked at her with calculating knowledge that extracting further information could be difficult.

'Then a girlfriend? Judith jutted her face forward and to one side as though she would have to strain to hear. Caprice's hesitancy spoke volumes to over-zealous curiosity.

'A friend,' Caprice had no intention of stating her real position.

'And how are you finding it?'

'What, Radburn?'

'Barri doesn't let his hair down.' Again, she assumed familiarity.

'What do you want?' the man behind the counter shouted to Judith above spitting vegetable oil.

'Four lots of chips, three fish and two tubs of mushy peas.'

'Fish will be a minute.' Three white fillets plopped into a slimy tray then into bubbling oil where they sank but quickly bobbed up into balloons of batter.

'The kids can share one of those, too bloody expensive for one each.'

'Just chips for me,' the red-head remarked. 'I fancied a bag as soon as I smelt them.'

'I thought you'd want something far grander, coming from a house worth a million.' Judith decided to extend her fishing line and waited for Caprice to be caught. 'How about, some caviar to go with your chips?' and Judith smiled to reveal two layers of button teeth, her lips too large to reveal them fully.

'No, I had that earlier.'

Judith stopped smiling.

'Your fish is ready. How d'ya want it?' It was a timely interruption.

'Two fish with chips, one halved with the other two lots.' Judith pulled a bulging purse from inside her coat while weighing how she could ingratiate herself with her new acquaintance. 'We're having Sunday roast at Fernlea tomorrow. The Old Dears will be asleep after four, why don't you pop round for a cuppa?' The invite was a warm gesture but from a cold heart. Caprice imagined what Barri would say.

On Sunday, Barri awoke to the strains of a violin as it quietly echoed from the depths of his house. Its mournful but soothing voice reached out to him through bedroom walls. Staring up at the ceiling, he replayed the previous day's events in his mind, almost smelling vanilla. He imagined running his tongue along the wispy down on the back of Caprice's neck and was compelled to seek out his new purchases. Then, he was bitterly disappointed, they weren't long enough to fasten around his muscled neck. Instead, he lay with one across his windpipe and dozed within a cloud of fantasy until he saw red hair brushing against his throat. With a start, he sat upright thinking Caprice was on top and crushing his windpipe.

Late afternoon, he was in a funny mood and loath to return to his office. He paced around the parlour like a hound awaiting the hunt. The house was becoming too small and its walls too thin. With indecision tearing him in two, Barri wearily decided: *I'm right to wait. To do it too soon and blindly won't satisfy. The moment has to be just right.* When he visualised a conclusion, his chest tightened. *Just a few days more and I'll be ready.* His nugget of secret longing was unbearable yet beautiful. If he clung on to its beauty then he could last. *Perhaps, if I should make an effort to look sociable? It would have to be something that didn't involve other people.*

'I'll take you out for a drive. Get ready.'

'I can't. I have somewhere to go.'

Barri's control slipped like fingers withdrawn from a comfy glove, 'Where?'

'Not far, I was invited out.'

Fighting through a fresh onslaught of rash blindness, Barri stormed to his office. Caprice nursed her nugget of petty power again. *Serves him right, any other man would have gone to the cinema with me when I'd asked. I can't be taken for granted.* She half-expected Barri to return and ask again but he didn't. It fuelled her curiosity about what he was doing in the evenings. Suddenly, Judith's invite didn't seem such a bad idea. 'Maybe I'll find out if he has a woman stashed away. The reptile woman talked about Barri as though she'd known him for years.'

Upon his return at two-thirty a.m. Barri was tempted to look into Caprice's room. He hovered with intent outside her door listening for the slightest sound, which eventually came when her bed creaked. It later replayed in troubled dreams. In his dreams he strained to hear a violin but it was too far away. 'You can't listen to it,' a shrill female hissed in his ear. He thought it was Miss Rogers. The creak then deafened him.

'Shut up!' he heard himself shout. It was six a.m. Barri decided to shower then go to the office. He hadn't slept much that weekend. The manifestation of unexpected physical side-effects had been as much a surprise as his compulsion to go to work early Monday morning. It was only when he fastened his car seatbelt that some normality returned. His physical side-effect returned to a flaccid state.

During the journey, Barri debated inwardly if it was Caprice or a combination of unexpected occurrences that knocked his world out of kilter. 'Is having her at home a necessary evil or pleasure?'

Whereas hormones and ego should have nudged a teenage Barri towards female company he'd lived with the sexual awareness of a nun in a confessional box, so devout to his one true desire. There could be only one remedy. Glancing down from his forearm to his crotch, Barri wished only the hair on his forearm would stand to attention, like during his kills. A new connection between Barri's mental and physical pleasure was forged and he grappled with his continuing see-saw. His

123

physical side-effect wasn't safe to drive with. Barri's fingers gripped the steering wheel as though it was the bar of a rollercoaster carriage.

The receptionist's greeting confused him. 'Good Morning Mr George!' she chirped.

Barri glared at the desk, not the woman behind it. Immediately he was a boy again, eager to pay a surprise visit but ignorant of what he would find. The receptionist had too bubbly a nature to allow the boss to deter her. It was the reason why she was so good at her job. 'It's so nice to see you in the land of the living.'

'Thank you,' Barri replied feebly, using two rare words.

Barri's assistant smiled at a silver envelope on top of a pile of weekend post. He put it to one side, hoping it would contain an invite to another free meal with drinks. *I'll save the best for last.* He then looked at the addressee on each envelope beneath and to his annoyance they were all addressed to his boss. He'd come in especially early to fish around then work on his game plan. Shuffling through again, he stopped and peered at a post mark franked with a company logo, *Mandrakes Cakes*. 'This should have come directly to me,' he muttered. He searched for his letter-opener. 'Nobody's going to take my position away!'

The tip of the letter opener edged into the envelope piercing a hole through the "*M*" of its logo. It gave little satisfaction but it was easy then to slide the blade while enjoying a ripping sound. Before the assistant could pull out contents, a shadow fell across his desk. An open palm appeared at the tip of his nose. 'I'll take my post with me.'

The assistant scanned his watch before he looked up with disbelief. 'That's right, I'm here early,' Barri confirmed. He scooped up the post and waited while his assistant reluctantly handed him the open envelope. 'I'll take that one too.' Barri pointed to a silver envelope. 'I was expecting it.' His assistant couldn't mask his disappointment.

Opening the post was a novelty. Barri needed something to do and he would need two cups of strong coffee to help him.

Voices buzzed in the outer office but he couldn't hear them through a closed door.

The assistant's surliness returned tenfold. *It's time to update my CV.* He could take advantage of a lighter workload but having his boss around during the day would require constant vigilance. The assistant threw his letter opener into a drawer then smiled slyly as he opened another to remove a wedge of paper. He reached for the telephone, dialled three numbers and waited for an internal department to pick up.

'Hi, it's me. Yes, I'm fine. Is he in? Good. Could you tell him I'll be down to see him later? Barri wanted me to go over the latest figures. Oh, and by the way, could you dig out the next six months sales predictions? Cheers.'

Unlike his assistant, Barri decided to open the silver envelope first. A grained card had sloping black font. Barri read it, wafted it in front of his face, read it again then continued to waft. He'd ignored the email in his inbox but couldn't ignore this. *My dad would have greased palms for a chance like this. I achieved something he couldn't.* For two years Barri had led the business in name only, allowed it to tick-over, delegation his only management style. He now saw his father's face, proud but envious. *He would have loved to wave this in front of his old rival's face.*

Barri had been nominated for the award, not his father. Radburn's was his now. Barri looked at the invite again. *"Five-course dinner... black tie... press..."*

'The owner of Whiskers Hotel is certainly aiming to please, a great way to promote a new business.'

Barri's curt email response to Mandrake's business proposal had been: *"No. It's out of the question."*

Mandrake had replied with: *"Before you make a decision, we should at least talk. I'll phone you."*

Barry had then emailed: *"It would be a waste of my valuable time and you already know the answer."*

Not content with allowing Barri to have the final word, Mandrake had quickly fired off: *"Then, I'll see you at Whiskers*

125

Hotel."

'That man should have learned by now.' Barri wafted the invite again then thought about the long feud Mandrake had instigated with his father.

Mandrake's Cakes produced branded cake products but Niall Mandrake hadn't been content to own the UKs biggest bakery. He wanted Radburn's Confectionery added to his logo. Although Barri didn't feel the intensity of competition, he appreciated his father's fight to maintain a non-reactionary stance to Mandrake's wheeling and dealing. Mandrake had tried to claw some of Radburn's market share, his prime weapon being a biscuit coated with caramel and chocolate. It had gone head-to-head with one of Radburn's famous products. 'Where will it go, on supermarket shelves with biscuits or with chocolate and sweets?' That question changed the balance. Other products then crept into supermarkets at a cheaper retail price.

Barri slotted the invite into the sleeve of his laptop bag and as he did so felt his heart quicken. His desk phone rang. 'Mr George, there's a lady here to see you.' Ignorant of Caprice's visit to Fernlea, Barri had tried not to think about where she'd gone to for her night out but, the receptionist's cheery voice now brought a vision. *She'll be waiting downstairs with an explanation.* 'Send her up.' Barri replaced the receiver, his stomach fluttered then he panicked when he realised everyone would see her.

The assistant acted peculiarly. He swung his wheeled chair back, kicked both feet up then held up open palms as though backing off from a fight while sitting down. People noticed and exchanged wary expressions. He hadn't been quick enough to respond to a flashing light on his phone. Reception had a visitor waiting. Yet another task had been greedily snatched away, his boss had no right to answer his own phone. After having larger tasks removed, only the menial could be claimed. The assistant quickly saw how foolish his display of frustration looked to others and with a red face rechecked Barri's online calendar but was at a loss. Jumping from his chair, he sucked his stomach in then took purposeful strides through the office. He would greet the visitor and act as though he expected one.

The smug young man stared at an open lift then blushed with embarrassment. *Things are far worse than I thought.* Barri's visitor was then escorted through the office. The assistant held his head high, looked directly ahead and ignored gaping mouths. Once at Barri's closed door, he rapped his knuckles once then swung it open. The boss had prepared himself by staring intently at his laptop screen and busily tapped at keys. 'Take a seat.'

Two shapely long legs crossed the far side of the desk and Barri saw movement from the corner of his eye. His visitor chose not to sit opposite but in one of the comfier Italian leather side-seats. When his eyes followed the legs upwards, the look of surprise on his face openly pleased his visitor.

'I expected someone else!' Barri exclaimed.

'I'll only take a minute of your time.' The sultry visitor had a soft voice but with perfect elocution.

'I can only spare you a minute.' Barri leaned back and placed both elbows on chair arms. 'What is it you want?' He was alarmed. It seemed even at work he had no escape from a treadmill of uncertainty.

The pretty young woman was a couple of years older than Caprice but her natural charms enhanced by cleverly applied make-up and a closely fitting skirt-suit. She smiled just enough to reveal unnaturally white teeth. Auburn hair rested stiffly around the tops of her shoulders. Barri noticed it had been treated to highlights.

'I've come on a mission of mercy.' She was clearly delighted in an interesting development; Barri was not at all as expected. She was now eager to embrace her task.

'And what part do I play in this mission?'

The young woman stifled her amusement. 'An important one, my father received an invitation from the Civic Trust. As you know, it will be a high-profile event. Unfortunately, he can't go and asked me to stand in for him. I'm not sure if you are aware, but my step-mother passed away recently.'

'I'm sorry to hear that.' Barri knew when to apply the graces expected. 'I don't know who you are.' The young woman's smile vanished and her eyes widened but she remained poised.

'I'm Purl, Purl Mandrake.'

Barri looked down to rest the tip of his nose on clasped hands. Purl took this to be a moment of allowing the importance of her revelation to sink in but Barri hid a smirk. 'I wasn't aware Mandrake had been nominated for an award.' Barri looked up, raised a brow and awaited his visitor's reason for arriving without an appointment.

'I believe invites were sent to all local major players.'

'Mandrake is not local therefore I don't understand why he would be invited.' Purl could have taken offence but she was smitten by Barri's looks and authoritative manner. Like her father, she wasn't easily sent off course.

'My father is acquainted with the new owner of Whiskers Hotel. I don't wish to attend such an important business function unaccompanied. As you are in a similar line, my mission is simple. I came in person to ask that we go together.' Purl then watched Barri's face. He leapt to the conclusion that Purl had a different agenda than the one suggested.

If I appeared at Whiskers with this woman on my arm then it would give the wrong impression to guests and media. My father was right, Mandrake will use any means necessary.

'Purl...' The name didn't feel right on Barri's lips. 'I already have a date for the evening.' Purl's expression didn't alter but her eyes told a different story.

'Oh, I see.' Her long shapely legs remained crossed and still. She was unprepared for a negative response. In an act of finality, Barri stood then walked around the side of his desk expecting his visitor to take a hint but, she remained seated and said: 'Before I go, think of the opportunity this presents.'

'It is an opportunity for me,' Barri observed, 'an opportunity for Radburn's to be heralded for its contribution to

Mistlethrop.'

'Yes, that goes without saying, but there could be more to it than that.'

'If by "*that*", you mean an opportunity to present a united front of our two... sorry... your father's business and Radburn's, then your mission is a fool's errand.'

Purl's soft smile vanished. 'Then I'll not take up any more of your time.' The visitor vacated her chair and the office with the swift elegance of a catwalk model.

Barri settled in his chair and sighed. One troublesome woman was enough to contend with. He was pleased to have handled another with enough directness to ensure there wasn't any room for misunderstanding. He couldn't care less what Purl reported back to her father.

Purl phoned her father as soon as she returned to her Porsche. She tapped a false fingernail on its steering wheel until her father answered. 'Well?'

'He's already taking someone. I thought you said he'd been checked out?'

'I did. I was told he lives alone and spends every night at the office. Are you sure he's taking someone?'

'As sure as I am of anything,' Purl was still smarting from the humility of a rejection and wasted trip. She didn't like missions of mercy that ended like a slap in the face and hers was smarting. She hung up. Purl was used to getting everything she wanted even if the novelty lasted briefly. It included men. She continued to tap her fingernails impatiently.

Having been told that Barri was totally unlike his father she'd expected him to instantly appreciate their compatibility and the opportunity. It riled that he'd been so good looking but indifferent.

'I love a challenge,' she whispered to her compact mirror while applying a fresh coat of lip gloss. Inadvertently, Barri had just set Purl's world alight.

14. Empty Words

Caprice doubted the soundness of recent decisions, her acceptance of temporary employment then stepping over Fernlea's threshold. *Should I make an effort with the reptile woman or am I here because I have nothing better to do?* She stayed for just under an hour but it felt like three. She was frustrated and tired. *When will I make a decision without it blowing up in my face?*

At first Judith gushed with heady gratitude as Caprice was shown to a communal lounge. She was genuinely surprised to see her visitor. When introducing her guest to the Old Dears, Judith displayed pride but as introductions progressed around a semi-circle of frail bodies in wheelchairs, she dwindled to flippancy. Caprice was then referred to as: 'The girl next door.' Judith's guest cringed, aware of a first warning shot. Caprice's discomfort increased the longer she stayed. *This was a huge mistake.*

During the visit, Judith adopted various attitudes. One-by-one, they were tested and replaced as though playing a game of chess. Flippancy replaced gratitude, followed by smug pride, familiarity then superiority with lots of advice thrown in.

'Will you be staying much longer at Radburn?'

'I'll stay as long as I'm needed.'

'What will Barri do when you're gone?'

'That's for him to decide.'

'Barri would be mad to let you go.'

'His interests lie elsewhere.'

'He needs someone to keep an eye on him.'

'He's a capable man so I doubt he would take kindly to anyone keeping an eye on him.'

'Well if you ask me, he definitely needs someone to keep an

eye on him. You should think about it. What on earth is he going to do with that tree-house?'

'It will be repaired and painted.'

'Why?'

'It's better than allowing it to rot and fall down.'

'Are you sure?'

What a stupid question, Caprice was tired of a barrage of questions.

Finally, there was suspicion; Judith's old faithful after her methods of extraction were unsuccessful. Caprice couldn't wait to return to Radburn. *No wonder I hate the company of women.* Caprice avoided Judith's eyes, they'd become abhorrent. She had a lot to hide and hated forthright nosiness.

The further Judith probed, the more her eyes glossed with anticipation. Caprice caught her own tiny reflection in them then Judith stared without blinking. She waited for a gesture, a facial expression to reveal Caprice's soft underbelly. It was obvious there was a lot more going on in Judith's mind than empty words she ejaculated but all Caprice could think of was escape. *I wish I'd never met the woman.*

'Are you on Facebook?' Judith pulled a wide mobile from her pocket then slid a podgy finger across its screen. 'You must send me a friend request and let me have your number.' Judith had over a thousand friends using the basis that even the smallest conversation could result in another number added, not realising that friendship should be earned. She needed to feel popular, involve herself with the minutia of others therefore bolstering her assertion that she was a vital presence.

Caprice cringed. She had only one friend and for safety, hadn't revealed her plans or whereabouts. Being anywhere near could drag her friend into a dangerous situation. *Is Barri a friend?*

As she looked at Judith's smug face leering at her phone as though it was the Ark of the Covenant, Caprice realised that a short train journey hadn't been far enough. Fernlea and Judith's glassy eyes then became intolerable.

131

'I'm sorry.' Caprice feigned an apology. 'I'm not on Facebook. I don't have time for it and can't give my number because it's my work phone.'

'Oh!' Judith exclaimed with disappointment. 'Where do you work?'

'Close by...' Caprice stated calmly then quickly made an excuse to go, 'which reminds me, I have an early start tomorrow.'

The only information Judith gleamed was that Caprice was single, had travelled a great deal but hadn't said from where. She was also on a temporary stop-over with her friend Barrington (Caprice wouldn't call him Barri in front of Judith. She'd seen his full name on household bills). Half-way through their conversation, Judith came to the conclusion that Caprice was deliberately elusive. It left a bitter taste in the carer's mouth and poisoned her thoughts. *She's a stuck-up bitch obviously covering for Barri.*

Caprice however, learned a great deal. She found out Barri's parents had died a couple of years ago and of Barri's quiet existence since. This could account for his odd behaviour. Judith had also relayed what she knew of the George's, all third and fourth-hand information but, as Judith imparted gossip she gave a distinct impression that she'd been there personally and witnessed everything.

Once Caprice returned to Radburn, Judith absent-mindedly complained to a deaf old woman. 'Barrington's bitch; who the hell does she think she is and, who has a name like that?'

'What's that about Burlington?' the old crone asked.

'Burlington? What do you mean?'

'Burlington Birtie dear, you were talking about him.' Judith ignored her.

On Monday morning when Barri had gone, Caprice had plenty of time to take stock. She was feeling more frustrated than the night before. She wasn't sure she could face Barri after another long day of Radburn's cold emptiness. Her decision to work there could be reversed despite Christmas being just two weeks away. She could take a plane to somewhere warm and sandy but at that time of year she'd find it difficult to find a job. Bar and restaurants would be closed out of season. She could work down South then go abroad in spring but living expenses would be extortionately high. With the washing machine loaded she had to escape the house.

Judith saw Caprice walk down Radburn's driveway then along Dandelion View to a bus stop. It kicked up unjustified fury in an already suspicious nature. 'She lied!' Judith felt searing flames of belittlement then was instantly reborn into a harder and more dangerous bird. It was the end of her shift so she raced to her car and drove out of Fernlea's driveway in a fury. The Ka braked hard near the bus stop and a window lowered. 'I thought you had an early start?'

Caprice couldn't see Judith's face because of billowing clouds reflected across the windscreen so she bent low. 'I did,' she confirmed. 'I've finished work and I'm meeting someone on the bus.' Her mouth smiled warmly but her eyes didn't crease. By the rapidity of her answer, it seemed plausible and so Judith was unsure what to think.

'I was going to offer you a lift,' Judith shouted although it hadn't been her intention.

'No need, really, but thank you anyway.'

Judith had overreacted. Her notion that Caprice was an upstart was a deep indication that below Judith's facade lay a woman who battled a huge inferiority complex. She over-compensated with a brassy mouth. 'I'll get you another time then!' She drove off with her inferiority complex as a permanent passenger.

Barri, heavy with fatigue, arrived home just before seven. He threw a bunch of keys onto the tub-chair, then realised he'd used the front entrance. He thought about this as he laid his laptop bag against the side of the chair. He'd parked his car in its usual spot at the back of the house but instead of favouring the kitchen door he'd walked to the front. *Is it a subconscious way of saying I'm still master of my house?*

Shrugging it off, Barri paused to listen to muffled tinkling from the annexe. 'She must be in there with all the doors open.' Barri wondered what Caprice watched on TV, then, he proceeded through a dark dining room into the kitchen, also in darkness except for a red dot of light like an assassin's gun aimed at a target. Something in the oven bubbled on a low setting. Barri could only think of food then bed, eager to return to a normal routine as soon as possible. 'I must stay awake.'

An oval dish sent a burst of steam into Barri's face when he opened the oven. He struggled with a tea-towel to manoeuvre it. He was so tired that he was tempted to grab a spoon and dig in but his upbringing prevented it. He took his meal and a bottle of red to the dining room. In all things there had to be a system and to eat his meal anywhere else was sacrilegious. Barri ate in silence under a yellow glow from a sideboard lamp, overhead crystal too harsh for dry eyes.

When he'd finished, he returned his plate to the kitchen then turned off lights as he went to the hallway. He removed keys from the tub-chair to sit while he finished his second glass of wine but laid his head back, closing his eyes to listen to a muffled TV.

To have lived a life devoid of commonplace feelings, without restraint of worry for others or events, he found new emotions mentally and physically taxing. *I wish they would return to their rightful place.* He wanted to release the few he favoured only at meticulously calculated moments. As he eased back into the chair he felt confliction gently pulse. Barri had relied on two basic senses, touch and sound, the warmth of a soft throat yielding beneath increasing pressure then, a delightful crunch. As he allowed his imagination to drift, Barri thought of another chemical sense, the sweet aroma of Caprice's cupcake vanilla. *They are all the emotions I need*, he thought as he drifted, confusing keen senses for emotion.

Barri nodded violently forward then looked around him with exasperation. Before he went to his bed, Barri pulled out the invite from his laptop and left it propped against his wineglass.

Caprice received a text twenty minutes later and it was her first. The eerie echo of a pulsed message alert made her jump. *"I've left a card on the hall table. You need to buy a dress."* Confused, she read the message a couple of times. 'Is he home then? Why doesn't he speak to me? It's downright rude!' She jumped up and tried not to slip as her socked feet slid across parquet.

The hall was in darkness so she went directly to the light switch then shook her head in disbelief when she saw an empty wine glass with a card. She picked both up then followed her suspicion into the kitchen to seek further evidence. What was left of her cooking had congealed into a gel-like mess; a dirty plate had been left next to it.

'Do I have to do everything around here?' Caprice asked the air. She grabbed a re-corked wine bottle and a clean glass then headed back to the annexe. 'He will have to open another tomorrow!' She gulped half a glass in frustration. 'Unbelievable! He can't be bothered to talk to me in person!' After reading the card she needed the rest of the wine. She was celebrating because despite the way the request had been delivered, she'd been invited as Barri's *"plus one."* She imagined her old teacher's hand, held out towards her.

The awards ceremony was a week away. Caprice smiled and reached for her phone. *"What kind of dress - full length or cocktail? I won't be able to afford a decent dress on my salary."* She pressed *Send* then looked up at the ceiling as though she could see through it. 'What if I phone him?' Just as she was about to select *Contacts*, an alert vibrated.

"Full length and charge it to Radburn's, use the card in the study top drawer."

Who needs a fairy godmother? Caprice mused then pulled her knees onto the settee. She looked at the TV screen but didn't see it. Then, she thought of Judith and shuddered. 'With a fairy godmother like her then there'd be no need for a wicked witch.'

The following day Caprice set out of Radburn with a credit card in her purse and a receipt from one of her clothes bags. The

135

receipt had the name and address of an East Gate boutique. From what she'd seen of the town centre, there wouldn't be many shops selling evening gowns and she couldn't venture farther afield. The invite had swayed her to stay at Radburn but she wouldn't take unnecessary risks.

'Darling, you're a walking advert for our store!' the boutique owner exclaimed as soon as she saw Caprice. She wore an ensemble Barri had bought. 'I can't remember seeing you before?'

'That's because I haven't been here before,' Caprice replied cheerily, eager to look at rails.

'May I ask where you bought the clothes you're wearing?' the woman now worried that a rival also stocked them.

'They came from here,' Caprice confirmed. 'They were bought for me.' The shop owner looked puzzled then beamed.

'Ah! I remember. He was handsome. There'd been some sort of emergency?'

'Yes that's right. My suitcase was stolen and I was left only with the clothes I wore.'

'What? How awful! Did they find the culprits?'

Caprice laughed and tossed back her hair. 'No but no matter, I much prefer the clothes I have now.'

'So, what can I do for you today?'

'I'm looking for a dress, an evening dress.'

'It's for a special occasion?'

'Yes, Mistlethrop Civic Awards.'

'How wonderful, you're lucky to work for such a generous employer.'

Caprice was confused by the woman's words and the woman was then unsure if she'd said something out of place. She clarified matters. 'Will the dress be charged to Radburn's Confectionery, as last time?'

This information came as a great disappointment; Barri hadn't paid for clothes from his personal pocket. Caprice tried not to show her reaction then thought: *To hell with him.* 'I also need a coat, shoes, bag and the name of a taxi company to then take me home to Radburn House.'

'Oh, please forgive me. I assumed you worked for Mr George.'

'No,' Caprice stated firmly but quivered with emotion. *Why on earth did I just say that?*

15. Strings

An ice-cream van broke the speed limit along Dandelion View but came to an abrupt halt opposite Radburn House. The van's driver caught sight of a heavily coated boy on the play-frame. The boy waved his arms frantically and reflective patches on his padded coat caught the van headlights. The van continued its sinister tinkling while children climbed through a wire fence hole then ran to a window. Wintry wind nipped at fingertips and ends of snub noses but, for children, it would always be the right time for a Whippy with sprinkles.

From her bedroom, Caprice heard a screech then electronic bells play a vaguely familiar melody. She found herself humming it as she descended Radburn's staircase, careful to pull up long skirts at each step. Caprice continued to hum until she reached the music room by which time outside tinkling had ceased. She couldn't figure out why it had disturbed her so.

Meanwhile, one of Judith's colleagues had sprinted across the road brandishing a large plastic bowl to join a queue. The van's musical call-to-arms had reached the old folk. A man with a dog also joined the queue, drawn by the infectious sound of expectant children. The queue watched a cone fill with long tendrils of vanilla then sink into a plump helter-skelter. A drooling dog was fed bone-shaped biscuits from the man's pocket.

Dressed in chic evening attire, Caprice rustled through old music sheets until she found a yellowed page and took it to the piano. She pulled her legs to one side so as not to crush her beautiful dress then slowly picked out the tune, the same played by bells.

'I got no strings....' She tried to quietly sing along but struggled with a cheerful tempo. Her fingers slipped from the keys and her arms dropped heavily to her sides.

'What were you playing?' Barri stood in a dark doorway. Caprice immediately straightened.

'It's a song from a Disney film - Pinocchio.' As she said it, she thought: *How apt? It describes how I used to live.* Even though her arms still rested at her sides they suddenly felt lighter as she realised her strings had been cut. She stood and Barri gaped at her.

Now, things don't seem so bad. So what if we're seen together? She was due to leave anyway. If she's found later then, it will have nothing to do with me. Barri tried to convince himself that Caprice was still just a subject but he was surprised by the simple elegance of her dress. Charcoal-grey, normally dull and formal, had been captured elegantly in velvet devoré. It made Caprice's red hair all the more striking. Her glorious mane cascaded around her shoulders and tops of bare creamy arms. From a round neckline, sumptuous velvet clung to curves until it pleated out above knees to fall into folding pleats that softly-touched parquet. As Barri examined his Plus-One closer, he noticed semi-transparent gauze against more solid fabric and how it appeared to be a shimmering web of circles and ovals.

Caprice saw an appreciative glint in Barri's eyes after nervously anticipating his reaction. The striking young woman hadn't worn a dress since the light cotton of early school years.

As Barri emerged from darkness into the light of the music room, his Plus-One gasped then looked at him from head to toe. 'I see great minds think alike.' He was dressed mainly in black; a velvet evening jacket with charcoal lapel over a charcoal crushed-cotton waistcoat gave him gothic sophistication. His white silk shirt didn't have the formality of a tie. Barri's attire complemented Caprice's dress so perfectly that it looked as though they'd consulted prior to dressing. A thin leather twine rested around his neck. It fell across his top waistcoat button and held a platinum pendant.

Barri's hair was feathered around the right side of his face,

139

his fringe prevented from covering blue eyes by being brushed to the left. A hint of stubble shaded his upper lip then both sides of his mouth to form a U-shape around the cleft of his chin. Caprice imagined him stepping out of a glossy magazine with rugged but alluring rawness to weaken any young girl's knees but she changed her mind. *Not a magazine, a gothic mansion, waiting for his first taste of warm virgin blood.*

Barri saw that Caprice had removed her new choker. He reached into a pocket then stepped closer with something clasped in his hand. 'I have something I know will look well on you.' He then opened his hand to reveal a thin platinum chain. It held a similar pendant to the one he wore. Barri's hand was still but his heart throbbed with force.

Caprice stared at an engraved crucifix encrusted with tiny diamonds but with its horizontal bar lopsided. 'It's a rune, isn't it?'

'Yes, it was my mother's. I want you to wear it... just for tonight.' Relieved that Caprice hadn't asked the rune's meaning, Barri waited expectantly for her to turn around and lift her hair as she'd done when accepting his choker. He needed some excuse to feel his fingers close to her neck. His compulsion went against the runes meaning, *Necessity, Need and Constraint*. There was an awkward silence before Caprice opened her right hand then held it out. She'd been hit by confusion again, so badly wanting the necklace to belong to her. "*Just for tonight*" had hit a raw nerve. Now, she was wary. Similar tastes in outfit plus a matching rune motif was worrying, almost brotherly and this sudden shift in perspective upset her. She put on the necklace while Barri stared helplessly at her fingers and flexed his with disappointment.

'Are you ready to go?'

'Yes.'

The ice-cream van had gone by the time the striking couple vacated Radburn House. A quietly purring stretch-limo conveyed them along its driveway into Dandelion View.

It was Friday night, six-thirty but the night had already been invasive for two hours. Old people in Fernlea still sucked the backs of spoons. The man with a dog wrestled a dripping nougat-wafer while his dog looked on and panted. The van had been a timely intervention for children tired of playing. They now sat in a row along the play-frame and fought against brain-freeze while rapidly licking ice-cream. A high overhanging streetlight illuminated them.

'Wow, look at that car!' Rosebud spluttered.

Armoured gushed: 'Sick! I can't see who's in it. Its windows are black.' His oversized headwear didn't help. The children turned their heads to their right in unison, tips of tongues still searching insides of cones as they watched the car grow smaller. Then, they all turned their heads to look at Radburn House.

'No lights,' Inky observed. 'Reckon no one's home now.' He tossed the soggy end of a cone into his mouth, chewed then looked at Rose. 'It's now or never.'

'What d'ya mean?'

'We can look at the tree-house. Men were doing something to it, my dad told me. He saw 'em when he drove past.'

Armoured jumped to attention, sensing his protective presence would be required then held out a hand to Rosebud. Sophie remained seated and waited for Inky to do likewise but he stepped over her and jumped to the ground. Awesome quickly held out his hand then Sophie accepted it sulkily. She grumbled as she was tugged upwards. 'He makes more fuss over your dog Citizen than he does me!'

'I'm here, aren't I?' Awesome complained but Sophie wouldn't look at him. She released his hand as soon as she was upright.

The road on the other side of the wire fence was quiet. A couple of cars drove by then the children raced across to then stand idly around stumped hydrangeas while peering into Radburn's driveway. Inky knew, as leader, his friends would wait for him to signal an advance.

'What if that nutty woman from the home sees us?' Awesome asked. The children immediately averted their eyes to Fernlea.

141

Inky weighed up the risk.

'Aw, she won't be able to see without night-vision goggles.'

'I don't think she's in,' Armoured chirped. 'One of her kids said they were going to his grandma's big party at The Varsity.'

'My dad says she pisses him off,' Inky stated and both Sophie and Rosebud glared at him.

'You shouldn't say that!' Rosebud warned but Inky looked innocent.

'Why not, my dad says it all the time? There's always something he's pissed-off at.'

'Yeah, my dad says that about your dad.' Words tumbled out of Awesome's mouth and Inky shot him a dark look.

'What's he been saying about my dad?'

Awesome wondered why Inky's tone had changed so quickly. He replied first with a shoulder shrug then: 'Like you said, just that he's always pissed-off.' Inky accepted it hadn't been a sneaky dig at his dad which encouraged Awesome to then ask: 'What's that woman done to piss him off?' He liked the sound of "*piss*." It felt good to swear and join the ranks of older boys.

'My dad said that wherever there's anything free to be had, you'll find 'em and they're a bunch of scroungers.'

'What's that mean?' Armoured asked from within his helmet.

'I don't know but, it pisses him off.'

'Are we going to stand here much longer? Only my mum's coming in ten minutes.' Sophie was losing her patience. Inky made a move and the others followed as he kept close to the side of the driveway into Radburn. When he arrived adjacent to the tree he quickly darted into a gap between bushes to make his way across the lawn. The others followed suit until they all stood at the base of a tree-house ladder.

Workman had restored the tree-house to its former state and then some. The children looked up with envy but changed their minds about wanting to see inside. It was a lot higher than anticipated, certainly a lot higher than their play-frame. From the ground, the tree-house ladder looked like a vertical climb. 'It's too-oo dar-rrk!' Rosebud chanted nervously.

'You wanted to see it,' Inky pointed out. 'I wouldn't have come over here otherwise.' Inky saw Rosebud's mouth quiver and became agitated. 'Look, do you want to go up or not?'

'I'll go!' Armoured shouted from somewhere inside a hooded helmet.

'No, you can stand guard, that's what you're best at but keep your voice down.' Inky lowered his too. The children then watched him ascend but as he climbed higher it became increasingly harder. He could barely see anything through a heavy mass of branches and clinging night. When he looked up to assess his progress, it appeared he was now climbing into pitch-black. He stopped near the top and held tightly onto ladder sides to look down. His friends' faces were faintly lit orbs and looked miles away. 'I can't see a thing up 'ere,' he whispered hoarsely.

'What?'

'I said...' this time a little louder, 'I can't see where I'm going.'

Armoured made the call: 'Don't bother. We'll come back when its light.'

'It's really pissing me off!' Inky replied.

Sophie made a contribution: 'You're really pissing me off!' she hissed. 'My mum's just parked across the road.' Inky descended a lot quicker than he went up.

Rosebud held Armoured's hand as she crossed the road. 'I bagsy the back seat with Armoured!' she sang as her personal bodyguard opened a car door for her.

'I'll sit up front,' Awesome said reluctantly. Sophie interrupted his melancholy:

'No you won't, Inky can sit up front. You can sit in the back with us.' As she clambered into the back of the car, she nudged Rosebud and whispered so that her mum wouldn't hear: 'He can tell my mum how pissed-off he is.' She giggled. A strong odour of vinegar drifted through from the boot and the children forgot about hastily eaten ice-cream. They craved chips.

Meanwhile, a stretch limo with black windows pulled across the entrance of Whiskers Hotel. Barri got out and nodded at its driver who held open a door then waited patiently for Caprice to alight. Barri knew when to add a flourish but now that he'd arrived he was suddenly eager to get the evening underway. People still tested his patience, the award ceremony just another necessary evil.

Barri stood rigidly facing the car and almost blocked Caprice's way forward but then offered his arm. When she slid her arm beneath to rest long slender fingers across it, Barri looked down. Gunmetal polished nails looked like a row of bullets laid out on his sleeve. He could feel their gentle weight, the same as a leather thong across his neck in the sanctuary of his bedroom. His arm trembled. He had to suddenly avert his attention before it reached a limb he didn't want to move. Breathing in heavily, night air brought a sweet cacophony of perfume, so understated that its simplicity matched Caprice's exquisite choice of dress. Barri was pleased.

The hotel entrance was ablaze with reflections from mirrored walls, chandeliers and glass doors so highly polished that it was difficult to discern if they were open or closed. A sign in the foyer stated: *Mistlethrop Civic Awards* with an arrow pointing towards double doors to the right. A receptionist beamed and raised plucked eyebrows, her blood-orange lips as bright as the lighting. Barri ignored the greeting and briskly turned to his right but, before he could take hold of a handle, a doorman clad in purple pulled it open then stood aside.

A buzz greeted the couple, audible above tasteful whining from a string quartet in a far corner. A cellist looked as though he had the weight of the world on his shoulders, a lanky man grasped a viola and two female violinists had hair so elaborately piled high that one firm shake could dislodge it. They played Brahms. Caprice ignored the rest of the room. Her heart lifted and again she felt that her strings had been cut.

Another woman with harsh lipstick and dressed in purple asked to see their invite which Barri presented. She looked at it then at Caprice as though she was about to say something but changed her mind and said: 'I'll take you to your table.'

144

Barri continued to support his Plus-One as they weaved between tables covered in silver cloth and sparkling cutlery. By the cameras and equipment strewn across one, it was obvious journalists had been given a table opposite a small stage. Reporters took more than a passing interest in the reclusive young man they'd heard so much about but rarely seen. Caprice didn't take her eyes from the quartet and only glanced in the direction they were being taken. The room was huge, as bright as the foyer and just as reflective. Caprice could see distorted reflections of herself and Barri in far walls.

All eyes in the ballroom focussed on the glamorous couple. There was an increase in buzzing as mouths discussed them except three who remained tight-lipped. A sea of faces stared as they walked by; some with genuine smiles, others with a seriousness to mask either envy or judgment. *'Where will they sit? Who is she?'*

When they'd reached the middle of the room, eyes were still upon them. 'This is your table.' The event organiser gestured to a wine-waiter who hovered expectantly. He pulled a dripping bottle from a silver ice-bucket.

'There must be some mistake!' Barri's mood changed rapidly. 'This cannot be my table!' To his immediate displeasure he saw Purl and Niall Mandrake staring up at him but he didn't recognise another man in their company. Mandrake pursed his lips then attempted a smile but his eyes flashed uncertainty.

Purl smiled sweetly but her rigid mask hid disappointment and anger. *So he does have a date. Who is she? How dare she spoil my evening?* She'd so looked forward to having Barri to herself and had run through her plan while waiting. If he did bring someone then his guest couldn't outshine her obvious beauty, wit and advantages. Purl looked at Caprice's dress, her figure, her hair then finally her face, all far superior to what she'd expected. *Who is she?* Purl racked her brains to think of all eligible partners within a twenty-mile vicinity. She knew everybody worth knowing but now found it difficult to stop her eyes from wondering back and forth between a beautiful dress and brilliant red tresses. Dismayed, Purl took a deep breath. *I'm the daughter of a business tycoon. Only I can heal the divide of past feuds to create a new future, a new dynasty.* Both Purl and her father considered it their table even though Mandrakes Cakes hadn't been nominated for a reward and they'd ensured Barri would have no choice but to sit at it.

'Oh this is your table, I assure you.' The red-lipped organiser had been forewarned. 'Guests from similar businesses are seated together, especially our two main award winners. You have much in common.' She quickly turned to weave back around the tables before Barri could say anything. He was far from amused by her error and looked at neighbouring full tables before realising he would have no alternative.

Caprice looked dreamily away from the musicians then adopted a fake smile as she looked from face-to-face at the table. Her row of gunmetal nails then gripped Barri's arm like a vice. He looked down at them then up at her face. Caprice was pale and trembled. He gently patted the backs of her fingers and she released them. The wine-waiter offered a chair but she shook her head, refusing to sit.

'Please, take a seat. Permit me to introduce you to my daughter, Purl. I'm sure you two will get along famously.' Niall Mandrake stood and waited expectantly for Barri's guest to sit. He first gestured to his daughter at his right who continued to mask her real reaction. 'This is Mr. Phestoz, the new owner of Whiskers Hotel. He is an award nominee.' Niall gestured to a grotesque man sitting to his left. Barri looked at a starched corner of a handkerchief poking stiffly from a black evening jacket; it matched an equally stiff tie. For some reason the name seemed familiar but he didn't know why. Mr. Phestoz was a wiry older man with thin silver hair swept severely across a deathly white scalp. Thin veins in his pallid forehead stood pale blue through translucent skin. He didn't look up to acknowledge Barri but tapped long but deeply yellowed fingernails. They seemed an extraordinary length and claw-like, his bony hands also marred by blue veins.

Caprice had frozen. Phestoz slowly raised black eyes to meet startled violet. 'It's nice to meet you my dear,' he drawled in a deliberately articulated way. He allowed his eyes to linger, taking delight in the young woman's reaction before dropping them slowly to her dress. He'd been careful to disguise his own surprise and a swift surge of anger. *She's here, dressed so finely, so expensively, so prettily and, for a man I don't know. I would never have allowed her to.* He also sensed she caused considerable disquiet to his friend's daughter. Then, the grotesque sinister man turned expressionless orbs on Barri's cold ones before lowering them to absorb every inch visible. 'Please, take a seat, I don't bite.'

Barri scowled but held in his distaste. 'Come, you must sit!' he ordered as though Caprice was the only one causing a delay. He rudely nudged the waiter to one side while he held a silver-sprayed chair until his Plus-One reluctantly lowered herself into it.

Caprice lowered herself into a terrifying, repetitive nightmare. As she descended into it, she was numbed. She trembled uncontrollably then it tore breath from her body, freezing her limbs and facial expression. *He's found me.* The striking young woman cursed her decision to remain at Mistlethrop and like Purl, feigned a smile. Her strings were reinstated.

16. Strange Bedfellows

'Are you going to introduce us to this delightful young lady?' Niall asked before sneaking a sideways glance at his daughter. Purl glowered.

Barri took a seat then looked his adversary directly in the eye deciding that his father's enemy would now be his. He suspected a blatantly planned ruse. *The hotel's new owner must control seating arrangements and by the looks of him he's in cahoots.* To what end? Barri hadn't yet surmised.

Phestoz spoke: 'Yes, please do. Now that we're all in the same bed so to speak...' The evil-looking man set black unemotional eyes upon Caprice. 'I'd love to know all about you and your lovely companion. I'm sure you Purl...' Phestoz didn't take his eyes from Caprice, '...are equally curious.' Purl's face was starting to ache but she made an extra effort. She couldn't speak yet, seriously upset that her own choice of pink chiffon had been outclassed.

'This is my.... This is Caprice,' Barri obliged but the table's occupants had caught his hesitation. Rarely were three master interpreters of body language and voice tone gathered in one place at one time.

Mandrake was alert to the power of withheld information and used what he thought was his no-nonsense business-head to ponder suspicions. *Either the beauty with him is more than just a date and he isn't ready to admit so in public, in which case Purl will have her work cut out, or, she means a lot less.* This possibility intrigued him. Mandrake had seen a dossier on Barri. *Perhaps he deliberately chose the wrong gender and is still encased in his closet.* This seemed a more plausible idea and Mandrake thought of Barri's assistant. *Back-stabbing and readily supplying information could be the actions of a jilted lover.* Mandrake sneered then made mental comparisons between Barri and his father. *I wonder who he inherited his looks and inclinations from.* Once again Barri was unaware that he was the subject of another irrational speculation.

Purl had inherited her father's wolf-like curiosity to seek weaker prey. She took Barri's hesitation as an indication that his companion was a definite presence. *By the end of tonight I'll find out whether she is a real threat or just a passing fling.* In her experience, one half of a relationship was always stronger and she would determine who had the greater bond. If it was Barri, then she would have to resort to devious methods.

As for Mr Phestoz or *"Mephisto"* as he was known to only a chosen few, he relished any opportunity to play games but soon lost interest leaving chaos in his wake. Inwardly, he celebrated because he'd found Caprice. It had taken longer than usual but it was as much a surprise to him as to his adopted daughter. He hoped she was ignorant of this fact. Not only hadn't he expected her to appear at his new hotel but wondered why she'd stayed so near Macefield, particularly after her last futile escape attempt then a close call with death. She'd recently attempted suicide, a half-arsed attempt from what he'd heard but it had given him an even sicker sense of power. Caprice made a surprising first course. *This is going to be so entertaining.*

The wine-waiter ignored Barri's brusque disregard. Caprice was first to seek out her glass and use its contents to steady her nerves. She continued to avert her eyes, looking down at her glass then her lap. Suddenly, her dress didn't feel so glamorous. She compared it with the scanty, debasing outer-casings that her step-father had forced her to wear. *What did he think when he saw me in this?* She couldn't escape his excellent periphery vision and knew he would constantly look at her but only seeing what lay beneath her dress. Eyes from surrounding tables found other things to look at, but two pairs still looked with intent.

The boutique owner had earned her place as a guest by bringing a breath of haute-couture to Mistlethrop. Her eyes now shone with pride as she looked at Caprice. She focussed on the dress not the young woman wearing it then her eyes sought out the journalists' table. *I must say something to one of the reporters about it.*

Barri's resentful assistant also had shining eyes, inflamed by having an invite snatched away. His dinner suit had seen a lot of wear during the last two years but he wasn't ready to retire it. His excuse to the event organiser had been: 'Barri has the invite and I said I'd meet him here.' It had granted him entry but he'd side-stepped his cosmetically-challenged escort by saying with a false chuckle: 'I'll wait at the bar until he arrives.' He'd assumed Barri would arrive alone and it would then be easy to wheedle a seat next to his boss. He'd practised his lines while waiting. *Oh, hello Barri, I was at another table then noticed you here. Don't you think it more appropriate if I join you?* There would be a sweet irony in sitting with both an old boss and new, however, the event organiser soon made her way to the bar once she'd deposited Barri and guest.

'Mr George has arrived with someone.' Harsh red lips were not smiling.

'Yes, I can see that.' The resentful young man yawned, trying to play it cool. 'I must have been misinformed. The woman is unknown to me and therefore must have been a last-minute decision.'

'Well, I'm sorry but we will not be able to sit you at a table.'

'Can't you add another chair?'

Red lips remained closed for a moment then said: 'I'm afraid that would inconvenience our other *guests.*'

The young man in a cheap suit was not a guest and therefore, not a VIP. 'I see,' the assistant had been reduced once again to the role of hired help, ironically a position Caprice had suffered recently. 'Then, if you don't mind I'll remain here until I speak to Barri. I'll let him know how helpful you've been.' He glared at red lips which quickly closed into a grim slit. The organiser nodded at a bartender.

'Give this gentleman one drink on the house before he

leaves.'

As the assistant eyed a glass podium on the stage, he seethed. *I did all the work for that award. It was me who co-ordinated the whole thing,* then, he looked enviously at tables. He could just see the back of Barri's head.

Double doors near the bar flung open and a flotilla of laden trolleys wheeled by. The assistant was hissed at from the other side of the bar: 'Here's your drink, if you want it.'

'Ay, I'll 'ave it.' The assistant's accent lapsed now that he was no longer part of official activities.

'You didn't really mind joining us?' Niall ventured, aiming to placate Barri's visual annoyance but his comment was barbed.

'I suppose you invited this man and his daughter?' Barri ignored Mandrake to address the grotesque old man who took an instant dislike to his questioner and guessed why Caprice was with him. Phestoz looked forward to testing him.

'I did, we're old, old friends.' Phestoz narrowed his nostrils, swinging back his bony head as though he was to embark on a lengthy tale. Niall smiled broadly. Barri had greater concern not to trust or underestimate them.

'I knew Phestoz before he was in the hotel business,' Niall interjected.

'And what business did you used to be in?' Barri mimicked Caprice by throwing back his wine. *Why does the old man's name seem familiar? I'll need more of this stuff. Thank God I hired a limo and driver.*

Caprice was startled. *Does this mean that the others have seen me before?* She examined the two Mandrakes.

Phestoz's eyes narrowed. 'Niall, you know that this hotel is just my latest venture.' He looked again at Caprice who hadn't yet mustered the will to look fully at her tormentor. 'I own a string of nightclubs across the country but I now stretch to a more salubrious clientele. This hotel is ideally situated for my business contacts in The North.' The sound of his voice made Caprice feel sick, she'd done her best to forget how deliberately he could pronounce each word.

'Phestoz is always on the look-out for new talent.' Niall first winked at Barri then looked meaningfully at Caprice who shrank into her chair. *God I was right.*

'His nightclubs are filled with beautiful dancers. Tell me Caprice, do you dance?' Niall was extremely amused by his question, believing the young woman's company had been for sale, possibly from a club similar to one of his friend's. Caprice nearly choked on her wine but didn't splutter. It was then that she found inner strength and raised her eyes to Phestoz then, Niall.

'No hardly ever. I'm particular what music I dance to.'

Purl detected a hint of bitterness in Caprice's voice. 'Now I'm the opposite...' she said, throwing two-tone hair over her shoulder. 'I love to dance and don't mind what I dance to. There'll be dancing later; Barri you must be my partner!'

Barri snorted. 'I don't dance either.'

'What a shame you don't both dance,' Phestoz drawled. 'Perhaps I can persuade you, afterwards,' he aimed at Caprice with amusement. She was balanced upon an emotional tightrope but returned sly innuendo with an icy look.

'I see they're bringing the first course.' Niall picked up a menu. He pretended to read while he said: 'I hate to speak of business during dinner but we could have a lot more to celebrate than just the receipt of an award.'

'You're not here to receive an award,' Barri remarked and he stared into an empty glass.

'Ah, but I am!' Phestoz gave a sickly smug smile.

Purl was astute enough to pull the wine bottle from its bucket and refill Barri's glass. Her father was grateful for the distraction. 'No, unfortunately I'm not but, you must agree, this is a timely occasion, one we could turn to our advantage? You read my offer but hadn't given me the chance to discuss it.'

'No, just as there isn't an award for you, there isn't an advantage for me.'

Focus changed from Caprice but she was curious by, what she guessed by their resemblance, appeared to be father and daughter. They hadn't been introduced. It was either an oversight or they arrogantly assumed that everyone knew who they were. She guessed the latter. *The father couldn't have recognised me or he would have said something by now.*

Appetisers were crab cakes around a king crab claw. An empty bottle was replaced with a citrus-tinged white. Phestoz stabbed a cake with one of his talons. It fell into halves then he withdrew his nail and sucked it through thin white lips while staring at Caprice. The inside of his mouth was as red as the event organiser's lipstick. Barri looked around his plate as though it was much bigger and filled with a huge selection. He ignored the cakes and went straight for the king-crab claw.

'You've provided a feast,' Purl complimented her father's friend. 'The menu looks good, but without meat?' Mephisto removed his nail from his mouth, bringing with it a strand of saliva.

'I shied from the usual hotel fare. This is a meaty choice.'

Barri cracked a claw to reveal dense white meat that tasted sweet when he placed his lips against it. He closed his eyes, still savouring the sound of the claw cracking. Caprice barely touched her food whereas Niall attacked his with gusto. He then pushed his plate away and watched Barri, who seemed to still thoroughly enjoy his first tastes. 'Here have mine...' Niall prodded his untouched claw with a fork. 'I'll swap for your canapés, if you're not having them.'

Purl ate little, preferring to destroy the perfection of crab rounds with her fork then pick at them. She would pick at all food, eat enough to get by but not enough to threaten her slender figure. Barri helped himself to Niall's claw, pushing his plate forwards so that his foe could reach his cakes. Phestoz didn't eat anything but was fascinated by Barri's enrapt expression whenever he cracked shell then raised meat to his lips.

'I'm extending my business Barri, doing something I'm sure your father would have done if he was still with us.' Niall wasn't about to give up his goal yet.

Barri ignored him; he helped himself to Caprice's claw having cracked what he could of the other two on his plate. They'd been picked clean. 'You should eat more!' he said quietly to Caprice after seeing she had pushed food around her plate. *She didn't hold back when she cooked crab risotto.*

'I know, I know!' Purl answered for Caprice. 'We girls must look after our figures, especially if no one else will.' Purl's barbed comment could apply equally to her.

Caprice didn't care what Purl had to say, she knew that Barri only tolerated present company. It was he that her thoughts turned to. *Is it only a brotherly concern for my eating habits? Do I want it to be anything else?* She now wished it was, especially as Barri provided a protective barrier between her and her step-father, Phestoz. As long as she remained with him then she'd be safe. This time she was with someone with as much, if not more, clout as her step-father Phestoz.

'As I was saying Barri...' Niall wasn't accustomed to being ignored. 'Your father would have diversified his business and eventually gone into desserts.'

'How do you know what my father would have done?' Barri asked, his voice immediately changing from concern for Caprice to the abrupt minimum. He snapped a claw in two and it sent a satisfying vibration along his fingers but he didn't attempt to eat its meat. 'What you meant to say, is that if my father was still here he would have bought YOU out by now!'

Niall grimaced and Purl was turned-on. Phestoz watched Barri's hands, which continued to break the remainder of the claw. He was content to allow Niall and Barri cross swords for a while.

'I doubt that.' Niall counteracted. 'It would take a great deal of money and a huge pair of balls to buy me out.'

'There shouldn't be talk of buying anyone out,' Purl interrupted. 'We're old family friends, well, all of us here except for you of course Caprice, and as old friends we should stick together. God knows, it's competitive enough out there without this delicious meal turning into another competition.' Purl glowingly saw herself as arbitrator and thought it better to attract flies with honey than vinegar whereas Barri thought she was interfering. Caprice didn't see her as a threat, just a spoilt bitch.

A second course of sun-dried tomato soup came with Parma crisps. Barri was dismayed as his plate of crab splinters were taken away. He had a two spoonfuls but wasn't keen on the soups aftertaste so he picked a crisp from a plate in the centre of the table. To his delight it was brittle and snapped into crumbs. A strong cheesy aroma was instantly released tempting table companions to reach for a crisp. Phestoz noticed Barri's disappointment when the plate emptied quickly. 'You can have mine.'

Barri looked at the offer held between two skeletal fingers with yellowed nails. They matched the colour of the crisp. *It's not nicotine. His fingers would be yellow too.* Barri shook his head with disgust then glanced to his right, Caprice held hers out. 'Here have mine.' Barri accepted, nibbled the edge then waited for everyone to return their attention to soup. He took the brittle wafer between his finger and thumb and squeezed slowly.

Soup was eaten in silence. Caprice tried to focus on the string quartet as they began Vivaldi's *Winter*. Purl watched Caprice from beneath false eyelashes, curious that there was so little body language between her and Barri. Then, she saw Barri look at Caprice, or more precisely, the necklace she wore and it prompted her to also look. She was alarmed when she saw Barri wore one too.

'That's an unusual necklace,' she remarked to Barri.

Caprice's hand went to the pendant at her throat. 'Yes,' Caprice agreed. 'It belonged to Barri's mother.' Purl feigned a smile but was instantly gutted.

Niall was surprised. Then, after contemplation came another conclusion. *She's obviously a relative, but I can't remember reading about any in the files his assistant gave me.*

'We should cherish our families...' Phestoz didn't have to

155

feign a smile. 'Where would we be if we didn't have people to rely on?'

'I agree.' Caprice surprised Phestoz. She'd gathered the troops of her remaining strength. 'You cannot rely on family enough!'

Phestoz stopped smiling but Niall remembered something. "Whatever happened to that darling little girl I used to see you with years ago?' Caprice's heart jumped and Phestoz's smiled.

'Oh, she's not that far away.'

'Then why didn't you bring her?' Phestoz didn't reply but winked at Caprice. Niall thought about what he'd asked. His own daughter wouldn't have been pleased with more competition. He now knew that dealing with Barri wouldn't be easy.

Phestoz slurped soup loudly. Barri and Caprice couldn't look at blood-red soup entering his blood-red mouth. He then gathered more soup on his spoon and gently sucked. Caprice waited for the inevitable but it didn't come.

'Well wherever she is, the child is missing a treat,' Purl commented.

'Oh don't worry,' Phestoz eventually drawled. 'I'll make sure she gets some dessert.'

The third course arrived. It was lobster and Barri's eyes widened with anticipation. Firm white meat was served in a red shell which had been cut lengthwise. It oozed butter but claws were also provided. Large napkins served as bibs and another bottle graced the wine bucket. There was only enough for one glass apiece but it was a perfect, medium-bodied white with undertones of aged oak. 'This is superb!' Niall exclaimed.

'That may be the only thing we agree on,' Barri remarked before immediately attacking his lobster claw. This meal was tailor-made for him.

'Ah, but don't you agree that my daughter is also a superb specimen?' Niall wanted to test Barri's immediate reaction. Purl was put-out at being compared to a crustacean. Barri paid her only a cursory glance.

'I prefer something with a softer shell.'

Caprice kicked Barri's leg under the table but was secretly delighted by his curt response. He dropped his claw then looked innocently beneath the cloth before resuming his task with renewed vigour. Purl was cut to the quick but before she could diffuse it with a playful response Phestoz chimed-in. 'I would have said that's the opposite of what you would really prefer Barri...' he emphasised the last letter of his name a little too long, '...judging by how you attack crab and lobster.' Just as he said this a loud crack came from Barri's plate. Buttery juice launched as fine spray.

'With lobster....' Barri explained, using a tiny fork to spoon it into his mouth. 'A hard shell hides a soft and sweet interior. Unfortunately, with people, this is seldom the case.' An insult was clear.

'Well this material is a little stiff,' Purl raised her fingers to her dress neckline but was mortified, her delayed playful response sounded feeble.

Barri is on form, Caprice thought. She'd relaxed a little; Barri's brutish charm provided a protective umbrella.

Niall pushed his lobster away but without offering a claw to his nemesis. 'I for one prefer pink meat,' he said with sarcasm. 'Not the brown I'd say you savour.'

Purl's mouth dropped open. *What is he inferring?*

'I have no idea what you're talking about.' Barri eyed Niall's plate. 'And, I doubt you do either!' Barri couldn't care less.

This is a dance, Phestoz mused to himself then, out loud: 'You'll particularly enjoy the dessert Barri. Niall, you'll find it too simple and sweet but Purl, despite Barri's preferences, whatever they may be, it will suit you. A firm interior takes real effort to reveal, whereas a superficial display may take little and have little taste.' Purl beamed and looked at Caprice. Phestoz chuckled. His eyes were placed firmly on his step-daughter. Niall smiled at his friend's timely intervention.

Lobster remnants were cleared and tiny glasses of Sauternes placed on the table. Barri raised an eyebrow but didn't have long to wait for the dessert. Crème Brulee had a crusty topping, blow-torched to create islands of brown in brittle gold. Everyone waited for Barri to either say something or be the first to tap the back of a spoon on brittle crust. Before he tapped, he looked around then said to Caprice: 'This dessert looks good but I doubt it will reach the standard of that delicious cheesecake you made yesterday.' Purl reeled from an almost physical blow.

'You cook?' Niall asked Caprice. This also surprised Phestoz.

'Most days, but Barri and I sometimes order-in,' another heavy blow to Purl. Niall was forced to reassess his hasty assumption.

Phestoz scowled. *She hasn't wasted any time then. The fish she's landed may prove harder to reel in.*

Whether Barri had deliberately given the impression that he was one half of a serious couple only he could say. He was heartedly tired of conversation. Although food provided some relief and sensations to be relished above those of sight and taste, they now paled in comparison to a prize beside him. His eyes turned to Caprice and they were filled with new warmth before he returned them to his Brulee. Purl quickly averted hers and lapsed into deep thought. She upturned her spoon to stab the centre of her dessert. Barri cracked his with enough force to create floating pieces. He scooped one up to rest gently on his tongue then quickly manoeuvred it to one side before it melted. He crunched bitter-sweet wafer. The others were unable to hear cracking but Barri could and he felt it along his jaw. It reminded him of Space Dust, a confectionery long gone from sweetshop shelves.

The dessert was eaten in silence and the table cleared. Niall looked at the menu, *Cheese, Coffee, Awards. I should have settled things by now but opportunities to discuss business slip with each course.* He waited for cheese which arrived with a glass of port. A platter contained a selection plus biscuits and grapes. Diners were given small bamboo boards and curved cheese knives. The atmosphere changed from formal dining to a more relaxed air and Niall decided to change tack. He looked long and hard at his young rival. 'I apologise Barri...' he offered. Phestoz shifted in his seat. *Caprice's man must be someone of note for Niall to kowtow.*

'I meant no disrespect to your father. If he was here with us today I'd offer him my apology. At heart I'm a business man and I don't like bad blood.' Niall then kept quiet to see how Barri would take an apology. It may be what he needed to hear. There was a pregnant pause.

Barri focussed on a piece of Yorkshire Blue he carefully loaded onto a cracker. When he had prodded cheese so that it matched the shape of his cracker, he said: 'I accept your apology on behalf of my father, but in reality, Mandrake, I doubt he would have been so gracious. He had no interest in false sentiment and neither do I. Let things end with your apology; do not discuss business with me. The only reason I came here tonight is to accept an award to Radburn Confectionery.' The silence that followed was stagnant.

Niall looked at Purl then slowly nodded. It would now be her sole task to win over Barri. Phestoz had weighed Barri as he spoke, resenting arrogance in one so young. His attention had been drawn away from Caprice and his triumph at finding her, tarnished. Coffee was served but he found it too bitter then added several sugar-lumps. As he stirred, he thought about how he could manipulate Barri into a less bitter opponent for Niall but then crush him as readily as the sugar lumps dissolving in his cup.

'We've hardly spoken,' Purl aimed at Caprice but was aware of Barri in her periphery. She had to ascertain how big an obstacle she faced. 'Friendship is obviously not on the menu for the men tonight but that doesn't have to apply to us.'

'No,' Caprice admitted. 'True friendship is earned.' She heard Barri sigh but didn't look at him. He was thinking of Elspeth's bracelet.

Purl was perplexed but not thwarted. 'When we know each other better then I hope we'll become true friends.' The fake smile appeared. Purl waited for Caprice to say something but

159

she just sat and sipped coffee. Purl pushed for another opportunity. 'I'm doing my Christmas shopping tomorrow; would you like to join me? We can do lunch.'

Barri jumped in: 'You'd be wasting your time. Caprice won't be around much longer and so friendship will be short-lived.' He was then angry with himself.

Caprice kept her coffee cup near her mouth, her heart skipped a beat. *I wish he hadn't said that. Mephisto will jump on it then me.* Mandrake smiled, his daughter would have a clear field ahead. Purl's smile changed to a genuine one.

'Oh, is that so? How unfortunate, tell me are you returning home?' The last word sent a thrill through Purl.

'That's Caprice's business,' Barri answered. 'We have an arrangement.' Mandrake's smile grew. Phestoz leered through thin lips but Caprice was mortified. She kept her cup raised to cover deep embarrassment.

'I see!' Purl exclaimed. 'It's just like that film, Pretty Woman.' She beamed then turned up her nose. Caprice's vision instantly clouded with tears. Barri didn't know what Purl was talking about and so couldn't offer a retort but everyone else at the table knew exactly what she'd inferred. Purl saw her knife go in and followed her remark up with: 'I'll withdraw my invite to lunch then. Oh look, the awards are about to start.'

The chairman of Mistlethrop Civic Trust navigated his way towards the glass podium. A triumphant Purl immediately stood, turned her chair towards the stage then sat down abruptly, with her back to Caprice.

17. Tired of Playing

Barri was bewildered. Events at the hotel replayed in his mind. He had to wrestle these thoughts so that he could grasp onto routine and sketchy control. He also sensed something was wrong. By Tuesday, Caprice didn't look well. She hadn't eaten much at the hotel or since. It annoyed Barri intensely, *Last breaths should be sweet. I hope she's not coming down with something.*

By Wednesday, he was frantic. Whatever ailed Caprice interfered with a domestic routine he now relied on it to take him to New Year's Eve. His goal had been put back repeatedly but he'd made a final decision, a frustrating year would end and with it, his craving. By Thursday, pervading silence within Radburn was torture. Used to hearing a violin whenever he was in his room or the basement gym, Barri realised that Caprice hadn't played since the day of the awards.

What happened at the hotel? Barri couldn't see a connection. *I didn't realise this house could be so quiet.* Silence now surrounded him and a trip to the music room confirmed his suspicion. The violin had gathered dust and, when he went to the piano, Pinocchio's sheet music was still on its stand. *Something is most definitely wrong.* The music room was no longer just another room. Over the weeks he'd frequently visited it just to see what music Caprice favoured. He'd entered their titles into *Notes* on his phone. He would miss her music after New Year.

Barri looked for Caprice in the kitchen, then, after searching other rooms, he was alarmed when it crossed his mind that she could have gone out. Later, when he'd taken his customary walk around the gardens and returned expecting a hot meal, he was even more perplexed. There was no sign of Caprice. The table

161

was bare and the kitchen cold and silent. With great concern he reached for his phone and paced. Eventually, Caprice's voice drawled: 'What?' Her tone took him by surprise.

'Where are you?'

A long drawn-out silence, then: 'I'm in my room.'

'Are you ill?' In his mind, Barri thought: *Say no, say no.*

Another long silence, then: 'No.'

Barri hung up, instantly relieved. Caprice had slept the day away. Her phone dropped onto crumpled sheets. 'He can get his own dinner.'

Barri's bewilderment then grew from the moment he stepped into his office. He had arrived a lot later having sat for a long while, alone and without light, without food, in his dining room. Caprice stayed in her bed thinking about what she would do the following day.

Entering his glass box Barri was unable to concentrate. 'I should have asked her what was wrong and not hung up.' Out of habit, he reached across his desk for his iPhone but found to his surprise that it wasn't in its usual place. After a thorough search of pockets and his laptop bag he realised he'd left it at home; the office phone would have to do.

'Why won't she answer?' he asked the plastic receiver after waiting two minutes. He hung up, pressed redial and waited again but, Caprice didn't answer. Her mobile also yielded an unsatisfactory result. When he'd tried several times, he slammed the phone down so hard it cracked its cradle. Self-control slipped and in a fit of frustration Barri strode along the open-plan office to clear his head then noticed a Christmas tree at the end.

Clear-desk policy had also wavered; each had a Radburn Advent calendar. Barri bent to admire old-fashioned lettering used for the Radburn logo but then saw plastic indents where chocolate had been. There were five closed doors, the fifth a larger door. His heart raced. New Year seemed closer, within reach. Barri forced his finger against the larger door until it folded. He continued to push until he felt chocolate beneath his fingernail. 'If only I could push through to the other side, into New Years Eve.' He stopped. 'There are no "ifs" in life.' He remembered his father's words.

The following day, every child in Mistlethrop dragged their reluctant feet to class hoping the last day of the term wouldn't mean the usual formal lessons. The longest term had been a succession of increasingly longer nights, the outdoors only seen clearly during school hours or weekends. Parents had warned fractious children that Santa would be informed if behaviour didn't improve.

One little girl decided that another school day was too much to ask and became conveniently ill in the morning. Miraculously, she recovered an hour before electronic bells were due to sound the end of term. She cheered-up whereas in classrooms, anxious faces counted the seconds. Fidgeting increased.

Rosebud sat on a swing hanging from the play-frame and kicked the toe of a shoe against hard ground until it crumbled. She didn't care if it scuffed, they were school shoes and she hated them. She looked at a vacant swing next to her and was lonely, regretting her blackmail tactics of persistent high-pitched pleas until her mother had finally granted permission for her to leave the house. Her mind raced for an excuse as to why she'd left the safety of her back garden. 'Maybe I should run home, get Citizen then say I wanted to take him for a walk.'

She stopped kicking the ground and examined her worn shoe then looked with doughy eyes at the sky. 'Please don't bring me new school shoes Mr. Claus.' Rosebud spat on her fingertips and was about to rub them across her shoes when she heard church bells. It was three o'clock and school would be out soon. All thoughts of returning home vanished. 'What if I was in the tree-house when the others come?' The child turned her head to look across Dandelion View then tip-toed across to the wire fence as though stealth mode would disguise her presence in the park. The small redhead leaned forwards resting her fingers claw-like on wire. She pressed the tip of her nose through mesh and searched for signs of life at Radburn House. The sky turned gloomy purple, a sign that the year's shortest day was due.

Caprice was also feeling lonely but unlike Rosebud, out of fresh ideas. One week ago, she'd looked forward to a glamorous night with Barri. She longed to still be within that timeframe of innocence and expectation. 'If only you knew of the danger you'd walk into,' she mouthed to a reflection in an oven window. The kitchen and her bedroom were the only rooms Caprice frequented. Radburn House was a prison, only she wasn't on parole and awaiting release, she awaited a death sentence. *Mephisto* had cast a long shadow.

She hadn't heard anything more about hotel guests after that horrible evening but Caprice now feared the sound of Radburn's telephone. It rang several times, each time for longer. The landline's sudden activity could only mean one thing and she didn't need Caller ID to confirm it. She expected her step-father to turn up on the doorstep and only felt safe while Barri was home. He may have let her down at the hotel but she knew he wouldn't tolerate Mephisto in his home.

She'd been alone, vulnerable and depressed after six each evening, routinely dragging her body to her room after ensuring all lights were out. Rather than enjoying flicking switches to illuminate, her mood sank and she needed darkness. Nights had passed slowly. Lying tightly wrapped in quilt, her mind's roving eye had searched frantically for a plan. Intense thought had made her wretched.

For a couple of nights she dreamt of shuffling outside her door and awoke in terror before realising it had to be Barri. He sounded so close and she didn't know why, his room was at the other end of the hall. 'He's not interested in me; his attitude at the hotel and since, confirms it.' Caprice was drowning. then, thrown onto the cold shores of abject misery, left to sink in its quicksand. Just before her train journey to Mistlethrop, unyielding mental pain had consumed her reason, her being. Radburn had been a brief break but she had been foolish to think she could permanently escape it. *I have to figure out*

164

what I should do before it's too late. The weight of the previous week was like freshly forged chains. She knew she'd have to face what could be her most difficult weekend.

On Friday afternoon, Barri was fractious. He hadn't slept well. An Advent calendar had grown in size and significance in his dreams. He now roamed the upper stories of Radburn like a lion with a toothache then came to rest outside Caprice's bedroom. He hovered and listened intently, then turned the door knob.

The room was dark, its curtains hadn't been opened for a week and an odour of sickly sweetness assaulted Barri's sensitive nostrils. He stretched his neck around the door. Her bed had been neatly made. He was about to close the door when a sudden thought caused him to break one of his rules: *What if she left last night and that's why she didn't answer the phone?*

Barri opened the door wide and went in, opening the curtains. Everything, except the odour and bedding, seemed exactly as it was before Caprice had arrived. Barri's heart was in his boots as he stared at the wardrobe. *What will I do if it's empty? Caprice is perfect; if I had to find someone else it would ruin my entire year and next.* He was hesitant to touch the wardrobe door and felt the same loss as when sitting at the dining table with Caprice in his mother's chair. Barri slowly pushed his fingers towards the wardrobe door thinking of the Advent calendar then, pulled it open.

Clothes swayed on hangers. He ran fingertips along them before leaning forward and slowly pushing his face into them, much as Rosebud was presently doing to wire mesh. He inhaled with deliberation. Different materials brushed against his skin, so sensual a moment that it made him light-headed. He reluctantly drew back with eyes half-closed, then, he opened them wide. 'She could have left them here and taken only what she arrived with.'

A quick dash to the dresser quietened his panic. The top drawer was filled with underwear. 'She may have left these behind?' A larger drawer beneath held a broken black box, its red velvet innards ripped but within their folds lay a tiny ballerina with one leg folded, its other leg stretched into a pointed tip toe. It was the broken box he'd seen on cobbles. Barri guessed it held sentimental value therefore she hadn't left him, yet. His heart lifted and he stroked the ballerina's minute throat with the tip of his finger then, dropped it onto red velvet. He had to get out of the room before Caprice knew he was there.

As he descended stairs Barri could smell roasting meat and his heart leapt. Everything seemed right in the world until he saw a timetable on the tub-chair. It was for trains from Mistlethrop to Blackpool North and times had been ringed in red ink. 'Why go to Blackpool?' He replaced the timetable then stood before the dining room door hovering with indecision before heading for the music room. Barri couldn't face Caprice yet, for fear of what he'd do in haste.

Meanwhile, outside Radburn house Rosebud had removed her fingers and nose from wire mesh and crawled through to venture as far as Radburn's tree. She admired a small row of five wooden crucifixes beneath the skeleton of a nearby shrub. It was difficult to read some of the names, their paint cracked and flaked. She read with awe, imagining the names had belonged to magical creatures. She felt sad but also excited. 'Brandy... Beauty... Bronson... Toots... Sherry.' It seemed right that they would be buried near a magical tree.

Confident that nobody was home, Rosebud placed a scuffed shoe on the first rung of the tree-house ladder. She looked up to first admire how wonderful the tree-house looked from that angle. It had not only been repaired but clad with an extra layer of semi-logs painted tree-bark brown, doors and window sashes, sage-green. The now magnificent tree-house looked like something out of a fairy tale and Rosebud felt strongly drawn, her coat the same sage green. She instantly felt connected. 'Please Mr Claus...' she whispered, 'let me have a house like this for Christmas.'

The small redhead looked over at the play-frame then squinted to look beyond in the direction of her home. She imagined the look on her friends faces when she waved her scarf out of one of the tree-house windows. She began to ascend. It wasn't so difficult. She didn't look down and in her child-like way saw bare tree limbs as welcoming arms when they began to close in. She made it to the top quickly then gurgled with delight as she pulled herself up the final rung and across a threshold.

Once inside, she felt safer but the interior was gloomy. She had to squint until her eyes adjusted. 'It's everything I wanted.' It was her ivory tower. She pulled her scarf from around her neck and red hair sprang out then clung with static across her coat. The climb had made her warm so she unbuttoned top buttons.

Inside Radburn House Barri sulked all the way to the music room. He sat at the piano and stared at Pinocchio's music then turned in a trance to stare at his feet. Two songs span around in his head, the tune from The Sound of Music followed by Pinocchio's.

'What should I do?' he asked himself over and over. 'For God's sake, I'm a...' He couldn't say it. He would be announcing his addiction at an AA meeting for one. 'I'm a total pussy.' he admitted instead and absent-mindedly kicked a boot against wood until it was scuffed. 'I should never have brought her to the house and I should never have allowed things to get this far.' His limbs suddenly felt heavy and he stopped kicking. The troubled man then thought of how he'd sleep-walked when he should have been wide awake. 'She's turned me into a pussy.' Barri angrily swept music sheets onto the floor. For the first time in his life Barri despised himself. He knew he had to transfer this new emotion to somebody else.

Caprice had become automated, preparing meals mechanically but with the lethargy of a prisoner about to enjoy a last cigarette. Every action was laborious, every second another blow to her already heavy heart. It would be a meal for one.

Barri heard the hum of the electric knife as he entered the dining room and he took his usual seat and waited. A bottle had been opened then left to breathe at his end. The lone diner could have happily filled a glass to the brim and made short work of it.

Five minutes passed then the kitchen door opened. Caprice appeared bringing with her a tantalising aroma of roast beef. She silently set the table even though only one setting would be used. Her face was grim and she didn't once look at Barri. 'Where's your plate?' he asked when his arrived. 'We're not going to have a repeat of your past performance are we?'

Caprice wearily sat down at the table, plonked elbows down firmly then looked Barri directly in the eye. 'Are you ever civil?'

'Civil? What's that got to do with anything?'

The young woman rested her chin on the backs of clasped hands and she struggled with what she'd planned to say. Barri was unnerved by her hesitation. His heart sank but he couldn't think what he'd done to upset her so. His plate remained untouched, hunger dissipated with steam above his plate. Barri wanted to reach out, touch Caprice's hair and could imagine pressing his face into it as he had with clothes in her wardrobe. At the same time he wanted to taste it, feel its strands in his mouth, against his lips then, wrap it slowly around her neck and tighten it.

'I've already eaten,' she lied.

'Are you leaving?' Barri found himself asking. Words escaped with calm acceptance but formed by a person he didn't know, they materialised from an earlier self. Tired violet eyes answered him and the bewildered person at the head of the table felt their weight crush him.

'Yes, I have... I have an unexpected problem to deal with.' Caprice sighed.

'Let me help you.'

'No, you've done enough already. You've been generous and I'm grateful but this is something I have to do by myself.' Her tone didn't soften and her vagueness added to Barri's disorientation. He looked down at a full plate not seeing the food.

'When?' He heard buzzing.

'The fridge and kitchen cupboards are stocked for the weekend and I've emailed a list of any outstanding invoices to you.' It sounded so impersonal, a role reversal.

'I'm not...bothered by that,' Barri erupted briefly but managed to contain his voice after the second word. Caprice sat back quickly, surprised by what could have been an outburst then, silence. Her eyes watered. *Was I wrong about him?*

'I'm not at all happy that you can't see your obligation through to the end.' Barri clawed back his dignity but only by a hair's width.

'I'm sorry. If there was any other way, but...'

'I asked you when?'

'I'm going today.'

Barri's left eyebrow arched sharply and the left corner of his mouth twitched before he picked up his fork to force a slice of beef into his mouth. He folded it inwards so quickly that fork prongs scraped his upper teeth. The vibration made him wince. Caprice arose and left the dining room and Barri spat out his beef.

Rosebud sat by the tree-house outer window to stare at Paxton Park. It was almost dark now and her friends and brother overdue. She hadn't paid any heed to time because in her mind she sat at the window of an ivory tower. She was ready to let down her hair. She had her scarf ready and stroked straggly end tassels as it lay across her lap. Traffic along Dandelion View had increased for a while during school pick-up times. The dull roar of engines had lulled Rosebud into her fairy-tale fantasy. She gazed out across the road to the Park and beyond then, a noise from outside startled her.

Barri had left his food to go cold. Gravy congealed around petit pois and baby carrots, wine remained in a glass. Panic gripped him, the like of which he hadn't experienced since children had arrived at a birthday party, only this time his only welcome guest was leaving. He wanted to stop her but knew he didn't have the skill to craft words to make her stay. He wanted to crush her but not yet, not during a frenzied attack. It had to be calm, deliberated, enjoyed. *What about money? Will she stay for that?* His father had once told him it was all women were really interested in. With enough of it there would never be an excuse to be lonely. After grabbing a coat and car keys Barri stormed out of his house. Both Caprice and Rosebud heard a door slam.

'God, I hate doing this!' Caprice left her evening gown in its plastic wrapper in the wardrobe. The final item she would pack would be the remains of her music box. Barri got into his car then out again before pacing around the side of the house. He wanted to leave, drive as far away as possible but was compelled to stay. Rosebud poked her head out the window and peered through a gap in branches but couldn't see anything. Looking back into the tree-house, its interior now looked bleak except for a shaft of light angled as a slant across wood. Daylight disappeared around the back of Radburn. It had turned pink behind purple.

Soft grass cushioned heavy footsteps but it would soon stiffen as temperature dropped. Barri kept his head down, looking at the toe of his scuffed boot as he strode purposefully towards the tree. When he reached its base, he thrust his hands into his pockets and looked up. Dark purple sky was not yet as dark as branches above. Barri wanted to climb, take haven but, his tree-house couldn't be a hiding place. In there, he could feel as though he was part of something bigger, a part of the outside world. If he sat near a window he could dangle his fingers outside, sense height as opposing as his house, be above road and cars, above Mistlethrop. He could feel breeze between fingers, open top shirt buttons to allow coldness to grip his throat. Only up there could he rise above everything and see clearly.

'I've left the front door unlocked.' Barri swiftly turned. Caprice stood behind him, he hadn't heard her approach. His mouth dropped open then he took in cold air. 'Does it have to be so soon?' A large holdall had been left at his front door.

'Yes, I'm going now but I didn't want to go without saying goodbye and thank you.'

'This seems stupid. You don't have long to go. What if I offered you more money?' It wasn't a plea, his voice hadn't softened, it had a barb of arrogance so inbred that he couldn't lose it if he tried. Surprise had gotten the better of him.

'I don't want more money, you've been generous. I feel awful doing this right now. I hope you find someone to buy your lovely house.'

Barri's jaw stiffened as a taxi pulled into the driveway. It drove slowly up to the house then stopped. The driver got out and automatically went for the holdall and was then surprised when Caprice appeared from a direction he wasn't expecting.

Barri turned to the tree, his heart pounding. He couldn't bring himself to look at the taxi as it drove back along the driveway then pulled out into Dandelion View.

He placed a scuffed boot on the first rung of the ladder.

18. Nails

Pink streaks in the sky had been a sign, they signalled the end of a colourful episode in Barri's life and the beginning of a dark one. From her far window seat Rosebud saw a salmon-pink gash. It reminded her that she would have to forget her fantasy and return to solid ground. She made a move but only made it as far as the tree-house entrance. Muted voices drifted up from below. She strained to hear what they said but they weren't clearly audible. She returned to her window seat and waited.

When murmuring stopped Rosebud shivered and blew out a blast of cold breath that couldn't be seen in the gloom. She looked out at Dandelion View. A car drove by and the tree-house interior was then plunged into darkness, only it seemed denser.

Barri began to ascend. Rosebud heard heavy creaking as boots met each rung. With each step, Barri's need to be within his tree-house increased, his hands grabbed the ladder to pull him upwards. His physical fitness should have made it easy but he was weighted with a loss so heavy that climbing became a difficult task. His strength of purpose had left with Caprice and only in his tree-house could he return to the time when she was unknown to him and he could nurse his new grief.

Maybe it's Awesome or Inky? Did they go to the park then, saw me? Rosebud was ready to cry out but sudden doubt prevented her; sinister creaking told her that it couldn't be her friends. *I would have heard them talking by now.* It was then that the girl realised she was the intruder. She pulled up her knees to cower into a small ball of fear.

Creaking stopped and Rosebud held her breath waiting anxiously for a figure to appear at the entrance. Her heart and mind raced. She quickly unfurled to look out the window. If she could spot a branch nearby then she could climb out onto it to avoid confrontation. She would have to jump down to it. With a child's simplicity of logic, Rosebud threw one end of her long scarf out the window towards a branch. End tassels snagged onto gnarled protrusions, wooden fingers grabbed one end of her lifeline then her scarf hung between the branch and her hands. It was an extension of another childish fantasy, one where she had the confidence and talent of a trapeze artist. Looking ruefully at the sagging scarf, Rosebud now realised that her mind played cruel tricks. She tugged at the long woollen rope and it tightened but she couldn't pull it free. Wool stretched but it was so tightly knitted that it wouldn't give. The small redhead stopped pulling and listened again for any sound. The pink gash in the sky changed to a thin but wide grin.

As Barri ascended, his coat sleeve caught on a splinter but shadows and his body bulk prevented him from seeing it. He yanked his left arm upwards and was freed easily but heard something fall through the branches. It sounded like a broken twig so he ignored it.

Slow, laboured creaking recommenced. Rosebud panicked then quickly threw her end of the scarf out the window. She returned to a cowering position. *If I hold my breath and squeeze really tight into the corner then I might not be noticed.* When she tried to, it was too hard to do. In an effort to have some control, she thrust her fingertips into her mouth and closed shivering lips around them. *I'll only breathe a little bit between my fingers so that I won't make any sound.*

Creaking grew louder and the pink grin out the window thinner then, smothered by purple. A head-shaped mass appeared over the threshold and Rosebud bit down on her fingers.

By force of habit Barri stretched up a hand to grope for the torch at the side of the doorway before realising that not only hadn't he been there for years but workmen had cleared it out. Rosebud heard scratching around the entrance and held her breath, hoping the dark mass would only look briefly in before descending.

Barri's hand returned to the top of the ladder and he heaved himself upwards and over the threshold. He had to arch his neck and shoulders then bend his head low but his hair brushed the ceiling. He tried to stare into the darkness. It was so dense that he thought it touched his skin then, gradually his eyes grew accustomed. A tiny shaft of light trickled in through a far window.

Rosebud bit down harder on her fingertips. There was a sharp snap, she'd bitten through a fingernail and it fell onto her tongue. The dark mass stood still and Rosebud stiffened. They both listened intently. The sudden snap awakened Barri to an unknown presence. He could feel there was someone in the tree-house and an unexpected but pleasurable sound reminded him of a happier time. 'Who's there?' He waited for a response but didn't get one.

Rosebud's fingernail remained where it fell but slowly, she edged her tongue towards her teeth and slipped its tip against her bottom row so that it arched. The nail slipped into a gap between fingers then fell out. Instantly, Rosebuds mouth began to water and it interfered with her breathing; she needed to swallow but fear kept it in check.

'I know there's someone here. I can see your knee.' The trickle of light reached as far as Rosebud's left knee. Luminescence of pale skin caught the light and held it. Slowly, she unfurled and Barri watched agog as a small pair of shoes, socks at half-mast then thin legs appeared. The legs straightened, stretched and stood but the rest of the body remained shrouded in darkness. Barri could tell the legs belonged to a child, a girl. 'What are you doing here?' he asked calmly but disappointed that his longing to return to childhood had been penetrated.

A timid voice answered: 'I was just sitting here.'

'Why?' The voice was as thin as the sky's pink gash and Rosebud now swallowed hard so that she could reply:

'I don't know. I saw your tree-house from the park and

wanted to see inside.'

'How long have you been here?' Barri was suddenly concerned that someone could be looking for the girl.

'Not long.' Rosebud had no concept of time; fantasies had cut through it like a hot knife through butter.

'You must leave here!' Barri demanded, a little too harshly and Rosebud whimpered.

'I will,' she whined, 'What about my scarf!'

'Where is it?'

'It's caught on the tree outside.'

'Leave it where it is!'

'Okay,' the girl answered, wanting to return to her corner and curl up. 'My dad can come for it tomorrow.' The girl's response conjured a vision of another unwanted intrusion. Barri stood in silence, clenching and unclenching his fists then looked towards the window near the girl.

'No, I'll get it for you.' His voice softened a fraction and he didn't realise it. It was enough for Rosebud to step forward. Barri couldn't see the girl's face or the colour of her hair but it was obvious from the disparity in their heights that she was not yet approaching her teens. This was a little girl with the innocence and acceptance of Elspeth. Barri thought of his first taste of death and wished he hadn't killed Elspeth so soon but then, he thought of Caprice and wished he'd been more level-headed and able to kill sooner.

Barri's realised that his heart may never be the same. He stooped, shuffled to the far window, placed one knee on cold wood then stuck his head out. He smelt the dampness of approaching night mingled with the pungency of freshly applied wood-preservative but it did little to sooth sinking emotions. Meanwhile, Rosebud climbed upon the thick ledge that had held her when sitting. She kneeled and gripped the sides of the bottom ledge to look over.

'Where is it? I can't see it,' Barri informed the child and as he stretched his neck out to the side. Bones cracked and Rosebud jumped.

'Oh no!' she exclaimed. She thought the ledge had given way with their combined weight. Barri swayed back with surprise. The child's voice was practically in his ear.

'What's wrong?'

'Nothing, I thought we were going to fall out.'

'It was the bones in my neck.'

'Are they okay?'

Barri hesitated to reply, a new aroma reached his nostrils then: 'Yes... My joints are hypermobile.'

'Hyper...? Mum says Awesome gets that when he's had too many sweets.'

'Who's Awesome?'

'My brother, he's the same as me, except he's a boy.'

'You're twins?'

'Yes, but only he gets hyper.'

Barri automatically responded: 'In my case it doesn't mean that. My ligaments are lax so the joints move more than they should then muscles tighten. They crack if muscles are stretched for a moment.'

'Does it hurt?'

Again, Barri hesitated. 'No, but I must roll my head now otherwise other ligaments will make my muscles tighten again.' Barri rolled his head slowly clockwise then anti-clockwise while Rosebud watched a black solid shape move. She breathed clouds of warm air across his face. Her fear evaporated.

As Barri rolled his head, his chin meeting his chest between rolls, he felt more relaxed. *I've talked to a lot of people lately, to strangers but, this feels odd, to talk to a child.* She smelled sweet and he stopped rolling his head.

'Do you like it here?' he asked the child, noticing the outline of long, bushy hair. Her small face was a dark orb in its centre.

'Yes, I wish I could stay here forever,' she replied simply.

'What would you do?'

Rosebud didn't need to think about it and responded with enthusiasm: 'That's easy! I'd wait by this window.'

'Wait for what?'

'I'd wait for someone to come and rescue me.'

'I don't understand.'

'I told you, it's easy! Me being a princess an' all, I'd wait for a prince to come then he'd rescue me.'

Barri listened to the little girl's explanation with disbelief. He didn't move a muscle. She spoke so innocently and with such belief that his perspective capsized. She reminded him of Caprice. She had done that to him too. He now lived a fantasy of having conversed with Elspeth before she was crushed and, at the same time, he took a step into a world he hadn't realised existed. People had dreams, feelings and lives. It had been so easy to snuff one out, to crush it into silence then hear its last gasp as it snapped, to smell its last sweetness.

The little girl continued; she had found someone to listen. 'You saw me once, don't you remember?'

Barri shook his head, then realised how stupid that was in the dark. 'No, when was it?'

'It was ages ago. I was in the park, on the play-frame with Awesome and we shouted over. I waved.'

Barri cast his mind back not realising that "*ages*" to a little girl meant a few weeks, then, he remembered the girl whose hat fell off and that she had red hair. 'That was you?' Now, Rosebud nodded but didn't answer. 'You have red hair,' Barri stated and he peered through the dark at the girl's head. The little girl was pleased that the man had called it red and not ginger.

'Yes, but it's not as red as that sad lady's who lives with you.'

'You saw her too? Was she sad? When did you see her?' There was urgency in Barri's voice and he hated it.

'That was ages ago too. She was in your garden and when she looked at this tree-house, she looked like she was going to cry. She's got beautiful hair; I hope mine grows like that when I'm older.' Again, the child's simple, accepting way captured Barri unexpectedly but, he felt his heart near his toes again when he heard that Caprice had been so sad.

I let her down in some way. His perspective shifted to new ground. His house guest, his employee had told him she had a problem to deal with. It must have been there all along but he hadn't even known about it until that afternoon. People had dreams, feelings and lives and they hadn't touched him until he had spoken with this little girl. He looked towards the child's face, seeing a small dot of reflected light in her eyes and instantly he saw Elspeth and Caprice rolled into one. He saw Caprice's hair in its colour by daylight but saw Elspeth's eyes looking at him. They held the same expression as the time he'd bared his bum to a hateful class only, they were a deep, deep violet.

He leaned forward to slowly breathe in the little girl's sweetness. A mother's hairspray had landed on her daughter's coat that morning. It had mingled with something else and Barri couldn't quite put his finger on it but it was exquisite. Then, it came to him, an old memory of a smell from his schooldays; the essence of sherbet. Barri became intoxicated by the mixture of aromas. *It would be so easy to reach out and take that sweetness to make it mine.*

With eyes like slits, breathing steady and a longing to be a boy again with Elspeth, Barri slowly raised his right hand to reach out. His fingertips were millimetres from the girl's throat. *I could take it in my hands, circumference it easily. She would fill a gap.*

'What about my scarf? Look, I can see it!' Barri snapped out of his trance. He followed the girl's outstretched arm as it brushed against the side of his face then past him. Barri leaned out, reached and slid his fingers along log cladding until they reached the scarf. He fumbled around. The scarf had slipped down the side of the tree-house and snagged on a bent nail just below the window. He yanked and brought it back into the tree-house.

'You did it, yeah!' Rosebud cheered and clapped her hands. 'Now, all you have to do is get the other end.'

Barri tugged as Rosebud had done previously until the scarf was taut between a branch and his hand. With one quick movement, he pulled up and back until the scarf whiplashed

178

into the tree-house. It lost three of its tassels.

'Yeah! Yeah! Yeah!' Rosebud grabbed the scarf and darted back towards the tree-house exit. Without time to be orientated to height above ground, the little girl descended fearlessly and disappeared out of sight. Barri was left alone with a sweet mixture of aromas and a feeling that he had been the one to narrowly escape danger.

'Bye!' he heard the girl shout from somewhere below the tree-house. 'Thank you! I'll see you again! I've left you a present!' the little girl sang as she plonked scuffed shoes down each rung. Her heart soared but that would change after she crossed the road. *I'm going to be in so much trouble when I get home.*

Barri wondered what the little girl meant by "*a present*" then tried to stand without bones cracking. His head was angled again and his knees stiff but they soon loosened as he mirrored the little girl's descent. There was no sign of her by the time a scuffed boot hit the grass. Barri walked wearily back to his house and felt his heavy loss again. He wouldn't go to work that night, now that he'd returned to the ground, his motivation to leave Radburn had gone in the same direction as his heart. A piece of him had left with Caprice. As he reached into his right pocket to retrieve his car remote so that he could lock it, he found a bag of candy Love Hearts with sherbet dip.

Next door to Radburn, Judith watched aghast as Barri lumbered wearily across his lawn towards the house, her nose pressed so firmly against a window that it left a smudge. She stretched her neck to watch him until the angle was too difficult to maintain. A little girl's shouting had brought her to the window, but it had been too dark in Radburn's front garden to see anything until she saw a small figure dart along the driveway to the road. Judith waited, glued to the window, but not for long. When she saw Barri emerge from long shadows beneath the tree, her sponge-like mind jumped to a conclusion that would have sickened him if he had known.

Without delay, the sour little women made hasty farewells to two old ladies then bustled away as fast as stubby legs could carry her. She finished work ten-minutes early and couldn't get to the police station fast enough. Her eyes were all the proof she needed. *If I had my way, then he'd be hanged from that damned tree.* 'Who the hell has huge trees like that in their garden anyway?' she mumbled. She was livid when her Ka pulled up outside the station but it was closed. 'Bloody budget cuts!' she shouted at a sign across double fronted glass doors. She remained in her car and reported her crime by mobile.

'Did you recognise the girl?' a well-spoken voice asked Judith.

'No,' she had to be truthful. 'She could be one of the kids from the park.'

'Did you see what they were doing?'

'No, but I know exactly what they were doing, that filthy bastard, he's been planning it.'

'In what way planning it?'

'He's been getting the tree-house ready and he's been taunting the kids with it, watching them whenever he can. He just stands in his garden and watches them for ages.' In truth, Judith had only seen Barri on one occasion when Awesome and Rosebud had waved at him but, he could have been watching children each time he took his late afternoon stroll. The tree had been in the way for her to see anything clearly from Fernlea's ground floor. By the time she made it up to the second floor, Barri was usually gone.

'I see,' the voice drawled then sounded apologetic. 'It sounds like suspicious behaviour. I'll send someone to take a look.'

'Is that ALL you're going to do?' Judith spat at her mobile.

'That's all we can do for now,' the voice explained. 'Unless an actual crime is reported, there's little we can do except make enquiries.'

'I HAVE reported a crime!' Judith yelled.

The voice hesitated to answer then said: 'Strictly speaking, a crime hasn't been committed and if it was, we will receive a call from the girl's parents.'

'WHAT? That's stupid, what if they don't know about it?'

180

'If the child is missing like you said, then they'll soon know about it. I'll send a couple of men to search the park immediately then pay a visit to Mr George. You say he'll be at work, at Radburn's?'

'Yes, yes! That's where he is every night. That weirdo can't be seen during daylight! I've been trained in mental issues.' It was part of her three-month training course, lightly touched upon.

'Yes well, we have your details Mrs Gormey and we'll contact you if we need to.'

'Yes, you do that and I'll testify if I have to.'

'Thank you Mrs Gormey.'

Judith was wound tightly and ready to explode. She wanted to race home and tell her husband so that they could both return to Dandelion View and hold vigil. She didn't want Bobbies or Community Police to handle this with kid gloves. Judith had stored up her venom and now salivated with excitement and there was no bottom to the depth of her hatred for a person she didn't know. She had to be content with setting Barri's comeuppance in motion.

Inside Radburn House, Barri covered a congealed meal in cling-wrap then placed it in his fridge. He took a bottle of red wine and a glass with him to his bedroom. The rest of Radburn was dark and silent. Later, he was sprawled with his laptop across his four-poster staring at Caprice's last email to him. She had been true to her word; her email was a straight-forward list, nothing more except for one small personal touch at the end.

"The cleaner came on Wednesday night and as you know, next Wednesday is Christmas day, so she said she would come on Monday next week, instead. I might have upset her. I mentioned I wouldn't be at Radburn much longer and somehow it slipped out that the house could be sold but, I said you could put a good word in for her with the new owners. I've left the evening dress in the wardrobe, thank you but I don't think I will have another occasion to wear it. The mobile and notebook are in my room." It ended simply: *"Caprice."*

The dress now lay across the end of Barri's bed and after he'd re-read the email twenty or so times, he stared at the dress but didn't touch it. Automatically, he went to his left wrist. 'Where's the bracelet?' He'd lost Elspeth's gift but it had to be somewhere in the tree-house or around it. Its loss was a final straw. For ten-minutes, he struggled in the dark outside with a torch that kept cutting out.

Judith's husband told her: 'It's none of our business what he does. Let the police deal with it.' Barri was spared an ordeal of having to explain to a lynch mob what he was doing. Judith had to make do instead with tapping slander into her Facebook timeline.

Barri didn't find his bracelet but he found bitten fingernails in the corner of the tree-house. He kneeled and felt around the floor beneath the window before gathering them up then turned their small crescents over in his hand with a fingertip. They were a reminder of lost opportunities. He gave up his search and returned to his room in a rage, which soon turned to the next phases of despair and self-pity.

By his fifth glass of wine, Caprice's dress lay across his bedroom floor with Barri's new leather bracelets strewn across it. Barri lay on top, completely naked while he perversely held his bare forearm in place as though the dress was still occupied.

Two policemen drove past the chip shop towards the entrance to Paxton Park then drove as far as they could before the roadway narrowed and they had to go on foot. Their search was fruitless. They warned a group of teenagers who swigged Red Bull and cider near the bandstand and a man wearing a Santa hat who was about to urinate in a bin. The men expected the last Friday night before Christmas to be particularly busy when office parties erupted into brawls in bars then spilled out onto streets. Also, theft was rife over the festive season. After checking back to base they were advised that as yet a crime hadn't been reported so a visit to Mr George was no longer a priority.

Rosebud had been sent to her room, grounded until after

Christmas. She hadn't mentioned Barri or his tree-house because she didn't see any need to. The girl lay sprawled across her bedroom floor but not particularly bothered by her punishment. Christmas day would soon come and she knew her mother didn't have a will iron enough to mar her enjoyment. The little redhead had enjoyed a grand adventure. In her mind, Barri had been a gentle giant. He'd climbed into her tower so that he could rescue her scarf.

'There's no reason why that lady with the beautiful red hair should be so sad.'

19. A Push in the Right Direction

Purl was, for the first time in her life, thoroughly discontent and burning with curiosity. Her evening at Whiskers Hotel hadn't ended with a straight-forward seduction and it was incomprehensible. *I should be basking in the glow of another victory and telling daddy that Barri was such a sweetheart. He's come round to our way of thinking.* Instead, the troubled young woman spent the weekend trying to decide what had gone wrong. She put on a brave face with her painted smile. Back in her home town she shopped and dined but all the while her mind replayed her blatant insult and subsequent snub to Caprice.

The unexpected rival had crawled beneath Purl's skin and it riled her no end. Caprice had outshone Purl's polished facade with natural attractiveness and said so little to distinguish or defend herself. Purl had a suspicion, particularly after her bitchy remark about Pretty Woman. To help her bruised ego, she reached a conclusion to suit her better than the one she suspected. *It's more plausible that Barri was deliberately obtuse to avoid the embarrassment of being with a paid escort.*

Purl's father suffered no illusions. 'If he's not gay then he must like a racy woman.' Her father's comment poured fuel onto Purl's new worry that perhaps she didn't possess the charms her superior position in life required for her challenge.

'Of course he's not gay daddy! I cannot see what's racy about that woman, she was a mouse.' Purl recalled how Barri had looked at Caprice during the meal. 'If he hired an escort then you shouldn't have goaded him and he wouldn't have reacted the way he did.' Purl's father was to blame for any unpleasantness at the table and she had told him on more than one occasion much to his surprise. Mandrake replied with stern impatience:

'Perhaps that damned assistant of his should have known about the company he keeps instead of giving me bum information! It would have made things a lot easier.' Then, he gave his daughter further cause for alarm. 'What the hell was the George boy doing with a whore in public? I wouldn't have thought him stupid enough to flaunt her at a high-profile event. Look into it Purl! If that girl was hired goods then get confirmation because I can use it. There's nothing like scandal to make a man think again about his business reputation. Speak to Phestoz. He's got contacts in that sort of thing.' Mandrake handed his daughter a business card and shook his head before concluding: 'I still can't see Barri putting his head into a media noose, can you? The number of the hotel is on the card.'

Purl knew that if she didn't initiate enquiries quickly then her father would. She phoned Whiskers to speak with her father's old friend. Her challenge became a personal crusade and she was excited. Her father's grotesque friend was surprised but intrigued why Purl, not her father, contacted him. 'Come to the hotel and we can discuss it over a drink. I never discuss important business over the phone.' It would mean another long drive back to Mistlethrop but Purl thought it could be worth it.

Once at the hotel, she wasn't put-off by Phestoz's physical features but the horrible man's eyes betrayed that his thoughts weren't always in union with his words. Phestoz chose his words with deliberation. He knew Purl was a devious soul.

'I have a confession,' she offered with a flurry of fake modesty and eyelashes. Phestoz looked at coated lashes, rigidly spaced. Amusement glided over his face before he pursed thin white lips. Her words reminded him of a Reverend he despised and had recently tried to ensnare in one of his games.

'You do?' The wily old man's tone sounded sarcastic.

'Yes, and it's something I thought you could help me with?'

'Something you cannot ask of your father?'

Purl feigned modesty and tried to smile sweetly but her

confessor could see that her eyes were quite still. 'I'd be too embarrassed.'

Phestoz slowly brushed non-existent crumbs from his crossed trouser leg with the back of bony, clawed fingers. He enjoyed a first flush of pleasure. *I so love the beginning of a new game with a willing victim.* 'You flatter me; tell me how I can help.'

'You remember the man who came to the awards?'

'Yes and his lovely companion.' Phestoz watched Purl's face.

'Well, it is she I came to ask you about.'

Phestoz immediately became wary. 'What makes you think I can?'

'Daddy said you could. You have ways to look into someone's background or can point me in the direction of someone who can.'

Phestoz's pleasure returned. He saw where Purl was going with this. 'You like the man?'

'Let's say, I'd like to get to know him better.'

'So, is this for your own sake or your father's?'

Purl's eyes shone a little too brightly and her eyes creased at their corners. 'Mine,' she said genuinely and Phestoz leered.

I could get Purl do my dirty work for me but first, I'll make her say exactly what she wants. 'What do you want me to find out?' Phestoz rested one elbow on the arm of his chair to support his angular chin while gazing at Purl. It was disconcerting but Purl relaxed, she was relieved by the inference that he would do the digging for her.

'I want you to find out what you can about Caprice, I think that was her name. I had the impression she wasn't all that she at first appeared.'

'And what do you think she really is?'

Purl licked her lips then replied with a forced degree of earnestness. 'The type of woman to latch onto men with money or, is paid to.' She looked pleased with the way she'd phrased this and the irony of her statement didn't go unmissed by Phestoz. He looked at Purl's pristine make-up and hair, designer chic and matching shoes as the epitome of bait for high stakes.

'If I was to discover that this young woman's company was due to a monetary transaction would it deter you from pursuing your interest?' His question temporarily dislodged Purl's equilibrium but her eyes then hardened with business-like intensity.

'No,' she stated plainly. 'There may be circumstances.'

'That's accommodating of you.'

'I'm sure you know what I mean when I say dedicated business men don't always find time for social niceties. They're often unable to develop relationships everyone else takes for granted.'

Phestoz's eyes hardened. Purl had touched upon a sensitive subject. 'On the contrary...' the old man drawled, 'in my line of business, my work brings me into daily contact with *the* social niceties.' What he omitted to say was that a relationship he'd taken years to develop had temporarily escaped him. Then, he thought how he would shortly repossess it, with Purl's aid. 'I can see that for someone immersed in less rewarding business it would be difficult. What would you do if Caprice was more?'

A tightening around Purl's glossed lips provided her answer but she said: 'Then, I would have to reconsider.'

'You don't strike me as the type of person to accept defeat.'

'I wouldn't call it that!' Purl snapped then, regained composure. 'Let's say I would have to test the waters.' The genuine smile appeared again. The thin, pale confessor returned her smile.

'Well, as it happens, you are in luck today.'

'Why is that?'

'I already know something about the young woman in question.' Phestoz was quick to add: 'I heard reporters discussing her then made tentative enquiries.' Only half of this was true, he'd overheard the boutique owner talking to a reporter but had no need to ask questions.

'Oh! Did I guess correctly?'

187

'Let's say, you were right on both counts.' Phestoz wanted to implant urgency into Purl's mission. He could think of no better way than by giving her a problem to encourage her. Anything easily gained would soon lose its appeal and knowing what he did of Mandrake he guessed his daughter would tire easily if granted her wish too soon. Purl looked crestfallen. Phestoz waited for her dismay to take root before continuing.

'The woman hasn't been with Barri long and she is the sole recipient of his generosity.' Again, he hesitated to allow his words to take weight. 'He favours a certain type and Caprice simply fulfils it.' He mixed half-truths with personal interpretation of what he'd seen at the hotel, Caprice's past misdemeanours and what he suspected her motives now were. He had seen how Barri had looked at her during the meal and his close attention to her welfare. Purl's *"Pretty Woman"* slur had passed over Phestoz's head. The devious man knew that his words now fell upon ears that would soon discover the real truth. Purl would then return to relay that truth with either delight or reproach. Either way, Phestoz wouldn't have to lift a finger until he was certain Purl had discovered what he could not. Reclaiming his property would then be a lot easier.

'What do you mean by a certain type?' Purl was eager to know and stared at Phestoz with pretend innocence. She jumped to the conclusion that Barri preferred women with prowess and sexual freedom but had been irritated by Phestoz's reply, which was exactly what he intended.

'Barri is a strong character, a man who has a high opinion of himself and little of others, by all accounts. However, when it comes to women, he favours weaker personalities but with strong looks. That way he'll always be in charge.'

'Are you sure?' Purl asked. 'Daddy is a strong character but a weak woman wouldn't stand a chance, he would walk over her in a trice.'

'Barri is not Daddy,' Phestoz stated as though he knew the young man well. What he lacked in direct knowledge, he assumed after expert assessment by eye only and by Barri's tone and manner it had been evident that the young man held iron intensity. It had to shield a volcano of emotion. *Who better was able to tap into it than Caprice? I groomed her specifically to entice.*

'For Barri, the weaker nature is to be cherished and protected. Caprice appeals to his masculinity. And, as for her looks: her unusual hair, simplicity of dress and lack of external tweaking...' Phestoz waved a bony finger, gesturing to Purl's neat and perfect presentation. 'He obviously likes women without all the fuss of make-up and tweaking.'

His assessment made sense and Purl was quick to accept it. She looked at her lap then her shapely legs, crossed at the ankle and to the side, her calves made prominent by high heels. *What man would prefer to look at a bare natural leg and foot without silk stockings and heels?* A shallow personality found this incomprehensible but there it was again, a nagging doubt that Purl wasn't everything a rational man would want.

'I will need a room for tonight,' Purl informed her new collaborator. 'On second thoughts, keep one free for me.'

Phestoz could have grinned if his facial muscles had been used to it.

20. Curiosity and the Fox

Monday morning, Purl phoned friends to say that she would shop alone for Christmas outfits. Despite protests and offers to drop what they were doing, she remained steadfast. She'd given a great deal of thought to what Phestoz had said and she didn't want anyone to know that she would be visiting a backwater boutique. Phestoz had casually mentioned the place where Caprice had bought her dress knowing that Purl would be curious to visit it and possible gleam more information from the owner.

Purl explored the boutique, much to the delight of the owner who was more than accommodating to yet another high-profile customer. She instantly recognised Purl from the Hotel dinner and exclaimed: 'Oh Caprice must have told you to come here!'

Purl bristled but replied demurely: 'Yes, she did. She had such good things to say.'

'I knew she would. It was Barri of course who first pointed her in my direction.'

'Barri?'

'Yes, the poor boy needed our help urgently. Poor Caprice did so well to overcome her trouble.' The owner assumed that Purl was a good friend and knew all about it.

'She did, didn't she?' To confidently acknowledge a strange snippet of information could lead to revelations.

'I don't know what I would have done in her place. She couldn't leave the house until Barri had bought everything afresh. Lucky for her, he had the good taste to come here. We are discreet.' As she spoke, the owner preened herself by removing stray strands of dyed blond hair from her black dress. Purl didn't respond, prompting the woman to elucidate. 'Theft is such an ugly crime and it was a shame they didn't find the

190

culprits.'

Purl had a rounder picture and thought: *Phestoz was right, Barri needed a victim.* She couldn't have guessed how right she was.

The cunning young woman returned home and threw herself into pre-Christmas engagements but by the end of it, she had clear purpose. She would visit Radburn Confectionery again then, Radburn House. She had to find out if Barri's Christmas would include her rival and in what capacity.

Barri's assistant was buzzed at his desk and when he'd spoken with Reception went to greet a visitor at the lift. Purl was all smiles as she alighted. The assistant accompanied her along the open-plan office into Barri's empty office where he then threw himself eagerly into his boss's chair. He gestured towards the chair Purl had favoured during her last visit.

'Where is he?' she asked, ruffled that Barri wasn't where he was supposed to be. His assistant's exuberant but smug manner was most annoying.

'He generally doesn't work during the day,' the assistant replied, relieved that his boss had resumed old ways. He didn't know that Barri hadn't been to the office since the early hours of the previous Friday morning.

'So, where is he?'

The assistant looked at his watch. 'He'll be at home. He won't come to the office until later when people have gone home.' Then, the arrogant young man leaned casually back in Barri's chair to look at Purl from down his nose.

'It's an odd way of doing business, at night.'

'Tell me about it!' The assistant's smugness increased. 'He has me to rely on during the day.'

'I hear that you hope it won't be for too much longer.' Purl sat with her usual sideway ankle-cross but she didn't like the way the man opposite looked at her legs.

'Ah, your father let the cat out of the bag.'

'We work closely together.'

'You work with your father at Mandrake's?' The assistant

was surprised; all his digging for information hadn't revealed this fact.

'Yes, but like Barri, I don't sit in an office during the day. Behind every great man is a great woman.'

'Waiting to get his job,' the assistant quickly interjected and he smiled at his joke. Purl wasn't amused.

'We are a family.' she said tightly.

'Can I help you in Barri's absence?' the assistant ventured, sensing his joke hadn't been well-received.

'No!' Purl stated sharply and stood to leave. 'I don't deal with the oily rag, only the engineer!' She then strode out of the office back to the elevator. The assistant's face turned red and he smacked the arm of Barri's chair.

Back in her car, Purl contemplated whether a visit to Radburn House would be wise. *Barri should be at home, but will Caprice be there too?* Purl took a moment to decide but her steely determination made up her mind. She didn't notice a Police Community Officer in her rear mirror. He walked through the car park. Going to Barri's place of work hadn't been his first choice. He'd already been to Radburn House.

Earlier, Judith Gormey had been too busy helping a wrinkled old body into a bath tub to see the officer walk along Radburn's driveway. After no response from the front door, he'd peered through kitchen windows before walking around a large oak tree. The toe of a highly polished boot had pushed through undergrowth but he hadn't seen anything out of the ordinary until he'd looked upwards. Something had fluttered in breeze above. With the peak of his hat pulled low to blot winter sun, he'd peered through branches at woollen strands stuck to bark. Rather than climb, the officer had made a mental note. If he'd averted his eyes to a lower group of twiggy branches to the right of his head, then he would have seen a leather bracelet dangling. Instead, the officer had used his radio to say that Mr George wasn't home.

As Purl drove out of the car park, the Officer entered Reception. Barri's assistant was further enraged when

192

Reception buzzed Barri's desk. The angry young man had returned to his workstation. He grabbed his phone then dialled zero.

'I told you a few minutes ago that Barri isn't here so why did you buzz his office? You should talk to me!'

The voice at the other end of the line said chirpily: 'He has another unexpected visitor and you must let me know which desk you're at. Use the *Follow Me* function on your phone.'

Exasperated, the assistant let loose. 'I have too many things on my mind right now to bother with minor details. I also have a mobile to answer and it's your job to find me! Where's the visitor now? Who is it?'

The chirpiness continued, which made the young man even angrier: 'It's a police officer and I told him Barri isn't in.'

'You did what? Why on earth would you do that?'

'Well, he isn't.'

'Yes, but I am!'

'The policeman said it was a personal matter and not business-related.'

There was a brief silence then the phone crackled. 'So, where is he now?'

'He's in the visitor's lounge. He wants Barri's personal phone number and I said I'd get it for him.'

'I'll give it to him. I'll be straight down.'

While he waited, the officer helped himself to a cup of tea from the hospitality bar. It was surprising how many chocolate wafers he was able to dunk and suck-up before the assistant appeared.

'Hello there!' the assistant held out a smooth hand. 'Can I help you? Barri isn't in right now.'

'So the receptionist informed me.' The officer reluctantly abandoned tea and wafers and stood, donned his hat then accepted a limp handshake with disdain. 'I want a contact number for Mr George or, do you know where I can find him?'

'He should be at home; he doesn't normally come to the office until evening. Is it something I can help you with?'

'No, I've already been to his home. This is an enquiry only, nothing to do with his work.' Then, the officer paused before saying: 'Do you know if Mr George has a young daughter?'

The assistant's dormant smile didn't falter. To reply "*No*" wouldn't have been satisfying. 'Why do you ask?'

The officer ignored the question and said: 'I know he is unmarried - a child or a young relative?'

'No, not that I know of,' the assistant was dissatisfied but held out a card. 'Here's his mobile number. I haven't spoken to him but if he calls, do you want me to relay a message?' The officer looked at the card then noticed that he'd smudged chocolate on it, which, he covered with his thumb.

'No message.'

Purl, in the meantime, arrived at Radburn House, parked her car then waited impatiently at the front door.

'He won't be in,' a voice informed her. She turned to see a coated dowdy figure. The cleaner, true to her word arrived early during Christmas week.

'Do you know where he is?' Purl asked and sniffed, offended at being forced to talk to such a lowly-looking person. The cleaner also sniffed and approached with a key in her hand.

'He's away till Christmas Eve, gone to his holiday home.'

Purl stood aside while the cleaner inserted the key and opened the door but only enough for the cleaner to put her foot inside. She kept one gloved hand on the key and the other on the door. She'd intended to use her usual entrance at the back but Purl's presence prompted her to take the front. Having a key in her hand gave a modicum of power. Purl looked at the key then the crack in the door. The cleaner recognised curiosity, the second she'd encountered since the weekend.

Judith had also been true to her word and had tried to extract information from the cleaner while shopping in Tesco. Thinly disguised as an attempt to strike-up yet another flimsy friendship, Judith had been transparent. The cleaner didn't class her own proclivity for gossip as in the same league as Judith's. Judith had puffed her bloated body with false superiority at having to deal with a woman in an inferior profession. The cleaner had thought: *I only touch household liquids whereas you have to clean up bodily fluids.*

'Tell me,' Judith had ventured. 'Did you like working for Barri? Did you know what he was planning?' The cleaner had been taken aback.

How does she know Barri's selling his house and that I'd be out of a job? It was too sensitive a subject to discuss with a woman whose reputation had preceded her. 'His plans are his own business, not mine to discuss with you.'

'Will Caprice be home soon?' Purl shivered.

'No, she's gone too.'

'Oh, they've both gone? I was delivering a Christmas card.' It was then that Purl's snootiness disappeared. As the cleaner watched the young woman pull an envelope from her bag, she saw that beneath a painted exterior was an upset young woman. It momentarily melted an uncomplicated heart.

'Come in for a cuppa. You look frozen. You should put on warmer clothes at this time of year.' The door opened fully and Purl followed the cleaner inside.

A lot was going through the cleaner's mind. Barri had phoned her on Saturday afternoon and she'd been surprised. He'd been brief. He was going to Whitby for a few days, Caprice had gone and the house could be cleaned whenever it suited. When she'd asked about Radburn being put up for sale, he'd replied that he hadn't yet decided. She'd concluded that the couple had fallen out, unsurprising considering Barri's lifestyle and Christmas always brought out the worst in people. The arrival of yet another young woman however, added a curious angle. *Maybe he had a love triangle going on. She looks upset. I'll show some sympathy. This could be another potential Mrs. George.*

Purl was led through to the parlour and the cleaner played hostess. She was as comfortable in a stately wingback as Barri's assistant had been in his office. While Purl waited for tea to be poured, she took a long look around her, pleasantly surprised.

It didn't stop her from imagining what she would do with the room if she had free reign. The cleaner was informative. 'I think Barri has gone away to lick his wounds.'

'Oh?'

'Caprice had mentioned she'd be leaving, but I didn't realise it would be this side of Christmas. They must have had words for her to go so soon. Barri plays his cards close to his chest.' The cleaner sipped her tea, safe in the knowledge that for now she could do whatever she liked in Radburn House. Purl looked more cheerful.

'You said he'll be back on Christmas Eve.'

'That's what he told me and he's always spot-on with what he says.'

'You don't know what time?'

'No, but he's a night-creature so it could be anytime.'

'He didn't tell me he had a holiday home.'

'Oh the George's had it for years and Barri uses it now. Whitby isn't that far.'

'You haven't got a Christmas tree I noticed.' Purl changed the subject and sipped tea from a china cup leaving a ring of lipstick.

'No, he never has one. I don't think he's bothered, just another day to him.'

'It's not for religious reasons then?' Purl delved.

'God, no!' and the cleaner laughed.

'Will it be alright to leave this card then?'

The cleaner thought otherwise and Purl put her card away. Purl had been handed an early Christmas present. The Gods had smiled upon her by removing her only obstacle. The following day would be Christmas Eve and Purl was thrilled that she could continue with her plan. *By New Year, he'll be mine. Perhaps Christmas isn't the best time?*

Once inside her car, Purl pulled out another envelope from her bag. It contained a time-worn photograph and she gazed at it before carefully replacing it then starting her car. She had found the photo in a folder on her father's desk. The folder bulged with information about Radburn Confectionery but contained little about its owner. The photo however, had caught her eye. It was a class photo, the only one of Barri as a child. He stood at the back, one of tallest but he looked down at a girl in front. Although her body faced forwards her head was angled to look back at him. It was the girl that interested Purl. Colour may have faded but there was no mistaking the girl's red hair.

Meanwhile, Barri had retreated to the fishing port of his youth. He had driven to Whitby late Saturday afternoon still suffering the remnants of a hangover. Two bottles of wine had seen him through Friday night but he hadn't been used to drinking so much so quickly and awoken naked in Caprice's bed without memory of how he got there.

Caprice had abandoned him too soon. He'd counted on her agreeing to take a short break with him. Christmas at Whitby would have served two purposes. An excuse to get his subject alone, seclude her from the outside world and, he could dispose of a body after a drive along the coast. He knew just the place, an isolated cove. It lay beneath an overhanging cliff with a row of cottages above it but after weather erosion, its houses were dangerously close to the edge.

Drawn to danger, Barri had hunted out a route around the base of the cliff to the cove where as a boy he'd once fished for crabs so that he could break their shells. A hollowed gap in rock face had half-filled with boulders from a previous landslide. A deep chasm in the centre held water that was stagnant during the day but replaced whenever the tide came in. Barri could dump a body in it, cover it with rocks then add a few bags of ready-mixed cement. He'd planned exactly what he was going to do and when. Caprice wouldn't have been missed.

Barri traipsed through the centre of Whitby like a man under a spell. Wailing seagulls serenaded haunting fog horns as he waited patiently for the swing-bridge to move until it spanned the River Esk. The intense young man relished the cold North Sea wind on his face and wanted to gulp it down, feel it deaden his chest and the tumultuous emotions that had kept him awake at night and then gnawed during daylight. Caprice's departure had left him vulnerable, added to by the surprise presence of a little girl in his tree-house. She had somehow combined the past with the present and now it was up to him to decide the future. *I don't want to feel anymore.*

The swing-bridge groaned and clunked into place. Barri pushed hands into pockets as he braced himself against wind. The last time he'd roamed through the old east side of town then climbed one-hundred-and-ninety-nine steps to the beautiful but eerie Abbey ruins, he'd bought a leather-bound book in its gift shop. He recalled the occasion and how happy he'd felt. His heart skipped a beat. *What if instead of moping around here I look for Caprice?*

Barri decided to buy a new clock he'd planned on getting if Caprice had been with him. She could have picked one out, something special and he could have enjoyed the irony of it. He found a spring to his step. Once he'd crossed the bridge and turned right down Grape Lane he was gratified that the shop past the Grape Vine Cafe was open. He pushed his nose against a window to peer through it. Two walls of clocks lined the narrow store. Barri entered and smiled.

21. Fishing for Info

Phestoz chuckled into a long glass of pure vodka. He admired a reflection of his right eye pupil as it stared back at him from a bobbing ice cube. Mandrake watched, amused by his odd friend's hiccupping chuckle. 'What are you so happy about?' The older man took a large mouthful and gulped like a snake swallowing a mouse, his wiry grey throat displayed every internal movement.

'Oh I'm just high on life,' Phestoz replied and he mused to himself, which peeved the younger man who didn't like secrets. He could tell that Phestoz was brimming with them.

'You must have passed Purl on the motorway.'

'Ah, she's taken another trip then?' Phestoz tried to sound surprised.

'Back to Mistlethrop, she went early. You two must have passed each other. I'm surprised you came so close to Christmas, won't it be busy at your new hotel?'

Phestoz waved limp, tapering fingers and brushed Mandrake's question to one side. 'My minions take care of everything. Anyway, what's Purl up to at Mistlethrop?'

'You know,' Mandrake snorted and Phestoz shot him a smug look.

'She must be serious about your interests; won't it interfere with your Christmas plans?' He was careful to imply Mandrake was the force behind Purl's mission.

'Purl is a determined young woman,' Mandrake replied with pride.

'She takes after her old man,' Mephisto observed. 'What if she's on a wild goose chase?'

'I doubt it; besides, if she's successful then, it will be mutually beneficial.'

'How so?'

'As the new owner of Radburn Confectionery, I could bring a lot of business your way.'

'Would your head office relocate?'

'No, Radburn's office will become a regional admin but I'll need somewhere for business visitors to stay and catering facilities for Northern promotional functions.'

'I see...' Phestoz didn't smile, not yet.

'Anyway...' Mandrake threw his chin upwards with fresh interest. 'You haven't told me why you're here.'

The older man's throat writhed again, emphasising a bulging Adam's apple as a last swig of vodka made its way down then, he looked seriously at Mandrake. 'As you're going after Radburn, I want to know if the family home is included in its assets. I took a look at it the other day. It would be a good place to have my own head office. If you take on the business then I'd be interested in taking on the house.'

The younger man stared into space for a moment then said: 'Let me find out. It's not something I've looked at. I'm more concerned with the factory and renovated Mill.'

'Are you able to find out now?' Mephisto was impatient for his query to be resolved. Mandrake hesitated and searched his old friend's almost skeletal face.

'Why do you need a head office Phestoz? I thought you liked flexibility.'

The old man's sallow cheek quivered before he replied: 'Radburn House would also make an ideal place to settle down with a... a loved one, an ideal place to combine both pleasure AND business.' His words held truth but Mandrake laughed. He arose from his chair, walked to a leather-topped desk, looked back at the old man then laughed again. Taking a folder back to his seat, he opened it. Phestoz watched with bated breath, willing the answer to be found within the folder and it to be in his favour.

He'd come to realise since seeing Caprice, so free and settled with a new suitor, that he missed her more than he could have thought possible. He missed his private recitals, his private dance. *Where else but Radburn, could I fully relish old rituals made new again? She would be a bird within a gilded cage.* The irony of being the new master of Radburn House would add sweetness to his pleasure.

It was also true that Mephisto had taken a good look at the outside of Radburn House, albeit from the pavement of Dandelion View. He'd committed every detail to memory, including a tree-house and what looked like woollen tassels hanging from bark. Phestoz watched Mandrake shuffling paper. 'I have a list of assets here... can't see the house though.' Paper rustled again. Annoyed, Phestoz tapped bony fingers on his hard bony kneecap which, looked like the head of a golf-driver beneath trousers, so angular that there didn't look to be any flesh around it. 'No. No, it's not included.'

'Are you sure? Can't you check with your man at Radburn's?' Phestoz's usual calm and deliberate manner portrayed annoyance.

'Can't do it, I'm going to burn that bridge this afternoon. The man is a hapless sycophant.'

'Then check or, let me check before you cut ties.' Phestoz's voice had urgency which, he quickly checked by sitting back in his chair and sniffing loudly.

'As a favour to you, I'll phone him.'

'Good, that's all I ask.' Phestoz regained composure and waited with elbows resting either side of his chair, long wrists hanging limply. Tapering fingernails were so translucent that it was hard to fathom how they could have grown so long and not snapped.

As Mandrake began to dial out, he said: 'You could have phoned me you know. You didn't need to come this far to find out.'

'Yes I could have but, I have other business in this area and it's no skin off my nose to make a detour.'

Mandrake thought to himself: *Skin is not a commodity you can afford to lose, there's so little of it stretched across your bones.*

'Ah yes, Mandrake here, I want you to check something for me.' There was silence for a moment then: 'Yes, I know that! Look to see if Radburn House is part of the assets, will you?' Silence again for a longer period then: 'No, I didn't think so... Yes! I know about the apartments, that's a separate matter.'

Phestoz heard a scratching noise from Mandrake's earpiece and guessed the voice at the other end had overstretched its zealousness. When it had become annoying, Mandrake continued: 'Look, let me stop you right there! Are you listening? Do not try to talk over me!' He threw a look of disbelief at Phestoz who shook his head then pursed white lips in sympathy. Mandrake didn't wait to finish what he'd intended to say. Instead, he replaced the receiver and aped Phestoz by also shaking his head. 'Like I said, the man's a buffoon!'

'What did you promise him for supplying information?' Phestoz asked without reserve. Mandrake resumed his seat. The wily businessman noticed how his old friend had pushed his empty glass forward across the table between them.

'Aren't you driving?' Mandrake had to get up again to fetch the vodka.

'I was but I'm staying nearby, within walking distance.'

Mandrake reluctantly refilled his friend's glass but remained standing and said: 'I may have hinted that Radburn's offices would fall under that fool's control.'

'You said as much?'

'We've only had verbal communication whereas he has been stupid enough to email and use the post. I may have said something along the lines that Radburn's offices would require a Regional Manager but that didn't mean that he would fill those shoes.' Both men smiled at each other in recognition of astute business practice. Mandrake returned to his desk.

'So, how will you cut the connection?'

'His latest email will be returned to the current owner of Radburn Confectionery.' Mandrake bent over a laptop, tapped keys then pressed *Send*. Both smiles increased in width, but the old man's could only make it as far as the width of his nose.

'What are you going to do about the house?' Mandrake asked.

'That depends how successful Purl is.'

'Then, let's drink to Purl's success,' and Mandrake decided to join his friend and complete the toast by adding a tot of whisky to his flat ginger-ale. 'It's a shame Purl is so enamoured with Barri.' The proud father didn't think Purl's latest whim would cause a problem.

'I thought she was there to encourage Barri to hand over Radburn, nothing more.' Phestoz feigned innocence but he watched Mandrake closely as he sipped his drink.

'Oh, she will succeed but, there's no harm in her having a little fun along the way. When she's done she'll return home and from her conversation last night I think she wants to settle down. If it wasn't for the age difference then you would be in with a chance. You would have someone to help line your new love nest.' Mandrake smirked into his glass. He couldn't resist the opportunity to tease Phestoz with false flattery. Having him as a son-in-law would be such a big joke that Mandrake had to stifle his mirth.

The older man winced. Mandrake's words held irony. *Purl - too old for me! With her cosmetics, dress sense and pushy attempts at beguilement, she looks older than her years. She would appeal to other men but definitely not me.* Caprice was and would always be the little girl he'd taken under his wing. He would always see her that way. Her lack of forced attributes appealed to more than just men with an appreciation for natural assets. She was malleable enough to bend to darker wills.

'Purl could make a man happy!' Phestoz exclaimed forcing false sincerity.

'You mean she would make a happy man feel old,' Mandrake cackled but Phestoz was offended.

'Age is just a concept,' he said calmly. He then thought about Radburn House and the one female who could occupy it. As he slipped deeper into thought, he gripped his glass so hard that his knuckles appeared white and angular. Mandrake stared at his friend's hands wondering what pre-occupied him so much.

Phestoz recalled his visit to Dandelion View then his last stroke of genius, a visit to Fernlea on the pretence of being a benefactor. Judith had sat next to him. He'd occupied a chair his step-daughter had once sat in but Judith hadn't suspected a connection. She had however, recognised deviousness, so immersed in it herself on a daily basis that she too was painted in its dark colours. Dour bitterness, etched around the old man's thin lips, also lay at the corners of Judith's.

She had joked about his generous donation and asked if it was because he hoped to be a resident. It hadn't gone down well. Phestoz had wanted to see the inside of Radburn but had to make do with the house next door. What he'd seen had disgusted him and to have been included even jokingly in the company of Old Dears, abhorrent. He could have cheerfully strangled Judith, only her thickset neck, brown with sun-bed abuse would be difficult to throttle.

He'd deliberately let-slip that he could be the future owner of Radburn and this had been welcome news to a podgy ball of resentment. Judith had taken yet another leap. *Barri's been shamed into putting Radburn up for sale*. Then, she'd gushed. Her joke had opened a possibility; the old man would need personal care. Judith had discussed Barri with unleashed fervour and when Phestoz had stepped back onto Fernlea's front step he'd exhaled the stench of old age but had the pleasure of knowing new and intriguing facts.

In the meantime, Caprice hadn't left Mistlethrop, preferring to leave an impression that she had. Having once tried unsuccessfully at Macefield to hoodwink her pursuer she'd since thought how it could have been better executed. Barri would think she'd travelled by train to her fresh start and Phestoz would expect that after their last encounter, she wouldn't be cunning enough to remain so close. She did however, need somewhere to lie low until after the festive holidays.

Caprice hadn't been so idle during her last days at Radburn. She may not have slept much but her dreams had remained intact. She had to find somewhere she could go without anyone knowing and be close enough to the town centre and station so that she could, if necessary, make a hasty departure. A sneaky visit to Barri's bedroom had provided the means.

A gem-cut glass award stood on a chest of drawers next to Barri's bed and with it, a set of keys and a glossy mock-up of property details to be used by estate agents. Apartments in Hebble Mill were fully plumbed and had electricity. All were empty except one showcase apartment, the rest to be made ready for occupancy after New Year. Building contractors had included a private report and a security company had been requested to patrol the area at nights. Although security camera equipment had been installed only a few cameras were live. Caprice had rocked back and forth, hugging her knees with delight.

She knew which of the mill security cameras were working, knew the internal layout and knew the times a guard would visit but was surprised that his personal inspection consisted only of a drive around the exterior. The wary redhead had implanted herself within the showcase apartment on the top floor. It boasted the best views of both surrounding countryside and Mistlethrop.

Back at Dandelion View, like Purl, Judith also burned with intense curiosity. 'Hello! Yes, I want to know if my crime report was investigated as I haven't heard anything.'

'Have you got the crime report reference?'

'No, I wasn't given one.'

There was a pause, then: 'Did you report it to the station using this number?'

'I tried to but you told me to ring the main number.'

'Then, you would have been quoted a crime report reference. Give me your name and the date you reported it and I'll access it from here.' Judith supplied the details and waited. 'Sorry madam, there isn't a reference but there is a record of your call and that it has been investigated.'

'What happened?'

'We didn't receive any report of a crime and after officers searched the area then followed-up, it seems there had been a misunderstanding. A crime hadn't taken place; Mr. George had dealt with a trespasser who had placed herself in a dangerous situation upon his property.'

'Too right, she was in a dangerous situation! Are you telling me you just took his word for it?' Judith's voice increased in pitch and volume.

'As I said Mrs. Gormey, a crime hadn't been reported and there was no evidence of one. It was a misinterpretation of events.'

Judith's voice broke with emotion: 'Are you calling me a liar? I know what I saw!'

'You weren't physically there Mrs. Gormey and we can only act if we have evidence. We are fully satisfied with Mr. George's explanation and have closed the matter.'

'That's not good enough! What am I paying my council tax for? I have kids and I want to know they're safe!'

'I understand Mrs. Gormey but rest-assured that it was fully investigated. I can only repeat that the matter is now closed. Goodbye.'

Judith's phone was covered with spittle.

22. Good Will to All

Feverishly optimistic during his drive back to Mistlethrop, Barri's heart leapt when he saw his home town, then, the reality of being back hit him. He had an impossible task ahead when it had all seemed so easy while he was at Whitby. He slammed the driving wheel with the flat of his hand.

Radburn's annexe had become an extension of his tree-house. It provided the same comforting space in which to devote one's thoughts to a higher plane but Barri couldn't return, not yet. In the tree-house he'd recently seen Elspeth's shadow, at his dining table, his mother's but the annexe now held Caprice's, the girl upon the stool. Barri hated what had become of him. 'I'll find her and crush her,' he growled. 'Then, there will be no more shadows!' He slammed the driving wheel again, feeling pain across his palm. 'Why didn't I do anything? This has been one long battle with myself.' Dreading the silence of Radburn House, Barri decided to drive to his office and ignored constant buzzing from his iPhone. Like a damn about to burst, Barri had held back repeatedly but his brief time in Whitby served only to cement cracks.

The young man stormed along the open-plan office, ignored his assistant's desk, which was unoccupied then, entered his glass box. Its door closed with a satisfying clunk and instantly, the outer office hum stopped. Barri's tension lifted but he found it odd that his usual preference to work in solitude during unsociable hours hadn't appealed as much as wanting to see activity and bustle through glass. Signs of life going about its usual daytime business added a reality to Caprice's planned demise. He wanted to be the only person to be still and silent, an observer, so that he could imagine what he would do, then, he would will it into the world and reality.

Ensconced behind a desk, Barri indulged in a pleasure almost as sweet as a kill. He lowered his head to a piece of paper but was blind to its surface, seeing only the results of a feverish imagination let loose. He allowed the first buds of a scheme to grow and as he lived it in his mind, his mouth widened so that he looked maniacal by the time his assistant returned.

Prompted by Mandrake's interest in Barri's house, the assistant had been busy researching its history. He now sat agape, his boss's manic expression only just visible through distorted reflections. In his box, Barri swam in deep waters of psyche, unheeding exterior activity or the alarm his expression now raised. He remained enrapt until cerebral energy had run its course, only then did Barri move. A heavy sigh of intense satisfaction escaped from his open, grimacing mouth.

The assistant had been concerned by Barri's unexpected presence then, worried. *What's he been staring at for so long and now laughing at? Is he laughing?* As he tried to decide, he became increasingly uneasy then became flippant. *I shouldn't care. The two-day Christmas break is nearly here. I won't have to look at his stupid face or put up with his madness much longer.*

All office personnel had hoped that they could leave early on Christmas Eve but Barri's unexpected arrival dampened their enthusiasm. The assistant's unease spread. Some quickly adapted, reluctantly accepting that they would have to see out the working day whereas others harboured sulky resentment. Minutes ticked by relentlessly reminding them that they would miss quality time with loved ones.

Desks held open boxes of chocolates and mince pies. They slid across surfaces at regular intervals and chatter increased but it wasn't the chatter of merriment. Not one person dared to ask how soon they could stop working, tacit guilt associated with abandoning work-stations too early. As ambient noise increased, the office atmosphere grew thicker.

The assistant fidgeted and squirmed in his chair. His reluctance to speak to Barri about business matters wasn't due

208

to guilt over recent betrayals. He'd grown in ego and self-confidence and in doing so had outgrown his position at Radburn. He glared at Barri's maniacal face. *He's only sitting there temporarily. It will soon be my office.* He thought about changes he would make and couldn't conceal his smugness but it soon turned into a snarl when he noticed his colleagues' secret clock-watching. He quietly waited. *If they're so serious about their careers then they won't be so keen to bolt out the door. I'll make sure only the seriously-minded remain working here.* As Barri brought his plotting to a satisfying conclusion his scheming assistant entered his own private world of fantasy.

With eyes shining with anticipation, Barri looked towards the outer office. He hadn't been aware of his extreme facial expressions but his face now ached, touching it he became embarrassed. *I'll have to make it seem as though I was heavily into my work,* so he quickly turned to his email inbox. Christmas confectionery, sales, promotions and publicity had already been decided at the beginning of the year. Valentine's Day was already in hand and so Barri saw only one subject heading each email, *"Easter... Easter... Easter..."*, that is, until he noticed one flagged as: *"Who's been a naughty boy then?"* As he read, Barri's expression changed from concentration to simpering anger. The shine remained in his eyes but for a different reason as he forwarded the email to his Personnel Department then added detailed instructions. Once sent, he snatched up his phone to speak quietly at length.

Thirty minutes later, Barri nodded his head at a thin woman dressed in a smart navy suit as she walked through the outer office. She nodded back. She was accompanied by a burly security guard and they both came to a halt at the side of the assistant's desk. The assistant didn't look up from a folder he studied intently but the office buzz hushed. Office staff had recognised the woman and wondered why a security guard was with her. Nervous eyes darted between the glass box and the assistant's desk.

'You must open this immediately.' The woman's sombre

voice alerted the assistant to her presence. He started, looked up, recognised the Personnel Manager then looked confused when he saw the guard. He was handed a white envelope. The assistant gawped at it while nervously looking at the guard. Barri returned his focus to his laptop. He'd insisted that his instructions be executed within the main office, ignoring advice to find a more appropriate and private venue.

"GROSS MISCONDUCT," the first words the assistant read. He shook his head in disbelief as he read the remainder of the dismissal letter while the whole office watched. Once he'd finished, unable to comprehend anything after the first paragraph, he gawped again and spluttered but words wouldn't come. His face flooded beetroot-red. Without murmur he grabbed his jacket, mobile phone and laptop case.

'I must insist all company property remains here!' the woman demanded. 'That includes your phone, laptop, identity pass plus the keys to your company car.' She held out her hand. The assistant glared at it then the guard who hovered expectantly, unable to gauge whether a fracas would ensue. The assistant's face looked like it was about to explode, so purplish that a navy blue vein in his forehead was lost in skin tone. He darted a look of intense hatred towards the glass box and his eyes widened, flabbergasted that Barri hadn't at least raised his head.

Humiliated and crushed, the ex-assistant unclipped a pass from his shirt pocket then dropped it. With the same deliberate movement, he picked up his car keys like an amusement arcade grabber then mechanically opened fingers so that they too dropped to the floor while placing one foot on the pass as he pulled his chair slowly back. He stood erect, throwing his head back and up before walking silently through the office, the woman and guard one step behind. The assistant's face remained purple but his tightly clasped lips were white.

Barri's face was granite but his eyes shined. His assistant's betrayal would have been swiftly dealt with and without personal involvement anyway but, it had come when he was able to feel its full force. Deviousness had been waved like a trophy in his face. Whereas Barri had successfully vanquished his father's shadow, his father's nemesis had cast a fresh one. Mandrake's email was brief and without a mocking tone except for its title but nevertheless, it freshly opened Barri to the fact that his perception of everyday matters couldn't be relied upon. Betrayal was also now associated with Caprice and his feelings. *She left me without fulfilling her end of the bargain. I was unprepared.*

'Good riddance to bad rubbish!' Barri wouldn't miss his assistant but when he tried to think the same of Caprice, he knew his emotions and judgment were clouded. The familiar roller-coaster ride began when he had so sorely hoped it had stopped for good. Barri's eyes glistened as he stared out of his glass box; they felt gritty. They began to water profusely but he averted them and caught sight of a discarded Advent calendar near his window. The calendar was empty and propped against a box of Radburn truffles. He remembered trying to punch his finger through a cardboard door when the office had been deserted. His eyes smarted again.

'I suppose I should say something.' A yellow post-it note had one word on it: *"Christmas,"* to remind him that the office would close for a couple of days. Barri glowered at his ex-assistant's desk; vacated by the one person within his business he'd relied on for two years to be his mouth-piece, his puppet. He vowed never to be so foolish again.

After another phone call to Personnel, Barri was ready to face a sea of faces with worried expressions. Although phones had been mostly silent, as soon as people saw Barri emerge many pressed buttons to ensure *Voicemail* was activated. Norman, the janitor and the security guard appeared. Again, Barri nodded in acknowledgement then went to corner desks outside his glass box where he sat, lifted one leg slightly so that he could face his staff but also observe the janitor and guard. The two men approached either end of the ex-assistant's desk, stooped and picked it up. There was total silence as everybody watched the desk ceremoniously carried out thereby removing all traces of the ex-assistant.

'It's half past four!' Barri announced. His voice was confident but its customary arrogance now absent. He then searched the sea of faces but didn't feel any of the warmth associated with final working hours before Christmas. The office atmosphere was stagnant. All eyes were upon the boss, behind them the expectation of an unwelcome business announcement or even worse, redundancy.

'Now, if you had gone at three o'clock like I was expecting you to then you wouldn't have witnessed the departure of someone who had blighted the good name of Radburn.' Barri then attempted to smile, which encouraged a nervous flutter.

A stout man asked the burning question on everyone's mind: 'What did he do? It was a bit harsh to get rid of him just before Christmas.'

Barri turned his chin to look at buttons holding a taut shirt together, the wearer had eaten more than a fair share of chocolate samples over a long period of time. 'I won't go into details,' Barri replied with enough solemnity to discourage further interrogation. 'It would have been a serious error to continue to employ someone who had so clearly gone against the best interests of the business.' He then paused to add weight to his words before adding: 'If you all do your jobs within your remit then there's nothing any of you need worry about. *His* misdemeanours came back to bite him.'

'So has his role gone then?' Another man, slim and suave with a stubble head, raised the question hoping it meant a new opportunity.

Again, Barri looked around the office before he replied: 'No, but his desk has.' Stating the obvious caused amusement. At that point Barri knew that his staff had little recourse to be upset by the expulsion, most of them looked relieved. A few had surmised that the public expulsion was meant to be a warning shot.

'Anyway...' Barri then continued. 'What happened is

unfortunate and it will mean extra work for some. We will have to tighten procedures after the holidays which, brings me back to the only thing you need worry about...' again, Barri paused and because his facial expression didn't flinch, the level of nervous expectancy around him increased. 'That there should be no further delay to your departure. Go home and enjoy Christmas.' A group sigh escaped then, the stout man raised his voice:

'Some of us are back in on Friday!' he tried to sound jovial. Barri shook his head.

'No, I've asked that the office be closed until next week so you've all got an extra day. One person received his punishment today for letting me and the business down, the rest will be rewarded.' Immediately, all remaining expressions of concern vanished, replaced by joyous surprise.

The ex-assistant wouldn't be forgotten. Wagging tongues would be busy before and after the holidays but Barri dismissed all thought of him as soon as he put foot back inside his safe haven. The stout man with bursting buttons leaned over and said to the suave, stubble-headed guy: 'He's like a different man! I'd heard rumours from Processing that he'd finally learnt to open his mouth.'

'Perhaps he's grown a pair at last.' Both men smirked. Barri had executed a daunting duty but speaking to the whole office hadn't been as uncomfortable as anticipated.

After being escorted from Radburn Confectionery the ex-assistant's searing anger turned to numbed shock. He reeled from the brutality of the previous ten-minutes, so publically stripped of the tools of his trade in front of perceived inferiors. Faced with a full car park but no means to leave it other than by shanks' pony, the bitter young man was forced to walk through rows of cars but, by the time he left it his head was held higher. 'I'll be back soon!' He had no doubt that he would, as Mandrake's right-hand man. 'There's only one place I can go now. I'll have a word with that Phestoz bloke then I'll phone Mandrake.' With each step, his optimism grew and his intentions crystallized. 'Looks like I'll have to take my changes to Radburn up a notch, a more radical change to staffing.' This thought cheered him immensely.

The previous evening, Phestoz had contemplated his checkerboard moves, greatly aided by a bottle of the finest Russian vodka. He was now fractious and had for the last hour sought the solace of a leather wing-back in Whiskers public bar. Copious amounts of black sweet coffee settled his hangover. From his vantage point he watched guests come and go but not before mentally dismantling them. He watched for signs of weakness, people-watching being a favourite past time plus, it helped obliterate a caustic memory of Fernlea's lounge.

After four, the bar almost emptied except for a few drinkers who waited for friends who were still working. Mephisto noticed a young man enter but didn't recognise him as Mandrake's snitch. The man ordered a drink then pulled-up a chair.

'Mr Phestoz!' the young man snorted with false and over-exuberant cheerfulness. 'I was hoping to find you.'

'Why? Do I know you?' Phestoz snorted too but with derision; his time for musing rudely interrupted.

'I recognised you as Mandrake's associate.'

'No you're mistaken, Mandrake is my friend,' the wily old man objected, rolling the "*r*" in "friend" with exaggerated articulacy.

'Then, as one of Mandrake's friends to another...' mimicking the old man's emphasis, 'I hope we'll have opportunity to do business together in the near future.'

'You do?'

'Most definitely, after I take up my new position at Radburn's, I'll need a good place to hold interviews.'

'This is the first I've heard of interviews, what for?'

'You must know, for the positions at Mandrake's new office of course!'

The corners of the old man's mouth twitched upwards but only for a second. He quickly disguised amusement by then

214

pursing his thin lips but at no time did he look at the young man. Steely eyes roamed the room but were acutely aware of the young man's every move and expression, gifted with periphery vision that had taken years to perfect. 'Mandrake has already mentioned that HE will be using my facilities for visitors. Your own interview has been confirmed then?' The uninvited guest was momentarily lost for words.

Phestoz brushed imaginary tobacco ash from his crossed trouser leg, an old habit hard to change after sacrificing one of his vices for the sake of changes to UK smoking laws. Not being able to enjoy a slender cheroot in a public drinking hole had been the only downside to ownership of a chain of clubs and a hotel. His body language distracted the bitter young man who had tried to swallow resurfacing anger by reaching for his drink and taking a large gulp to keep it down. 'There's no need for an interview; Mandrake will be giving ME the prime position at Radburn's.'

'Are you absolutely sure? I'm sure I heard him say that he already had someone in mind.' Phestoz couldn't resist an opportunity to stir troubled waters.

'I don't understand.'

'No, it appears you don't, perhaps you should speak to Mandrake to clarify matters.'

'That's exactly what I was about to do.' The bewildered young man then reached inside his jacket for his mobile before remembering it had been confiscated. His look of panic gave away his predicament. In a second gulp, he finished his drink.

'Have you lost something?' Phestoz looked at the young man's troubled face.

'Eh, no... I must have left my phone at the office.'

'There's a phone at the reception desk and I'm sure the receptionist will let you use it, if you ask nicely enough.' Phestoz continued to brush away imaginary ash but this time six inches above his crossed leg and in the direction of the worried young man.

A few minutes later, the seat next to him was occupied by a

distraught and haggard looking man; youth having faded between his steps from the reception desk back to the bar. 'You look as though you could do with a drink,' Phestoz observed with concealed amusement.

'Aye, aye, I could do with 'un, that's decent of you.'

Phestoz also noticed the drop in the young man's accent. 'No, you know where the bar is.' Phestoz sniffed loudly but although the ex-assistant looked directly at the bar he didn't see it. Phestoz then remembered what his friend had said about the young man and it blew away all cobwebs of his previous nights over-indulgence. 'What did Mandrake say?'

With a purple face, the young man stated feebly: 'I didn't get to speak to 'im, too busy to come to' phone but 'is secretary told me that nothin' was agreed.' In an effort to make his dilemma seem more acceptable the young man then added: 'He'll be in touch once the deal has gone through.'

'I wouldn't be so sure. IF, it does go through then Mandrake will want to hire someone new.'

'How do you know?'

'He told me.'

It was the ex-assistant's turn to now experience betrayal. He could have burst into tears but bitter anger overrode them. 'What a fool!'

'Who is?' Is it you or, Mandrake?' Phestoz already knew the answer.

'Mandrake...'; the defeated young man whispered hoarsely. 'I could have told 'im things about Barri he didn't know, things that could have ensured the deal went through.'

Phestoz's spine then stiffened. 'Let me get you that drink.' He remained seated but raised a bony forefinger, which brought an alert bartender with the alacrity of a greyhound released from a racing trap. The bartender hadn't yet received a Christmas bonus but was expecting one.

Hours later, the defunct employee suffered the humility of public transport after remembering taxi-drivers charged double at Christmas. He didn't want to be taken advantage of again but was forced to sit with the working class. He chose an upper-deck seat positioned behind spiralling steps.

Bus windows were steamed by hot breath from coughing passengers. Two stops into the journey everyone heard the loud slurring of a passenger too drunk to care how much he paid in fare. He pulled coat pockets inside-out. A sound like gunfire indicated most of his change hit bus windows, then, as the bus moved forward, he decided to climb the spiral steps.

'Whoa there...' He slipped half-way and belched loudly. Everyone on the upper deck hoped it would deter him but where there's no sense, there's no feeling. The drunkard continued to climb, singing and swearing, until two hands gripped metal rails at the top of the stairs, his arms so outstretched that there was no sign of a body beneath. Everyone on the upper deck waited with dread.

There were just two seats available, one next to a bald man opposite the stairs and the other, next to the ex-assistant. They would have no escape. The bald man was unaware of the drunkard's options, too busy swirling the back of a coat sleeve around the window so that he didn't miss his stop.

After an age, the drunkard's head and shoulders appeared and after another age, his upper torso, unkempt and unbuttoned. His coat was flapped open, half-way down his arms and he glared at it then, hiccuped so violently that he had to quickly grip a metal rail to prevent falling. The bus driver's keen use of brakes didn't help and all passengers gasped as the drunkard seemed to dip and his arms over-extend, with fingers slipping around greasy metal. The bus lurched forward again to repeat the process. The drunkard swung like a rag doll. He clung with two fingers to the metal rail. His loose arm flayed and his head swayed back before he yanked his body up and over the last step but as he did so his head was thrown forward to release a torrent of vomit. It landed on top of the bald man's shiny pate. The busy bald man was soaked. Steam from hot beer arose from his bald pate and he held out his hands and arms but didn't say a word. The smell was atrocious and once excess beer had been ejaculated, the drunkard slipped slowly back down the steps and sloped off at the next stop.

The ex-assistant considered it a lucky escape until he remembered that in future a bus would be his only transport. He tried then to feebly hold on to one small satisfaction, he'd successfully ejaculated his own venom and it had spilled easily into Phestoz's receptive ears. Those ears had received a disillusioned man's speculations. Booze loosened lips to release information thought to be of no further use but to Phestoz it had been new cards for his game.

He'd heard about expenses for woman's clothing, including underwear and also how someone employed at Barri's home was listed as a cash payment. Then, the police visit and inquiry, whether Barri had a daughter, a child somewhere. Part of Radburn House's history included the death of a little girl during a birthday party.

After venom had been discharged, its bearer had quickly sobered whereas its recipient had made fresh speculations. Latest information joined Judith's gossip - Barri's tendencies for children particularly a redhead, this being the one physical feature Judith remembered about a child fleeing from a tree-house.

While the sobered assistant reeled from a stench of vomit, Barri took a stroll to a taxi-rank outside the train station. He relieved his wallet of twenty pounds then held it between two fingers while an eager-eyed taxi driver looked at it. A promise of reward without working for it yielded an interesting result. The driver remembered going to Radburn House and a redheaded beauty who'd occupied his back seat.

'Yeah, she got out here but instead of going into the station she turned and walked back the way we'd come. I watched her in my rear-view mirror. A few minutes later, after I'd picked up another fare, I saw her walking along the road to the left of the junction. Why ask for the station if she wanted dropping-off somewhere else?'

So, Caprice could still be in Mistlethrop, but where?

23. Dangerous Assault Courses

On Christmas morning, wrapping paper was ripped and scrunched into balls then deposited in recycling bins. Tired parents dosed themselves with Bucks Fizz or something stronger after struggling with children too excited to sleep past six a.m. A drink wouldn't help when navigating dangerous assault courses covering living-room floors but it would lull parents into the belief that they'd given their children true Christmas happiness. It had been ripped out of each carefully-wrapped present. Credit card statements would wait until a new year.

Barri's father had once used Christmas as an opportunity to have a good meal, wine and smoke cigars. His mother hadn't hid her disappointment, another day without any spirit of Christmas except that in her glass. On this particular Christmas Day, Barri stayed in bed until early afternoon then fixed himself a cheese sandwich. As with all celebrated holidays it was just another day for him but this morning his head was clear and he felt fit to burst. 'Perhaps I won't have to spend the rest of the day alone?' He'd slept soundly; making up for a previous night of sulky disquiet when he'd dreamt of flying inches above Mistlethrop's streets, a giant owl with outspread wings.

In the meantime, his ex-assistant had imploded into a white-heat ball so intense that he thought that his insides were eating him. Antacid couldn't ease his burning. Christmas Eve's events would leave emotional scars.

For gainfully employed Radburn staff, they had the extra joy of not having to return to work until the following week. Their Christmas would seem never-ending, a see-saw of gluttony, alcohol and television repeats. They would later complain that it was over before they had a chance to do anything worthwhile.

For people who would pass the day alone and lonely, it was the worst time of year. If they could, they'd eagerly swap peace and empty fantasies for a blazing argument with someone who loved them, all, that is, except for the terminally independent and there were three among their number, the ex-assistant, Phestoz and Barri. One spent his day in twisted torment and on the loo because of an overdose of antacid. One waited quietly for the day to end so that he could renew his fact-finding. The other, took a long slow drive around Mistlethrop.

Main roads were quiet but side-streets were dotted with children on new bikes, rollerblades, skate boards or peddle-cars. Christmas lights twinkled from every window; including houses whose inhabitants had gone elsewhere so as to fool would-be thieves. As Barri drove, he searched for clues, trying to put himself into the shoes of a young woman. 'Where would she go to at Christmas?'

He'd driven a dozen times along the road the taxi-driver had recommended. If he had branched-off to take a narrow left side-street then, he would have come to the Hebble Mill complex at its end. Instead, he drove past and followed the main road until it bore right and came to a T-junction. As his car stopped at Give-way lines he saw a bus stop. Barri looked at the worn sign, made a mental note of numbers and had to park-up to use *Google* search. Two services travelled through Mistlethrop towards Macefield but took different routes, one over The Tops and one through villages. He drove back to town, parked and walked along the cobbles at the back of The Varsity. He spent a few minutes gazing with longing at the stones.

When back at Radburn House, Barri closely examined a map spread across his dining room table. A bottle of red wine helped ease tumultuous yearning while he used a black marker to make rings. 'You're somewhere on this map but where?' He knew that he would have to phone B&B's plus the Whiskers orange-mouthed receptionist.

As daylight faded, Barri's fingers were covered with blotches of ink. The stains made him feel closer to Caprice, so close that after most of his wine he abandoned his marker to roll a bare arm across the map as a blotter. It was a flimsy connection but that was all he had.

Later, in the shower, he tried to scrub the marks away, every movement a sensual pleasure, rubbing a nailbrush so hard across skin that his arm was lobster-red. The pleasure continued. Seated in a comfortable leather niche in the annexe he laid his arm along the cold arm of the settee, sitting where she'd once sat. His skin's soreness sent electric shocks of pain so pleasurable that Barri groaned softly. He laid back his head, allowing his vision to haze in the blackness of a blank TV screen. Then, he allowed his imagination to run wild.

Caprice's Christmas hadn't been so thrilling. She had withdrawn from the world, albeit in a modern apartment decorated with luxurious furniture and fittings to entice the right kind of buyer but nevertheless, an ivory tower. She'd isolated herself from society and as such had to hide any sign of inhabitation in case of unexpected visitors. Unlike Rosebud within her tower, Caprice wasn't waiting for a prince but there was a constant threat that she could be found by a troll.

Her provisions had been bought with great trepidation on Christmas Eve having roamed only as far as a mini-market on the outskirts of Mistlethrop. While procuring them, an unexpected visitor had called briefly at the Mill to look at a temporary pied-à-terre, Radburn House being an ultimate goal. It would be necessary to have a property close to the centre of Mistlethrop. Whiskers Hotel had drawbacks; noisy people too close for comfort; privacy being a valuable commodity.

Christmas Day offered peace and not knowing of the previous day's visitor to the Mill, Caprice felt safe. During the previous few days she'd grown stronger, *or, is it I feel less afraid?* Objectivity increased, the uncertainty of her predicament slotted into an acceptable place. She ate a solitary meal of thickly sliced turkey with Aunt Bessie's mash, nuked in a microwave then smothered in gravy made from granules and boiling water. To celebrate Christmas she had enough wine in a mini-bottle to provide a glass and a half but it did little to cheer her. Outside and in, the apartment was quiet and so cold that she had to wear a coat and scarf. Caprice was one of the terminally alone and lonely.

Looking down on the world on a day when people shared precious moments, it was easy for Caprice to shed tears; some out of self-pity, some out of anger that her life could have been different if only Phestoz hadn't met her mother. This maudlin train preoccupied her as she picked at pieces of dry turkey. She then used the back of a fork to slowly flatten mashed potato into a thin pancake before pushing the plate away.

'Perhaps I should have bought a large bottle.' She rued her decision of restraint then thought of Barri and how he would cork a bottle so that he could finish it another day. She smiled. 'What will he be doing right now? Will he be sitting alone at that huge table and drinking wine with his dinner? Will he put a cork in the bottle so that he can save it for Boxing Day, or, will he let loose for once and drink a whole bottle?' The image brought another wry smile to Caprice's face.

Her wine, her distance from Barri, the passing of time, imagining how Christmas Day could and should be celebrated, all came into play. Caprice did what most people do when feelings have settled, her mind wandered back to times when petty resentments hadn't yet festered. 'What if I hadn't met him?' It troubled her, and then, she was consumed with warm gratitude. 'What if he hadn't been there to rescue me from those horrible hoodies?' A fresh downfall of tears released her loneliness. She had a hankering to see cobbles again, return to the moment when she'd opened her eyes to see a blurred vision above her. 'Was I right to run away?' That was what she had done, was going to do. 'If only he'd shown his tender side at the hotel.' She'd glimpsed it once when he spoke of the girl on the stool. She recognised a shell, having carried her own around with her for years, not allowing emotions to surface until they'd smothered her. *My heart had almost stopped beating at Macefield but what is it telling me now?*

The troubled young woman looked at a tiny ballerina figure propped against her empty wine bottle then, a folded paper next to it. It was a copy of a letter she'd written before leaving Macefield having taken great pains to ensure she kept a copy. It had summed up her raison d'être and she had to continually remind herself of it. Having the letter was a connection to the only other person who had been there for her when she needed someone.

"Dear Kim,

Thank you for putting up with me but too much has happened for me to stay. I couldn't face people and their wagging tongues, despite now knowing I'm no longer alone in this world and you are there for me. I don't want you to get involved with Mephisto's games but I fear that if I stay then you will, sooner or later.

I cannot hide in your house forever and now that I've faced myself, having sunk lower than I ever thought possible, I have to look for that fresh start I so desperately need. I won't say where I'm going, just that maybe, one day, we will see each other again but I'm afraid it won't be a for a very long time, not until I've built a secure life for myself.

I've been thinking over what we talked about the other night, the music box and when you told me the story of Carousel. I didn't realise the box's music was from our father's, my real father's favourite musical, I always thought it was just a fairground tune. I'd like to think there was a Star-Keeper, someone who watches everything that happens from the heavens and every now and then he intervenes. My only solace used to be in playing my violin and I could escape to wherever I imagined I wanted to go. Now, I will think of the Star-Keeper whenever I play because I'm convinced there was more than coincidence in our finding each other.

You told me of how a father asks for permission from the Star-Keeper to be sent down from heaven for just one day to make amends for the mistakes he made in life. He got to see the unhappy daughter he never knew and even though she couldn't see or hear him he could ease her pain. You told the story well and it stayed with me. Maybe us getting to know each other, the music boxes, were our father's way of easing pain.

While you were at work yesterday, I searched on the internet and Carousel's final words made-up my mind, "You've got to go out and find it for yourselves"

As for happiness, I'll never find that here, I know that now. I have to become my own Star-Keeper. Please don't look for me. I will find you when I am ready to.

With love
Caprice X"

24. The Lesser Evil

Whereas Barri was a murderer, driven by hunger for physical sensory relief, Judith was a lesser murderer of sorts. In her own way, she crushed everything that didn't suit her natural order of things but kept emotions constantly on her sleeve; they drove her. Although she controlled them as best she could while working, they constantly bubbled beneath her surface. She watched, much like Phestoz, for evidence that people were inferior, thereby proving by default that she had to be superior and only then, would a nagging, small inner voice quieten.

Her husband, who suffered from small-man-syndrome and proud to be married to a younger woman, acquiesced to her every whim but had the mistaken idea that he was in charge. Every few months, she had him ripping out their house interior to install a do-it-yourself project with the emphasis on cheap rather than quality. Decorating and redecorating, tinkering with plumbing, hammering and climbing ladders, all done with determination so that his wife could compete with her neighbours. All their efforts were tasteless and didn't last long, following trends Judith saw in other people's houses then thought of as her own.

Working on Boxing Day meant double-time plus a day in lieu so Judith left her kids at home with her better half. He sprawled at an awkward angle on a two-seater settee, one of three stuffed into a small lounge. He watched a wall-mounted TV hanging over a hole in the wall with an aquarium in it. His wife had asked that all signs of Christmas be packed into boxes before she returned. It was cramped enough inside the small room.

As well as extra pay, Judith looked forward to unwanted gifts. The Old Dears would hand over anything that cluttered their limited personal space. Judith could fill her car and at the same time commit a charitable act. Boxes of chocolates unable to be eaten by dentures, scented candles unable to be lit because of Fernlea health and safety policy, hardly-worn clothes replaced with new and boxes of toiletries. *They don't want them so why should they go to a charity shop. What a waste!* Chocolate would be eaten and everything else sold on eBay.

Boxing Day morning was painfully bright but the sun's heat hadn't reached Mistlethrop, it sent blinding shafts through branches to be reflected off windows. Driving anywhere was a challenge. By eleven-thirty sun hid behind swirls of two-toned clouds.

The tree-house beckoned Barri. He would take a short stroll to look at it then reminisce about a redheaded girl, optimistic that he could repeat that pleasure, possibly that day. With a thick coat collar pulled high and, wearing a sheepskin hat with hanging earflaps, Barri trod a familiar path along Radburn's expansive front lawn. Air was crisp and icy but warm and foggy when exhaled. He didn't hear children playing in the park but Judith did. Barri didn't spend long at the tree. Once at the base, all he could think about was: *She should be waiting at the dining room table with a hot meal.*

Children's yelps of enjoyment could be heard as far as Fernlea. Judith was in the hallway, preparing a wheelchair for a frail old woman with wasted limbs and hands curled into arthritic claws. The self-righteous carer poked her head out the door, heard yelps then espied Barri in his front garden. *He's there again. I knew it! As soon as children come out, he's there watching them.* She couldn't wait to find out what Barri was doing. She manhandled the old lady into the wheelchair then checked her phone to ensure it had enough battery life. *I'll film him.* She imagined him being dragged out of Radburn in handcuffs then she gurgled with glee. If she hadn't been delayed so by the old lady then she would have seen Barri walk back to the side of his house and then heard his car drive away.

Another well-wrapped figure strolled along Dandelion View. His car was parked near a closed chip shop. He was so wrapped

226

in layers with thick coat collar pulled high and a sheepskin hat with earflaps pulled down low that at first glance it would have been easy to think it was Barri but, there were subtle differences. His height may have been the same (and he looked a lot bulkier in a thick coat and hat) but stiff, skeletal legs hardly filled his trousers which flapped with each step. Barri wouldn't have worn suit trousers unless he was dressed for an occasion, or narrow-laced shoes so highly polished that their toes looked like mirrors.

By the time Judith had manoeuvred an occupied wheelchair through doors and down a ramp, she panicked when she couldn't see Barri. Putting all her weight behind the chair, she strained along the driveway then came to an abrupt halt once she'd broached Dandelion View. She saw Barri standing on the opposite side of the road and talking to children on the play-frame. He had his back towards her but she could see it was him and, quickly reaching into her pocket, she pulled out her phone and began recording.

Phestoz had stopped to watch children playing, armed with Judith's gossip and the ex-assistant's venom, his interest was drawn to a little girl with red hair and a long scarf. Eagle-eyed and a stickler for details, he'd quickly fathomed that woollen strands on Radburn's tree were from the girl's scarf. One end was bare except for straggly tufts.

Inky had seen the stranger from the corner of his eye as he tried to load glass marbles into a new pop-gun. He'd intended to get one over the road and hit the tree-house but first the stranger would have to move on so that he wouldn't get into trouble. The boy laid his gun flat on the play-frame and waited impatiently, peering at a horrible face hidden within a huge hat then recognising it. 'Weren't you here the other day?' Inky shouted, which was just the opening Phestoz needed to come close to wire mesh. He looked up at the beefy boy but his peripheral was set on a girl who had walked near, sat down and dangled her legs over the play-frame side.

She looks so like Caprice when she was little. Phestoz sighed

227

then replied: 'Yes, just before Christmas, very observant!'

Rosebud was both repulsed and fascinated by the old man's face. He looked like evil incarnate but his hat was so comical that it prevented her from being too scared. She wondered how old he was.

'Why were you looking at that house over there?' Inky didn't want his friends to see that anything or anyone scared him but his sixth-sense told him there was something definitely not right with the man. By then, Awesome had joined them, he hadn't liked the way the old man had been looking at Rosebud.

'I'm thinking of buying it.'

'What about the tree-house? What will happen to that?' Rosebud ventured in a timid voice. She looked with longing and regret at the object of her dreams. Now Phestoz turned his full attention to the girl and both Inky and Awesome wished she hadn't said anything.

'It will stay.' He examined Rosebud's features, his sunken eyes hidden in shade beneath the rim of his hat but their pupils pinpointed with light.

'Good,' Rosebud stated, relieved.

'Of course, you, all of you, would be welcome to use it whenever you liked.'

Judith caught the back of Phestoz on video but she had also panned upwards and filmed the children. She'd been careful to balance the phone in her right hand, using her wrist propped against the wheelchair to hold it still. Then, she raised her hand to span the scene. It had been a problem to push the wheelchair but once she had mastered momentum she was able to guide it with her left hand, pushing her thick torso against it while keeping one eye on her phone screen. Phestoz's voice didn't travel well across the road and a passing car muffled it but Judith distinctly heard Barri invite the children to his tree-house. She hoped her phone had picked it up.

'It's too cold!' the Old Dear complained into her muffler.

'What?'

'It's too cold, take me back.'

228

Judith clucked her tongue but was grateful not to proceed, far too interested in what the children would do next so that she could add to her film. To her perplexity Barri decided to walk further along Dandelion View away from the children. She popped her phone back into her pocket then turned the wheelchair around. 'What a bloody fuss for five minutes!' Judith hissed between her teeth.

'What's that?'

'I said, lucky for us we were only out for five minutes!'

'Yes dear, maybe you can push me around the conservatory instead.'

'Great!' Judith hissed but then had an idea and quickly applied the handbrake. 'I won't be a minute,' she was ready to leap away but then bent and shouted into the old woman's face: 'I'll be right back in a minute!'

'Where are you going?' but Judith didn't reply, she'd darted across the road then thrown herself against wire mesh.

'Hey kids, what did he say to you?'

Inky span round with a loaded gun in hand then dropped it guiltily. All the children recognised the mad woman from the home. 'Nothing,' Inky stated.

'What did he say? It's important.'

'Nowt really.'

Armoured poked his head around one of the frame's posts. He could be needed but didn't know in what capacity with regard to a threatening grown-up.

'Where do you live?'

'Why do you want to know that?' Awesome got scared and it was infectious.

'The police will need to know.'

As soon as police were mentioned, Inky grabbed his weapon and shouted: 'We've done nothing wrong!' Then, at his mates: 'Come on! Let's get away from her, she's off her head!' The children clambered down and fled. Judith crossed to the other side of the road, visibly annoyed but she had a fall-back plan:

'My kids will know them,' and she tapped her phone with

stubby fingers. She would first send the video to her husband so that he could get her kids to identify the children. She would also show it to the police so that they could see and hear what kind of predator Barri really was. 'Now, I've got evidence. Not such a waste of five minutes after all.'

'What's that dear? What were you doing over there?'

'I said: they should change that fence, not that safe if it falls.'

'You know what your trouble is? You care too much for other people.'

'That's right Aggie. At least someone appreciates me.'

Phestoz had continued his stroll along Dandelion View, not aware of Judith and her madness, but later he crossed the road to return along the opposite side. He returned to his car. *Looks like that awful woman may have been right,* he mused as he clunked his seat belt. *First, I must deal with Caprice, then Barri. It's a shame that buffoon of an assistant got himself fired. He could have been useful. I could have asked him to place incriminating material on Barri's office computer. Looks like I'll have to get Purl to do it.*

Later that day, much to Judith's smug satisfaction, the police paid another visit to Radburn House but this time Barri was at home. The snoop hung around front windows waiting excitedly for Barri to be dragged out in handcuffs and thrown into the back of a car. She was disappointed that she couldn't see around the far side of Radburn, despite opening a window as far as she could.

The police were satisfied that the man in Judith's video wasn't Barri but had to pay him a visit anyway. Children they'd visited described a different man. Barri had been at The Varsity where the landlord and staff could vouch for him if necessary. 'I don't understand why you're here,' Barri said to two policemen whose eyes roamed around Radburn's parlour with a mixture of envy and awe.

'You've rubbed someone up the wrong way,' one of the officers replied. 'We can't say who, but this is the second report we've received from this person and we have a duty to follow it up. Turns out that there is someone hanging around and he's been watching and talking to the children. It's looking suspicious. He may also have been hanging around your garden, probably using your tree-house to start up a conversation so keep a look out for anyone loitering.'

'The report hasn't come from a man has it?' Barri was keen to ask, thinking of his disgraced assistant.

The policemen looked at each other before one of them said: 'No, we can tell you that much. Is there a reason you think it's a man?'

'It's just that I had to fire someone on Tuesday and he could hold a grudge.'

'Is he an older man? It could be him trying to drop you in it?'

'No, he's in his twenties.'

'It's not him then. Like I say, keep a look-out.'

'What about the woman, what are you going to do about her? She can't go around pointing fingers. I've a business to run and if nonsense like this gets out it will have serious repercussions, not only for me personally but on the working population if Radburn's name is dragged through mud.'

The officers looked at each other again, but neither gave clues to their private opinion. Judith was known to them. She'd battled with neighbours and moving house had only given her new people to have a go at. 'Leave this with us, we'll talk to her.'

'Tell her that if there is any repeat then I'll sue for slander.' Barri was livid, clenching and unclenching his hands. The officers couldn't blame him. He had every right to be mad about allegations of sexual deviancy.

Not only was there a mysterious trouble-maker but Barri had only just discovered that an officer had been to his business. He thought of Purl. *I can't think of anyone else who would try to ruin me using underhand methods. It won't be Caprice. She has no reason to do it.* It was another betrayal.

To his knowledge, Barri had never been suspected of crime and this type of crime sickened him. A police visit was like having a bucket of cold water thrown over him. It instantly washed away any desire for murder but, as soon as the police had gone, his yearning returned with overwhelming urgency. Barri groaned in abject misery and slumped to the floor with the burden of unseen forces. For once, he couldn't run to the office, sit in the annexe or be anywhere close to the dining room. It was as though sections of his house had become no-go areas and it had now over-spilled to his office. Barri's coolness deserted him.

Judith saw a police car back out of Radburn's driveway but it was too dark to see its occupants.

'When are we going to see Judith Gormey?' one of the officers asked his partner.

'Leave it till after New Year. It can wait, finding that man is more important. We will thank her for the info but let her know just how dangerous it can be if she shoots her mouth off. The kids' description though was something else, wasn't it?'

'Sounded like a Bogey Man, but that's kids for you.'

'One thing I've learned mate is that Bogey Men come in many forms and some of them wear a skirt.'

25. Getting Ready to Usher-in

Leading up to New Year, a time for change and resolutions, six people plotted and waited. Each was a coin to be tilted on its side, spun between thumb and finger to whirl like Bugs Bunny's Tasmanian devil. The danger of plotting in isolation is that coins could collide. New Year's Eve was the timeframe they shared when some would never spin again.

Caprice sat in her ivory tower and waited, her plan was to finally escape a shadow and it meant leaving Mistlethrop on New Year's Eve. She knew Phestoz would be looking for her but at New Year he would be far too busy with his entertainment empire. This would be her game and a crafty jump over him on her checkerboard would leave him unprepared, she could then sweep him from her life. Alone, and with only ivory-coloured walls to look at, she now questioned her heart and where it should reside. She resented self-imposed confinement. Open spaces called to her, freedom to walk among people without guilty secrets and without her turmoil of inner cowering.

Although Mandrake had confidence in his daughter's capabilities, he had Plan B. up his sleeve. If need be; he'd play a dirtier game and Phestoz had come up with a gem. At first it seemed a step too far but when the old man had spoken about a police visit to Radburn and why, Mandrake wiped out a chalk line between ethical business practice and destroying a person who stood between him and progress. He was as devilish as his friend except his physical being didn't portray clues of twisted machinations.

Phestoz knew how to word a suggestion so that it progressed from an idea to fact, more easily achieved by phrasing it as a challenge. 'I didn't realise that the world of cakes and biscuits was so intriguing. You're the J.R. of the sugar business but

233

without the Stetson.'

Mandrake appreciated the comparison but suspected it was disguised sarcasm and defended his choice of enterprise: 'UK confectionery made five-point-one billion last year. Don't underestimate it. Selling sugar is better for the planet and its people than selling oil.'

Phestoz looked surprised but after reflection: 'So as a leader in your business you take no responsibility for rising obesity then?'

'Too right I don't. I can't control what people choose to put in their mouths.'

'With the acquisition of Radburn's you could have greater control of who puts it on their plate. If you don't act quickly enough then you'll find Radburn's have control. Perhaps the real intrigue will be if you are able to destroy the man without destroying the business.'

'It's ironic,' Mandrake scoffed. 'Mothers warn their children not to take sweets from strangers and there's Barri owning the whole sweet shop.'

Phestoz was confident that Purl would eventually humiliate herself. Then, while she was still raw and smarting he would use her to plant the gem he'd presented to her father so plausibly.

Barri was physically active, desperately hoping to override manic phases by returning to the comfort of well-worn obsessive-compulsive habits. As such, he had to execute his plan in defined steps. It meant visiting each circled location on his map and he'd been busy. There were now just two to visit and he found himself precariously balanced between feverish craving and wanton despair that his search could take longer. The latter worry he pushed to the back of his mind which, was so cramped with unwanted thoughts and emotions that he felt fit to implode.

Purl was also active. She'd initiated her plan on Christmas Eve but left all physical activity to lesser mortals paid to do it. She would host a New Years Eve party at Whiskers Hotel. Its former ballroom would be the stage on which she would enact a play. It didn't take much to convince Phestoz that it was a good idea. 'Leave it all to me. You'll make a huge profit instead of pennies. Why host a small-town affair only a few of your lonely hotel guests will attend? With my contacts, I'll put this place on the map and...' Purl smiled then giggled before saying: 'Barrington George the Third will look back on it as the day he met the woman who changed his life.'

Phestoz looked down his needle-nose with syrupy fake admiration, raising a wispy brow that looked as though barbed-wire grew through it. 'Of course Purl, my place is entirely at your disposal but aren't you planning this a little too close to the knuckle?'

'Had you already planned a New Year party?'

'I had. I'd advertised it in the local press but, if you want to spend your father's money and can put my efforts to shame then, please feel free to do so.'

Purl clapped her hands like an excited three-year-old. 'You've already done some of the work. I'll do the rest.'

The clever young woman used her many contacts to take the party to new heights but, timing was everything. Guests had to be notified and she insisted her friends abandon plans and join her, which they did. 'Why pass up an offer of free food, drink and accommodation in a backwater hotel surrounded by scenic hills?' The Mandrakes would foot the bill.

Purl was keen to take centre stage with Barri as her leading man but she had to control scenery, lighting and supporting cast. The excited painted-doll wanted a show and it would be spectacular. As is so often the case with people with too much time and money, she fixated on a picture in her head. 'Barri won't know what hit him but first, I must ensure he comes to my party.'

Personal invites were quickly couriered to recipients; another expense. As an extra push Purl paid a printing firm to produce A4 posters which were distributed to all local stores. 'I'm doing this for the business so I'm sure Daddy will treat it as a business expense.' Mandrake wasn't aware of his daughter's extravagance. Bills wouldn't arrive until after New Year.

Barri's invite was worded differently and Purl laboured to ensure it was one he couldn't refuse. *"All recipients of Mistlethrop Civic Trust Awards are cordially invited to attend a New Year party at Whiskers Hotel. This will be an opportunity to celebrate local achievements at the end of a difficult economic year. As a major contributor to our community, your support will be highly publicised thereby demonstrating your continued interest in promoting Mistlethrop as an enterprising area for both business and conservation."* A business angle would obligate Barri to personally attend.

A courier had made several trips on Boxing Day but hadn't grumbled, grateful for an unexpected opportunity to make cash. He'd shuffled from foot-to-foot on the step outside Radburn's front door. Purl had been implicit. 'This invite MUST be delivered as soon as possible!'

Barri had accepted a silver envelope then shoved it into a coat pocket. The invite remained untouched and forgotten until he set out for his penultimate search. 'What's this?' Barri looked at his watch to check the date then clucked his tongue. 'I'm in no mood for a party and I doubt I will be tomorrow.' Then, Barri thought of his map. 'If all goes according to plan then I will want to celebrate and, I should be seen somewhere public.' Barri warmed to possibilities. 'Perhaps I'll need a higher public profile? I handled that award thing and it wasn't so difficult to deal with the office. Maybe the betrayal and the police visit did me some good?' In retrospective though, his lifestyle seen through the eyes of an outsider could seem odd. 'Why can't people mind their own business?' He was conflicted again. 'Putting myself out there, might invite more interest from busy-bodies.' Barri wrestled with confliction. 'It could also prove that I'm just a normal guy.'

Caprice stared out at an ocean of sky visible through a wide window. Except for a few cotton-wool waves, the sky was calm and the palest blue. She'd returned from another visit to the mini-market with enough food and drink to get her through the next twenty-four hours but, she thought about a poster she'd seen. *A party at Whiskers Hotel, award winners will be there so Barri must be going.* She now felt trapped as opposed to lying low. *If I stay here I'll sink into a depression so deep that I won't pull myself out. I can't stand another twenty-four hours of this.* She thought of dark days she'd spent at Macefield and how depression led her to deaths door.

'Will I feel any better if I run from here?' she asked a cloud. She raised a tight fist to her breastbone. 'What if I returned to Radburn? What if I told Barri I needed just a few more days? She contemplated possibilities. 'Should I tell him everything?' She knew she couldn't, he would balk. 'Should I just go back then see how I feel?' She surprised herself. 'Or, should I just move on to the new life I want?' Confliction gripped her. 'If only I had one more night to face my fear as it should have been a long time ago but, this time, do it with Barri, knowing something about me, as moral support. How much can I tell him?'

Looking at a clear sky and thinking of a fresh start, Caprice found courage. 'I'm not going to face a new year with regrets.' With clarity, she saw that she had only one complication and running away wouldn't solve anything. 'Who am I fooling? If I continue to run then I'll constantly look over my shoulder but, with Barri's help I could face him.'

She thought of the hotel and how Barri had let her down. 'Did he really let me down? He only told the truth, we did have an arrangement.' She then remembered Barri's dejection when she'd told him she was leaving.

Leaving her dress behind at Radburn House was a small problem in comparison with greater needs. She'd left a front door key on Radburn's hall table but had a backdoor key in her coat inner pocket. She could fetch her dress. 'I can go to the party, speak to Barri then face down Mephisto.' Caprice didn't feel trapped anymore but she sensed finality. 'Perhaps it's the approaching death of an old year?'

With a surge of energy Caprice left the apartment. She was certain that Barri would be true to his habits and on his way to his office but their paths crossed. Caprice looked out of a bus window, hidden inside a coat hood while peering at people on pavements. She wasn't concerned by other passengers who wouldn't recognise her whereas someone looking towards the bus just might. Barri drove by but she didn't see him and he didn't see her, two coins spinning, one of them nearly out of control only Barri wasn't going to the office as Caprice surmised. His final search took precedence.

Pale blue sky turned to a smoky hue as day waned to another long and dark night but Caprice was glad of its cloak. Her soft traipsing along Dandelion View and Radburn's driveway went unobserved. With trepidation she crossed Radburn's kitchen threshold then looked about her with invigorated reminiscence. At first she felt foolish. *I knew I'd left here too soon.* She'd been premature but as she passed through the dining room and ran her fingers along cold wood she shook her head. *I just wish Barri hadn't said anything about our arrangement at the hotel. Richard Gere climbed up a fire-escape for Julia Roberts but all you thought about was climbing up a tree!* When she'd left Radburn in a taxi she'd seen Barri place a foot on the tree-house ladder.

As Caprice climbed Radburn's stairs, Barri climbed the steps at the far end of Hebble Mill preferring to use physical stealth than a noisy elevator. Poking his head into bare apartments he didn't see any signs of life but as he neared the showcase apartment his pace slowed. *I should have thought of this sooner. Of course she'll be here.* His breathing quickened.

Back at Radburn House, Caprice was shocked to see her dress wasn't hanging in the last place she'd left it. 'He's thrown it out!' her new plan immediately scuppered. *Perhaps this was never meant to be and the dress is a sign?* Disappointed, the redhead left her old room but as she closed the door to face a long corridor ahead, she looked at Barri's door at the end and was drawn to it. Floor boards softly creaked beneath carpet. When a wooden expanse blocked her way Caprice rested her forehead against its cold surface. She licked her lips nervously then opened it.

Everything was in its designated place. She paused in the doorway to take it all in but it wasn't until she'd poked her head in that she saw something at the side of her eye. Her dress was hung at the back of the door and grasping hold of its folds, she hugged it to her cheek. 'If I take it, he'll notice. Why is it here?' Reaching up, Caprice removed the beautiful but simple dress from its hanger and walked to Barri's bed where she laid it across then sat next to it. She sighed when she caught her reflection in a dresser mirror. 'I look a mess.' She tugged at her hair then ran a forefinger around shaded eye sockets.

At Hebble Mill, Barri put on a fresh pair of surgical gloves, removed his shoes in the corridor then, slowly eased his body through a gap in a doorway. Swiftly but silently, he prowled around the ivory apartment in his socks. 'I needn't have bothered,' he scolded then, stopped. He sniffed the air and stretched his chin upwards like a predator on a fresh trail. His sensitive nose led him to an open kitchen.

Sniffing around units, Barri came to an abrupt stop in front of a microwave and he opened its smoked-glass door. Inside it was gleaming but the aroma from steam, dried and imbedded within an outlet grid, was barely discernible. Anyone else wouldn't have noticed an instant release of sage. Barri's pupils expanded. He flew at every cupboard, drawer and door in a cyclone of blind panic.

After searching a bedroom but not finding anything, the predator bent double to hyper-ventilate. He wheezed frustration out and sucked despair in until eventually he became so worn-out out that he plonked down on a bed to moan softly. The bed hadn't been slept in; its tasteful display of pillows and cushions undisturbed. He didn't know that Caprice had slept in her coat, in a chair.

Barri stared at the hunched individual in the reflection of a

239

vertical wall-mirror. He placed elbows on his knees and his head flopped down in defeat. It was then that Barri noticed a drawer between his feet, one designed to hold spare bedding or anything else that could eat into storage space. It fit snugly into the bed but could be opened by placing fingertips beneath. Barri pulled.

'Thank God!' he whispered. There was no room for a deity in Barri's darkened soul. Joy, pure joy, the joy of a child when opening Christmas presents was Barri's that late afternoon. Barri's joy overwhelmed him. He wanted to bathe in it, roll around on the floor in it, swipe at the air and rip off his clothes. It was a joy so intense and deliriously extravagant that he didn't feel fit for it, not yet. He wanted a holy ritual, a mystical rite, an anointing of his body so that it could be pure and ready for a greater gift it was about to receive.

Slowly, joy subsided and Barri became pious, silent and serious as he crouched into a ball, pulling his knees up to his chest then wrapping arms around them to hug them tight. 'I don't ever want to release this feeling.' Holding his breath, Barri squeezed then swallowed hard, cementing his emotion. Then, with a clearer head he raised his body up and used the toe of his shoe to close the drawer so that its contents were once again safely hidden. Strength of purpose renewed, Barri knew he had to prepare himself for a return visit later.

Once more, Barri and Caprice passed each other on the road but this time under a thick cloak of darkness. Christmas lights still twinkled from house and shop windows. For the first time Barri noticed illuminations hanging from the tops of lamp posts. He belatedly felt both cheerful and festive. He wanted to release new found joy, celebrate it with champagne and fireworks. 'First,' he told his car mirror, 'I have to grasp back my life by taking another.'

Radburn House was in darkness, silent and looming at the end of its driveway but Barri smiled at the oak tree as he drove by. He still smiled as he entered his home, ascended stairs and walked along the hallway to his bedroom. The smile didn't leave his face as he turned on the shower and waited for water to run hot. All the while Barri thought intently about what he would do when he returned to the Mill. *I could wait in the upper corridor and surprise her or, if she's already there, I could wait until she's asleep. A hard surface beneath my subject will help but what if the bed is too soft?*

As he contemplated, Barri's eyes roamed instinctively to the back of his bedroom door. His usual visual stimulation would spur ingenuity but, the dress was missing. Rushing over to the door, Barri pulled it open but didn't know why. He looked out into the hallway then spun quickly to look around his room before taking slow deliberate steps back to his bed. Confused, suspicious and highly agitated, Barri sat on the end of his bed and stared into a dresser mirror.

He sat still for five-minutes, allowing panic to wash over him, sending him hot then cold then lukewarm when he realised what a missing dress meant. Barri ran to his iPhone and quickly searched for Caprice's last email then found what he wanted to read. *"...I've left the evening dress in the wardrobe.... I don't think I will have another occasion to wear it."*

'She must have another occasion,' Barri reasoned. His lower jaw twitched repeatedly. 'The only place she could need such a dress would be at hotel party but why would she go?' The perplexed young man closed his eyes and recalled how the hotel dinner had triggered a turning point. Caprice hadn't been the same afterwards but as Barri racked his brains he still couldn't see the reason for her sudden change. 'She was miserable,' he concluded. He mentally searched again. 'There was no fault with how I behaved or anything I said.'

Barri read the email again then thought dismissively: *It's irrelevant. In future, I will not get close to my subjects.* When Barri thought briefly about past subjects he came to another conclusion: *They were all happy before I crushed them. Caprice must be happy too, she must enjoy her party.* It wouldn't be Barri's New Year until he'd despatched his subject. Now, the party had a new significance, the death of a subject

241

with the death of an old year and Barri appreciated the poetry in that.

He dressed slowly and decided he wouldn't go out again that evening. Feeling much calmer, Barri glanced fondly at the back of his bedroom door imagining Caprice hanging there in her dress, her long red hair cascading. 'It will be worth the wait. I can add a few extra touches. I know where you'll be before the party and where you'll go to after it. There won't be a soul around to interrupt and there won't be a soul to worry about you afterwards.'

Barri left his room and descended the stairs, too wired to think of sleep, his body-clock used to activity until early hours. He ran his fingers along the dining table's cold surface but as he passed the chair where Caprice had sat, he paused and pulled it out to chivalrously allow a phantom to arise. Then, he leaned on the chair, peered down at its seat before looking wistfully at his own, favoured chair.

Barri furrowed his brow, swept aside dirty-blond hair where it had grown a fraction too long so that it now touched dirty-blond lashes. His fingers lingered. With one hand holding the chair and the other against his hair, he closed his eyes. His hand fell slowly down from hair to shoulders, along one side of his chest, lower and lower until he had found the warm, hard bulge in his jeans. His brow creased further. Opening his eyes, moist and stinging, Barri felt suddenly dizzy, terribly sad then, terribly confused.

26. Parlour Games

New Year's Eve dawned slowly with overcast skies that became streaked with bright lilac and peach. Whiskers ballroom was going through a transformation and Purl was overseeing every detail. Her eyes sparkled with anticipation as brightly as winking spotlights overhead, festooned among folds of black satin to form a midnight sky. It may have been bright outside but within the ballroom it was dark and magical, an enchanted glade in a pretend night.

Garlands of silver-laced ivy weaved through silver chairs, up table legs and around pillars. Urns sprouted bushy sprigs of eucalyptus with contrasts of silver poinsettia. Interspersed, tapering pine and holly cones added green with polystyrene red apples. Berry spotlights of electric blue shone from boxed topiary. Table tops gleamed, ovals of glass covering scattered moss with green leaves. It would be easy to imagine Little Red Riding Hood skipping merrily through tables while sprinkling handfuls of berries from her basket.

Under the make-believe sky with its myriad of twinkling stars, hired decorators chuckled while trying to perfect an illusion. Purl had asked for a fairy-tale forest. Later, a low mist of dry ice would give the impression that mythical creatures could emerge but, the enchanted forest was false and Purl was used to masking reality.

Mandrake kept out of his daughter's way by escaping to the south of England, it was now her turn to release her particular brand of magic and the poison apple hadn't fallen far from the tree. He walked up and down an eighteen-hole golf course in Torquay while watery bright sunshine lit a bald spot just forming at his crown. He may not have been physically beside his daughter but Mandrake was with her in spirit. He knew she

243

had planned something special.

The middle-aged business man brooded. The prospect of his daughter being successful made Mandrake's eyes squint more than necessary in winter sunshine. He'd promised that he would phone and wish her happy new year at midnight to which, she'd replied: 'If you don't get an answer then don't worry. It will only mean that I'm enjoying the fruits of success.' Mandrake was worried in case Purl was going overboard and half-hoped that she'd be unsuccessful. He hadn't yet told her that it didn't matter if she wasn't. *I hate to burst her bubble.* Either way, he would use the gem that Phestoz had offered him.

Meanwhile, Phestoz had driven to his nearest nightclub, Toffee Neon in Macefield. He met a shady contact displeased to be awake at such an ungodly hour. Once he'd accepted a memory-stick there had been no need to mention payment, a favour long overdue. With the gem safely secreted in his jacket breast pocket, neatly held behind a starched and crisply-cornered handkerchief, Phestoz was on his way back to Mistlethrop. He smirked at the road then softly hummed *Auld Lang Syne.*

At Radburn House, Barri snoozed fitfully in a stately wingback in Radburn's parlour. He'd sat rigidly still and stared into darkness for most of the night, the air so heavily pitch-black around him that he'd sensed its touch. The fraught young man had been a raw nerve open to all and any stimuli, so intoxicated with fantasies that they'd obliterated all else. Barri had stared wildly into a portal of twisted thoughts and willed himself there until he had finally been sucked in. Eventually, his head had nodded forward before swinging back to snore quietly. Armorial griffins at fireside pillars watched with dead eyes.

Caprice, however, had taken a morning walk, breathing in damp air and looking at a cloudy sky then worrying how she would later get to Whiskers in all her finery. By the time she turned back towards the Mill, the sky lifted and wet patches on pavements evaporated. She would be able to walk to the party that evening but it would be a long way to go in high heels. With some reserve she considered pre-ordering a taxi but after walking for thirty minutes, her reserve vanished. She could walk to the taxi-rank and get one from there.

Bright afternoon turned gloomy. Darkness descended but within Whiskers ballroom a false night sky still twinkled. The forest now bereft of humans would remain so until seven when its doors would be flung wide to reveal misty innards. By that time, a vine-leaved bar would be manned, a D.J. secreted in a grotto with a spinning green spotlight. It would give him a Shrek-like quality even if he saw himself more as a Hulk.

The instigator of the mystical glade was busy in a hotel room, adding final touches to her costume. It wasn't the sort of dress she would normally have chosen but Purl admired her reflection. Her eyes shone more brightly. It was hard to stop her mouth from grinning so she practised pouting instead, blowing kisses to the mirror. She admired her sleek contours and her lips pursed seductively. 'I just might keep this look. I didn't think it could be so exhilarating.' She gently hummed an old Kate Bush song as it had poignancy just then. 'Perhaps this is the real me?' Purl turned slowly to look at herself from every angle. She leaned forward. With long nails she flicked an imaginary speck from her cheekbone then looked earnest and whispered: 'Someone is going to get *so* lucky tonight.'

Before seven, revellers assembled in Whiskers bar to resemble a colony of flapping impatient penguins, squawking their presence with animated excitement. Black formal tuxedos and variations of the little black dress occupied every chair, draped across barstools or leaned against tables.

As Phestoz stuck his head around the doorway, the bartender winked. He anticipated generous tips as well as double wages. As the gaunt old man approached, he was jostled from behind by a group of tipsy Hooray-Henrys who made a beeline en-masse for the bar.

During the afternoon, Purl's friends had ordered champagne then drifted in and out of each other's rooms. They'd taken a glass of bubbly in each but their tastes now called for vibrant cocktails. Purl's absence hadn't been noticed. It was such a hoot to be in a quaint old place they hadn't heard of or would want to again. Their animated squawks could be heard above others.

Phestoz steadied himself against a doorframe then placed his bony fingertips together as though in prayer but then pointed joined hands outwards as he pushed through the crowd. He approached the bar like Moses parting the seas, only black instead of red. 'Make way, make way,' he sang as he pushed with as much regard for Purl's friends as they'd shown him. Then, he snapped his fingers in the air and a tall glass, misty with icy condensation, appeared on the bar into which the smiling bartender poured neat Russian vodka. He ignored penguin newcomers who glared at the old man and his vodka.

At seven, the hotel owner ensured he was first to be ushered through gaping ballroom doors. He was also first to grab a fresh drink from the ballroom bar then take a high-backed seat at its far end. It would be a great night to people-watch and from a ringside seat he could observe Purl's plan in action. She hadn't said anything about it but Phestoz was sure it would fail abysmally.

Just before nine, there was still no sign of Purl, her friends lost in a jostling monotone out of place in an enchanted forest. Bow ties dangled from unbuttoned shirt collars splashed with booze; mascara smudged cheeks, hair held high and tight with clips had escaped but, these details were hardly noticeable among a writhing mass. It seemed to move up and down from a steadily ascending knee-high mist as one undulating wave.

Rap and Blues pounded their bass beats. Old favourites crooned. Still, Phestoz sat cross-legged on a high-backed seat. He didn't care how tipsy the penguins became as long as a huge bar bill could later be presented to Purl. He looked forward to seeing her reaction, more so to her father's when he discovered her extravagance. The old man grew stiff and impatient, on his third large drink but still favouring his tipple of vodka which, he'd take over food any day.

At ten-past-nine Phestoz's eyes peered at dancers and examined tables to seek out newcomers. His steely eyes were now accustomed to forest light, more shade than luminance. It served equally to hide him from the thick of the crowd. He didn't converse with anyone or listen to conversation as he was so enthralled by watching bodies gyrate and pulse. He waited, increasingly impatiently, to catch a glimpse of Barri or Purl so that the main entertainment could begin. As minutes passed Phestoz sensed something was about to happen. He drew his spine quickly forward and upright when he saw a sudden vibrancy of colour that flashed for a second between dancers, then, it was gone. 'Did my eyes deceive me?'

Uncrossing his legs, Phestoz laid the toe of a shiny shoe down and slipped from his seat. He slowly walked towards the edge of the crowd then stood still, mechanically moving his head from side-to-side as he searched gaps between bodies. The floor vibrated beneath his shoes when a familiar song boomed from amplifiers hidden among eucalyptus. He recognised *Heaven Seventeen*'s most famous song. The old man quickly glanced behind him. The song inflamed a sense of danger. It reminded him of an old friend, although he doubted the owner of that title would see himself as one. A young Reverend had been the only man not to succumb to one of Phestoz's games. He'd been the only thorn in the old man's side. *I'll get you one day.*

To Phestoz, everyone was his friend. He refused to acknowledge enemies, only people who didn't see things his way and that could be remedied given the right circumstances and persuasion. At that moment there was one individual he could not be without. He continued to look for a splash of colour to give her presence away. Then, he saw her.

She was talking to a stranger. Her long red hair looked like the leaves of a flame-tree during spring's first blush. Her slender but curvy figure wore the same dress she'd worn the last time Caprice graced the ballroom. In profile she looked even more tantalising than Phestoz remembered. 'You always knew how to fill a dress.' He sighed with a rasp but clasped his bony

247

hands together and then, rocking gently from heel to toe, considered what to do about this unexpected complication. *Purl would be on the war path if she knew.* He was delighted.

Barri's car pulled up near the hotel but a row of taxis had taken free spaces outside. As he emerged from his vehicle he looked up at the renovated building. Curtains tightly drawn showed little activity on any floor above ground level but a thud of music rattled ballroom windows. They were so densely forested that it was difficult to discern what was happening on the other side.

As he neared the entrance, Barri hesitated and remained on the pavement, his heart beating the same time as the music. He had to breathe slowly and hard to prevent his mounting excitement from exploding. His breath escaped as swirling wisps around him. Faced with the hotel and the treasure it held, he felt giddy. Barri was a tightly coiled spring, a jack-in-the-box waiting to be released. He inhaled deeply and began to walk towards the entrance.

Inside, penguins were on the march again and this time they gathered near Phestoz, alcohol spilling from their glasses as they squawked louder and flapped with abandon. Droplets splashed onto the old man's suit and he angrily took a few steps back but when he looked up again, Caprice had disappeared. Music was so loud that the penguins didn't hear his torrent of profanity. The sudden force of his anger shook the old man then, he became even more annoyed. This hadn't happened before even when vexed by drunken behaviour at one of his clubs.

Caprice stayed at the party for only a short while. Like Phestoz, she'd also perused a pulsing crowd before being targeted by a lone wolf. He'd salivated as soon as he saw delicious curves appear in a misty entrance. The wolf prowled around her for a few minutes, admiring the view from various angles while waiting expectantly for her partner to appear. When he saw that she was alone, the wolf made his move.

A lothario in a white dickey-bow, the man crept up to

Caprice's side, leaned forward so that he could speak into her ear: 'It's too dangerous for you to be here.' Then, he leaned back expectantly. Immediately, Caprice turned her head and from the alarm then confusion in her eyes, the wolf knew he'd gained her attention. He didn't realise that he'd also struck fear into the trembling vision before him. Caprice hadn't expected to face her tormentor just yet. 'What do you mean?' She had to shout to be heard above music and she felt uncomfortable doing so. This man had frightened her deeply, immediately dispersing the self-confidence she'd arrived with.

The wolf leaned forward, his breath smelt of fresh menthol. Under the illusion that he possessed animal magnetism and a new little lamb would be naturally drawn, he said: 'You need protection and I will provide it.'

'I do not!' Caprice felt like shouting now. The wolf stared at her with a whimsical smile, confident that his chat-up opening would work.

'Ah, but you do!'

'What makes you think so?' She said words he'd expected.

'Every man in this room will want you and I cannot allow that. Beauty such as yours should be worshipped. I will be both your humble slave and protector for the rest of the evening, if you allow me to.'

Caprice looked at the man's smugly-smiling face then slowly shook her head in disbelief. She couldn't be bothered to reply to cheesiness so openly served in a chunky wedge. The wolf thought she was toying with him and offered his arm. Then, he leaned forward again, closing his eyes. When he didn't feel the soft touch of a female hand on his forearm his simpering expression altered. He opened eyes in surprise but his lamb had gone. There was an even greater urgency for her to seek out Barri so that she could rid herself of sudden vulnerability; her sensitivity magnified.

The magical forest was densely crowded; more people arrived and surged gleefully into the glade to join infectious party atmosphere. It was difficult to see anything clearly except the fake night sky above and people within one's immediate vicinity. Caprice thought Barri would be uncomfortable in such a crowded place, trying to ignore her own discomfort and increasing vulnerability. She edged her way to black foliage at the side of the room.

With slightly more air to breathe and less whiffy odours, she made her way clockwise around the ballroom, expecting to see Barri at a peripheral table or standing near an urn but she was disappointed. She also expected to see Phestoz and her heart raced as she tried frantically to recall her memorised speech. By now the older man had seen her but she didn't see him.

The red-haired beauty passed a grotto, having to push between bodies gathered around it then, she was startled to look up and see a Grinch-green face twisted into contortions. A D.J. strained to listen through one earphone while preparing another track. She progressed as far as the bar before realising Barri wasn't in the ballroom. *Maybe he's outside?*

Phestoz picked up her trail, having shoved his way through penguins and emerging at the other side just in time to see the back of Caprice's head as she edged towards eucalyptus. From there it was easy to mirror her movements and he saw logic in what she was doing. *She's looking for Barri. You foolish girl...* he thought with satisfaction, thoroughly enjoying the game. *It's not you Barri's interested in.* Then, with haughty confidence: *Neither is Purl.*

After this macabre game of hide and seek, Caprice left the ballroom through a billow of dry-ice mist that danced around her like old London fog. Phestoz wisely held back. He didn't want her to know just yet that he'd seen her.

If Caprice had looked behind her before disappearing into thick swirling mist, she would have seen Barri. He now occupied her old spot in the ballroom and the lone wolf was still close by, polishing his chat-up delivery. He practised a different line on each girl he took a fancy to. He was used to disappointment but it didn't hold him back, The Terminator of Romance.

Barri was of much the same mood and like the wolf wouldn't take one step beyond a vantage point. He stared at the offending crowd, not listening to music but its deafening pulse feeding a new fantasy. In the misty gloom, where deafening noise and crowds made time slower and an island of an onlooker, Barri imagined Caprice before him. She played a violin. *What would it be like to take one of the strings and wind it around her neck? How white would her skin become before it shed blood? Would it be as red as her hair?* The image was strong, so strong that the dreamer forgot to blink. When dry-ice wisped upwards, his eyes smarted painfully. Barri was forced reluctantly out of his dream.

Eyes had turned upon Barri. Some recognised his face whereas others looked through alcohol-fuelled lust. He turned on his heels and took two steps towards the door to take up a fresh position. White mist clouded the doorway, freshly blown from a dry-ice machine meant to be facing the opposite way but it had been kicked by a penguin.

Caprice looked into the bar area and visibly shook with disappointment. She hesitated near the entrance and looked nervously into clouds, seeing the back of heads appear and disappear. Just as the reality of a cold, damp morning had given her dogged determination, the humid, dry evening robbed her of it. She lost heart completely. *Why on earth did I come here?* Now feeling lower than ever, the red-head turned around to leave the hotel and its fake magic behind her.

The train station wouldn't provide any income to cab drivers that night and so vehicles lined Whiskers kerb, their drivers confident that there would be no danger of a parking ticket. As Caprice's taxi departed, another cab was then occupied.

'This will sound awfully cliché...' a mature voice rasped behind the driver's head. 'Follow that car will you? Don't get too close. When I tell you to stop you'll be paid handsomely.' The driver examined a skeletal face in his rear-view mirror and shuddered.

Purl descended Whiskers staircase, using her fingertips to lift

251

long skirts so that she could make a safe and graceful descent. Her eyes still held an excited sparkle but it soon vanished as she entered the ballroom mist. A man's hand grabbed Purl's arm to spin her round and she almost fell. Her high heel caught on her dress but she managed to regain balance. Nevertheless, it shook her and as soon as she turned towards her aggressor, the hand was removed. Its owner gaped, he looked disorientated. Purl's skin smarted where she'd been grabbed and her hand instinctively went to the tender spot to rub it. The offender stepped back with confusion and swayed.

'Why on earth did you do that?' Purl hissed.

'I... I... Who? !.. I want to know...'

'Well? Out with it?'

The swaying figure didn't reply but turned, lunged forward and staggered along the hotel lobby as far as the entrance then swiftly went through it. Two taxis waited outside and as the man grabbed a door, its driver shouted over his shoulder: 'Where to?'

'Anywhere but here!' then the man projected vile vomit into the back of the cab.

Purl was furious; not only had her heel ripped a hole in the bottom of her gown but it had buckled at an angle. She knew by putting weight on it that it would soon snap in two. She examined the heel, bending down as far as she could without losing further dignity. Then, looking back along the lobby at the staircase, she realised the only spare pair at the hotel were those she'd arrived in and they were bright blue. 'This simply won't do!'

Close to angry tears, she lifted her chin and glanced over her shoulder through a shroud of sleek hair. Her carefully planned entrance was ruined but there was a chance yet, her victim had seen her. She saw Barri looking at her with a strange look on his face, almost as surprised as the man who had grabbed her arm. Thinking at the speed of a fired bullet, Purl quickly straightened, stifled a smile and dabbed at her eyes as though tears were falling. Then she limped with exaggerated effort along the lobby taking the same path as her aggressor. Purl got into the last taxi at the kerb. *I'll have to change my plan slightly.* It could bring events closer to her desired conclusion.

Barri had instantly recognised the attacker. What his ex-assistant expected to achieve by coming to the party was a mystery but judging by the way he'd swayed and his subsequent behaviour it was now easy to guess. *Why take it out on a defenceless woman?* The irony of his thoughts wasted, Barri had gazed at the victim bent in the entrance, her lower half obliterated by mist but saw something was wrong. Then he'd seen her rise, rub her eyes before mist thickened again. Just as he was about to offer his help, he was pulled by ivy garlands thrown around him.

'Hi, handsome, come and dance!' Three giggly girls pawed at Barri's arms while ivy pulled taught across his chest and shoulders. Long French-polished fingernails tried to pull him one way then the other before he lost patience, tugged at the garlands across his chest and broke them in two. 'Wow! Get you Tarzan!'

Barri may have been able to discard garlands but he couldn't get rid of the girls so easily. They saw his ivy-tearing as shameless bravado to impress them. After trying to pry their roaming hands off his body, he totally lost his cool. 'Go away!' he yelled, 'I'm with someone,' then he patted his inside pocket; his iPhone was vibrating.

Running out of the ballroom and out of the hotel, Barri's eyes smarted but this time with the contrast of cold night air. He was just in time to see a cab pull-up at the kerbside. Barri stared down the road then up it. The driver looked expectantly at Barri but looked away when Barri walked back to the hotel doorway while looking at his phone. A vibration in Bari's pocket alerted him to a text message. He couldn't think of anyone who would contact him on New Year's Eve.

"I hope we can talk. Come to Hebble Mill's showpiece apartment." Barri read the message several times, his heart quickening when he realised there could only be one person

who could have sent it. *I won't have to wait for Caprice, she can wait for me.*

Barri looked up just as a woman barged past, almost knocking him over. She was swiftly followed by a dreary-eyed man who shouted: 'You know I didn't mean it!' A couple of seconds later the taxi had left with only one new occupant. Barri headed back to his car.

A short while later Caprice paid her cabdriver then slowly walked along a row of dilapidated cottages lining the narrow side-road to the Mill. She walked so slowly that she heard the cab reverse onto the main road then squeal away after a speedy u-turn. She also heard a single toot a couple of seconds later but thought nothing of it. The toot was one driver acknowledging another. Another cab had pulled up just before the junction but the driver too busy counting a large tip to wave his response. He pocketed folded blue notes he'd been handed by an evil-looking old gentleman.

'He paid me handsomely...' the cabdriver nodded then chortled. 'What an ugly bastard!'

27. Red

She was wearing that dress, the charcoal dress so elegant yet so sexily alluring. Phestoz waited in darkness, standing sideways behind a doorframe and peering into a bedroom semi-bathed in pale moonlight. He'd left his shoes at the entrance. He didn't want to give any warning of his presence, having slithered socked feet effortlessly along smooth wood until he'd found the source of a low but repetitive *thud, thud, thud*. He heard that dress rustle gently, crisp gauze against sumptuous velvet as Caprice's legs brushed the side of a bed. *You won't wear it for long.* A purple slimy tongue flicked forward to lick thin white lips. The old man anticipated overdue joy with his step-daughter.

Caprice paced, having kicked off high heels to feel the coldness of bare wood beneath her feet. Its icy touch made her shiver more than the piercing first bite of the lifeless apartment when she'd first entered. The lack of warmth offered uneasy solace. She wanted the cold bitterness of reality and it had crept through the souls of her feet so that her bones now ached with it.

The distraught young woman gathered up long velvet skirts so that she could walk freely over smooth cold boards. The crinkly outer gauze of her hem scratched bare ankles. The cold was also sweet torture, reminding her that her whole life had been numbingly-cold and it was sick comfort to appreciate that she deserved no less. A cold floor brought her back to her senses then her senses were flooded with self-reproach. *I've been so stupid.* She admonished herself for having savoured the hope, no matter how briefly, that she could have faced her demon then tried to rise like a phoenix. *I've never lived...* she admitted while clutching her skirts tightly with clawed fingertips, 'I've existed.'

Her thoughts became finally audible but she whispered them between gritted teeth. She gripped her dress tighter and her self-reproach turned to anger.

Phestoz continued to spy, seeing a glimpse of red when Caprice's vibrant hair was momentarily lit by moonlight then, her painted red toenails when she stepped away. He closed his eyes imagining himself at her feet. Just as Rosebud had once pressed her nose against wire mesh to look at a tree-house, Phestoz imagined his nose pressed against gauze. His slimy purple tongue darted forward. *I could put my tongue against it then push until I tasted bare skin.* The vision aroused him and he grinned, a distorted grimace, now finding it easy to grin from thin wrinkly ear to thin wrinkly ear. His eyes creased with delight then he opened them and his tongue was sucked back into his mouth. Stealthily, he entered the bedroom.

Caprice halted in front of a window to stare at Mistlethrop's surrounding hills. Moonlight disappeared fast behind clouds that looked like black swirling smoke. *I wish I was with you and able to vanish so easily.* Then, her fingers snapped rigid and her skirt hems fell heavily to the floor. The tip of an icy but sharp fingernail slowly drew an invisible line down the back of her left arm from its shoulder to her elbow. She froze and stood with her palms and fingers spanned, stretched like the bride of Frankenstein awakened to her groom.

'I've found you.' Three words were whispered in her ear through her hair but Caprice couldn't feel any warmth from the breath behind them. For a moment all she could think of was her bare feet and how cold the floor felt beneath them. She remained frozen and rigid then, pulled her unblinking eyes away from the black horizon where the moon had vanished completely. She slowly lowered them to a bedside table. It was a black block with a black shape upon it made even darker by the withdrawal of light. Her pupils instinctively widened but all she saw was deep red and it began to swirl like night sky clouds.

Silently, she reached out as two cold lips brushed her shoulder where the fingernail had first alighted. Silently, she snatched the black shape from the black block then swung it, spinning her body so violently and quickly that the object found a target. She didn't feel the object connect or hear a surprised groan followed immediately by a loud crack as a head hit a bedpost. Then, there was another sound as a body fell sideways onto the floor. Nor did she see a pool of red slowly accumulate around the head then nestle into a halo across bare boards. Caprice remained frozen and rigid and stared at a crumpled shape at her feet. She waited for it to move. It didn't.

A car dimmed its lights as it entered the side road leading to the Mill then slowly made its way towards its destination. Its driver didn't want to draw attention to his vehicle, not that the cottages along one side of the road showed signs of life within. Their exteriors were yet to be given a make-over and their interiors, unoccupied but the driver wasn't to know.

When Barri slowed his car, he could hear his own heart beating. It pulsed and pushed blood and as it did so adrenalin increased, he was suddenly aware of the backs of his ears. His car rolled next to a skip at the rear of the Mill and he felt the vibration of an engine purr softly like a kitten beneath him. The tip of his tongue darted forward then sideways to the corner of his mouth. It wasn't the only pink muscle to move.

He patted his forearm, pressing his jacket and shirtsleeve against its preparation of cling-wrap. It was an odd but thrilling sensation and he repeated the motion so that the wrap crinkled across his skin. Barri was ecstatic, looked forward to release and relief but he had to sit still and drip-feed his rush of adrenalin. He would wait until he stopped shaking, only then would he be able to don surgical gloves.

It was overbearingly erotic to just sit in a dark car, looking out at what waited for him inside the building then, fell the soft kiss of icy air on his face as he emerged. He removed his jacket and carefully folded it back onto his seat and rolled-up his sleeves.

As the killer made his way along corridors and up steps he had to pause to control his tremors. Wave after wave of electric-

257

like shocks travelled through him, tingling and so sensuous that it nearly brought him to his knees. Barri looked up dark steps. It was his stairway to heaven. He had to feel his way up it.

The door to the apartment was ajar and a shaft of moonlight spilled out. Caprice stood with her hands on her hips, a black silhouette in a black narrow hallway but the ends of her hair lit vibrantly where it fell over one shoulder.

She was wearing that dress; the dress Barri had pressed his face and naked body against when lying on his bedroom floor. It was the dress he'd used as a prop for private fantasy. It was the dress he wanted so desperately to feel filled and writhing beneath his body. The gauze on one side glimmered where light touched it. In the darkness Barri had to close his eyes for a moment to enjoy a clear recollection of crisp gauze scratching seductively then, soft velvet folds. In his room he'd sank into it; pressing his hardness into softness beneath a fragile outer shell. Barri was delirious. His facial muscles relaxed, the corners of his mouth went up.

There was a rustle. It was that dress and Barri's eyelids sprang open. There was no need for words, she was waiting for him. It was as though she knew he craved darkness in order to do what he had to. There were just six steps towards his subject, he took one to take him nearer but Caprice turned her back, dropped her arms and took a step into darkness beyond. Her fingers were rigid, stretched. Barri caught a hint of her perfume but it was tainted by a smell of paint.

When Caprice turned, Barri had paused with disappointment. He then swiftly took final steps to bring him immediately behind her, the top of her head close to his open mouth. The beating of his heart now pulsed in his ears. As he moved, delirium overtook him and although Caprice had stepped out of the light, all Barri could see was red. His fingers stiffened. In one swift movement he'd spun her around, pressed his forearm against her neck and pushed her body against the wall where he listened feverishly to gasps of surprise. They sounded odd and not as expected. *Is she enjoying it?*

In a dark hallway, pinned against a wall, Caprice's body was slowly pushed downwards. Barri's strong forearm held her, his right hand spanned her waist and he continued to push what seemed to be a willing victim. *She's not fighting back but if she did, would it matter?* As she crumpled to the floor, Barri straddled his subject, lifting his hand from her waist, his forearm relinquishing pressure from her neck for only a second. His subject lay on cold bare wood. Barri hovered over her, his mouth now close to her face. His muscled legs gripped either side of her arms, pinning them in.

She whispered softly: 'So that's how you like it.' He didn't hear her words; he was mentally and sensually beyond them. Warm sweet breath caressed his face then, he felt the awe and excitement of having that dress beneath him. This time it was infinitely more pleasurable because that dress was occupied by a warm and willing body.

The killer's delirium increased a thousand-fold and he almost screamed out in ecstasy but, then, it stopped. Flashes of Elspeth's face taunted him, mixed with a shadowy image of the little girl he'd discovered in his tree-house. Two faces blended then morphed into Caprice's. He looked down into darkness but their faces had been as clear as daylight. Elspeth had survived, grown up. The little girl in the tree-house was a ghost to remind him of something.

'What is it?' Barri asked the darkness. All other victims were now instantly forgotten, they'd led to this one superior kill. Like a curious animal, Barri placed his head on one side then increased pressure on a warm throat. He heard ticking and thought of the new clock he'd bought not realising it was the sound of his watch and the beating of his heart. It felt fit to burst so huge had it grown, so loud.

Arms against his inner thighs moved and Caprice's lower body squirmed but Barri brought his face so close to the back of his forearm that it was easy to slide his full body downwards. He covered his victim completely, mirroring movements he'd made when lying alone upon an empty dress on a bedroom floor.

An arm escaped, flayed up and a small tightly clenched fist rained down hard to hit Barri swiftly beneath his left shoulder blade. The physical blow forced him to gasp with exquisite pain but instead of bringing him to his senses, they were magnified and beyond control. He drowned in fitful ecstasy, contorted into spasms of rapture.

Quickly and efficiently, he heard the sound he'd longed to hear, a sharp and distinct crack. The sound echoed around him then hastened him to quickly remove his forearm so that the exquisite soft breeze of a final breath could gurgle unhindered. It spluttered against his face. He breathed it in and it became his, a last moment before death to give him release.

Something is wrong. There was a strange odour. Barri continued to lie on top of his subject. His body shook in spasms, aftershocks that slowly subsided until he was able to discern that the slight odour was some kind of synthetic. Barri tried to regain control. When he thought he had, he quickly jumped up to stand at the side of the corpse. The smell had gone. He bent to sniff above Caprice then he smelt it again, snapped his spine erect and stood listening to the increasing boom in his chest as it began to shake him from the inside out. Taking a huge breath, he sprang into action, this time to pull Caprice's body into the shaft of light across her midriff.

Despite being a dead weight, Caprice was easy to manoeuvre; the outer gauze of her dress allowed her body to slide effortlessly along smooth wooden flooring. Barri hovered above and looked down at the shaft of light as first white cleavage then crushed throat were a luminous shimmer like the moon's surface when it emerges from a swirling cloud. Her face slowly came out of the darkness and into a sliver of pale moonlight. The killer gasped when her mouth became visible. A thick lock of beautiful red hair had been caught around her face. She'd died with it sucked into her teeth which were bared with lips tightly drawn back.

Caught in white amber, the lower face that looked up at Barri was cruelly frozen in acute pain. A wide scream had been captured, its escape prevented at its apex, there for all eternity. It was an expression he hadn't seen in such intensity, but, it wasn't the tortured expression that caused Barri to shake so much that he lost what was left of his sense. Panic seized him. That expression, on that face, that body in that dress, all cut through him like a knife through butter. It pierced his heart as readily and pushed through to the other side. He could still feel where Caprice had hit him with her fist. He tried to stand. He had to get away from that face.

'Whose face is it?' he cried out. 'Is it you Elspeth?' His knees buckled and he sank heavily down, his knees on either side of the lifeless form still morphing in and out of identities.

There was a loud crack and Barri froze, unsure whether he'd imagined it. He listened intently but all was still. Hot tears toppled as tiny beads rolled slowly down his face. Barri gazed at the tormented face beneath him and his throat tightened. It sent a sharp pain along his gullet. More tears fell onto his shirt. Utter misery consumed him, blacker than the darkness of a cold, unoccupied mill. He wallowed in his misery, groaning softly then looked up into dense blackness but, as he did so, he felt another uncontrollable burst of emotion. Tears continued to fall but now down a face twisted in hopeless laughter.

When he'd exhaled all air from his lungs after maniacal howls, Barri quietened. He took another long look at the dead body beneath. Again, he thought he heard a crack, but something within Barri had snapped. 'Happy New Year!' he cheerily sang at frozen, snarled lips and their veil of red tresses. The maniacal smile froze and he stared through watery eyes.

'Was it too soon? Is it not midnight yet?' There was no sound of fireworks or flashes of gunpowder to send shafts of light into the hallway. The silence was all he was left with.

'Why?' Barri pleaded then waited for a reply. 'Everything was so perfect. I wanted you to be special.' Barri owned the kill, it was his murder. 'Why didn't you stop me?'

Barri paused again, putting his head on one side, still waiting

261

for the corpse to contribute to his bizarre one-sided conversation. This time there was a definite cracking but Barri ignored the spasm in his neck before automatically rolling his head to the opposite side then slowly rolling it around and around. Silence surrounded the man and his subject then, a smell of synthetics mixed with Caprice's perfume and it was intolerable.

'I murdered you.' the killer laughed: 'Ha!' then moaning, looked up at a black ceiling in a black hallway. 'What do I do now? You were so perfect. It was supposed to be so perfect.' The smell hit him and he had to hold his breath.

'I shouldn't have done this to you, not here,' he whispered to a still-warm body beneath. 'I'm sorry I chose this place, it reeks.' He bent his face further so that his warm breath brushed lips that had lost their heat. The ache within him was far stronger that the ache of a thumped shoulder blade. His heart was full, his adrenalin still flowing and his longing, his need for release still with him.

'Why won't it leave me?' For the first time Barri felt remorse. 'It's an animal!' he yelled into an empty hallway. It echoed and Barri began to howl with disbelief, throwing back his head and guffawing with lunatic force. His body began to spasm again, hot tears cascading and mingling with the dirty blond of over-long hair until it was sodden and limp.

'What do I do now?' Barri uttered repeatedly between maniacal laughter and tears. In one wrench, he pulled the rest of Caprice's face into the shaft of light and looked down at it. 'I want to see what I did to you,' he tenderly told the face staring up at him. He tried to blink away tears to focus.

Beautiful red hair had wrapped itself across Caprice's distorted features and Barri stared at it, not comprehending what he was looking at. As his vision cleared something again snapped within him. Barri fled.

Afterwards, he couldn't remember how he drove back to the hotel. Nor could he remember leaving his car unnoticed at the spot it previously vacated outside the hotel then walking home.

Survival instinct kicked-in. Barri had been swept along on its tidal wave. Once safely within the grounds of Radburn House there was only one place he wanted to be. The tree-house was colder and darker than when he last remembered it.

Meanwhile, back at the Mill, the body Barri abandoned was slowly tugged back into the apartment, making a swishing sound as its dress slid over the floor. It took effort to ensure that the dress suffered no harm in the process. It took considerably more effort to then slide the occupied dress gently an inch at a time, so that it turned one-hundred-and-eighty degrees. It was positioned in front of the bedroom window. The body lying behind it had also been changed, its trouser zip undone.

Gloved hands picked up a heavy lamp that lay on the floor, wiped it clean and carefully laid the prints of dead fingers upon it before returning it to its previous position. A new victim had been caught unaware by an attack from the rear and had then lashed out during final moments. Whereas Barri had lost his mind, the only person to survive death, apart from a killer with intent, had found cold clarity.

'What would my father say if he saw what I'd just done to this woman?' Then, the survivor stood over two bodies, too wired to shed tears. Adrenalin still surged through her veins, relief at being alive but, she also had power. It was so magnificent but a glorious terror in comparison to the fright the old man had tried to instil in his prey.

Not realising the irony of her words, the wired young woman then said: 'More importantly, how do I solve a problem, like Barri?'

28. Out with the Old

Barri sat hunched with eyes squeezed tight in the corner of a dark dank tree-house. He tried to focus solely on the sound of his breath. He winced when church bells clanged then writhed in agony when a clamour of whining whistles and echoing bangs followed, the loudest from the rear of Whiskers Hotel in the distance. Each explosion was a bullet ripping through him, killing his reason to be. He clasped his arms tight around him.

As the cacophony increased his agony magnified and he brought his shoulders closer to his ears. He groaned. Intense pink flashes of light infiltrated closed eyelids with each bang. Soon faces appeared and stared at him from the back of squeezed lids until they blended. Barri tried not to open his eyes and look out but flashing continued.

'Light, dark... light, dark...' He began a mantra in time with the bursts of light and noise. Each time he thought they'd stopped and opened his eyes, he saw shadows in the tree-house. The cacophony began again and surrounded the tree until Barri was forced to halt his mantra, open his eyes and look out.

'They're celebrating,' he told the shadows. He watched the glittering sky. Fireworks released a final multicolour splurge which cascaded as drops that disappeared on their descent.

'I did it!' he wanted to shout to the explosions but words stuck in his throat. 'I did it,' he whispered instead.

Barri had been plunged into deep waters then put through a wringer. He hadn't had time to wear new emotions before they'd been thrown into the wash. Maybe if they'd been allowed to air years ago, instead of being wrapped in plastic and left to hang in the bare wardrobe of a young boy's introversion, Barri may have had a normal life. It is a topic best left to the myriads of doctors who spend careers producing papers about such things but don't cure, just manage. The killer had intended to manage in his own way but it hadn't brought the expected result. Caprice had been his past, present and now a challenge to his future.

'Do I just look for another, repeatedly feeding my need...until? What?'

The fireworks stopped. Fading waterfalls of light lingered then, Patsy Cline's soulful voice drifted quietly through the night. It came from Fernlea. Barri imagined himself covered in a blanket and sitting in a wheelchair. *What if it was made from bracelets?* He tried to count how many subjects it would take, so bitterly ridiculous that he shuddered.

'Is this what it's like? ...To mourn death?' he asked a burnt orange glow that appeared on the parks horizon. He turned his eyes back to a pitch interior to close them again to all external influence.

Inhale, exhale... Inhale, exhale... He set up a rhythm, practised this meditation for hours, taking into each contracting nostril an odour of damp wood and traces of gunpowder drifting across from the park. The most difficult part was trying to quieten his heartbeat as he pushed air out. *I must breathe,* he told his chest, over and over. *Just breathe.* Eventually all that remained was deathly silence and his mantra. His breath turned to fog. Time passed slowly.

'Why did you do it?' A soft voice whispered its question. Barri was startled and gasped.

What new madness is this? Slowly he opened his eyelids a fraction but was too disturbed to look in the direction the voice came from. With his elbows resting on his knees and hands held as though in prayer, he started again when he saw yet another shadowy vision had presented itself in a corner. They had visited him throughout the night. He waited for it to fade but recognised the voice. The pain of recognition brought fresh agonies.

'Why?' the voice whispered again. Barri raised his eyes to see an outline. She knelt in a corner, sitting back on her heels.

If only I could see her properly, see the colour, the bright beauty of her hair. It was too dark and his vision, too densely black. Some had changed form and size.

'It's you Elspeth, isn't it?' His voice cracked and he took a moment. 'I always thought it was you. I knew you'd come back.'

The vision didn't move. Barri's heart rang as loudly as church bells in his ears. Tears sprang to his eyes, their saltiness stinging them painfully as he waited hopelessly for this vision to fade. He had acknowledged her at last.

'I had to come back.'

'Will you stay with me now Elsp...?'

He was interrupted. 'No, I'm not Elspeth.'

'I was foolish to think so.' Barri's voice faltered with disbelief.

'Do you know who I am?'

'Yes... No...I don't want it to be you.'

'It is me. Why?' the vision whispered her question again.

'I can smell you.' Barri's voice cracked again in his throat. He blinked to allow tears to fall like firework raindrops. 'You always smelt so good. That was part of it you see...you were right, just right for me.'

The vision remained silent and still. Barri searched his soul but found nothing, just the essence of who he once was. 'You reminded me of her, even your smell. You reminded me of so many things. Killing you was killing her again.'

'Was that what you wanted?'

'Yes... No...I don't know. It *was* what I wanted.'

'So what do you want now?'

Barri fell into heavy silence and closed his eyes again, wishing the vision would disappear yet at the same time willing it to be real. There was overwhelming beauty in acute pain.

It was deathly quiet for a long time. With his eyes still closed, Barri whispered: 'I just want to do what I do then come home.' He gasped the last two words then turned his head towards the window and opened his eyes to see the first stirrings of another day, a new day. It was then, from the corner of his eye that he realised the vision hadn't stirred. He swallowed, tasting salt as

266

his tongue rolled over his lips.

'Look at me.' The vision's demand was hoarsely whispered.

Dreading what he would see, Barri turned his head towards it. There wasn't yet enough light in the tree-house to see clearly, but the presence seemed real. Barri remained seated and hunched. The vision remained kneeling until black shadows lifted to a lighter tone. Both stared at each other in deathly quiet; Barri's tears not quite finished but not heavy enough to add to the previous slow trickle. Every now and then he blinked to force a lone tear to tip over sore eyelids.

'I can see red,' he eventually broke the silence. A dull hint of crimson, like the smoky residue of fireworks, surrounded the vision.

'It's my hair,' the vision replied but this time the whisper had increased to a low female voice.

'I killed you.' Barri's voice sighed acceptance.

The vision was silent for a while then, as though answering a question that hadn't been asked: 'Yes... No.'

Barri's heart leapt and in his confusion his hands dropped to the floor. The thud of his knuckles as they hit bare wood sent tremors through his arms, up his shoulders to the back of his ears. 'How long will you be here?' he asked with the simplicity of a small boy.

'As long as you need me... Do you need me?'

'Yes.' It was the only positive affirmation Barri made.

The vision moved, its torso moved forward and then upwards until almost standing but the tree-house roof was too low. 'Come. Follow me.'

Barri tried to raise his body, limbs stiff, legs numb and unwilling but somehow he managed to stretch then roll sideways until he turned onto his knees. He crawled towards the door. The vision was already descending.

As the confused young man reached the doorway, he looked out expecting the vision to have disappeared. He gasped. The gasp turned to happy relief. His heart began to thump then became quieter. Barri followed until he was on the ground and standing next to the big oak's trunk.

'It is you, isn't it?' Barri heaved out words, his eyes moist again. He shivered, feeling the cold of dawn for the first time. Glistening eyes beamed warmth. Caprice looked into them and shivered. She now felt tremors move through her. It was warmth she hadn't seen in anyone's eyes. She reached out her hand.

'Come, we'll go home together.'

Barri took her small cold hand and they both walked towards Radburn House, she leading the way and he shyly following. They walked towards her bag, left on Radburn's steps. Barri sniffed the air now enjoying the smell of burnt wood and gunpowder. Flashes of colour still exploded in his head, everywhere was quiet but not so deathly.

When they reached the dining room, Caprice led Barri to the chair at the head of the table. She then took the seat to its right but didn't relinquish his hand. Both hands were cold but their palms, warming. Barri could now look fully at Caprice and she at him. 'Tell me?' he asked.

'I went away and you knew where to.'

'Why?'

'I had to get away from someone who had made my life a misery.'

'Was that me?'

'No. I thought I wouldn't see him again but we saw him at the hotel. One day I will tell you about it but not today.'

Barri searched Caprice's face in wonder. As with the girl in his tree-house, he was made starkly aware that people had lives and whereas he hadn't been interested, he now wanted to know about Caprice's. She spoke. 'I went to the hotel to see you, to speak to you but, when I didn't find you I returned to the mill.'

'I got your message.'

'I didn't send one.'

'I don't understand.'

'You will.' Caprice paused. Barri was slowly regaining his faculties, feeling like he'd brushed against his own death. He noticed his vision wore a plain lambs-wool sweater. She wore his choker and his eyes dropped to it but gazed at her throat, expecting to see brutal evidence of force. Caprice saw him look then deliberately stopped her fingers from going to it. She shivered.

'Are you cold?'

'Yes, a bit.'

'The radiators will be coming on soon.'

'I know.'

Caprice saw warmth in his eyes again, radiating out and into her. She stopped shivering. He reached out to run his thumb over the back of her hand, stroking it softly while gazing at her. His vision was real.

'You saw me.' Barri whispered the last word, suddenly repugnant after the first two. He had to say it; to know.

'I saw the results but, you haven't told me why.'

Barri's thumb continued to stroke the back of Caprice's hand. Rhythmic movement added to euphoric calm, his emotions made soft and new. *My subject...my victim...my future...whatever she is, is sitting in the chair she belongs in. What can I tell her?*

'Because of Elspeth,' to his surprise the sound of her name didn't jar. 'She died a long time ago.' He was surprised that he'd phrased it that way. 'In the tree-house...I was there.' Despite remorse and all the crazy emotions he'd discharged when alone and hallucinating, he still couldn't tell his resurrected love everything.

Caprice looked at him with equal calm but he detected something behind deep violet eyes. *Does she know?* He thought she did but it would remain unspoken, a bittersweet pain but a penance he was happy to carry around him forever if necessary. *As long as she stays and never talks of going away again.*

Barri didn't blink; his warmth still glowing and Caprice looked into it searching for what lay beneath. Barri's voice had lost any note of arrogance, it was softer. 'I lived with it until I saw you. You remind me so much of her.' Barri's eyes roamed across Caprice's hair, took in its splendour before he brought focus back to her skin, the curve of her chin. To her surprise he looked upwards until he found what he wanted to look into. Caprice's violet eyes saw his warmth increase and pupils grow wider. 'You tested me.'

'I did?'

'You tested a part of me that didn't know what it wanted. I thought I knew what would be next.' There was a ring of appeal in Barri's voice. 'When you went away I had to get back to what I was before.' He searched Caprice's eyes, the back of her hand and his thumb still caressing hers.

'Does that explain what you did?'

'Yes... No...' He couldn't find the words to explain and Caprice saw panic wipe over his face then it was gone. 'Before you came here, I remembered Elspeth. Then, I found a little girl in the tree-house one day. She came from the park and I thought it was her. I knew it couldn't be but wasn't sure. I thought she was going to tell me all the things she had wanted to, all the things others would tell me if they'd had a chance.' Barri wasn't sure if he made sense but could see that Caprice understood.

She does understand, doesn't she? She's come back from there. She's spoken to them.

In the same matter-of-fact tone, he continued: 'I saw you at the party then, I got your... a message. I had to follow. At the mill, you were waiting. You taunted me.'

Caprice weighed his words which, didn't fully explain, but she knew she wouldn't hear his true feelings. She was silent and gazed at him, watching Barri's warmth turn to fear and then felt a power she thought she'd left at the mill. 'We weren't the only people to go to the Mill.'

'People?' the use of plural confused Barri and his fear turned to bewilderment.

'When I saw what you'd done, it solved a problem.'

Barri's bewilderment increased. His thumb strokes stopped

270

then continued. Caprice spoke in hushed gentle tones as though telling a story to a young child. Her voice soothed, Barri was mesmerised, his eyes going from her lips to her eyes and back again. All thoughts of a throat's milky creaminess beneath the choker vanquished as he heard her speak. 'I had to change when I got out of there. It made sense.'

'Where's your dress?'

'It's in my bag but I must get rid of it.'

'No, don't do that!'

'I may need to Barri.' When she said his name it sent tremors through him.

'She wore a dress, the same, except hers was dark blue. You wouldn't have known.'

'She had your hair.'

'No, she had a wig. I have no idea why she pretended to be me.'

'Who pretended?'

'The woman from the hotel, Purl, the one who was so rude to me but you didn't mind.' Caprice watched Barri's confusion change to panic. 'You don't remember do you?'

'Yes... No... Was she rude to you?'

'Yes and that's partly why I had to leave. You see, the man I hated was also at our table and when you didn't care much what was said, I was upset, extremely upset.'

'It was Mandrake?' Barri thought of that invisible world where things happened to other people all the time except he'd been present. Something had happened in front of him but he'd been too deep in his world to notice.

'No, Mephisto, his friend!' Caprice almost spat the name.

'The old man, it was clear now, Barri remembered the name, Caprice's first word but, that wasn't the name given at the hotel. He mouthed it phonetically and Caprice watched him.

'What are you doing?'

'He had a different name at the hotel, didn't he?' Barri was no longer sure of anything.

'Phestoz, Mr. Phestoz, it's the same surname as mine.'

Barri couldn't remember ever asking Caprice for a surname but he must have. He looked at her with fresh surprise then confusion.

'He'd followed me back to the Mill. He was the problem.' Caprice tried to enlighten him. 'I had to defend myself physically this time. I ended up with a result like yours only mine wasn't intended, it just happened.'

Caprice searched Barri's face but kept her cool. Barri looked as though he was going to say something but she interrupted his chance: 'I moved your problem to the bedroom with my problem so that it would look like they were each other's.'

'You did that last night?' Barri was incredulous but suddenly, admiringly proud.

'Not long after you'd gone.'

'Where did you go then?'

'I went to the hotel and waited outside for a while but then I saw your car wasn't locked and your jacket on the seat, it was crumpled. I knew something was wrong because I know how particular you are with your things.'

'You knew where I'd be.'

'I had an idea.' Caprice was almost emotionless and Barri admired that in her. She could be relied upon. He relaxed. His heart beat quietly, adrenalin now at an even keel while he welcomed a warm flush of calm euphoria.

I'm home. We're home. Barri now wanted his own reliability to return and with it a new future. For a moment his heart leapt with possibilities. 'What do we do now?'

'Wait.'

Barri nodded his assent and Caprice knew that for now, he meant it. Her fingers went to her choker and Barri followed them with his eyes.

'We will both wait and live,' he said with finality. Warmth sprang from his eyes to embrace Caprice.

29. Knowing When to be Quiet

A few days later, two bodies were discovered by a security guard who reluctantly inspected Hebble Mill before workmen were due. The discovery not only took him by surprise but almost cost him his job. He had a hard time explaining how he hadn't seen Purl's car parked in the private underground car park. As far as he knew, she hadn't arranged a moving-in date, her new apartment wasn't ready.

The police found a memory-stick in Mephisto's pocket. It contained some disgusting stuff. When dots were connected, the man owning it matched the description of one seen prowling the park and talking to children. Later, hotel guests confirmed that he'd also acted oddly at the party. As Purl was the daughter of his close friend, one he'd known for years, then, who knew how long he'd been her special acquaintance?

News of Mephisto's death, the contents of his pockets and Purl's demise was broken to Caprice at Barri's house. He sat by her side while a detective spoke softly to the next of kin. Two policemen stood near.

'Is there anything you can tell us about your step-father?' A detective peered at her hair then his jaw-line stiffened.

Barri had recovered. His natural confidence was back in its rightful place but with it a deep sense of satisfaction. He was able to remain composed when he heard *"step-father."* However, details were now emerging that could either fog the situation or mask it completely so Barri watched Caprice as eagerly as the police.

'He wasn't, by any means, a caring relative.' Caprice sighed. 'He looked after me after mother died.'

The two policemen looked at each other, the detective hesitant to ask what he needed to. He looked earnest before speaking. 'The disturbing images of children on the memory-stick, as his daugh...' he corrected himself, '...his step-daughter, does this come as a surprise to you?'

One of the policemen glanced at his colleague who raised his eyebrows in reply. The detective had chosen his words well. The policeman then kept their eyes on Caprice. All men noted a startled look in her eyes but there wasn't a flush of colour to tarnish her pale complexion or give away her true knowledge. She looked genuinely surprised, which she was. She had a lightning suspicion that her own image was on the stick but that lightning didn't hit ground. Caprice knew that Mephisto had never used electronic equipment; his private dance was always by candlelight, *Mephisto and his shadows*. This made sense; any other aids to his depravity, or borrowed from someone else's, came as a genuine surprise.

'I don't understand it. He was always so fond of children,' she lied. 'He always said it was a pity I didn't have friends. We moved about so much.' Caprice paused then, raised trembling white fingers to her hair and her eyes filled. Barri looked at her hair and thought about his tree-house.

'I can't believe it,' she finally said with such effort to control her voice that her audience were instantly convinced. The policemen and detective looked at each other but said nothing further. She didn't need to know about the incident at the park. The policemen, however, looked apologetically at Barri then the detective gestured to have a quiet word.

'Caprice confirmed you were both at the party and you left your car near the hotel?'

'Yes, I don't drink and drive. Caprice got me home. I was in no fit state,' another half-truth and it suited Barri.

'We found a text message to you on Purl's phone. Can you shed any light? It was sent not long before her death.'

Barri pulled out his phone and looked at it. 'Yes, here it is.' He passed his phone to the man. 'It's no secret she was interested in me, in fact she came to my business on a couple of occasions without an appointment, demanding to be seen. She went out of her way to gate-crash an awards ceremony I was at, making sure she sat at my table.' Barri became quite animated, now realising that he could spin what happened in the best possible light.

'She was also rude to Caprice, seemed to take it for granted that I'd leave her. The woman thought she could influence my decision not to take up her father's offer to buy my business. I was explicit in my refusals on both counts then she became resentful, probably because she knew I was about to propose to Caprice, Phestoz more so. I was going to deprive him of his step-daughter.'

This information added a further dimension to the machinations of New Year's Eve. Barri used logic, his cool logic which, had been added to by Caprice's even cooler logic to fill in all gaps.

'You're quite a lady's man,' one of the officers remarked, looking closely at Barri. *How could a care-assistant next door have thought otherwise?*

'Money always attracts women.' Barri looked at the officer and inhaled sharply. 'However...' He now creased his eyes a little to hint at a smile. 'Money isn't everything.'

'Ah, but it helps,' the officer replied then thought to himself: *And looks help too.* He would happily swap long working hours dealing with scum for a day in Barri's life except two things held him back, money and looks.

'Purl's friends said they hadn't seen much of her at the party and thought it odd. She'd spent a lot of time in this town lately, not their usual scene. A shop owner also confirmed Purl had insisted on buying a dress much the same as one worn by your intended, and the wig?' The detective shook his head. 'Well, when we went through her phone, her father had sent a text saying he and Phestoz had discussed the future. It more or less said that if she hadn't been successful with you then he was a possible suitor.' It was a sarcastic jibe from Mandrake which, the police had interpreted literally.

Barri saw the men out. As he closed the door he thought

about what he'd told them, pleased it had gone so well. Caprice had said it would. The proposal was a spur-of-the-moment inclusion to show commitment but now that he'd said it, difficult to erase. He took a short detour before he returned to his intended and stopped at a chair to the right of the dining table head. Looking down, he gently stroked its back and smiled.

News of the deaths was briefly covered in newspapers and on TV but they were just two of many tragic incidents over the festive period. It was a time when broken-family arguments had been replaced by resentment and anger.

Judith's husband had a volatile nature but if forced to quit his home, his marriage and see his kids only at weekends then he would have drifted into it without acquiesce. Eventually, he would have drunk himself to death while making a complete nuisance to everyone outside his family; his wife being a stronger force. The Force however, could withhold volatile turmoil, be mild-mannered and soft-voiced but without a flicker of empathy to back it up. She let loose at home as neighbours could testify; a loud nature and loud mouth, but, beneath her brashness, she loved her husband. They were nothing apart, but together, they were something - mostly annoying, self-centred, sly and sneaky, with a bolstered superiority that varnished inferiority.

Give either one of them a certificate or diploma and they could be dangerous but not to their own flesh and blood. Qualifications have become so easy to come by. Judith knew how to make a bed, take a temperature, follow a medication chart, assist, but did she know how to care? Judith's New Year had been eventful. Shortly after her return to work she'd received a phone call informing her that an ambulance was on its way to her house. Mr. Gormey had collapsed.

'A serious infection,' she told neighbours, hiding the truth that he had drunk so much over New Year that he was toxic.

'Funny,' one neighbour remarked a day later when he saw the short fat man on his roof, fixing a broken tile. 'It couldn't have been that serious.'

Judith returned to work and turned her thoughts to greater things. By then, the police had been to Radburn. Both Caprice and Barri had absorbed the news and allowed it to drift silently into their new world of understanding. Afterwards, what they didn't say to each other was equally important.

'So I told the police all about it,' Judith told her colleagues and Old Dears. She related the story of Barri and the red-headed child then the incident at the park. 'I posted a warning on Facebook over New Year, told people to keep an eye on their kids. It's disgusting how him next door is still out and about.' Judith had seen patrolling policemen frequently, saying to herself: *That was all my doing.* It was safe to spread the word; she had the confidence of her own conviction. If she had checked her FB then she would have seen her Friend Count fall.

Police spoke to the parents of the play-frame gang telling them that paedophile danger had been resolved. He wasn't local. News then spread. Children returned to the park with a vengeance.

'I saw most of it from here.' Judith pointed out a window then gawped when she saw Barri in his garden. Her colleagues gathered at the window and looked out.

'Look, he's at it again. What did I tell you? He can't get enough. Look, he's perving at the park and his bloody tree-house!' She'd make sure there were witnesses this time and felt the weight of her importance.

It was a crisp, bright January morning. Stunted grass crunched underfoot. A silvery, watery sun remained aloof but hinted at more promising weather. Barri stood at the foot of the oak tree and peered up through one hand.

Judith guessed Barri was talking to someone in the tree-house then, she saw what she wanted to. A shock of red hair appeared for a second at the doorway. The bitter woman snorted: 'See, See! What did I tell you?' A bubble of spittle appeared at the corner of Judith's mouth, the first two words squeaked in falsetto. Judith's throng jumped, not so much at the loudness of the sound but that it was so full of excitement and hatred.

In the Radburn garden a head briefly popped out of the tree-house to reply to Barri but its face masked by a long flow of red hair. Judith couldn't hear anything, windows were closed but without a second thought, she turned and ordered over her shoulder: 'Come away or he'll see you!' Shuffling feet immediately did as they were told to but Judith had disappeared, amazingly agile for a short dumpy woman. She rummaged in her bag for her phone, compelled to take action. 'Now the police will have to do something. They can catch him red-handed,' she snorted. 'Ha, red-handed,' and she smirked at an unintentional pun.

'Well, what do you think?' Barri shouted up at the tree-house. Watery sun hurt his eyes but he couldn't get enough of seeing Caprice, especially as she was in his tree-house and about to make an important decision. 'Do you want me to come up?'

Caprice popped her head out briefly. 'No, stay where you are!' the redhead giggled as she pulled her head back in. 'You wouldn't be able to keep your hands off me.'

Barri could hear musical laughter and he grinned from ear to ear. 'What did you say? What are you laughing at?' When a reply wasn't forthcoming, the changed young man became impatient and stomped sulkily around the tree before coming to a halt at the other side.

Caprice stuck her head out of a far window to look down at the top of Barri's. She dropped a small chunk of wood. There were plenty from drilled holes after workmen had finished. The chunk hit the dirty-blond head smack-bang at its centre whirl. Caprice giggled again in triumph.

'Hey!' Barri shouted and turned his chin up to see Caprice's red hair now hanging around her pale face. His impatience and sulkiness vanished. *I just can't get enough of her.*

'Things look different from up here.'

'They don't look so bad from down here.' Barri was learning, now a communicative human but with one burning question still waiting to be answered. 'Well, what's the verdict?'

Caprice stared down at Barri's upturned face then said: 'Do you honestly want a *For Sale* sign to spoil this lovely garden?' Ironically, she had reversed a conversation that Barri's father had once had with his mother.

'I said it was up to you.'

The face and red hair then disappeared. Caprice felt all-powerful but didn't want her face to portray it. She had two decisions to make, Radburn being the first.

Barri began to stomp around the tree trunk again, unused to indecision but fully prepared to make one exception. However, Caprice made the most of her position of power and sat on cold bare boards, hugging her knees while she looked around the tree-house. Before long, red hair orbiting a pale face appeared again at the tree-house window. Barri stopped pacing and looked up expectantly.

'This will be OUR home,' Caprice declared. 'And... The tree-house stays.'

Barri had thought of Radburn as his home but now it would be *"ours"*. Looking up at Caprice, he decided: *Only because it will contain a person I can be ME with.*

'Despite its history, the tree-house is part of your childhood and I won't deprive you of it. I don't know why you'd think I would want to?'

Barri's eyes creased, they'd done that a lot lately. 'It was just a thought.'

'You know what Barri?'

'What?'

'You're not normal,' and Caprice giggled again as she disappeared back into the tree-house.

Barri grinned, wider than he'd ever grinned before. 'I'm not normal,' he said quietly as he continued to look up, feeling as though he had just joined the world, the normal world. Its glorious wonders were now his.

Just then, a police car slowed down as it drove along Dandelion View but Barri didn't see it, he was still looking up.

The car came to a halt, a policeman got out but one remained seated. Barri didn't know until he heard a voice from beyond skeleton hydrangeas. 'Stay in the car, this shouldn't take long.' Barri turned to see a policeman on tiptoe peering back at him from over the barren shrub. 'Is everything okay?'

'Yes,' Barri replied. The creases from around his eyes disappeared. 'Is something the matter?'

'What's going on?' a female voice asked from the tree-house forcing the policeman to look up.

Crackling came from the car and the seated policeman listened, shook his head, let out a low whistle before saying to himself: 'That bloody woman. Unbelievable!' He continued to shake his head but then ducked a little so he could glare at Fernlea's exterior. His colleague heard the crackling. Barri came closer to the shrub. The policeman on the other side then looked sheepish. 'There's nothing the matter, we were just on our way to see someone and thought we'd check.'

'That's very considerate,' Caprice shouted down.

'Is that safe?' the policeman added, feeling obliged to have a genuine reason for intruding.

'Yes,' Barri replied. 'Just had it made like new again.'

'Ah!' The policeman took a long look at the tree and its tree-house. 'Well, when you get round to starting a family it'll come in handy, so I guess it must be soon then if you've had it worked on?'

Caprice gawped then had to shut her mouth quickly. Barri cleared his throat and looked up at Caprice. Warmth and embarrassment radiated from his eyes but the policeman recognised infatuation when he saw it and smiled to himself. The upright policeman guessed he had touched upon a delicate subject. *Maybe it will be official after the wedding.*

'Well, glad to see everything is okay. I won't disturb you any further.'

'Right,' Barri replied and he watched the policeman get back into his car and continued to watch as it pulled out slowly but instead of going down the road it turned right.

Caprice still looked out the window. 'Something must have happened next door,' she observed. Barri nodded, both ignorant of their part in yet another one of Judith's false reports.

The police were shown in. Judith at first basked in self-imposed celebrity status, she was pivotal in bringing justice to the world. She also felt gratified that police had come to her place of work. *It will look good in front of the manager,* proof of a conscientious citizen.

'Mrs Gormey,' one of the officers said with deadly seriousness. They'd been shown through to the lounge. 'Is there anywhere more private to talk?'

'No,' Judith lied, protuberant eyes unblinking. They shone with the joy of being proved correct and were quite disturbing. 'You caught him then? Is the girl alright?' Her last question was asked with such soft insincerity that Judith's head made a sideways nod. The policemen could see it was done with a confident but delighted tremor. One of the officers looked around at old people sitting in chairs, some pretending to be occupied with books or newspaper crosswords. He then looked at uniformed carers, pretending to be busy. Turning his head, he looked to his colleague who gave a weary nod.

'Mrs Gormey, there wasn't a girl. Once again, no crime committed or about to be.'

'I saw her; we all saw her.' Judith gestured to the room in general but was greeted by silence.

'I don't know who you thought you saw. Mr George and his fiancée are entitled to look at their tree-house on their own property.'

'No!' Judith interrupted. 'I saw her distinctly, that little girl from the park was in there.'

'No, she wasn't Mrs Gormey.'

'Did you go up there? I bet she was in there.' Judith sounded pathetic, a ring of panic in her voice.

'I didn't need to; Miss Phestoz was in there alone.'

'So, she's back on the scene again then? He just uses her as an alibi.'

'Mrs Gormey!' The officer raised his voice prompting his colleague to take over.

'Do you know about slander and defamation laws Mrs Gormey?' Judith's head wobbled and her eyes bulged. She turned pink.

'Miss Phestoz is grieving the loss of her step-father, one of the bodies we found at Hebble Mill recently. Haven't you seen the news or read the papers? No? We also found out who was responsible for hanging around the park. It wasn't Mr George.'

'Who was it then?' Judith scoffed, still wobbling and pink.

The first officer answered after he heard his colleague sigh openly. 'That is none of your concern. I suggest you not only familiarise yourself with the laws just mentioned but I warn you that any further false reports could result in a charge of wasting police time.'

Judith crossed her arms, her face now crimson. 'I haven't done anything wrong,' she hissed, then, she quickly unfolded her arms, leaned forward and pointed a stubby finger in Radburn's direction. 'He has!'

'You should listen to the officers,' a concerned voice said behind her. Judith swivelled her head and glared. Her popping eyes, scarlet face and more natural vocal tones had shocked her audience. She turned back to the policemen and refolded her arms.

'Take heed,' a policeman calmly continued. 'There'll be a record of this latest false report. If Mr George wants to bring a complaint against you then he'll be within his rights to do so. As the owner of a famous, long-established business he takes his reputation seriously. Any verbal slander or anything you post on social media will land you in hot water. So, I suggest you read-up, consider your position and I hope not to hear from you again.' The policeman gestured to his partner and they turned to go.

Judith was humiliated but totally convinced that she was the subject of a highly organized conspiracy. As soon as the policeman had gone, a voice behind her said: 'Mrs Gormey.'

Judith turned quickly, unable to hide her wrath and high colour but managed to choke it down.

'Yes, Mrs Keogh?'

'Accompany me to the office please.'

Judith obediently followed her manager to the office while everyone else looked on with one united thought: *I wonder if she'll still work here?*

Meanwhile, Barri and Caprice had gone for a stroll. It was such a lovely winter morning and Caprice had suggested it. 'I don't want to go back indoors just yet. Come on,' she said, taking hold of Barri's hand. Once again he found himself led away like an obedient child. 'Let's take a walk around the park.'

'You're sure about the tree-house?'

'Yes. Whatever happened there, it happened B.C.'

'B....C?'

'Before...Caprice,' she smiled and Barri's eyes creased. 'Another thing Barri, we must let the cleaner know her job is safe and increase her hours. The whole house needs a bloody good clean and she can put up that new clock you bought. It'll look good in your collection.'

The walk took some time; Barri hadn't been fully around the park before. They ambled along, hand-in-hand, not caring how fast they walked or how brisk the air was. It was part of the normal world. Through Barri's eyes it was as fresh as it was to Caprice, who'd only seen the park from across Dandelion View.

'Have you decided what to do with your step-father's businesses?' Barri asked quietly. He blinked up into a bright clear sky.

'My...it's a day for decisions,' Caprice remarked. 'I don't know yet. Sell probably.'

'I could help you with that.'

'I know and I'll need you to.' She then changed the subject. 'Should we send flowers to Mandrake, for the funeral?'

Barri considered this then said: 'No, it's not appropriate.'

'I wonder if he'll end up selling his business to you.'

Mandrake was heartbroken, crushed and defeated. He had

been through the events of News Year Eve a thousand times and still couldn't believe it. He searched a wretched mind, soaked in grief and helplessness but there was nothing he could do to take the pain away, a nightmare now filled his days.

Material found in Phestoz's possession had been intended for Barri but it hadn't stopped Mandrake from feeling shock and disgust. The man he thought of as an old friend had murdered his only child. He guessed why she had worn a wig, but didn't want his last thoughts of his daughter to be of a woman who had covered up her own identity with that of another.

'You were worth more than that,' he told the bottom of a glass. 'It was a stupid idea, a weakness and you shouldn't have resorted to it.'

His disgust was drowned in solace only found at the bottom of a whisky bottle but, even that became tasteless. The smallest drop remained in a smudged glass as he contemplated what he would have done to Phestoz if he'd found him with Purl. Deeply buried in his turmoil was guilt for having joked about something the dirty old man had obviously taken seriously.

'What was Caprice's role in all this, why is she still standing? Was Phestoz using my daughter and his, to ensure an interest in both sides? Was that why Caprice didn't acknowledge him at the hotel and he acted like a stranger?'

Mandrake became lost in loneliness and shattered confidence. The grieving father would remain like this for weeks, get the funeral out of the way then pull himself together. He knew he would have to eventually but couldn't imagine his business without an heir, flesh and blood to carry it forward.

Caprice had her own inner turmoil, new concerns and worries that she couldn't have conceived of a week ago. She kept them well hidden from Barri. *Should I stand before God's altar with Barri beside me? Would it then be a joke, a mockery or would it be a sign that I seek forgiveness? Would having Barri there be an abomination? Would we both be an abomination?* Security embraced Caprice, a fur-lined coat that could be snatched from her at any moment to leave her naked and unprotected. *Is this any different than the way I used to live? At least I won't be asked to do anything I don't want to do.*

There was so much to think about and Caprice had become tired of thinking yet, she had to. So much now depended on finding a way forward. *I have to be the stool.* She thought this while running fingers along her leather choker while her other hand nestled a miniature ballerina figure.

What was the name of that Reverend? She'd forgotten his name. A young man her step-father had ridiculed from the minute he'd read about him in a newspaper. She hadn't heard much about him but seen his name on a booking sheet for Mephisto's club. *Toffee Neon is my club now. Ah yes... Jacob,* she remembered. He "*spreads The Word in unconventional ways.*" If she was to stand before God then there was only one clergyman she would want to officiate, a man Mephisto had detested. *Do I believe in God?* She wanted to but felt like a hypocrite.

Caprice still danced. Each private dance for Mephisto had been a death in itself but the lure of finality had drawn her to Barri's. She would be his last dance until music stopped but somehow, somewhere within their relationship, was genuine love. Caprice smiled, she would control the music. Then, she realised something.

I have become my own Star-Keeper.

30. Strength in Silence

A few weeks later, Barri and Caprice lounged on a white-sand beach near the Mayan ruins of El Castillo. Caprice's crowning glory was gathered and secured beneath a large floppy hat, her pale skin doused in glistening factor-fifty. She stretched beneath a shady umbrella. She was getting used to a heavy pear-drop diamond on her left hand. It caught sunlight to reflect sheer brilliance.

Barri glistened too, but grains of sand were stuck to his feet and lower legs. His hair was almost white with the sun, his eyes closed. He had the look of a contented man but opened one eye occasionally to watch beachgoers pass by. He intermittently dozed and watched as they stopped to dip feet in shallow waves lapping against sand. He kept an eye open as a young woman walked by. Her red hair gathered and held fast by hair combs. Caprice noticed her too.

'It's nice to do nothing,' Caprice stated dreamily. She kept her vision on the young woman, designer sunglasses shielding her eyes.

'Yes,' Barri agreed.

'There's still plenty to do here.'

'Yes,' Barri agreed.

'There are lots of underground caverns.'

'Yes, I read about them.'

'There are caverns people aren't allowed in. I suppose they're not common knowledge.'

'I'd imagine you're right.'

'I read about them, did you?'

'No... Yes... I may have seen something.' Barri was still, observant and blissfully happy. A following silence was broken by the sound of a stray wave attempting to make its way up the

286

sand. Both sunbathers observed the young woman walk slowly along the water edge then up the beach.

'Barri?'

'Yes?'

'Did you pack everything?'

'Yes. Why, did you leave something?'

'My choker, the one you gave me.'

'We'll buy a new one here. I saw some at the gift shop.'

'I'm glad you noticed.' Caprice stroked her oily neck, where the choker would sit if she was wearing it. 'You can pick one out for me; you've got such good taste.'

'I'll go later, if you want.'

'I'd rather you did, I'm too settled here.' Caprice kept her head forward, as did Barri but their eyes followed the red-head. Two pert buttocks swayed as she walked into the distance.

'So that's all you left behind then?' Caprice again asked.

'Eh, yes.' They both turned their heads back to the ocean. 'I'll go to the gift shop now.' Barri stood and his shadow fell across the sand at Caprice's feet. 'Might as well, I'll bring back a drink, something cold and fruity.'

Caprice held her hand up to her eyes, even though they were shaded. Designer glasses were great for effect but did little to protect the eyes. 'That sounds nice.'

Barri bounded away. Caprice turned to watch him. He stopped suddenly, looked down, picked something up then continued on his way. A loud *crack* beneath one of Barri's feet had sent a sharp but pleasurable vibration through his foot, its cause a half-broken seashell. When Barri pulled it from the skin beneath his foot it disintegrated between his thumb and forefinger. Barri smiled. 'I love this place.'

In the gift shop he ran his fingertips along racks of necklaces and bracelets, some made of white moon-shells and they clacked satisfyingly against each other. He looked at a selection of maps and guidebooks then chose one. While getting a bottle out of a chiller he then dreamily returned to the trinkets picking out a choker, then, he picked up a rack of bracelets. A dark-skinned lad beamed with teeth whiter than moon-shells.

'It says outside you take bookings for the cavern tours,' Barri stated.

'Yes that's right.'

'Then book me one for tomorrow and I'll take these.'

'How many bracelets do you want?'

'All of them.'

'All?'

'Yes, they're presents for back home.' Barri returned the lad's smile.

Thirty-minutes later, the girl with red hair held by combs, returned along the beach and stopped at the water's edge. Warm water caressed hot, sandy feet and again, two pairs of eyes watched her.

'Are you sure you didn't forget anything?' Caprice lazily repeated her previous question then turned to look at Barri. His eyes were slits peering at the girl from down his nose.

'Yeah, I'm sure,' but, as an afterthought he added: 'besides, if I'd left anything it's because I no longer need it.'

Caprice stretched her neck then looked towards a designer beach-bag propped against her sun lounger. She used one fingernail to push aside a small towel to reveal an object inside. She was careful not to touch it in case she got sun-cream on its leather cover. Having it with her gave her immense satisfaction. *You haven't missed it so far.*

The leather journal lay at the bottom of her bag, protected from prying eyes. It wasn't holiday reading. She'd already consumed the contents during her first long days at Radburn. There was great comfort in knowing she carried it with her and Barri didn't miss it.

Barri smiled too. Something had changed. He was no longer alone. He would never again share his dark side but he knew that Caprice knew of it and he knew something of hers. His smile faded, totally confident that his life would now include all emotions. They could be mastered and used, recycled, released when needed but kept chained when he required peace.

288

Another loud *crack* caught his attention and he immediately turned towards it. A man was trying to erect a sun-lounger.

Barri turned his head to watch the redhead walk slowly into the distance. He waited for his current emotions to set into cold steel, the coldness of an animal about to hunt his prey. 'What do you want to do tomorrow?' he asked.

'Oh I don't know, nothing much.'

'Why don't you treat yourself to a day in the spa? A full work-up, you might not get chance when we go home.'

'That's a really good idea. You wouldn't mind?'

'No, not at all, I'm sure I can find something to do.' Barri sighed with contentment.

'Yes, I'm sure you will.'

www.ingramcontent.com/pod-product-compliance
Lightning Source LLC
Chambersburg PA
CBHW070835250626
47159CB00003B/788